THE

NEXT

THE NEXT

STEPHANIE GANGI

ST. MARTIN'S PRESS NEW YORK

This is a work of fiction. All of the characters, organizations, and events portrayed in this novel are either products of the author's imagination or are used fictitiously.

Printed in the United States of America. For information, address St. Martin's Press, 175 Fifth Avenue, New York, N.Y. 10010.

www.stmartins.com

Designed by Anna Gorovoy

The Library of Congress Cataloging-in-Publication Data is available upon request.

ISBN 978-1-250-11056-5 (hardcover)
ISBN 978-1-250-11058-9 (e-book)

Our books may be purchased in bulk for promotional, educational, or business use. Please contact your local bookseller or the Macmillan Corporate and Premium Sales Department at 1-800-221-7945, extension 5442, or by e-mail at MacmillanSpecialMarkets@macmillan.com.

First Edition: October 2016

10 9 8 7 6 5 4 3 2 1

DEDICATION

You know who you are

THE NEXT

1

This is not my beautiful life.

Far away, in the kitchen, water runs. What's that for? Tea? God help me, no more tea.

The water runs and runs, far more water than a kettle requires. I can't hear anything under the damned running water, but I know the conversation is intense. Anna's antennae are already up. Anytime she comes in here, she scans the room for my phone and drops her voice, assessing and conferring with her sister or the hospice nurse like she's the mother, not me.

I can feel the twitch at the corner of her right eye. I can feel Elena's mouth draw in and pucker with the effort not to cry. They are mine. Both girls, trying to do the right thing. It drags me like a rip current. I can't get pulled along. I have my own problems. I don't want them in here. I'm busy.

Yes, okay, yesterday I fell. Or was it the day before? I was on a mission, I needed my phone. I got out of bed and made my way over to the dresser to where it was charging. I leaned on Tom, he braced for me, he paced himself for me, he's a good dog, but I stumbled. Not his fault. Yes, I cracked a rib, my compromised bones gave way, yes, yes, high alert.

Now Anna wants caregivers around the clock. Now Anna wants to confiscate the phone. Now Anna wants me in a special bed, secured, so I can rest and revive and survive, for how long? Another week, another month? She wants to fix me, fix everything. She is trying to will a miracle.

Laney's stunned. I need to leverage that. She's still in her kid mind-set, waiting for direction, not wanting to disrespect me, wanting to believe I have enough mother left in me to rally, to assert control over this, too, the process of my dying. But I have only so much energy left and now with the rib, every breath hurts. They want to strap me down and take the phone. I need that phone. Like I said, I'm busy.

Let me think. Not easy. My bedroom hums with monitors. Soft, steady beeps track my . . . I was going to say "progress," but that's not right. What's the opposite of progress? Regress? If only I *could* go back.

I remember when this bed, surrounded now by equipment, was a raft that rocked and rolled as we navigated the briny seas of each other. In the mornings, after he left, waves rose in me again, knocked me off balance, made me blush as I untangled sheets, retrieved pillows, tried to restore order.

This bed is not that bed. Here, I am anchored by a line embedded in the back of my hand, and morphine keeps me bobbing and drifting, a little ways away from the pain. I've noticed everyone seems eager to press the button that releases the drug, on my behalf.

Not me. I prefer the pain. Anna cannot possibly understand that. The pain keeps me sharp. When I am sharp I go inside, and I make myself feel it again, how it was with him, how I was, when everything was slippery with the chemistry of new love greasing the rusty mechanisms of my heart, and—I'll say it—my soul.

I shouldn't do that. Idealize the past. It's not healthy. Ha.

But memory is seductive, especially here at the end, and I follow and it lures me down the same old hole, I follow it back, back, until it turns on me and I am where I started, without him, in the land of the left-behind, two hours out from the next morphine push. Swapping one pain for another, cancer for heartbreak, down in the hole, alone.

He's moved on. Meaning Ned.

Meaning, love of my life, mate to my soul, late-night listener curved around my body, with late-night fingers stepping across my lines and furrows, the terrain of me, and into me as the light rose pink like me over the Hudson River, through our window, and lit me up, and opened up my folded desire. I showed myself.

Ned put his hands on me and he stopped time. Ned put his hands on me and he stopped cells. I came alive. This, after chemo and the menopause that comes with it. I got my period again. That happened. My skin glowed. My hair, my wayward hair, flowed back shining. I trusted my body again, and forgot to run my visualization exercise, the daily action movie, bad cells in black Speedos and swim caps poised to jackknife into my bloodstream, while good cells, valiant surfer boys in board shorts and hippie hair, built dams.

I told Dr. Keswani, "He's younger," as if that fact might be another symptom, which, in retrospect, it was. She laughed and said, "The best medicine." Which, in retrospect, it was.

Well, the medicine was addictive, and then it was poisonous.

But that first night, when we were up against each other, I had to halt his hand. My shirt was off. He was working at my bra. "Wait, wait a second. I need to tell you something." He looked stricken. Sexually transmittable disease? Pre-op transgender? Or any number of other show-stoppers I was too old-school, or just too old, to count.

I reached behind and undid the hooks and let the bra drop to the floor. I said, "I've been sick. I have scars. Here. And here." I closed my eyes and took his fingertips on a walk along the ropy ridges underneath each new breast, and finger-stepped him along the scar higher on my chest, the one the bathing suit did not hide.

That was five years ago. I was a topless, middle-aged woman splayed on a grad-student sofa. Did we even pause to sweep away strewn papers, his mess of a dissertation? A window was open somewhere, the room was chilled and I was tense with the cold and the reveal, I was like a sensor, every nerve distended, my hand guiding his hand, feeling for the slightest recoil from him.

A recoil that did not come. I opened my eyes, expecting to see his face clouded with disappointment by my body. He pushed up. He looked into me. He said, "You okay?"

"Yes, yes, I'm fine. I think. I hope." I gave a little smile, a little shrug, to protect myself against the gods of irony, who were surely listening, waiting for me to get cocky, to drop my guard and let myself feel a future. "I mean, I am. I'm fine." I had to add another "I hope."

"Does this mean we can't . . . ?" He was concerned only that the slide inside, so close, was in jeopardy. It was so normal a thing to say that it took me by surprise. He was not repelled. He was worried he wasn't going to get laid. Ned had a reassuringly male, one-track mind that made cancer irrelevant for a little while.

I wanted him. I was wearing the pricey lingerie to prove it.

Even though technically they were nerveless, with cosmetic nipples, created from belly fat and tattoo ink, my new breasts remembered what my real breasts once responded to. Like phantom limbs, they were gone, but the yearning was still there.

"Does this mean we can't . . . ?"

Relief flowed, loosening my thighs. I pulled him in. After, he touched his lips to the ridges where his fingers walked, kissing away my self-consciousness. That's when I came up with the nickname. *Doc.* I felt healed.

I was forty-six and he was thirty-one. I was by far the oldest woman he'd ever been with. "Is it weird for you? Do I feel old?"

He said, "Of a certain vintage, maybe, but not old."

I hid my face. "Vintage! That's just code for 'old'!" He pulled my hands away.

He said, "Textured," in his smoke voice, and stroked the skin at the corners of my eyes.

He said, "Wise," and let his fingers flutter over a scar.

"Complex," he said, and put his hands between my legs. He moved over me again and pushed in again and whispered, "No more talking."

I am not healed. He did not stop time, he did not stop cells. Did I mention? Ned's moved on. Ned's living the high life now with someone younger, richer. Healthy. She's iconic. She's a celebrity skin doctor. She's one of the best-known female entrepreneurs in the world. She's everywhere and he's right next to her. Smiling. Can you believe that? He's smiling. Swipe, tap, scroll. See? There they are again, those lucky ducks, at last night's events. There you are again, Doc, you moved-on, up-trading, lucky-duck bastard. It's like I never existed.

Jealousy, whoa. I hadn't ever experienced it, never really related to the scorned-woman thing. Not like this. I guess I was always the dumper, rather than the dumpee. But now. Wow. I see them and my brain whirs like an old jukebox gearing up to search and reach and set the disc on the turntable and drop the needle into the open vein of an Adele song, any Adele song. I feel ennobled by jealousy, diva-like. I have been wronged. I have been betrayed on a level that is Adele-esque.

Still, I need to see Ned, even if it's only on the small screen in the palm of my hand.

Swipe, tap, scroll. I'm fascinated. I'm disgusted. The display, the showing off, the bragging. When did that become okay? Didn't that used to be discouraged? Look at our expensive objects, look at our famous friends. This is what we are eating, wearing. Here's where we are, here's where we're going. Everyone is healthy, everything is special. Everyone poses in a sunny, filtered future where the unphotogenic are not allowed. Well, I got older, I got sick, I got totally unphotogenic.

Refresh, refresh, refresh. Talk about ironic. I'm pushing my own buttons. I need my phone so I can check Twitter, Instagram, newsfeeds, posts. So I can see. Good morning, Doc. Good morning, Doc's new woman.

Trudi Mink, dermatologist to the stars.

Trudi. I don't like that name.

He's moved on. I have to accept it and move on too. If only.

If only he would acknowledge what we had. What we meant to each other.

If only he would apologize for walking out on me in the hour before my darkest hour.

If only he would stop ignoring me.

If only cyberstalking weren't so easy.

The truth is, I want nothing more than to move on. Except it's too late. Where am I going, in this condition?

Where is my fucking phone?

I'm sobbing now, that's what happens when the morphine is at the end of its shift. Sobbing brings coughing. I try and stifle myself with a pillow so my daughters don't hear, so they won't come in, and then the pain in my ribs sears me, and I can't hold the coughing back, and then the pain in my ribs sets me on fire. Tom, who has been resting heavy against me, like ballast, raises his big dog head and looks at me with anxious eyes. He steps off the bed. He paces. He pants.

The silence outside my door is full. Someone listening.

Someone entering. Here comes the tea. Elena murmurs and fusses, but now there is something formal in her voice, something harder than before, something not-Laney, something more Anna, adapted from the kitchen conference. Things have been decided.

Caregivers, around the clock. New bed, no phone. No phone, no reason. I can't face it. I push the button myself this time. The morphine blur spreads thick like gel across my brain, such as it is, and it doesn't take long, I fall away just as Laney enters, I mumble nonsense as she approaches, I'm going under and I won't have to face her. I pretend if I can't see her, she can't see me.

2

Joanna DeAngelis was dying wrong. It was one thing the sisters could agree upon.

She had fractured a rib, and now, surprise, an interloper, pneumonia, outpaced the cancer in her chest. Her breathing was inhibited; when she slept, half sitting up so she didn't choke, her breath sounded like it scraped her lungs. Keswani, the oncologist, recommended they install a high hospital bed, with railings and restraints, which she would not be able to leave without help.

Laney rinsed the porcelain cup and saucer, her grandmother's, for the third time that gray February day. She set the kettle under the faucet and let the water run cold, for tea, again. "You're not living here. I'm here all day. She's . . . she's okay."

"She is not okay, Lane. She's not. You have to deal with it."

"I am not saying she's fine. I said she was 'okay.' Not 'fine.' I'm not stupid. And stop telling me to 'deal with it.' You deal with it."

"We need someone here full-time. And she needs the special

bed. Or she's going to have to go back to Sloan. We can't have her wandering all over the place!"

"Anna, no one is wandering all over the place. She went from the bed to the . . . bathroom, probably. She had Tom to lean on. She's done it before with no problem."

"Well, it's a problem now, isn't it? I'm getting that bed installed this week." Anna tapped at her phone and waved it at Laney. "Jules agrees with me."

Laney said, "Well, Tom agrees with me, but neither of us are doctors, so I guess our votes don't count."

By nature, nurture, and now, profession as a pediatric resident, Anna was devoted to her mother's care. She'd put her own life on hold, or more accurately, double-timed it, fitting in long days of tending to the kids at Kravis, stealing time with Jules, and supervising an environment of efficiency at her mother's apartment. Captain of the team, guardian at their mother's door, Anna wanted only to protect Joanna—who seemed kind of deranged, frankly—from more pain, of any kind.

"I don't like the idea of Tom in there all the time, either. He's too big to be on the bed! What if he knocks into the machines? Or pulls out the line? And she's . . . recruited him or something, to help her get around. She's supposed to be using the bedpan, not the bathroom. He's her accomplice!"

"First you go for the bed, now you want to take away the dog. Tom's watching over her. He's not an accomplice. And Mama's not a criminal."

"Something's off, I'm telling you. She's not right. Maybe something going on in the brain? What is up with the phone thing? I never saw her so into her phone before. What's she doing on the internet all the time?"

"Tinder?"

"Is that supposed to be funny?" Anna watched Laney, who

assembled components for tea on a tray. "Lane, the water. Shut the water! You've got a flame open, and the water's running, and—"

"It might be hard for you to believe, but I do know how to make a cup of tea." Laney set the kettle on the stove. "Fine, see about the caregivers' schedule. Order the bed. But leave Tom alone." By giving Anna a win and throwing down about Tom, Laney thought she might distract her sister from their mother's obsession with her phone. Tom was not Joanna's only accomplice.

Anna scrolled her contacts, made the call, and set the date for the bed's delivery. "I have to go, Jules is waiting. It's Valentine's Day." She went to Laney and touched her forehead to her sister's. "We're okay, we're doing okay. Right?"

"It's Valentine's Day? I'm such a loser." Laney's eyes welled. "Yes, of course. We're okay."

The sisters hugged tight. Inside the hug, they were nearly identical in stature and build; apart, blonde Laney, blue-eyed, with pale skin and an open visage; brunette, brown-eyed Anna with tawny skin and a face that revealed itself slowly. Yet, definitively sisters.

Anna said, "You do make a fine cup of tea, I'll give you that. And . . ."

Laney waited for the parting shot.

"You're almost good at manipulating me. Do not let her have that phone."

Before Christmas, when Joanna came home from Sloan Kettering for the last time, Laney moved back home too, to help. She was secretly relieved to flee the clutter and grime of expensive floor-through rooms she shared with three others in Brooklyn. Aside from the circumstances, being home was a respite from watching for signs of what to do with her life, in her first year as an official grown-up after the four-year undergraduate fairy tale in Boston.

Laney was tired of her Boston-Brooklyn friends and their opinions, their naïveté and cynicism, their distressed clothes and hair and outlooks, and most of all, their healthy mothers. She was tired of alcohol and technology, which had turned once-friends into posers with poor eye contact, all of whom seemed unable to form a sentence without reaching for a device. She worked as an intern helping the former hippie-boomer publishers "deploy" social media at Personal Growth & Human Development Books, PGHD, the company where her mother had been an editor, but that gig was on hold for the duration. She'd had to leave every normal thing, pals and work and mindless fun, everything with which her friends were preoccupied, outside the dying-mother bubble she inhabited.

Tray in hand, she tapped her toe at the bedroom door, and whispered, "Mama?"

Her mother drifted, drugged, in her blue bed at the Titania, the Art Deco apartment building standing sentinel over 103rd Street and Riverside Drive. The bedroom's windows were high enough and wide enough so that the Hudson River was a presence. The river, flat glass or chop, showed on the mirrored closet doors. The watery reflection shimmered like a lure across the bed, catching the sun's rise and set and the moods of the moon.

Always cold, her mother had huddled and gone small under blue quilts. All Laney could see was the beanie that Anna bought a couple of years back at a skateboard shop downtown on Lafayette, white with an embroidered black skull, when the skull was still ironic. Joanna was attached to the hat. Laney hated seeing it on her mother's head, daring death.

Joanna had stopped eating. Bringing tea was all Laney could think to do. She set the tray down on the night table as quietly as she could. Joanna moaned from inside a dream.

They'd moved to the Titania five years before, and there were still unpacked boxes in basement storage, mostly her grandparents' things, or things in limbo from their old life that her mother hadn't been ready or willing to sort through. Laney had brought up a few boxes to go through, a project, something to distract her mother and herself from the exhausting mix of drama and tedium that is caregiving. She started with cartons that looked the oldest, liquor boxes advertising brands she never heard of, marked "Loretta," her grandmother's things.

She took up a spot on the floor at Joanna's bedside, slit through yellowed tape, opened cardboard flaps, unwrapped glass, ceramic, porcelain vessels and dishes, plaques and ashtrays, figurines, once precious, now useless, stopping now and then to smooth and read from crumpled newspaper. Laney, at least, was diverted by the treasures, and thought it would lift her mother's spirit to see Loretta's porcelain cup and saucer show up in rotation. Joanna had given Laney one dip of her head to acknowledge, days ago.

Laney wanted more. More Mama. She was finding it tough to stay connected—to stay kind—to this person, sunken in pillows, agitated or absent, in sleep or drugs or a private darkness all her own.

Anna felt it was their duty to make their mother's final days the experience Joanna said she wanted when she'd lobbied to leave Sloan Kettering: a tranquil passage at home with loved ones nearby. No fear, no worries, everything understood, everything absolved, and with luck, eyes would close, and she would sigh with acceptance, and simply stop.

Laney thought, *Like in the movies, like* Beaches. She was conflicted. It was Mama, after all, not an erratic stranger messing up the choreography of some big dying-with-dignity plan. Laney was trying to hold on to her, respect her, by keeping more strangers and equipment from encroaching, more indignities from accumulating.

It was hard to argue with Doctor Know-It-All, as Laney was

coming to think of her sister. But Anna did not know it all. Laney knew and Anna did not, that the phone expedition was not random. Joanna was technically still there, still with them, still alive, but she was secretly—secretly!—preoccupied to the point of online obsession with Ned, so much more compelling than food or daughters or her own life ebbing away. Laney could see it was a fierce force keeping Joanna going. But the force was overtaking her, hijacking her, which is why Anna, who thought Ned McGowan long out of their mother's life, assumed there was something wrong with her brain.

Laney was surprised her sister had not yet figured it out. She could tell Ned was back on the scene last summer by Joanna's voice on the telephone, girlish. She knew he was gone again a couple of months later, when her mother's voice fell heavy and flat. Laney hadn't shared this observation with Anna, who loathed Ned from the start, who'd never considered Ned anything *but* a hijacker. Now, once again, he had stolen their mother.

The room was dim but not dark. Laney could feel her mother's eyes slide, watching through the split of swollen eyelids. Tom lay against her and his eyes followed Laney, too, as she closed up the boxes as quietly as she could and set them in a corner for another day, another attempt at reclaiming something of her mother.

"Hey, Mama, hi." Laney sat at her mother's side. "You awake? You hot?" She reached to remove the beanie. Joanna moved away from Laney's touch.

"Okay, I'll leave it. What do you need? Tea? I brought some, fresh." She poured. "Can you try and sit up a little?" She reached to adjust the pillow. Joanna shut her eyes and turned her head.

"How about some water, then?" She went to the bathroom and filled a mint-green plastic hospital pitcher from the tap. She thought, *I need to get rid of this hideous pitcher. She must hate it.* Rejected, guilty, and angry all at the same time, she checked herself, *Then again, why bother? She can barely look at* me.

She knew it was ridiculous, but she was pissed at her mother. Where was the cancer-movie version, selfless and dying in a way that made everything okay for her kids? The three of them had watched *Beaches* enough times to know there was protocol, there was supposed to be a good ending, with cozy sweaters and cups of tea and looking out to sea, the three of them, their best, loving selves.

This was not that.

Laney pulled aqua sheets with white ruffled edges, her mother's favorites, up under Joanna's chin. She straightened and tucked. "It's Valentine's Day, Mama. Anna reminded me." She leaned down, touched her cheek to her mother's forehead. She couldn't judge Joanna for not dying according to Hollywood movie standards. Laney was twenty-two, it was the hallmark of her generation to *not* judge. And death, it was so heavy, so personal. Was it even possible to die wrong? On the other hand, it wasn't only happening to Joanna. Their mother's death was happening to Anna and Laney too. Chasing down an ex-boyfriend? Ignoring your kids?

Her mother was definitely not dying right.

"How about some drops?" Laney separated the sliver-thin skin of her mother's eyelids, easing them open. Joanna's eyes were blue and black, much darker than Laney's. The whites were yellow and the rims were flaked with dried tears.

Laney said, "This will feel really good," and carefully let a drop fall into each eye. Joanna squeezed them shut against this comfort, and again pulled from her daughter's touch. Weary tears ran. She coughed for a full minute, and Laney's heart raced for twice as long.

She dabbed at Joanna's eyes with a tissue. She murmured, "Oh, don't cry, Mama, don't cry. You're making it worse. I'm here." She used the same soggy tissue to dab at her own eyes.

Tom wriggled closer to Joanna on the bed, and dropped his heavy head onto her thigh. "No," Joanna rasped. "No." She shook her head.

Laney grabbed the dog's collar and dragged him away. "Come on, Tom, you gotta get off. You're too heavy. Come on, off now."

Joanna shook her head again.

"What is it, Mama? What are you trying to say?"

Joanna twisted under the mask.

"Are you in pain?

No, no. She shook her head. *No.*

"What do you need?" Laney adjusted the mask. "I can't take it off right now. You don't sound good. Try to relax a little bit, and then I can give you a break from the mask. Should I press the button?"

Again, Joanna shook her head, this time forcefully. She said, "Phone," and Laney stalled and pretended not to understand, an attempt to heed Anna's admonition, but she and her mother had made a wordless pact. It had become routine, when Anna wasn't around, to give in about the phone. What did it matter? Wasn't it better than leaving Joanna to struggle to find the phone again?

"You need to try and slow down your breathing. Concentrate on the oxygen."

Joanna said, "Elena," and grasped Laney's hand.

Tom watched as Laney-the-accomplice delivered the charged phone to Joanna and said, "Just for a few minutes." She brought Joanna her sunglasses, because the bright light and colors on the small screen hurt her mother's eyes. She pulled Tom along by his ruff and stepped out to give her mother privacy and to give herself a break. As she shut the door of the bedroom, she looked back to see a shadow of her mother, an apparition of her mother, surrounded by machinery, sprouting tubes, the white beanie with the black skull pulled down low on her brow, behind sunglasses, bent over the phone, Joanna DeAngelis, Mama, a stranger acting strange.

3

I fall into a morphine dream. We are in the Met, our old haunt. We circle a sculpture, the Kouros, the big, nude boy. I press my fingers along the cool, stone phallus, the round bulk of shoulders, the torpedo thighs. Marble calf and ass muscles undulate under my touch. I am turned on. I need Ned inside me, but he is gone, striding the way he does, down impossibly long hallways. Is he leading me or running away from me? I push through a door into an empty auditorium. Ned is onstage. A television camera circles, a woman blots his shine away, another tries to tame his famous hair. I want him and I am on him and he tries to fight me off. I get stronger and stronger and I tear at his clothes. I pull at the bristle of premature white that strafes his black mane, and it rips away from his scalp. I hold a handful. The camera circles. The auditorium is full. Hundreds of students, nineteen, twenty years old, film too, with their phones. I force Ned inside. My skin is tagged and mottled and rippled. It sways as I move. My breasts have broken off, leaving flat, rough stone where they had been. My hair, everywhere, is gray. An artillery of cell phones aims. I don't care. I move up and straddle his mouth. I bear down. He struggles. The students film.

I wake up hot, aroused, just like the old days, with a pulse between my legs. I don't want to move. I want to stay alive inside the dream. Traffic motors along on Riverside Drive. It must be rush hour. I hear the hum of the dishwasher in the kitchen. NPR plays on the radio in the living room, an unstoppable current of events. It all keeps going, even as the dream dissolves, even as I disintegrate.

"Tch tch tch." I attempt clicking sounds with my tongue for Tom. Laney slipped me the phone but forgot to bring the bedpan close. I need Tom for my trip to the bathroom, and then I can use the phone again, that's the important thing. I need to check in on Dr. Trudi and her boyfriend—my boyfriend. Tom noses in and puts his long muzzle along the bed, ready to be of service.

"Let's go, man." He positions himself, and stares intently at me as if to say, *Really? This didn't go so well last time we tried it.*

I take the oxygen mask off and detach the line embedded in a vein on the back of my hand. My poor veins. I'm covered in bruises in bloom, purple and green and gray and yellow. Lifting the quilt is an event. I am frustrated to the point of tears as I untangle my legs, so pale and thin they look like someone else's, from the bedding. Finally, I have feet on the floor, but I am sweaty and freezing and nauseated from the effort.

I sit a minute. Tom waits. I put a hand on his back, his long, strong back, ninety pounds of poodle covered in chocolate-brown curls, and I feel him shift to take my weight. He knows what to do. This, a couple of times a day, our little secret. This, the way his body braces for me, releases fresh tears. Tom. My friend.

I rasp out, "Thank you, buddy," and off we go, fifteen feet that might as well be fifteen miles. I am only half-upright, bent around the burn in my bones. I grip Tom and shuffle forward, shuffle again, two steps more. I have to gasp back a cough, I don't want Elena to come running.

Laney is the weak link. She's lying to Anna. Not only is she slipping me my smartphone, she knows what I'm doing with it. She's suspected about Ned since last summer. She will cave under pressure if—when—Anna exerts it. Allegiances are fluid right now.

Shuffle, cough, rest. Shuffle, cough, rest. Tom pants, too, with anxiety. It's not easy for a dog to measure his steps, it's awkward, he has to step and stop, step and stop. He presses—not too hard—against my leg for constant contact, to feel what I need from him. I lean against the wall to rest, and he noses my hand to ask if I'm okay. Not really, buddy.

I struggle to position myself properly on the cold bowl. I am queasy, I can feel a sheen of perspiration on the back of my neck. An awful essence rises up from inside me into my throat, a mouthful of foamy fluid, and I worry that I should be crouching instead of sitting.

Tom waits politely with his head turned away.

I pull myself up, I hang on to Tom for the trip back to bed. I rush a little, queasiness abated, I've got the hang of walking again for the moment, I've got the phone, and I'm busy. The phone's days are numbered, or mine are. Either way, I need to see. Swipe. Tap. Scroll.

Swipe. Here we go. Tap to parties, clubs, galleries, charity events. Scroll and score: new images. Last Night's Events. A red carpet. He's half a step behind her, with his arm extended and a hand on the small of her back.

I follow a Twitter trail of betrayal to The Cut, The Gloss, Style, the Style Section, the New York Social Register. It's incredible how intimate you become with strangers by following them online. I check Instagram to see how Trudi is doing, I interpret her emojis, I note her LOLs and exclamation points, I know what they are up to for the weekend. I'm familiar with her OMG besties, selfies, fancy plates, lush flower arrangements, wine labels, boutique shopping bags, her trending nail color.

Like the old song says, they gavotte. They cavort, they preen. I pinch my fingers and expand the screen to examine Ned's two-faced face. To see if I can find the taut upper lip, the tension that wires his smile when he is only pretending to be happy. Pinch, expand the screen. Ah, she's got a fresh mani-pedi. I know her fingers and her toes. Ah, there's the ring.

My boyfriend. I sound crazy, I know. Look, I'm sick, I'm on drugs, I don't know whether it's night or day, I am not feeling anything good, except good ol' pain over every inch of my ruined body, and from the corkscrew to my heart. I am hurting my daughters. Of course Anna wants to enforce lockdown. Of course Elena is terrified. But I'm not crazy.

I'm righteous.

I'm struggling to let go and move on, and I don't mean from the relationship. I mean from life, my life, mine, the version that began again last July when he knocked, again. He'd had a dream. He had to come. Of course I let him in.

Just last summer.

Here we go. Down the hole. I can't prop the pillows. My chest tightens.

Just last summer, only I knew I was sick and only I knew I was not getting better. Keswani showed me the film and I nodded, polite down to my radiant backlit bones, and I nodded at the luminous ghostly shapes gathered in my lungs, I nodded, understanding nothing, seeing nothing, hearing nothing, I just nodded, and Keswani gave me options—"It's your choice"—and none of the choices suggested a life worth living, the options being not-bad days and bad days and very bad days in a fight to the finish, more chemo, more hospital, more strangers and machinery with increasing authority over my body and my mind, more iterations of not-dead-yet, stops along the way, stops along the way. Caregiving. Submission.

That was me, just last summer. Alone, dying, dragging it out. No partner "in sickness," no partner "for worse." I thought about Anna and Laney, building their lives, interrupted, detoured, dutiful. For who knew how long. It felt immoral. I had dark thoughts of swift exits pursued to save us all.

Then there was Ned, in my in-box. He'd had a dream, he had to come. You can't make this stuff up. Can you imagine? I did not resist.

Just last summer. He still loved me, not her.

So yes, Doc, come in, come in, of course, yes, it's the beginning of the end of me, yes, come back, yes, come home and love me till my heart stops. Love of my life, my beautiful life, unto my beautiful death.

For eight weeks, hot as hell, he took care of me. Trudi Mink, his soon-to-be-ex—I believed him when he said, *It's over, I promise*—was globetrotting from fashion week to fashion week tending famous skin, doing business, he was free as a bird, he was nearly moved back in, walking Tom, whistling in the kitchen, washing my hair. He took notes at doctor's appointments.

I dodged my daughters. They didn't even know I'd recurred. Anna had started her residency, she'd met Jules, she was in love, she was in that bubble. Elena, newly graduated, was bumming around Brooklyn, piecing together dollars for rent and a social life. I, Mama, I was out of sight, I was out of mind, they were doing their lives, they were doing their twenties, so all-consuming, right? Normal! Exactly what it's supposed to be.

I put aside the ways he'd hurt me before. Burned me. Doc was back, and he loved me and I loved him, that fucker. Love. I told myself that was all that mattered. I let myself trust Ned to help me be strong.

We slow strolled the shady promenade on Riverside with Tom,

who looked over his shoulder, tongue lolling, grinning at his reunited puppy-parents. We watched television. Ned worked on his book, a thriller about a charismatic news anchor and his sexy-stalkery intern, year four or five since he'd begun, he'd lost count of his drafts. I read his pages, my trusty green Flair in hand. Our old routine. We retreated to bed, this bed, where we swayed and floated with desire. Ned on his knees. Cries of pleasure rising from my center. I remember looking to the window and mouthing, *Thank you, thank you,* to the sky, to the river, for giving me this, at this late stage. Cries of pleasure!

I showed myself. He promised. *I won't let you be alone. I'm here. I've got you.* He promised.

Imagine my surprise.

In humid August, I was tossing and turning on the sofa. I could not get comfortable. I'd lost weight, and my bones hurt. It was hard to find a way to be. It was hot but I was cold. I don't like air-conditioning in the first place, but air-conditioning when you're sick is a nightmare. The noise. The faint chemical smell, what is that? Freon? The steady chill. I could not get warm. Tom was stretched out on the floor next to me. Ned was set up in Laney's old room, tapping away, working on the book, excited by it, I could tell by the way he hit the keyboard. The tapping stopped, he came to me, he didn't ask, he didn't have to, he arranged a quilt on top of me, and he went to the air conditioner and adjusted the setting. He said, *Errands, I'll be home soon, you sleep.* He said, *Take care of her for me*, to Tom. He stepped out and he never came back. They call that an Irish exit.

Under the monitor's soft bleats, I remember his voice. *Errands.* I'm still waiting, Doc.

I bleat too, a noise like laughing, and I choke on it.

I'm not crazy. I'm righteous.

I have fallen past rational thinking. I have fallen past the edge of myself. I have fallen into purple despair, into red, red fury, into bloody black hatred deep and dark as, well, death. Me hating him has turned into me hating me. I'm unrecognizable to myself. Unrecognizable to my daughters.

A bitter mantra beats inside me: *You taught him how to treat you. You taught him how to treat you.*

Bitches are made, not born. What I taste, the foamy fluid in my throat, that's bile.

Whatever. I only care about the phone. Swipe, tap, scroll. There's Trudi. Did I mention the baby bump? No? Oh.

There. Behind the velvet and chrome stanchion. Ned has his arm around Trudi Mink. Her long black hair glimmers in the glare of step-and-repeat lighting. She is in couture, something Grecian, red, one-shouldered, fitted tight under her tiny breasts, from whence it flows and drapes over a tidy baby bump. A baby bump made by Ned. He fucked her and he knocked her up, probably right around the time he sent me the I-had-a-dream e-mail last July.

It's all over the internet, has been for a few months, so I'm not surprised, but the shock of the new photos—she's really popped—has me . . . I am at a loss. For words, comprehension, sanity.

Okay, maybe I am crazy. Maybe I am. I've earned it.

I'm sweating again. I'm freezing. My fingers tremble. I need to sit up, I'm choking, I need to stop crying, I'm choking, I need to stop crying and choking so I can see the screen. Pinch, expand. A new burn rises from my heart, up into my throat, up into my nostrils. My eyes boil. I blink to clear my vision. I imprint this image, the pregnant woman in the red dress, behind my eyes and it joins all the other invaders inside me, taking me down. I can't believe it.

He has an arm around her shoulders and a hand on her belly. I'm blind with pain and I'm sick, I'm dying, but I'm jealous, I'm blinking, I'm peering, I'm bent over the small screen, I'm dying but I'm trying to see: Is that his tight smile? Is he faking?

The phone flies from my grip, so I can't tell.

4

Anna swatted the phone away. Joanna grabbed for it and was swept up in a perfect storm of fury and coughing and crying. Gales chased her breath, raced her heart, shivered her bones, and frightened Anna.

Laney, guilty daughter, who had given Joanna the phone and taken a nap, rushed in. Tom, guilty dog, sides heaving, ears flattened, skulked out.

The storm was a final force occupying Joanna's body. She fought. The sisters worked to protect the tubes, to restore the oxygen mask, to push the button, to calm their distraught mother, flailing in their arms. The morphine took a couple of terrible minutes to do its work. Joanna slumped with the drug. The sobbing stopped. The coughing tapered off. Her eyes closed, but leaked tears. She was spent.

Anna turned to Laney. "What the fuck? Where were you? How did she get the phone?"

The phone had flown. The sunglasses had skittered. The white beanie had fallen. Laney picked up the knit cap and set it back on her mother's head. "I took a break, okay? Why are you still here?"

"I asked you how she got the phone." Anna picked it up and tapped to see. She shuddered and shook her head, as if she could not believe her eyes. She waved it at Laney, who refused to look.

Laney said, "Let's get out of the bedroom. She needs to sleep."

The sisters moved away from the late-day river, gray as the sky, from the deepening shadows of their mother's sickroom, away from the machines, the whoosh of traffic, into the dark living room.

Laney turned on lamps.

Anna showed the phone's screen to her sister again, and again Laney refused to look. "That's Ned. Is this what's been going on? Ned McGowan?"

"She just wanted her phone. I don't know what's been going on."

"That's not true, Lane! You always know what's going on with her! I mean, I can't believe you . . . you . . . enabled this."

"I wasn't enabling anything. I was just trying to keep her calm. That's all. That's it." Laney dropped to the sofa and held a pillow to her chest. Tom loped over, lay at her feet, and rested his head against her leg. The dog's kindness, his complicity, his loyalty, overwhelmed her. Tears welled.

Anna sat next to her sister. She set a light foot on Tom's paw. She said, tenderly, "You two. A couple of enablers." She took Laney's hands, and her own were still shaking with the dissipating energy of restraining their mother, and the failed effort to soothe her.

Laney said, "Anyway, what are you doing here? I thought you were doing your romantic evening with Jules."

"She got called in. I came back. I had a funny feeling."

"I like your scrubs."

"I know. And look!" Anna extended her leg and showed off black patent-leather clogs. "I'm official!"

This seemed the height of absurdity, of hilarity. Laney's tears turned to laughter, and the two of them dissolved, shushing and giggling. They were giddy, waiting for the worst.

Anna tapped their mother's phone to life. "Have you looked at this?"

Laney said, "No. God, no."

"I think you should. I mean, it's . . . bizarre. What is she doing, stalking him or something?"

Laney inhaled long and deep to quell her fluttery chest. She looked at Anna's intent brown eyes shining at her, at Anna's interrogative brow, furrowed, her burnished hair, everything about Anna questioning, always questioning, everything about Anna more familiar to Laney than her own face in a mirror. They were in this together now. It was just the two of them, from now on, and Tom, in his way. Laney understood it for the first time. Martin, their father, he would help, and Jules, of course, Anna's big love, and there were family and friends and people from Joanna's work.

But really, it was Anna and Laney, together. Only Joanna's daughters could travel from here into the mystery of the next minutes, hours, days, into all that gathered ahead of them. Sorrow had settled in, grief hovered, and there was nothing to do but keep going, right into it, united.

Laney loved her sister with a ferocity that felt like power. She wanted to harness that, not work against it. Especially now. Her heart lifted a little with that realization. She hadn't connected those dots before. She thought, *It's time to tell the truth.*

She took Joanna's phone from Anna and searched. She pointed to the pregnant woman in the red dress. "That's Trudi Mink. She's famous."

"She looks familiar. Is she an actress?"

Laney said, "Hold on," and went for a device with a bigger screen. She handed an iPad to Anna.

Ned's fiancée, known to her clients and fans as Dr. Trudi, was a dermatologist with an empire. She catered to socialites and moguls, celebrities and celebutants, fashion and music names in the news, those wealthy enough to try to erase time from their faces. To answer the needs of her core target market—Upper East Side girls with whom she had gone to school, all of whom had, unsurprisingly, excellent, face-forward, blogable, tweetable lives with their reality-show looks and wardrobes, studied and coveted and replicated by their followers—Dr. Trudi, proud descendant of a long line of high-cheekboned Prague women for whom beauty products had evolved from kitchen-table avocation to global domination, had cooked up a service and product pipeline called EternaPlast. It was a compelling concept: a members-only, lifelong subscription/prescription schedule of Botox, fillers, acids, resurfacing, and custom formulations in a jar. The EternaPlast lifestyle—philosophy, really—was holistic, comprehensive, calibrated for all ages, from tweens and teens on through every decade. Dr. Trudi, at great profit, franchised EternaPlast to an exclusive band of like-minded practitioners around the globe.

EternaPlast's tagline, *Control Your Face*, inspired a catchphrase craze. Politicians, artists, TED talkers, thought-leaders, and the culturati clamored, right behind the celebrities, to participate in the advertising campaign, shot by a famous photographer in the style of rec-room porn. EternaPlast clients of all ages posed nude in the positions of da Vinci's *Vitruvian Man*, wearing a Trudi Mink latex mask covering their faces.

Trudi was her own best marketing strategy. Her skin was soy milk–smooth. She had blue-black pin-straight hair that framed her huge eyes. She had champagne-shimmer lips thick with gloss, and kitty-shimmer eyelids sharply winged in black, and cobalt fingernails and toenails, her signature. Her nail color was so heavily tweeted it became the Pantone color of the year.

Anna and Laney swiped from screen to screen. There were countless pictures of Trudi Mink stopping to smile on red carpets or exiting an Escalade, tuxedoed Ned right behind her. They partied frequently at charity dinners and fund-raising events and museum exhibitions in important places all around the world, with the famous people of the world. They sat third row at couture shows, and ringside at model fight clubs. Dr. Trudi, now pregnant, her blue-tipped, beringed hand cradling a baby bump, beamed, with Ned McGowan at her side.

Laney said, "Hard to believe it's Ned, right?"

Anna said, "Eew. This is just . . . eew."

Laney laughed. "I agree, but what do you mean?"

"I don't know, it's just all so . . . shiny. Like they exist so we can look at them on an iPad. I can't explain it."

"Remember that movie Mama made us watch? That old black-and-white with those giant pod things incubating in the garage, body snatchers who take over when the humans fall asleep? Everyone has the same foreheads and cheekbones and smiles. It's depressing. This is what Ma's been looking at."

"The pregnant girlfriend."

"Yeah. And all their nice stuff. And the parties. While she's . . . you know. Not doing so well." Laney's voice caught.

"He is such a dick. I cannot believe it. What happened? They were back together?"

"For a while last summer, I think. Mama was sick by then. And then he was gone. She won't talk about it."

"How could I not have known any of this?"

"She didn't want us to know."

Anna's phone dinged. "Dad. He's on his way up."

"More fun." Laney powered off.

"Now I really am getting out of here. I'm going home, I'm exhausted. I'll be back in the morning." Anna rose.

"Noooooo. Don't leave me here. With them!"

"Enjoy it. Our parents are finally getting along."

"Yeah, how could they not? Drugs work."

In some primal pecking order, the advent of Martin, with his advantageous height and unruly gray hair, sent Tom from his post in the bedroom. Martin pulled a chair to his ex-wife's bedside. He tapped lightly at her arm and she raised her eyebrows slightly to acknowledge his presence.

"Some news?" Martin unfolded the *New York Post*, and gave the tabloid pages a shake. Reading the *Post* to Joanna was a habit left over from their marriage, and when she got sick, he visited her in the hospital and now, at home, to carry on the tradition. He picked oddball stories, not the hopeless, sad ones, and he read them in New York voices, nailing borough accents and ethnicities. Every story that cited a billionaire, a police chief, a cabbie, a bystander, or a hot dog vendor became a theatrical event, perfectly cast with Martin in all the roles. Joanna was too sick to reward Martin with even a smile.

When there were no more happy stories to read, Martin sat quiet for a long while. Joanna dozed. Finally he said, "Jo. I hope you can hear me. Maybe you can."

He moved closer and tilted his head and talked softly at the mother of his daughters. "I have one more piece of news. I was going to wait, see how you were coming along. But I think we'll just go ahead. I think that's best." He moved his warm fingers under hers, curled and damp and cold. He paused to see if she registered his touch or his words, but she was still.

"I'm going to marry Margaret. In the spring. I haven't told the girls yet; I wanted to tell you first."

Martin's eyes filled with tears. "I bought Margaret a ring. It's fine, it made her happy. The whole time we shopped for it, though, all I could think about was, how was it that I never bought you a ring? How did you let me get away with that? I twisted a piece of wire and put it on your finger. I bet if I opened your jewelry box, I'd find it, right?

"I have the impulse to apologize to you right now, although I know how mad that makes you. And I get it, I do. I'm too loose with the apologies, you've always said that.

"I love Margaret. But I still think of you as my wife. Isn't that crazy? I remember promising myself—promising you—that I would look out for you forever. I broke the promise. I know.

"Are you in there? Are you in pain?" Martin made useless adjustments to Joanna's knit cap, to the quilt. He looked into her face to find her beyond the drug, beyond exhaustion and acrimony, and there she was, she was there, he could see with no trouble the young woman he married. Her cheekbones were high. Her forehead was smooth. Her hair flowed from the cap, tangled as if by the wind.

"Jo," he said. "Remember when the girls were little? I was hardly ever around. I don't even know what I was so busy doing. How stupid. That house was filled with fun. You made it fun. I remember coming home late and all the lights would be off, you were all asleep, and I would take my shoes off and walk through in my socks and it would feel like the house itself was resting, catching its breath. I could practically hear the day you'd all had echoing in the walls, the music and the giggles and the squabbles, your voice steady underneath theirs, the beat they listened for, you, your girls. I would go from room to room to see the three of you recharging in sleep, all that female energy, all that girl power, and then the next morning I could hear you all in the kitchen right back at it, and that's how I woke up, to music and giggling and squabbling. I don't think I had any idea what to do with all that love. How to protect it. I think I thought it was all just automatic, it would turn out fine. It doesn't work like that. It's not automatic. Not by any means." Martin bowed his head. He squeezed the summit of his nose and sat straight.

"They were so surprised, that's what I remember when we sat them down to tell them we were splitting up. Laney, she thought she was in trouble for screwing up the plumbing in the upstairs bathroom. Anna, she went so silent, she was so hurt, she hates surprises, she hates to be out of the loop, doesn't she? I thought we'd ruined them, our girls, when we broke our home.

"Are you hearing me, Jo? They weren't ruined, were they? Not at all. They are . . ." He had to stop.

He started again. "I'll be here, I just want you to know that. But Jo? Joanna? I hope you can hear me. This is not easy to say." Martin entwined his big fingers through Joanna's. He held loosely but could feel an infinitesimal tightening of her grip, just enough tension in her hand to know she was listening.

"You're frightening them. Fighting and resisting everything. You're hurting yourself and you're frightening them, and you don't want that, you would never want that. I went along with the idea of bringing in the hospital bed, but I'm going to pull rank. I'm going to speak to Keswani about getting you back to Sloan. Or hospice. It's time for the professionals to take over. I don't like this." Martin waved at the glowing machines surrounding the bed. "This is too hard on them."

His voice stayed soft and low, he never changed his tone or his pitch, but he spoke with conviction, he held his voice steady, he closed his fingers around her fingers, and he cupped their clasped hands with his big hand, as if sealing a pact or a vow, and he said, "So, here I am, looking out for you. By looking out for them. Which I will do forever. Forever. I promise. Better late than never, right, Jo?"

He bent to Joanna, who kept her eyes closed but was very much part of the conversation. "Say it's okay."

Martin's once-wife nodded. *Okay.*

5

I said okay to Martin but it is not okay.

Come on, you know how he is. He'll talk to Keswani on Monday and he'll persuade the girls and before you know it, we're back on death row at Sloan. Or waiting it out in some hospice.

Hush. I'm not going to Sloan and I'm not going to hospice. Anyone looking at me (except Martin, focused, as usual, on his own agenda) can see I'm not leaving the bedroom alive. I'll be surprised if I even wake up on Sunday morning. And what's with the "we"? There is no "we" yet. Stop hurrying me along.

I'm looking out for you. Sound familiar? Marty's rationale.

Martin. Martin seems lovely but you have to know him to understand. He is a famous conversationalist. A great talker. Martin gets going, it's performance art. I remember a dinner with friends, it was Max and Alison, and he told a story, he was funny, he was the hero, of course, and everyone laughed and Max toasted him for his storytelling chops. Later we walked to the car and I said,

"Martin, I told you that story nearly word for word at breakfast. You stole it."

Why are we still talking about Marty? Hasn't he sucked up enough of our oxygen?

Let me finish. He dropped a heavy husband arm around my shoulders and said, "Jo," in his shut-me-down tone. "It's a good story. It's just better with me in it." That's one example, multiply it by years. Forgive me if I'm no longer susceptible to Martin's charms.

You taught him how to treat you.

For a long time, I navigated his anxieties. I tried to steer us past them. In other words, I let him drive me crazy. We weren't suited—like, biorhythmically—to each other. The Martin of my married life was an anxious, anxious guy. That manifested itself in all the usual ways, not enough money and then debt; workaholism and then loneliness; my disappointment in him and his retreat from that, from me; and then, naturally, no sex and then the dead air between us, a silent knell. All that was left was contempt, for him and for myself.

First comes love, then comes marriage and a baby carriage and mortgage payments and the death of desire, and presto change-o. Contempt. It's the circle of married life.

Along came Ned with his intent listening, his hunger for me, his light touch lighting me up in my forties, after divorce, after cancer.

It was supposed to be a fling.

We met at Harvey's on a Saturday night. Flirtation was instant, mutual. I could tell Ned was younger but in bar light, nothing suggested a fifteen-year age difference. I think my first question was, "How old are you?" which he waved off. Fifteen years, dismissed. That was nice.

Nice? Please. That was seduction. Ned needed an editor, a steady blow job, and a mother.

You're so cynical. Ned was—is—rugged and unkempt. He has the face of a 1940s studio star, a Cagney, a Bogie, the kind of face you no longer meet, an old-before-its-time face, idealistic, with a wide, soft jaw and a bull brow. It's obvious that something is off-kilter. A long, pale scar disrupts the planes on the left side. I locked in on that face, trying to understand the asymmetry. I couldn't even attempt to be cool or coy. I couldn't tear my eyes away. Very, very attractive. I didn't need much seducing.

It was supposed to be a fling.

Not to mention, another good talker. He told the story of a surprise line drive in second grade, just seven years old, within five minutes of taking the field at shortstop in his very first Little League game. A lot of blood and forty stitches later, the scar, faint by the time we met, ran from the top of his left cheekbone, up, two centimeters shy of his eye, through the eyebrow, across the forehead, ending a couple of inches into the hairline.

Because of the injury, his left cheek seems to sit higher than his right. The interrupted eyebrow begins late, leaving him with a crooked look. His eyes are heterochromatic—two different colors—as a result of the trauma. The right is the black-coffee brown it was meant to be; the left, which he's lucky he kept, is black-coffee-with-a-drop-of-milk. And the scar points the way to an impressive forelock, a white patch growing in his thick brush of black hair. That's how it grew back after his little-boy head was shaved to stitch up the laceration.

He should have caught the ball.

I loved his crooked face. His many faces. The weather that passed across, the repose I found there. The pleasure I took in reading the skies of his variant eyes, in knowing him without words, without touch. I thought I'd get to look at that face forever. I thought his face was my forever view.

You said it yourself, it was crooked. Two-faced! Face it, that mug was a lie factory. Behind those wonky eyes he was conniving. How much can

I get away with? How long can I keep this going? How can I dodge commitment with a capital C? You taught him how to treat you.

You're so cynical. When I spoke, he surrounded me with his long arms and legs. When I spoke, he listened with his whole body leaning to me. I felt cornered, thrilled. I hadn't been listened to in a long time, and I hadn't been backed into any corners in forever.

Five years later, I'm lying here hooked up to monitors, hooked on drugs, arguing with the next me—you've come for me, I get that—so I can remember the woman I was with Ned, desirable, for just a little longer. Just a little longer. I'm a block away from Harvey's and it's Saturday night again. Everything is still happening out in the city without me. That is hard to process, hard to process. Saturday nights will keep coming around, without me. Whoever I was. Am. May be.

Whatever. It's time to do something with all this self-pity. Let's exit memory lane. We're busy!

Look, here's Tom. Tom reminds me of the girls. I've neglected—ignored—them. I should feel bad. Where are they? Where's Laney? Someone must be home.

We're home. You and me. Or almost home, anyway.

Tom noses me. Tom distracts me. Where am I? I'm in bed now, aren't I? I'm just checking. I'm in the moonlight, it's Saturday night, did we come back here that first night? Let me think.

No. You went to his place, that crummy apartment a block over, the studio, the studio. I was a topless, middle-aged woman splayed on his grad-student sofa, I don't think we even paused to . . .

Wait. I already said that. Or maybe you did?

Wrinkles, scars, forty-six, thirty-one, none of it mattered, you showed yourselves. It's all a very big deal for a minute, the surfaces, and then nobody cares, after a minute. Once you get the whiff, once you inhale—you go for the neck—once you imbibe what you need to heat your blood and your groin, and your fingers tingle with the proximity, once it is moments away, you're going, you're a goer, you're a goner. Muffin tops, crow's-feet, sunspots be damned. With all due respect to Dr. Trudi and her empire.

What hope flooded my body at the cellular level, when Doc came back last summer.

You were all in again, heart and soul, cells too. You became unhinged when he left you. Understandable. It's science. Exactly the same receptors that must have nicotine, that must have cocaine, must have love. You can actually die of a broken heart. Loretta did, right? After Daddy? Despair kicks the door open and depression tramples the immune system. Strokes strike, hearts attack. Cancer flourishes. Keeps on flourishing, if I'm reading our current situation correctly.

Just last summer.

Misty watercolor memories of the way he fucked you over.

Breathe.

Next thing I know, I am sleeping, sick on the sofa, fucking sleeping, and Ned goes downtown and never comes back, and there he is all over the internet, Trudi Mink is Instagramming herself and her stuff, tweeting herself and her sonograms, tweeting Ned, too, for fuck's sake. I'm surprised more people don't take up weapons, I really am.

Breathe!

Are we still breathing? Tap tap tap. Is this thing on? What are we seeing? TEMP, EKG, RESP. The green and blue and red, the actual lines of our life, peaks and flats giving the play-by-play of what's happening inside of us, or technically, you. Those are your vitals giving notice. The waves of yellow, that's breath. Are they flatter? Are the crests farther apart? The beeps. Faster? Slower? What's Tom staring at? He sees something. The twitchy ears, what does he hear?

I need to stay calm! I need to breathe!

It was never a fling. It was never a fling. The stakes were high. The stakes were high. He knew that. He promised and he promised and he promised. His face. He put a twisted wire on my finger. He dropped his heavy arm around my shoulders. He kissed my scars.

Wait. Who were we talking about just now? Martin?

No, Ned.

Ned, Ned, Ned. Jealousy is green. I look down at myself in my blue bed and I am outlined in neon green, like a Kirlian image. Tom barks. Shhh, Tom, shhh. Where am I? Where are you? My chest rises and falls, I can see it from up high. Not alive, not dead, I hear my own voice, Ned Ned Ned.

A weak throb at my clit. The monitors glow bright green and yellow, green pulsates, yellow blurs. The lines, the lines, the waves, their crests, blood, beats, breath. The throb. Crests become flat lines. There's a relentless, hellish sound in my head. Beep and beep and bark. "Bark, bark, bark," Tom warns.

Tom? Is that you? Go, boy. Get someone. Get Anna. Elena! Laney! Who's home? Who's home?

Light telescopes to black. I go higher. My breath ceases. I'm rising and falling at the same time. I'm floating above it, and I am, and at the end of me, the end of Joanna, I'm wondering what's next. I'm only human. Aren't I? Wasn't I? I'm thinking that this part, this free fall, this fall and float, will end soon, and then the next part will begin as it always does, like that summer driving out east, a clear Fourth of July, rich kids in an oncoming BMW, a BMW barreling at us in the wrong lane, driving drunk at seven in the morning, they lost control, they skidded, and we swerved hard right and it was slow-motion chaos, waiting to hit that pole on Sunrise Highway but I was still there in real time. Waiting for whatever was next. My thoughts, in fact, were racing, are racing now, human thoughts racing, which is good, which is good, maybe I am still here, maybe I am not gone, maybe you are not gone, maybe I will find you again, maybe I will find myself again on the other side of chaos. And so. I make the thought, I voice the hope, and I hang on to that hope for dear life while I wait for impact and believe: *This will end. It has to. It's physics. It can't just be this, this waiting to hit, forever. Something must be next.*

Blackness like space. No direction, no light like in the movies, to know how to go. Beep beep beep, warning sounds. Bark, bark, bark. The smell, it's stale, the wasted body, it's done. Waiting, and waiting, and waiting.

I am literally trying to feel dead. Something's not right. I employ visualization techniques. I used these techniques in the quake of childbirth, in waiting rooms, in doctors' offices and infusion suites and surgical theaters and sick on the sofa last August waiting for Doc to come home.

I picture myself in long-ago Lamaze class on the floor, struggling to cross my legs and tipping back like a punching-bag clown, without Martin to lean on because Martin is not there, Martin is late, and I am doing breathing like they tell you to, knowing it's a technique, suspecting it's a scam, but huffpuff-dizzy and grateful for a distraction from the belly so big, the body so possessed.

Now I breathe and now I follow my last breath, to concentrate, to try to smell again baby scalp, and I find it, I do, it's so hard to call up scent but my last breath travels, then, to the day my little girls run to me up the beach and they smell like coconut lotion and sand and sunlight, yes, sand has a scent, bleached bones of the sea, crushed bones of the sea, and yes, sunlight has a scent, warm yeast like baby scalp, of course.

I focus. To see without sight, to intuit celestial signals, stars, a path, a way made for me, a way to go. I'm looking for light. Give me something, give me light.

Something isn't right. Terror and certainty collide.

This is not my beautiful life, this is not my beautiful death. I roll alone in a dark of my own making, trapped inside a flip-book of the last ten years:

My father, Ben, gone fast on a wet road, three minutes from home.

Loretta's exit four weeks later, massive coronary, boom, in what seemed like a choice, leaving me a grown-up orphan, and my little girls grandparent-less. All of us too young.

The lawyered-up, papered-over end of my marriage to Martin. Selling off the house on the hill. My kids, stunned, assembling game faces, for me.

Gray areas illuminated, deadly, on X-rays. Battle-ready every morning, at war with my own cells. The tyranny of numbers: dollars, centimeters, nodes, pounds, older, younger, time creep. Words said or unsaid. Risks untaken, or taken so often they became self-inflicted wounds. Grasping, trying, losing hold. Breasts, hair, skin, love. Everything imprinting itself on the body, inside the body.

And then desire. And then vanity. And then letting a fling fall into the future and rob me—rob my daughters—of the dwindling now.

You taught you how to treat you. You taught you how to treat you.

I have done everything wrong. There is no light. There is nothing to do but give over to black. The blackness is utter. It's a propellant, like estrogen.

Look back, look back, look back. There. There is a faint shimmer of an already-memory of the blue bed, there is a young woman there, Elena, my baby, bending over the body in the bed. Where is Anna? Tom looks up into my face, and I look down into his. If I could still listen I would hear his liquid eyes speak of devotion, of loyalty, of promises kept, but my senses are irrelevant now.

Elena says, "No, Mama, no, no."

My babies, my babies, I love you, I'm sorry.

Tom barks. The barking does not stop. My exit music, bark, bark, bark.

Here we go. Something is not right. I feel . . . strong. I roll faster, I gather all my pain and my fear. I wrap myself in it, the disappointments, betrayals, abandonments. This is what it is, this is what I'm left with, this is what I am. This is what's next. Here is the pull, the massive pull into black pitch, and I'm in the spin and I'm spun out and away, and my soul is cut loose, borne ceaselessly away from home.

I go deeper into this dark thing I am and that is chaos, and in chaos I am known to myself as not human, and I know that faith, the belief that there is something beyond the slam and the quake, faith has flown, and light and hope are gone too, fragile human things, gone, and I am left behind in the land of the left-behind, and this is not life nor is it death, this is neither there or not-there, but here where I split apart and reconstitute at the border of light and dark, matter and antimatter, here where I am a new element, now elemental, now ether, now risen, now doomed, and now ready to trespass against you as you trespassed against me.

Closure time, Doc.

As a transmigration took place in the next room, Laney, unaware, anxious to relax, chased an Ativan with a slug of wine. She did not like being left alone with her mother.

Her father was gone, but his scent lingered in the apartment, heavy wool holding a cedar-soap smell, and tobacco, his secret vice, with an overlay of mint for camouflage. His voice left traces, an old resonance she could replay, although she hadn't been able to make out his words, just Martin's up-from-the-diaphragm tonality and inflection. Laney knew it had been a serious, sad, one-sided conversation.

A box from storage had her name on it. It was stacked with papers from middle and high school, and spiral notebooks. She had been a doodler, and a writer. The notebook pages were worn smooth as cloth, all white space covered with a girl's hieroglyphics: flowers and eyes and spirals, lips, song lyrics, quotes, forgotten names emphatically underlined for forgotten reasons, her own name over and over, autograph practice, and long lists of wishes, established, revised, checked, of plans and prospects for the future, set down on paper with such force they were nearly carved.

Laney was a lefty, and the notebook pages were blurry because she couldn't write without dragging her hand across her own words, smearing them. She remembered late nights, writing, writing, writing, letters and poems and stories and sketches, journal pages branded with the intensity of her teenage struggle to make sense of her self. Then, groggy school mornings, worried about the time, starting to spin out. Her mother would stop her—*Ma, no, I'm late!*—and scrub the side of Laney's left hand with a wet cloth, from pinky to wrist, to clean the blue ink from her skin, and say, "Well, I guess you've found your passion."

It was a noisy New York night. Sirens approached and receded, intermittent shouts and barks cut through the cold, everything echoed short, sharp on the streets below. Laney flipped through old book reports and essays and smiled at her adolescent theories and conclusions, and her earnest energy. Seeing her own handwriting, how she had once so fervently practiced it, ignited a feeling of tenderness for her younger self, in the time before doubt, before the narrowing of possibility, before her mother got sick.

Laney hadn't written in a long time. She wanted to, and when he came on the scene, she had been encouraged to by Ned McGowan. She was a high school senior, just transferred from the suburbs to public school in Manhattan, working to navigate the urban environment with at least false confidence. And although it was strange, her mother with a boyfriend, she'd been impressed with Ned.

He taught a couple of Intro to Media classes to freshmen at Columbia's Journalism School, was finishing his dissertation, had a cool idea about a novel, and worked on his blog, ShameShame.com, to which people were beginning to pay attention.

ShameShame started as a simple linked list of "family values" politicians who were caught espousing a morality they themselves eschewed. In some cases, they were literally caught with their pants down. ShameShame visitors could click and be carried to the politician's website or public Facebook page, where the shamers shared their strong opinions about hypocritical behaviors. The blog's early band of followers was raucous and enthusiastic, and Ned's one dumb idea, a hobby, really, took on a life of its own. He was trying to figure out how to monetize it. Ned was ambitious. He had goals.

When Ned and Laney's mother were in full swing and he was living with them at the Titania, dinnertime became ShameShame brainstorming time. Ned and Jo riffed and laughed and Googled, and eventually the simple list idea grew. ShameShame became a kind of hypocrite aggregator, pulling together everything the internet was churning out by the hour about men in power behaving badly: irresistible gifs and video clips, silly blind-item innuendo, tips and cell phone photos sent in by the blog's readers. One big idea that was Ned's and Ned's alone: the StickyFigure. He'd drawn a suggestive stick figure, barely R-rated, that somehow resembled a sanctimonious politican even though it was just a dozen strokes on a napkin. Ned added a salacious caption, posted it the next day, and *voílà*—a meme was born. Ned was not a cartoonist, not a writer, had no real feel for technology or what constituted an internet business model, but he was famous-ish for StickyFigure, well-loved, well-linked.

Laney loved the dinners. First of all, her mother was happy. Joanna buzzed from kitchen to table, setting out roasted chicken on a platter, the big wooden bowl of salad greens, asking questions that led Ned to refine his ideas. She put her arms around Ned and nuzzled his neck and he leaned back into her, and Laney, hit by the realization that she had a sexually active mom with a young boyfriend, would look down at her plate or have a sudden need to clear the table.

But it was good, a good phase. Her mother was happy.

Laney wasn't much interested in ShameShame, not really, and she didn't care about monetizing the internet or aggregating content or click-through rates. What she did care about, what she heard loudest, was what was seldom discussed—the young women who were part of the scandal stories. They seemed vague and nameless to Laney, and indistinguishable from one another. A secretary, an intern, a dancer, a masseuse, an escort. It was a weird sisterhood of women with strict adherence to shared standards of artificial beauty—jutting breasts and lips, for starters—trading for . . . what? Money? Access to power? Laney couldn't stop thinking about it, long after the dinners.

As Laney struggled with college admissions essays, her mother's green-pen edits were extensive and intimidating. When Ned read the essays, he scrawled, nearly illegibly—*Good thought, say more*—in a way that helped her relax and write. Ned encouraged her to slow down and think harder and build her ideas, sentence by sentence.

Anna hated Ned, but Anna didn't know Ned like Laney did. Anna had finished her undergraduate years at Columbia, and was in Birmingham in med school, forging her separate self, completely distracted. She hadn't seen how happy Ned made Joanna. She had no idea how cool and supportive Ned had been to Laney. When Laney felt teenager-miserable and awkward and un-beautiful, Ned was a friend, without making a big deal about everything like her warring parents had.

Laney was drowsy. She leaned back on pillows. The mild effects of the Ativan loosened the knot at the base of her skull, the knot at the hinge of her jaw, the knot in her shoulder. Pages were scattered across her lap. Tom was nearby. He snuffled in sleep. She let one thought form and hover. *Maybe I'm a writer.* It seemed like something she could be good at, looking at the past through a young woman's eyes. Looking hard at the narratives of American history, long dominated by powerful men, and hearing the background voices of women rising, long unheard, and amplifying those voices, and writing them into the story. Maybe figure things out and then tell it from her perspective. Maybe.

Not maybe, definitely. She felt as though everything was cracking open, because . . . because women. Because the internet. Because superhero-level forces had converged, finally, and it was time for new stories and she had something to say. Laney pictured her words flying to join other young women's voices, euphonious, like birds seeking flock and flight pattern, across language, across economies and cultures, across differences, carried by technology on myriad currents.

Good thought, say more.

She felt an effervescence, just a tickle at the base of her spine, a gathering of resolve. She'd always been so fired up about things. She'd had commitment and persistence and big ideas. Then everything got shadowed by her mother's illness. Muted. Put on hold. She allowed herself the disloyal thought: *On hold, just for now.* She let that thought lead her, let herself follow it, let herself believe that this part would end, somehow, some way, maybe soon, and the next part would present itself. She could be tougher, more like Anna, and map out the future. Her future. She had to picture it, visualize the self she wanted to be, living the life she wanted. She wanted to write. Not maybe. Definitely. She was ready to reclaim . . .

Behind her closed door, for a full minute, in a drowsy dream about her future, Laney did not register that the shrill alarm and the chopped bark of a big dog were coming not from the streets below, but from closer. Much closer. When she finally did register that the alarm, the barking, the urgency was here, at home, she jumped from bed without untangling her feet from the covers, got caught, had to crawl toward the door until she was free of the sheets, and tried to stand but her socked foot slipped on the papers strewn across her bedroom floor, and then she got to her feet, finally, and ran.

"No, Mama, no, no." Laney held Joanna, tried to pull Joanna back. She reached for the phone, punched 911, and punched at the monitor to stop the alarm. Tom reared back and barked frantically, as Laney texted Anna, *Come home!*

Joanna whispered. Laney said, "What, Mama, what?!"

With a sudden lucidity that shocked Laney, Joanna fixed her gaze on Laney and insisted, in a clear voice, "Ned. Ned. Ned."

The words tattooed themselves on Laney's heart, deeper than grief. Laney held Joanna and looked down into her mother's face, and with those terrible last words vibrating in the atmosphere between them, she watched an emptiness invade her mother's eyes. "No, Mama, no, no."

Meanwhile, Anna sipped her cocktail. Anna was not where she was supposed to be.

She'd walked just one cold city block to the dive bar around the corner from the Titania, ordered a Tito's and soda, stuck her hand in her jacket pocket, and shut the phone off. She would not let herself look at the screen, equally dreading a cancellation or confirmation text of the assignation Kai had suggested: *Meet me.* Anna's curiosity about Kai was so intense she felt like she was already cheating on Jules, doubly so because it was Valentine's Day. Kai had stepped into her line of vision, impossible to classify, curved and muscled, soft and hard, womanly, manly.

At first she thought Tap-a-Keg was empty, but once inside she saw that nearly every table and bar stool was occupied by patrons sitting alone, resolute, fixated on the drink in front of them. The bartender moved fluently in the narrow space between a wall of ancient, mottled mirror, set with bottles set on stepped shelves, the stock multiplied by reflection, and the rutted old bar. Anna, nervous, guilty, with too much energy to wait patiently, made small talk with the bartender, who glided along, wiping, reaching, scooping, pouring.

"Quiet crowd."

The woman, tall and long-necked with a tight braid down her straight back like a second spine, shrugged. "Yeah, for now. These are my regulars. They don't get too excited about drinking anymore." She threw an experienced glance at Anna. "Waiting for someone?"

"Oh, yeah. A friend. From work." Anna had no idea why she dropped Kai into the friend-from-work category, why she needed to establish that distance for the bartender's benefit, but it was vaguely connected to being close to home, where her mother lay dying.

"Work nearby? Nurse?" She indicated the cocktail and smiled. "Hope you're not on your way to your shift."

Anna remembered she was still in scrubs. She pulled her down jacket around, to hide the hospital name embroidered above the pocket. She was irrationally self-conscious. "Oh, yeah. No. My mother lives near here. At the Titania. On Riverside. I was . . . visiting her."

The bartender nodded. "Well, give a shout when your friend shows up. I'm Wills."

Anna heard the word "friend," again, as if it held subtle emphasis, as if the bartender knew Anna was about to cheat on Jules with Kai. Kai, of the ink-black scrubs and the dark red clogs, Ninja of the nurses' station. Kai, whom the doctors sought out for consults on patient evaluations, who hauled equipment effortlessly through crowded corridors, who never used baby-talk or a singsong voice with the children, who didn't condescend or obfuscate to their worried parents. Kai who, with three diamond chips outlining the curve of an ear and a stethoscope that fell from the neck and snaked a course between compact breasts to dangle at the abdomen, flirted right past Jules, at Anna.

The game, now on, was the best kind of distraction: Anna's senses tuned to and scoped for Kai at work, texts had flown, and now here it was, their stolen hour of sexy, irresponsible fun. *Meet me.*

Anna was into her second vodka and soda, itching to fire up her phone but stopping herself from doing so, when two parallel events rose to compete for her attention at precisely the same time: one, a singular presence approached, and Anna did not have to turn to see that trouble, Kai, had just crossed the threshold; and two, the night was knifed by a siren so loud, the ambulance had to be pushing, urgent, through Broadway traffic right out in front of the bar and then careening around the corner to speed shrieking toward a building near the river.

The siren faded from Anna's perception into the near distance as Kai took the bar stool next to her.

7

What the hell.

I pictured something out of a Nancy Meyers movie: I follow a light through a meadow, up a slate walk to a many-windowed house with white sofas, and French doors open to an ocean in the sky and the sun, and because they are angels, all the dogs I've had to put down greet me and frisk around me. There is a to-die-for kitchen, a good chair, and a cloud-soft pashmina waiting. The floor is one big Apple screen, showing me those I love, Anna and Elena, and Tom, thriving below. I mean, what's the point of heaven if it's not utterly customizable?

Wrong, wrong, wrong.

I'm in a vast waiting room with an infinite number of beige plastic chairs, joined one to the next. There are no directions or signs or indicators. There is definitely no light. I am . . . progressing? regressing? . . . along the line of chairs, which extends so far that each is diminished until it is a tiny speck touching a black horizon that never gets closer, even as I move along.

My shoulder blades twitch. Are those wings? My legs jump, my fingers vibrate, my eyelids are pinned open, but there are no legs, there are no fingers, there are no eyes. I have no heart but it pounds. I am phantom-limbed, now a whole-body amputee. Leftover thoughts and memories spin around me like I'm a mad scientist in an old movie trying to work out the formula, zeros and Xs and Ys and brackets and equal signs swirling, searching for the solution so I can undo the dark hour of my death: my spirit intestate, in the throes of disappointment, choking on guilt. I closed my eyes against my daughters, away from love. Away from love. I withheld my touch. I left Ned's name ringing in Laney's ears, rocking her to the core.

Anna must be furious. I should care. I realize that.

I smell ether or maybe Freon. It's me. I'm a gas, I'm the stench of claustrophobia, the fumes of panic, stuck with myself and my sorry soul. I'm stinking up the joint.

I'm a ghost. Perfect. So much for a graceful exit.

Walls and ceiling and floor meet at precarious angles. Everything vibrates. At the far black horizon there is a tall, outsized maitre d' stand with a bad lean. The room, the chairs, the maitre d' stand, objects that once anchored the day-to-day no longer have substance. Everything wavers like a stage-set backdrop version of what it was. The show will go on without me.

I move along. Sinister file folders are piled in tall stacks behind us. Yes, us. There are others. Many others.

We are somewhere together, we are something together. I process the familiar shape of beings, once human, ahead of me and behind me in line. Men, over and over and over, loveless. There is a child, many children, unloved. There are women, lovelorn. We are multitudes, various, the same, mingling and massing, unlovable. We coil, tight around our ectoplasmic selves. We uncoil and extend. We reach and we reach and we recoil. We shift from spherical to elongated. We flow into each other, without boundaries. We are becoming fog. A susurrus comes up from under, a white-noise hiss we make. We plead: *Unsuffer me.*

We collectively know to shuffle along the queue. Gray lighting like garage fluorescence buzzes and echoes, the sound of insects, bugs hitting the zapper, and that's stressful, and the buzzing gray light is the only light, and it's not what I need, it's not what I expected, and that's stressful too.

I really don't want to be here. I'm not supposed to be here.

Let me think. It's not my fault. It's Ned's fault. Let me think. I was trying to stay alive, hoping love would save the day, while he was holding out for someone better. While he was trading up. I suffered for him.

Let me think. He needs to suffer too, for me.

I pointlessly, endlessly move along the line of chairs. I'm surrounded by entities on either side of me, trapped in the tilted room, and then I am there, right there, now it's my turn, I'm at the maitre d' stand, an enormous podium that looks like it might tip over. There is a gooseneck lamp, unlit. There are red velvet ropes on chrome stanchions that bar the way into a deeper black.

The black is a screen. I look hard to try to see where to go, to find a hidden horizon.

The screen flickers. I'm at the movies: Tom paces. His nails tick on the wood floor. Smartphones, landline, door buzzer bleat and fade, bleat and fade. Footsteps come and go. Voices rise and calibrate. An industrial zipper opens, *zzzrp.* I am lifted and folded by an EMS crew and set into a black vinyl bag on a gurney. The white knit beanie with the skull drops off. *Zzzrp.* An industrial zipper closes. Elena says, "Oh my God, is this happening?" Anna is clenched gray with remorse, glazed with what appears to be the effort to get sober.

I am steered out. The gurney bumps walls and the corners of my furniture. Laney winces. She says, "Be careful!"

Anna leads the EMS crew through the apartment. She thumbs

her phone, texting, talking, tears streaming. Laney shuffles behind, wearing a nightgown, a hoodie, battered boots.

Look at that. Tom stands stock still in the foreground. He stares. His stare burns. He stares not at the gurney where Joanna is bagged, but through the screen at me watching from this waiting room.

My movie's last shot shows the grim processional stalled: EMS crew, gurney and body bag, daughters, one in a nightgown, one in scrubs, all awkwardly waiting for the elevator. The End. But the screen never fades completely back to black. Tom's disembodied eyes, two pinpricks of not-black, still watch me through the luminiferous ether.

It's my turn. I am stopped at the border, Security, or Customs. Whatever. There is another other in authority who does not acknowledge me. Her back is to me. She is long and sinuous and gowned in shadow. She burns dark blue, but the burn is a freeze and the freeze makes me I shiver. I wait. I try to see. I catch glimpses of silver filaments that obscure her face where hair should be and extend from her fingertips where nails should be. She surveys countless manila folders—full of damning evidence, I guess. I wait.

At last, I am judged, I am found wanting in her flint eyes. She shifts shape and shows me my own old blue eyes, my own silver blonde, my own naked body, my desire, my vanity, and she runs me backward from deathbed—Christ, let's not go there again—to my first night home on earth when Loretta swaddled me, baby Joanna, and set me in a low drawer lined with a soft towel, while my father, young Ben, assembled a bassinet nearby.

Whiskery appendages beckon me closer. Lore is imparted to me over imponderable reaches of time and space, summed up with a singsong mission statement.

Well, hello, here you are, you've turned up between realms
Now heed your predicament, which no doubt overwhelms!

Your quest is impossible, it will never succeed,
To get to the Light, where you will be freed.
You missed it already, the moment so crucial—
The love of your girls, even that proved un-useful!
You'll haunt and you'll moan, it's New York, so you'll kvetch,
You'll knock once for 'yes' and you'll still be a wretch.
You'll fuck up the present, you'll be stuck in the past,
You'll wear out your welcome, forever outcast.
I've seen it before, my hopes are not high,
But give it a go! You're now doomed to try.

I feel hypnotized. I agree to something. The velvet rope drops. I pass through and I fall like in a falling dream, into the black. Through human habit, I'm worried about impact. I forget: I'm immaterial.

Words revolve around me: impossible, doomed. I pinwheel down, an ether-diver with no parachute. The zapped bug sound recedes. The *zzzrp* sound is forgotten. The susurrus doesn't stop. I need a strategy. Let me think. I need a plan. I need . . . A new word pops up in front of me.

Revenge. It feels right, it's a classic, why reinvent the wheel? Isn't revenge what ghosts do? I'm probably chock-full of ancient wisdom and contemporary tricks, the art and science of payback.

It's not my fault. I will make him pay. *Make Ned pay, make Ned pay.* Could be my new mantra.

The atmosphere changes. The black evaporates and the blue-green world is in my sights.

I'm closing in. I'm in the approach, I am the approach, I'm dead reckoning, on course, here I come. Here I come through satellite view and Earth 3D and now I zoom through high-res images and heat maps and population densities, I navigate and pan the paranormal panorama, I am close to the terrain, I zoom the city, I zoom the river.

Welcome to Morningside Heights.

There are ghosts, everywhere. They—we—mass like a cloud of no-see-ums over Broadway.

I join. I have to. I am a mote in the dust of the unresolved dead, geographically drawn to my old neighborhood, compelled to return to the scene of the crime, to have a look around, so to speak. Familiar energies loom and recede: a castaway marooned on the bench of the Broadway median, shirtless in all seasons; Charles, the retired Supreme Court justice from my floor at the Titania; the beautifully dressed blue-haired woman with the bent spine who forded the swamp of the 103rd Street subway platform every morning; a missing child I knew from posters in the market and on lampposts; the rescue-dog lady from Riverside Park, perpetually pulled along by her mutt pack; and the blind businessman I had a crush on; and millions more, millions, my neighbors, all of us defined at death by our failings, and so, failing to die right, doomed to keep trying.

We orbit instead of rise. We seek but look backward as we chase *hiraeth*, *saudade*, nostalgia, different words for the same indistinct need, those glimmers of ineffable human longing, abysmal and tantalizing but gone, gone, and we can't stop wanting what we cannot have, even though the glimmers have been obliterated by shadow and it is possible that nothing human remains.

Every unearthly earth hour is spent haunting alleys once avoided, streets once walked, the pocket parks and benches, coffee shops and dive bars, our lobbies and corridors, our bedrooms, our kitchens. Ghosts swoop through trees and buildings, pass through people, pace back, forth, and run, and roam, looking to tear a hole in a world to which we no longer belong but which we refuse to leave, which makes us moan and whine and beg for release, and keen relentlessly, and the collective sound is something like a bow drawn slow along a violin's E string, but infrasound, felt by the living in the teeth or at the back of the neck, and the keening translates to: *I'm here, I'm here, I'm here.*

Yes, we are legion. Yes, we are a pain in the ass.

Hey, wait. What's that? What do I hear? Adele?

It's Adele, coming out of her own dark despair, daring her ex to underestimate her, threatening to make her ex's head burn, if I'm hearing correctly. Every radio plays the same revenge anthem as I dance through the spirit-dense atmosphere.

Now I have a mantra and a sound track. I am delivered into a hot bad mood and a constant, roiling churn. The need to escape beats where my heart used to be. This is it, this is what remains, this is what I am.

At 116th Street, there are the black iron gates of Columbia University. The plaque reads "May All Who Enter Find Peace and Welcome."

Peace, that's the goal. Welcome? I'm guessing that's not the reception a relentless, needy entity gets.

Well, well, look who it is.

The professor walks with purpose across campus in his tweed jacket, his low-slung jeans, chalk dust in his hair. There he goes, dispensing smiles and clever remarks to colleagues and students. There he goes, so charming. He can't help himself.

Neither can I. I watch, I hover, I go close. He passes near me. *Hey, Doc.*

I make that thought and a chill runs through him. He turns up his collar. Doesn't help. He walks faster. Doesn't help. I'm almost on him.

Hang on. Let's slow it down. I have all the time in the world. The good news is I'm not weak or sick anymore. The good news is that I can't age out. *Hear that, Doc? We said forever and I meant it.*

Ned pauses at the top step of Low Library. He surveys his territory and waves to his students. His every gesture is more known to me than my own. The physicality of him. The reality of him. I watch him start down the steep steps, shifting his weight as he descends. The little sway in the hips. The bolt of white through his black hair. Something wry in the crooked expression, a little lift of the lip, a kind of a who's-zooming-whom look, and I remember that look, I remember being attracted to it. Like he was skeptical of everything except me. Himself included. Himself most of all.

I also remember my rage, the sputtering, coughing, choking rage, but I don't need to struggle anymore, I don't need to rant about being ignored, the change has come, now it's my mission, now it's revenge, now it's just let's get this thing done, now it's my turn to move on, move away from life, and I know what to do, I know how this has to go, and I make the thought and hit *Send* with the thought, it's just click bait, some bullshit thing about closure, and I see him feel his pocket rumble, and he goes for his phone, and I know my days of being ignored are done.

It's good to be invisible.

8

At the top step of Low Library, Edward McGowan Jr., known as Ned, stopped to look around. He felt like he was being watched but he was getting used to it. Between his students, who lifted phones or tablets to click or film as casually as they uncapped a pen; his Fox News fan base, who tuned in to hear him give blogger-guy insight to trending political imbroglios, and begged for selfies with him on the street; and his own image beaming alongside Trudi's on the internet, Ned was always on, and learning to adjust to always having an audience.

Ned raised his collar, pulled his scarf tight, and buttoned his jacket. He took the steps down two at a time, underdressed for the first week of March in his old tweed sports coat, the one he kept rescuing from Trudi's pile for Housing Works. Kids huddled and smoked and called to each other under a bright moon. The *Post*, rolled in Ned's jacket pocket, devoted an entire front page to it: Super Moon. Ned hated how they kept trying to turn the weather into a disaster movie—yesterday's headline was

"SNOWPOCALYPSE!"—but he couldn't remember ever seeing the moon so close and huge and low before. It hung stark behind water towers atop buildings west of campus, along Riverside, and cast its cold glare over Morningside Heights.

The phone in Ned's pocket rumbled. He squinted at the screen and although the words were clear in the super moonlight, he could not process them. He shook his head and blinked hard, like a sitcom character who can't believe his eyes, and looked at the text again.

Closure time, Doc. Use your keys.

Ned staggered, lost his step, and fumbled the phone. It skittered ahead on the cobblestones and he fell to one knee trying to grab for it. His students roused from their smokers' huddles under bare trees and hooted at him. "Hey, Professor, whaddup, you high?" He smiled and nodded and waved them off.

The phone twirled to a stop at the tips of Dean Peck's snow boots. "Professor McGowan, be careful. Watch your step."

"Dean! Yes, thanks, I will." Ned waggled his phone as he got to his feet. "Got away from me." He struggled to compartmentalize, for the moment, the shock of receiving a text from the grave in order to focus on the formidable dean. Every encounter was an opportunity to inch up and out of adjunct, closer to tenure at the Journalism School.

"How's the blog sideline going, Professor? I caught you the other morning on Fox as I was flipping past. Going on about . . . who was it? Another congressman?"

"Yes, from Maryland. Following in the footsteps of Weiner. So interesting, Dean, we've now added selfies to the proliferation of—"

"Selfies?"

"Selfies, yes. You know." Ned held his phone up and smiled at it, to demonstrate. "Pictures you take. Of yourself."

Peck was dismissive. "I know what selfies are, yes. I'm just not sure there's enough there." She moved away from Ned. "Keep in mind, Professor McGowan, that blogs and tweets won't bring you closer to publication."

Ned called after her, "Dean, no, I'm working on turning StickyFigures—that's my cartoon on ShameShame.com—into an e-book, it's a different thing, there's actually a substantial market for cartoons! And I'm nearly done with the first draft of my novel. . . ." But the clarification was lost on Peck, who hurried away.

Ned was thirty miles west of Syosset, the Long Island town where he grew up, and after a patchy undergraduate career, finally, he was a long way from where he started out, but still not on the inside at the J-School. Tenure, the grail, seemed unattainable. His journalism niche, blogging about the internet as a big-box store of sex enticing susceptible shoppers—men in power with a compulsion to digitally display themselves and hit *Send*—was more pop culture than news. The university was not interested in conferring legitimacy on either ShameShame or Ned.

The growing interest in gotcha reporting had gotten him pegged as an expert by Fox. He'd leveraged Jo's old nickname and become "Doc McGowan" on television. With cameras rolling, Ned would offer up a full plate of gossip, served in quasi-intellectual sound bites so viewers need not feel guilty about their appetite for the transgressions of politicians. Ned's narrative was swallowed by the internet and regurgitated over a twenty-four-hour news cycle. Viewers liked Doc McGowan.

So did his students. Teaching gave Ned another stage, where he performed for his captive audience. He knew how to get and hold a room. He arrived late to class, unshaven, in rumpled clothes and untied shoelaces, trailing a scarf, clutching a white plastic bag bulging with books, papers, manuscript pages, the newspaper, and a couple of water bottles, with the air of a man who'd had a late night.

Like a hip mime, silently he would set down his bag, unwind his scarf, shrug off his coat, shake it with flair, and deliberately let it drop to the floor. He rolled his sleeves with flourish. He shambled to the desk and ritualistically emptied his pockets of the detritus of his day. He patted and unpacked and examined items before placing them on the desk: pens, pencils, scraps of paper, chalk, a broken cigarette, a complicated key ring, and a plastic Tic Tac box that he rattled when he wanted their attention. Finally, when the students were quiet, expectant, he would look up, run his hand through his signature hair, and speak, or more accurately, bellow. His opening remarks about politicians caught in compromising situations were infamous.

"Wide-stance Senator Craig!"

"Dirty chat-happy Congressman Foley!"

"Governor Sanford's midlife hike!"

"Selfie-obsessed Representative Weiner!"

And so on. The whole shtick took sixty seconds, and they were in the palm of his hand for the next eighty-nine minutes as the real teaching took over.

Doc McGowan's annual fall semester kickoff field trip to the Museum of Television and Radio earned rave online reviews from his students. He was their guide, putting media front and center as a cultural influence with at least as much impact as the policies and institutions and best-known names and events of the twentieth century. He showed them how media shaped itself around events, and at the same time, how events were shaped by media. In the galleries, he pointed to artifacts of the early days: scratchy recordings, heavy typewriters or teletype machines, furniture-sized radios, the revolutionary television set. Ned opened their eyes to how the students' own media consumption was changing everything. Their worlds had become circumscribed by a mosaic of screens customized by physical size and shape, but also by content they themselves could create, design, curate. Audiences were dictating the formats and the content—he himself was a citizen journalist—and defining themselves based on how they clicked and tapped. In effect, if they weren't responsible, media-literate consumer-audiences, they would be curating current events so that they were hearing only what they wanted to hear, not necessarily the truth. The truth was becoming tangential.

The tour concluded in the library, where hundreds of thousands of programs from television and radio and the internet were available. Ned's students sat at consoles and watched Cronkite broadcasts, Martin Luther King's march on Washington, Super Bowl commercials, the Apollo 11 launch, the Challenger disaster, aerial footage of OJ's slow roll along a California freeway, and quick-cut minutes of thousands of hours of global coverage of the 9/11 attacks. They laughed at assembly-line antics and sledgehammered cats. Ned paced behind them and gave the backstory to what they were seeing on their screens. Old black-and-white, static, fixed cameras, and poor audio made long-concluded occurrences seem like fresh conspiracies. Contemporary saturated colors, increased volume, dizzying angles, and roving cameras made scripted drama seem like news. Phone footage made everything seem like an exposé.

Ned's whirlwind media field trip—insightful, politically incorrect, bawdy, condensed for the attention-disordered—helped the kids, some of them just landed in the U.S. from villages on the other side of the planet, relax and connect to the ideals of journalism, to the J-School itself, to the city of New York, and to the enthusiastic ambassador of all three, Doc McGowan.

All of which Dean Peck and the J-School had ignored. Nor did they acknowledge the student reviews Ned got, including tiny flaming Zippo lighter emojis to attest to his hotness on myhotprof .com. His television Q factor, 200,000-plus Google Search results, multiple-screen presence, and name-brand girlfriend had turned Ned into a rock-star professor. But he was still an adjunct professor. The J-School was not impressed. Neither was his mother.

Ned's academic career had been a delaying tactic in the long-game strategy of defying Pat McGowan's assumption that he, dutiful Irish only son, would become the lawyer in the family. Columbia had not unlocked the ivory tower so that he could put an end to his mother's question, the question she led with every time he picked up her call or stepped through the door of his childhood home. "What's new?"

His answer was always "Not much." He secretly wanted to hit the long ball—a bestselling novel—and obliterate that question, but for now, for years, "Not much" was the only answer he could give to avoid admitting heresy to the lawyer-son mandate.

The four words—*What's new? Not much*—were excavated, coded, exchanged, deciphered, catalogued, and archived like fossils from ancient times or moon rocks from the future by Ned and his mother. Having a blogger for a son who taught a couple of classes to undergraduates was not nearly the payoff for which she'd hoped. Drawing infantile cartoons, snickering about sex on Fox, being "internet-famous" were meaningless to Pat. She hardly knew the girlfriend, Trudi Mink, future mother of Pat's future grandchild, with whom the only meals shared so far were in too-dark restaurants where the skinny dermatologist poked at leaves and picked up the check.

Ned passed under the 116th Street gates. For the millionth time, he pointedly looked away from the university's plaque. He felt neither peaceful at Columbia nor welcomed. The phone in Ned's hand rumbled and glowed, again, insistent. *Closure time, Doc. Use your keys.*

Standing in the cold outside the iron arch, Ned shook his phone once, hard, to bring it to its senses, and looked at it again. The vertical view had gone horizontal and bigger, but the text from dead Joanna was still there. Ned scanned his limited knowledge of how technology worked. Maybe it was a weeks-old message delayed somehow in transit, just hitting his phone now? A glitch?

He tried to remember which button powered it down, gave up, pressed and held each tiny nub on the rectangle's top and sides. Finally the device went dark.

Ned waited an interminable minute or two, covering the phone with his hands, as if keeping it warm might ward off the text. He repeated to himself: *Go away go away go away.* He shook the phone and pressed the tiny buttons and the device came alive and buzzed its notification again, and there it was, still on the screen: *Closure time, Doc. Use your keys.* Ned tapped at her name, JO, and swiped and tapped to erase the contact, but the Delete function was nonresponsive. The text remained.

He said, "Fucking hell, leave me alone," out loud. It had been his mantra over the past six months.

After Ned walked out on Joanna last August, he'd electronically dodged her in his devices many times. He'd felt frightened and stalked. He'd deleted maybe a hundred e-mails and voice mails from her without reading or listening to them, and had forced himself not to see texts, blindly swiping and deleting, muttering "Fucking hell, leave me alone" each time, an abracadabra to mute her pleas. He just wanted Jo, sick Jo, desperate Jo, to go away. There had been nothing he could do for Jo. Now, fatherhood was less than two months off. Trudi needed to know his head was in the game. He couldn't let the Jo situation jeopardize his setup with Trudi.

He didn't feel good about it, but there it was.

Finally, Jo went silent. Ned had been even more freaked out. He'd half-expected her to show up at events in a nightgown and sickbed hair, pointing an accusing finger at him. Then came the e-mail from Laney. She'd blind-copied him on an evite sent out for a memorial gathering for her mother, "The Sad/Happy Hour," her way of letting him know Joanna was gone, while hiding contact with Ned from Anna.

Ned had been stunned to see the subject line, Joanna DeAngelis, formal, definitive, on his screen. Her name in his in-box evoked a torrent of denial, disbelief, and shame. Jo was dead, and he could no longer pretend there was time to make things right with her. He would have to live with how poorly he'd conducted himself at the end of Joanna's life. Jo, whom he had loved. Who had loved him.

Now, here, under the Super Moon—the memorial was tonight, over at Harvey's, a few blocks south on Broadway—a stray text hurtled itself from the great Wherever to the screen of his smartphone.

Harvey's was where they met. Ned was a grad student flummoxed by his meandering dissertation, *The Exigencies of Political Power: Adaptive Morality Through a Mass Media Lens.* After hours laying down bad writing about a depressing topic, he'd wandered out of his studio apartment on 102nd Street and stopped into Harvey's to clear his head with bar bustle and a drink and a Mets game on the television. He took the stool next to a woman and overheard her order exactly what he was about to order, Grey Goose and club soda. He said, "Good choice," and she tipped her glass toward him. He wheeled around to see her, and never went back to the game.

Her hands wrapped around the glass, the color of her skin, her soft eyes assessing him. Her face. He was knocked back into the future, into an idea of forever, something he hadn't believed existed. Yet here it was. Here she was. He physically lost his balance and grabbed for the bar to steady himself. Which, for years, she teased him about: *You literally fell.*

"Whoa," she'd said. "Hold on." Her first words to him.

"What's your name?" Ned asked, extending his hand. "Say it again," he demanded, not letting her hand leave his, looking into her eyes. "And again."

It was the way she pushed off the *n* and lingered on the final *a* of Joanna, the way her tongue hid behind her front teeth on the *D* of her surname, the slight pucker on the soft *g* in the middle. It was the way she complied without hesitation, saying her own name once, twice, three times just because he asked her to, playing with him, showing frank interest in him, with a smile suppressed in the curve of her lip. It was how her hand buzzed in his so that the current between them rendered Ned shocked and unable to let go, a victim of electrocution who can't release the object and sustains a fibrillation of the heart and an alteration of the nervous system.

Ned had previously dated self-protective academic women who were suspicious of him, unsure if he was marriage material. As astutely, they voiced complicated sexual concerns and demands that required attention and thoughtful negotiation, none of which Ned could muster. One too many times he found himself in cerebral conversations at three A.M., too drunk to give a fuck, if fucking was even viable. He did not know if this phenomenon was endemic to Gen-X women or academic women or was possibly provoked by him specifically—whether it was their problem or his—but sex wasn't fun. Then he'd walked into Harvey's, sat down, looked into the eyes of Joanna, and felt the strongest surge of desire—his own and hers—since his early twenties.

He had no choice but to hold on, exactly as she'd instructed, and try to tap into what felt like the source of who he could be.

She was forty-six and he was thirty-one.

Five drinks later they were pushing against each other in a doorway. Five months later they were living together at Jo's in the Titania on Riverside Drive, with Laney, too, who immediately became like a kid sister to Ned, minus the constant barbs he was dodging from his actual kid sisters, Irish twins Kristen and Keira.

The bonus, the stroke of luck for Ned, was that Joanna was an editor. Of self-help books, true, but she had the focus, the patience, and the deep ear he didn't have to listen for the dead spots in his dissertation. With her green pen, Joanna pushed Ned paragraph by paragraph, and then word by word, to strip out recycled anecdotes and unoriginal thinking. She challenged his formulaic, cherry-on-top conclusions about the media. He wasn't thinking hard enough. He wasn't thinking new enough. He wasn't making the leap from the old-school ways of the politicians and the press to right now. He was trying to build a blog, so it was time to think like a blogger.

On nearly every page she'd written: *Bump it up against the internet!*

At Harvey's, at Tap-a-Keg, Ned and Jo convened nightly to review the dissertation. Afterward, in Jo's apartment, six cozy rooms over the river that Ned now called home, she set simple plates for him and Laney as they continued talking about Ned's work. Ned's career.

A white segregationist senator's half-black daughter claimed her birthright. Leaked divorce papers of a Senate hopeful with a sex addiction showed he'd bullied his wife into bondage clubs. A closeted gay governor was spectacularly outed, and in the process, scripted the now-classic redemption story: powerful man exposed for his long-repressed fill-in-the-blank desires denies all to the cameras with a grim-faced good wife at his side. The blackout period follows, and then "rehab," public soul-searching, and one-on-one with a sanctified confessor, on television.

Joanna pushed. *Bump it up against the internet!* Ned wrote. His doctoral degree was awarded.

One night after a few drinks, she supplied a jokey title for the dissertation. *The Exigencies of Political Power: Adaptive Morality Through a Mass Media Lens* became *Pricks & Dick Pics: Politicians in the Digital Age.* Joanna passed it to an agent friend, and a book by Edward X. McGowan Jr., Ph.D., was born. Ned could no longer remember at what point his stunted thesis became this wonderful object, eight copies briefly occupying sixteen inches of shelf space in the Current Affairs and Politics section at the Barnes &

Noble on Eighty-third and Broadway, before *Pricks & Dick Pics'* rapid, remaindered retirement.

Along the way, ShameShame had taken shape. His having somehow elbowed his way into a couple of areas of accidental expertise—he wasn't a writer but he had a book, he wasn't a cartoonist but he had StickyFigure, he didn't know much about the internet but *The Huffington Post* was offering ShameShame.com a spot on its Polities page as a featured blog—television was Ned's next frontier.

When Fox called, Ned, with his slight smirk, mismatched eyes, and white streak of hair, was a telegenic, credible mix-master of relativisms: moral, cultural, and ethical, wrapped in cartoon commentary. He did *Meet the Press* a few times, and even *The View*, where the ladies giggled and eye-rolled as he expounded euphemistically on what makes a man called to public service, so often a Christian man with a deep reverence for God and country and family, bang strippers and teenagers and humiliate his wife and children and, probably, elderly parents on the national stage. None of it was new, but because of the internet, the transgressions seemed kinkier, the descriptions more explicit, and Ned, as adaptive as the next guy, was on hand to shake his shaggy head along with the viewers, *What a world, huh?*

Ned wanted to turn his attention back to his novel, tentative title: *The Angry Intern*. But television was fun. Short spots, cameras rolling, thirty seconds to commercial, the squint, the grin, a shrug, the hand through the hair, Doc McGowan delivered truthiness parsed from rumor, innuendo, frantically cycling news, leaked e-mail, tweeting tipsters, and the blogosphere. It was pretty unsavory but it paid the bills and Ned enjoyed the attention.

Bookings took Ned away from home. He was mightily distracted from academics, from *The Angry Intern*, from the comforts of monogamy. His expertise was needed at events, conferences, other television appearances, and it was so easy to work ShameShame from the road.

Ambition and attention, recognition, a little bit of money, all those things and then more of those things, as well as being young and callow, paved Ned's way right out of Joanna's bed, out of her home that he had made his home, and into the beds of other women. One night, after a lot to drink at a party, Ned found himself being pushed back onto a white silk duvet by Trudi Mink, celebrity skin mogul, in her very contemporary apartment overlooking the High Line.

Within a very short time, surprising even to Ned, Joanna became a stop along the way. Not that he'd planned that. He wasn't sure how it happened. He had gotten carried away and then carried along, and every now and then he tried to get back to Jo. Back home to where it felt like forever, back home to the source of who he could be. But he always strayed. Until last summer. Last summer, they reunited and he'd intended to stay.

The text reasserted itself. *Closure time, Doc. Use your keys.*

Probably to pick up a package, he assumed. Notebooks or drawings or copies of contracts or leftover clothes or something that she thought he'd want. Maybe that's what the communication barrage had been about before she died: She had something she thought he needed. Her family would be at the memorial service at Harvey's, maybe just Tom would be home, and he could use the keys and get in and out.

He couldn't make things right, it was too late for that, but maybe he could make things easier on himself. He could pick up the package and shut down his lingering guilt over leaving Jo. He would honor her last, texted wishes, and maybe wherever she was now, up there somewhere looking down on him, she would see that he was making an effort. That his intentions, finally, were good. That his intentions, maybe, had always been good. That he was—definitely—not so good at turning intentions into commitment.

Ned blinked to clear tears of cold and focused again on the text. "Closure." That was a good thing. He patted at his pockets. He still had keys to Jo's apartment hooked on his key ring, mingling with Trudi's. He looked up at the night sky over Broadway and thought, *Better late than never, right, Jo?*

9

I've got to laugh. I give that a try. What comes out is a weak, infrasonic hiss.

First Martin, now Ned. *Better late than never.* Easy for them to say! I'm the dead one! Now they can tell themselves what good guys they are, without me and my disappointment around as a rebuke.

I guess I have—oops, had—a pattern. I knew how to pick 'em, men who excelled at breaking promises and making apologies. For a human instant I wonder, how did I not notice this in real life? Was it my guy-dar that found the few, or are the many just so good at playing the promise/apology get-out-of-jail-free card?

Eh. Who cares. I am no longer obligated to own my own shit or cheerlead theirs. I don't have to be accountable. I can be as heedless about accountability as Martin was, as Ned was. What's good for the gander is now good for the ghost.

Better late than never. Ned tosses the thought off, and I shoot back immediately: *Speak for yourself, Doc!*

He gives a galvanic little shudder and I can see he is aware of a disturbance in the atmosphere. He feels me but he writes me off as a memory. Still, he's vulnerable to me. He's receptive. I'm giving him a surge, just like the old days. It's sexy. I wonder if he can actually hear me. I push a directive his way, as an experiment: *How about a little smile, Doc?*

Sure enough, the corners of his mouth rise. It might be a grimace, but I don't care. I put it there, that's what counts. This is my first good, long, off-screen look at Ned in months, since last summer when he planted the kiss of death, sort of, on my clammy forehead and took off.

He looks good, I'm not going to lie. He's still doing the tweedy-professor thing, so I guess he hasn't succumbed yet to Dr. Trudi's Euro wardrobe advisors. His hair, that never-ending source of vain satisfaction for Ned, looks a little less black and is threaded with gray, and the shock of white is a little less bright, all of which gives me pleasure. I swoop and I smell him, I smell him and I want him. I'm fleshless and bloodless but I'm riled up. I'm turned on.

I resend the text message to his phone, just for fun. Ned reads it again, pales, and tries to dislodge me from his device. He is struggling to make sense of the incursion. I can see it on him. Memory tugs guilt, the heavier boat, and he tries to shake me off, to square his shoulders, his beautiful, broad shoulders, but I read him, his brain runs through questions and analyses and scenarios, desperate to reach his reward, the luxury of denial. He is feeling me.

Of course he is. We were soul mates, although my soul is in grave jeopardy, and I am not sure he ever possessed one.

Ned walks south on Broadway. He's waylaid by students eager for attention from their cool professor. He bestows a tilt of his head and a little smile, his go-to seductive listening posture. A girl approaches, a couple of years older than the others, a grad student. Winter layers, puffy jacket, ski hat, scarf wound around to cover half her face, tight pants and Uggs. None of it camouflages her blonde intent. She gleams. She is three inches too close to him. Something in his head's tilt redirects, something in his smile deepens.

I can't believe what I'm seeing. No way. No fucking way.

I sputter and rage. I'm all over the place. I'm to-ing and fro-ing like a balloon, overinflated and not yet tied off, that escapes the grip of the knotter. This much Ned-doing-Ned is too much much too soon. I'm a sensitive instrument. There must be a motherboard to master to control the peripherals of my ghosty capabilities, or something.

Ned and the grad student step into a Starbucks, dense with energies I can't parse, the girl making her play, Ned's dumb desire like a leash she holds as he trots after her. They disappear into the caffeinated intensity of a crowd I can't penetrate.

I'm triggered, I'm without a plan, I churn and coil and spring and recoil uselessly, jealous—technically, I guess—on behalf of what looks like the pending betrayal of Trudi Mink.

I remember, oh, I remember. I died chewing betrayal like cud, and I'm still at it. Once upon a time he was the grad student. Once upon a time, I had blonde intent and a Grey Goose and club soda in my hand.

It was supposed to be a fling. I was single for the first time in two decades. My hair was back and good after chemo and I was so happy to be healthy—having swallowed the "survivor" bullshit along with my morning Tamoxifen—that I forgot to notice I was on the precipice of being un-young at forty-six.

In bar light, in conversation, in the vodka stream and the heat between us, the Ned-Joanna Venn diagram charted overlapping circles of collapsed Catholicism, a veneer of cynicism over reckless romanticism, intellectual compatibility, and a taste for dark vanilla dirty-sexy. Not to mention his heliotropic bend to any spotlight, and my polishing of him so he would shine there.

Who was the moth and who was the flame?

It was supposed to be a fling, but we fell into a fantasy future where we pretended the age difference didn't matter. Ashton and Demi were together, so high-profile, same age gap, but, holy smokes, I did not relate to being a cougar, the label that had been coined and gained currency in the tabloid mainstream. I told myself that didn't apply to us. We weren't a joke or a trend. We were real.

Sometimes too real. Sometimes his enthusiasm for ShameShame made me wonder, *What's his interest?* I remember watching him provide color commentary on television for the unfolding revelations about John Edwards, presidential candidate, a man whose hand I shook at a fund-raiser Ned and I attended in Soho, on a long-ago rainy night.

The candidate's wife had been there too. Elizabeth and I exchanged pleasantries, a couple of words about the heavy rain. She touched her reddish, unkempt hair and said, "It's ruined mine, but he's got a glam squad to make sure his stays perfect!" and she inclined her head to her husband and his infamous coif in that condescending, conspiratorial way women do to establish instant common ground at the expense of their men. I saw her eyes flicker to my scar, the one that edged past my v-neck, and just before she moved on to mingle she gave me a quick hug in acknowledgment of breast cancer sisterhood.

When Edwards, after torturing his family—I mean, families—with denials for so long, finally admitted the truth—*Better late than never*—Ned was booked on Fox to "provide context."

Edwards, the father of daughters and a child who died, husband to the woman with whom he endured that, a woman mortally ill with breast cancer but still working on his behalf while he sidled up to some younger someone and bantered and flirted and cheated.

Caught, he lied about everything with righteous indignation, so perversely entitled and deluded that he conspired to pretend the newer woman and the newer child belonged to his best buddy. Who, of course, had his back.

After the Edwards scandal broke, Ned and I met at Harvey's as usual at the end of his Fox day. I was rattled. I wanted to talk about Elizabeth, how terrible this betrayal must be for her. She and I had shared a moment in Soho. I was really rattled. Maybe I was feeling my age, my own compromised health. Maybe I was confronting how risky it was to entrust my dicey future to any man, especially one who was fifteen years younger than me.

All Ned wanted to do was talk about his performance on television. How did he do? How did he look? Did he strike the right note of authoritative-but-compassionate? How was his hair?

How was my hair? I remembered Elizabeth Edwards's bemused comment at the fund-raiser. John Edwards, Doc McGowan, brothers in hair obsession. And more, it turned out.

I felt confused, frustrated, by the sleazy detour Ned's career path was taking. He'd wanted to be a writer, not a blogger digging for dirt about semen stains and wide stances, recycling the same script on Fox, scandal after scandal. He seemed to relish what I found depressing. I couldn't help but consider the creeping possibility that Ned's interest in raking the muck of lying men was other than academic. That Ned was drawn to the topic and so very good at talking about it because on some level, he related. On top of which.

I felt unheard. My late-night listener wasn't listening unless we were talking about him.

On top of which.

Ned looked the same as the night we met, and I didn't. Forty-six to his thirty-one is one thing. Me, forty-eight, forty-nine, I'm in another country. I'm trying to course-correct backward in the mirror. Small, serious-looking jars and bottles proliferated on my bathroom shelf as I renewed and smoothed, toned and improved, repaired and corrected to stay youthful. I contoured and illuminated as if my life depended on it.

Ah, the EternaPlast irony. Considering the outcome, growing old would have been a gift.

On top of which.

I was newly shy to show myself. I shut the lights. I bought pajamas. At cocktail parties, I covered my arms, the scar on my chest, the latest sunspot, and I fumbled for my glasses as shiny, tiny, underdressed producers, editors, agents, and yes, grad students with perfect eyesight and firm upper arms waved Ned's latest interview at me from their phones.

I couldn't stop doing the math. *When I was X, you were Y. When you are Y, I will be Z.* One time, trying to make light of our age difference, unable to leave the topic alone, pushing at the topic, tongue to tender tooth, I said, "I was Witing-Out the date on my birth certificate to get into bars when your mother was pregnant with you."

Sly Ned said, "What's Wite-Out?"

I said, "Very funny, Doc," but point taken. From then on, I was on the lookout for everything obsolete: landlines and dictionaries, road maps and film, me, especially me, included.

The details are banal, honestly. I would wait, he would be late. His phone shimmied on the dresser in the middle of the night. When he was there he was not all there. He told me I was hearing things when I mentioned late-night text dings and call vibrations. He told me I was imagining things when I noted some ever-so-slight emphasis in the mention of a new associate's name. He told me I was being dramatic when I got angry at being kept waiting, everywhere, all the time. He told me I was projecting my own doubts onto our relationship, and in the process, I was undermining his commitment to me, to us.

He said, with the sincerest eyes, "My doubt is your doubt."

For years, and even now that I'm dead, I turn that phrase over and over. *My doubt is your doubt.* It's masterful! It's a mirage of meaning. I almost understand it. It sounds like something a politician simulating "earnest"—namely, John Edwards—might come up with. My doubt was simple: Fidelity!

We broke up, we reunited. The breakups were about me trying to get in front of the inevitable. The reunions were about Ned, guilty and tired, burnt out on drinking and being charming, wanting to detox back to a better self. Or, more like recharge at the power source. Me.

One reunion brought us to the brink of making it official. We were on a reconciliation vacation, naked in the sea under a tropical moon, such a cliché, and yet. He said, "I don't want to be apart anymore." He said, "Do you want to . . . ?" and I nodded. I really did want to marry him. I really did think—because my own parents had shown me—we could be better together than we were apart. In the sea, we never said any of the actual words. The word "marry" was never said, stayed unsaid, the word "yes," was never vocalized, but he theoretically asked and I theoretically answered. We spent the rest of our idyll announcing our engagement to strangers on vacation, people who didn't know us, whom we'd never see again.

Back in the city, Ned never mentioned the proposal again. I brought up making plans, once, twice, and then there was nothing left to do but seethe, stung, and count up the ways in which I had been affronted.

I wanted a fling but it was never a fling. The stakes were high. I was past young, he knew that. I was shell-shocked from loss, compounded: my parents, my marriage, life as a family in our house on the hill, my breasts and my health and quite possibly, on the horizon, the loss of my actual self. He knew. I whispered my fears to him as our breathing quieted after pleasure, before dreams. He knew it all. He promised—no, he vowed—that he would shelter me as I would shelter him. He vowed. Where do the naive whispers go? The thoughtless vows?

Now I, a ghost with no body, embody them. Now I, a ghost, am nothing but the chemtrails of those whispers and vows, breath once wasted on words poured into each other's ears, words I meant and he didn't mean. Lies.

Instead of putting a date on the calendar or a ring on my finger, we got Tom. I'm thankful for that. Tom was the perfect rebound man. I threw myself into that relationship with as much zeal as I did any.

Most telling, most egregious, the reddest of the red flags: Although Ned lived with me, he'd never gotten rid of the apartment on 102nd Street, where lately he was spending a night or two or three a month, "writing." I called it what it was, an expensive escape hatch, plain and simple. He deflected, vaguely, about Manhattan real estate, and I delivered the first and only ultimatum of our years together: Get rid of the bachelor pad. Six weeks later, ultimatum ignored, I threw a garbage bag full of his clothes out my twelfth-floor window onto Riverside Drive. Hey, I worked hard on Ned. I was his finishing school. I sucked up a grad student and spit out a minor celebrity. He snagged Dr. Trudi. That's how well I did my job.

These memories are chum, ground bone and blood that pull me into the toxic undersea where, sharky, I trawl the waters to feed the need now. I'm rolling in the deep. I churn, coil, spring, recoil. Ned and the blonde are still in Starbucks. I'm pissed but I pace myself. He got my text. I know where he'll end up tonight.

I'm above the trees, between the swarm of souls and the people who scurry over avenues below. I practice. I rise and glide and dive. Because misery loves company I join my cohorts, the gusting, dusty dead.

Talk about a power source. We gather in the glow of the moon, we charge and surge in every direction, we never acknowledge, we never bond, there is no contact between us because we are nothing, we don't exist, except we are in it together. We shriek in unison, *I'm here, I'm here, I'm here,* and it sounds to people who come and go on the streets below like the wind seesawing a rusty street sign that's lost a hinge.

I propel myself out of the mass. I swoop low, for kicks. Drunks stumble in my wake. Schizophrenics wave. Cyclists swerve into traffic and brakes scream. Old women shuffle and shift their burdens. I thread through alleys and stairwells and doorways and gated windows and fire escapes, my streets, my shops, I fly past Smoke, the jazz club, Hector Placeres Law/Abogado, past Suba Pharmacy and John's Frame Shop, past 103 Grocery and Jerusalem Restaurant Since 1989.

What do you know? Here we are, at Harvey's.

I blow past the "Closed for Private Party" sign. I spread myself thin and seep into a pixelated tableau: Familiar faces flicker with candlelight and grief, for me. I forget myself, my lack of self, I see my dog and I call out as if I'm human with a head and a voice, as if I'm just home from work, *Hey, buddy, hey boy, hey Tom!*

His big dog-head swivels. He strains against the leash. His wet eyes track me, and I realize, uh-oh, of course, dogs and ghosts, this is a thing, he's a dog and I'm his mistress dead or alive, I am the voice in his head. He hears me above all and above all I hover, trying to hide from Tom.

10

It was a good turnout for a weeknight in March. Only a little more than two weeks after Joanna's death, assessing turnout at her mother's memorial gathering—Laney couldn't call it a "service," there was nothing service-y about it, no religion, just remembrance—seemed like a sad train of thought and so Laney, who had already semi-guzzled Chianti straight from a fiasco at home (which, fittingly, was what the old-school straw-covered bottle was called, a fiasco), distracted herself with Keith the bartender and more red wine at Harvey's bar.

Joanna's friends and extended family had asked the sisters what the plans were—a wake, a funeral—but Joanna had wanted none of that. Their mother had loved the dark iconography and weirdness of Catholicism, but masses of cut flowers, a priest hired to officiate over a corpse with a scary-clown makeover, people inspecting the effects and the remains to be boxed up and dropped into a hole in the earth, the stages of decay, a favorite dress deflating and then disintegrating with the bones into dust, no. Laney pictured her mother pushed out to sea on a raft or carried off by the wind. Joanna wanted cremation, but for her daughters, there was the expectation of loved ones wanting to gather and share memories. Harvey's, their neighborhood go-to, seemed right.

Laney created the evite and dubbed the gathering "The Sad/ Happy Hour." Anna had gone through contacts from her mother's phone and an old Rolodex wheel and an even older address book, relics with Joanna's handwriting reaching, eerily, across cards and pages. She'd looked through dozens of pictures of their mother and found one she knew Laney liked, to avoid debate, and had it enlarged on posterboard. She'd scrolled through Joanna's music library and made a playlist.

Laney had focused only long enough to point out what Anna was getting wrong. She said, "Six o'clock is too early." "Dad can't read his own poem, that's tacky." "Don't forget John from her office, and don't forget the doormen!" "Tom Waits." "Mama hates cilantro." "Mavis Staples. Pink. Judy Garland. Rihanna." "No bruschetta?" "Where's Gang of Four?"

"Gang of Four?" Anna said. "This is a memorial service, with, like, grown-ups, not Irving Plaza in 1982. Pardon me, I left Gang of Four off the playlist."

"It was 1980. I found the T-shirt."

"You found a T-shirt? What else did you find? We're supposed to go through stuff together."

"And it's not a service, it's just Happy Hour. A couple of hours. The music is important. Anyone who knows Mama for five minutes—"

"Then you do the playlist. Take over. Do everything. Use all that energy you've stored up during the naps I interrupt every time I call you."

"And Tom. He's invited. If it's about people who loved Mama, Tom has to be there."

"Tom is a dog. Not people."

"He goes or I don't." One afternoon, in a rare outward exertion of effort, Laney had leveraged her grief face and walked to the corner and cajoled Harvey's manager into relaxing the no-dogs rule for the couple of hours during which the restaurant would be closed to other customers.

For days leading up to the gathering, she had wandered, motherless child, with a task list in hand she kept forgetting to consult. She waited on the "Walk" as pedestrians pushed past her and crossed on the "Don't Walk" as vehicles honked. She ate when she was hungry, which was all the time or never. She watched television all night, spooked by the flicker and shadows, afraid to head to bed because she had to walk past her mother's room. She slept through the day and woke at dusk from dreams that seemed embarrassingly obvious: Frantic search for lost keys. Stuck and sinking in quicksand. Calling through the empty house of her childhood and getting no response. Or worse, hearing her mother call, and losing her way trying to get to the voice.

Except for disruptions from Anna, who prompted her, goaded her, and nagged her, and Tom, who had to be walked three times a day, Laney stayed mired in thick grief, listing between denial and depression, anger and red wine. Her mother was just around every corner, and then *poof*, gone when Laney turned it.

She'd needed something appropriate to wear to Harvey's and so forced herself out to the shops on Broadway. In a favorite boutique, she realized that the last time she'd been there had been with her mother, whom, she realized, had still combed the racks for her, had still handed her flattering choices, had waited outside the fitting room, chatting, prompting, evaluating, and then paying, even though Laney was, supposedly, a grown woman.

Fogged in, blurry with loss, needing something for the service, needing to stop shopping, Laney grabbed a floaty, flowery skirt that looked like nothing else she owned. She overpaid, and fled the store.

Her mother's death resuscitated old griefs over other things she'd counted on—been led to count on, actually, if she were in a blaming mood, which she was—that had been lost or released: her parents' union, the family unit, her childhood home, the normal self-absorption of her teenage years, which her mother's cancer had nullified. And sure, Ned, who'd supported her without pressuring her. Who'd made her excited about her future.

Poof. Her own friends were scattered, in all senses of the word. And she'd closed herself off from them, so there was no one cheering her on into the unknown. Mama gone, Ned a stranger, Dad with Margaret, Anna completely preoccupied with everything, except Laney. And so she carelessly crossed avenues as if Joanna, the mother of her childhood, was about to say, "Hold my hand," and "Look both ways," as Laney stepped off curbs assuming, statistically, she could make it to the other side without getting hit by a bus, more often than not with judgment muddled by a pre-errand glass of wine.

Laney knew what Anna thought. She was being "selfish-and-childish," the old fighting phrase from their contentious phase when Anna was a teenager and Laney was not, yet, and the four years between them was vast. She did wish she could manage herself better, be less easily overwhelmed. She resented her sister for calling her out, even though she could see with her own eyes that Anna was doing all the work—setting everything up, checking items off the list, pulling Laney along to the next part.

At the bar, Laney arranged her flowered skirt, picked lint from her black tights, and lifted her chin to signal Keith. Small talk helped. Wine helped. Harvey's, just a corner joint, looked alive and expectant the way restaurants do before patrons occupy the space. A big moon lit the place, windowed on two sides. The dining room lights were low. Flames from candles threw shadows that swayed. Everything seemed set, ready, stocked, and aglow in anticipation of the memorial event.

At the bar, Laney thought, *Everything's lit, including me.* She sipped to hide a giggle.

The poster of Joanna was displayed on an easel near where food was set up. One track light pinpointed Joanna in a white bathing suit holding an orange drink on a pink float in a turquoise pool with her head thrown back in laughter and her arms wide open as if offering herself up to the sun and sky. From her mother's bliss, Laney had no doubt about who had captured the moment. In a small way, Ned was here.

Anna arrived, followed by Tom, pulling Jules. As soon as he entered, Tom's nose went up, twitching wildly in this forbidden land of wondrous aromas. Jules had offered to hold on to Tom until the handoff to Laney, but Laney did not seem in the right frame of mind for wrangling the dog.

Anna gave her sister a tight smile and indicated the sign outside. "'Closed for Private Party,' huh? You're taking that impressively literally." She reached for Laney's wineglass, too slow. Laney drained it, waggled it, and winked at Anna.

Anna ordered her own drink. "In high spirits, I see."

"Yes. I must be at the 'Happy' part."

Jules exhaled pointedly. Her bangs ruffled above the breeze of one exasperated breath. She said, "Why don't we all do water for a while. Doesn't that seem like a good idea?" She had great respect for presenting a pulled-together aspect, for not revealing private conflicts that might make other people uncomfortable. She was tall and easy in her body, and she observed the world through deep amber eyes, from under long brown bangs, and was unusual in that she had set herself the conscious goal of making kindness her default approach.

Anna snapped, "I don't need to 'do water,' but hey, thanks for the suggestion."

Laney said, "Uh-oh, you two having a little . . ." and then the doors opened and closed and opened, as Joanna's mourners gathered. Anna, in a narrow-cut navy suit, white shirt, and red Chuck Taylors, fixed her smile and greeted and pointed to the coatroom, the bar, the buffet. Tom could barely contain himself as one familiar face after another moved in, said his name, and gave him a scratch or a rub, everyone grateful for the novel distraction of a big dog in a restaurant. The food smells from the buffet table, so close, had Tom yearning and dancing at the end of his leash, held by Jules, who tugged and encouraged and reprimanded as best she could in a too-friendly voice that excited him more.

Guests sat or stood balancing plates and drinks, shaking their heads, stopped in their tracks by their own proximity, always, to transformative loss. Everyone drank. Outside the night deepened. Inside, it was cold. Sentimental songs played under hollow voices. Everything sounded distant and flatter than in life, like the sounds in an airplane or a tunnel. Condensation formed on mirrors and windows. The recesses of the room were black. Intermittently, someone called for attention with the tap of a knife against a glass.

Martin stood and spoke first. "Until Margaret"—he raised his glass in his fiancée's direction—"there was one love of my life. And that was Joanna." Margaret, big ring on her finger, nodded tolerantly.

"Joanna was . . ." Martin went silent. He swirled the ice in his scotch. He stared into the glass, slumped slightly with regret, words lost to him. He patted the thinning spot at his crown, and he looked up and shook his head. He said again, "Joanna, she was . . ." He gave a small shrug and studied his drink again, which caused the other guests to study theirs. The silence ticked. A chilly odor crept in, like a freezer door had been left ajar.

Laney glanced at Anna to confirm with her sister that their father was off-script and that one of them needed to step in and rescue Martin and the other guests from this maudlin moment. She waited for the return look, but Anna's head was lowered. She was absorbed in her phone. Her thumbs flew. Laney could see something suppressed at the corners of her sister's mouth. She looked to Jules, next best thing, and she caught Jules's eye and raised her palms slightly, a question, but Jules dimmed her attention from Laney like a light switch, and something tightened in her mouth too, and Jules turned away, pointedly attentive to Martin, pointedly ignoring Anna, and Laney thought, *What the hell is going on with them?*

Meanwhile, Martin rallied and took back the room. "Anyway. She was a beautiful woman. A sexy woman—can I say that? Is that allowed? So many wonderful memories. And these two, right?" He gestured to his daughters and Jules. "I should say 'three.' The. Best. That's it. Thank you all. I'm sorry. Just. Very, very sorry."

He finished his drink and set his glass down hard to punctuate the apology, to make it retroactive and definitive, to be done with thc topic of Joanna, to be done with regret, as if he realized, finally, that he'd gotten out of the past alive and there was nothing he could do to change it, and that all he could do was love the girls and move forward with Margaret, and he was looking forward to it, it was possible, maybe for the first time in twenty-five years. Margaret patted his arm.

Three or four beats after he set it down, Martin's glass exploded. Glass and ice shards flew. The interval between impact and the glass's destruction was remarkable. It had taken a long pause, too long, before it shattered after the slam-down.

He said to Margaret, "I didn't put it down that hard, did I?"

Waiters approached; Martin tried to help them and picked up what he thought was ice and sliced a finger. Margaret handed him a napkin. He wrapped the finger and said, as blood seeped through the white cloth, "Sorry, everyone, I'm fine. Please, let's continue."

Laney said to no one, "Jesus, whose idea was this again?"

Marie, Joanna's oldest friend, stood. Faces lifted to listen. "I'm sorry, I'm not much of a speaker." She kept her eyes on Anna and Laney. "I just wanted to say, I have known, knew, your mother"—Marie did a quick calculation—"for forty-five years! Forty-five!" She choked up, held on, pushed ahead. "She was just so much fun. So much fun. Fourteen years old, she started me smoking. She stole them from your grandma, Loretta."

Joanna, the antismoker. Everyone laughed. Marie said, "You girls and my kids were babies together. We sat you in a blow-up pool with the sprinkler going and we plopped down in lawn chairs, with red Solo cups full to the brim. Chardonnay on ice. Just talking and laughing. Stay-at-home moms! So lucky. We figured it out. You girls will too. You will too. I'm going to miss her. She was too young!"

Marie waved her hand as if to dispense with the injustice. "And I just want everyone to know, I'm going to have a cigarette today, just to make her mad. Maybe she'll come back and haunt me. Don't worry, Mayor Bloomberg, I'm going outside!"

More knives rang glasses. A cousin. A neighbor. Jason, Joanna's boss at Personal Growth & Human Development Books, stood up and presented Joanna-the-professional. He extolled her editorial acumen and her talent for building relationships with writers who had gone on to sell a lot of books, many of which were born from an idea of hers. She'd see an article online or hear something on the radio, track down the expert, the source, and convince them that the topic was book-worthy. And then she'd nurture and nudge them along, just as she'd done with Ned. She had an understanding and respect for the genre disdainfully referred to as "Self-Help," because there had been numerous times when she herself had reached for those books and found comfort in them, a phrase or an aphorism or even just a worn-out cliché that helped her pick herself up and make her way, again, through life's increasingly random challenges. Jason toasted Joanna as PGHD's survivor-book specialist and for the books she had acquired as cancer classics.

Survivor books. Cancer classics. Laney couldn't listen to Jason, technically her boss, too, even though she was only an intern. She knew she should be nice to Jason, he'd promised she could come back when she felt up to it, and she wanted to ask him to consider her for a freelance position, maybe copywriting, anything but tweeting publication dates for *Your Inner Vampire* or *Tantric-Cancer.* Being nice to Jason was complicated. His face was set in a permanent leer, he commented too freely on her looks and her clothes, and he made off-color jokes when he was sure no one else was around.

Laney turned away. She roamed, restless, drunk, and ready for the night to end. Her brain was cluttered with too much intense contact from people she knew too vaguely pressing too many memories she didn't share. Who was this Joanna they all claimed to know? Laney wasn't sure she knew the woman being memorialized, just as she had not known the woman in the blue bed at the end, shunning daughters and dog.

She pictured her real mother behind the wheel of a carful of girls, driving the gaggle to the mall, Anna's friends and hers, peppering them with questions about school and teachers, crushes and favorite movies and books, getting them to talk, listening, and then enthralling them with stories about her own long-gone loves, or her quirky friends. And Laney's favorite part, when Joanna would say, "Okay, ladies, let's dance this mess around," and she'd turn up the volume and play songs, driving songs, sing-out-loud songs, and make them do car-dancing, bouncing their butts and waving their arms as they all sang out loud, even the shy girls, or the girls whose families weren't crazy into music, like hers was. Blondie, the B52s, the Pretenders, Madonna, the Bangles, the Go-Go's, girl songs with unstoppable power and unexpected lyrics and harmonies, harmonies that she and Anna would mimic, making Mama whoop with delight—harmonies that made Laney's eyes well now, thinking about them, hearing them in memory.

She pictured her mother standing behind her in the long mirror in the upstairs bathroom, brushing Laney's tangled hair, not too gentle, not too rough, getting the job done, as Laney, blindsided by the rampant physicality of being twelve, an alien to herself, oppressed by her own body, kept her eyes squeezed shut rather than look in the mirror, self-exiled to that terrible place girls go of comparing and despairing. Joanna would make Laney open her eyes. She would agree to let Laney complain and be miserable, but first, before complaining, before pointing out every flaw, the rule was, Laney had to name five things out loud that she liked about her looks.

Then there was another Joanna, the woman Laney was trying to piece together, who was once Laney's age, and surely had her own dreams and aspirations, but stepped back instead of pushing forward, and stood behind Martin, and behind Ned, and behind Jason her boss and all those writers, hung back thinking up great ideas and handing them off so everyone else could run with them. Somehow, the relationship with Ned, its devolution into an obsession, fit in.

To Laney, at the edge of her own future, it seemed like an abdication of who Joanna was meant to be, of who she told her daughters they should be.

Laney made for the bar. Her head hurt. Each route she pursued between tables and chairs was dense with well-meaning guests and hands grasping hers, eyes searching hers. She hacked through a thicket of sympathy, a tangle of sincerity, the brambles of concern, and she hated it.

Jules was across the room, trying to get Tom to sit. Laney felt guilty. She should have taken Tom from Jules the moment they arrived, but she could not concentrate on anything but herself. She'd already misplaced her phone and lost a contact lens. Her boots looked more battered in the restaurant than when she'd pulled them on at home. She felt the familiar, comforting dread that her mother was about to notice the boots and throw her the look, the one that meant, *Really, Elena? Couldn't clean those up?*

She said out loud, "Ma, I'm doing it, okay?" Laney took a bar stool, grabbed a wad of cocktail napkins, dipped them in her vodka, and bent to shine the toes. Why she bothered she didn't know, because the look wasn't coming, ever again. Except she couldn't stop herself. It felt like her mother was watching.

Anna found her sister at the bar. "What are you doing?"

"My boots."

"Yeah? What about them?"

"They're a wreck. I'm cleaning them."

"Now?"

"Yes, now. Ma said."

"Okay." Anna shrugged. "Hey."

"What?"

"Nice skirt."

"I know. I don't know. I really don't. I was in some kind of altered state when I bought it."

Anna nodded. "Let's do a shot."

"A shot? What happened to the hard time you were giving me?"

"There's no other way to deal. I see the wisdom of it now."

"Perfect, I could drink all night, I'm like, post-drunk."

"So post-drunk you're cleaning your boots with vodka, 'cause our dead ma told you to?"

The sisters, shoulder to shoulder at the bar, clinked glasses. Laney tugged at Anna's lapel. She said, "Cheers to you. You did a really good job with all this," and tossed her shot back.

Anna said, "You, meh. You were supposed to deal with Tom. Jules is too nice. He's literally got her wrapped around his leash. He's pulling her all over the place."

"Jules is good people. I love Jules."

"I know. Me too." Anna nodded and went quiet.

Laney said, "Do you? Love her? Like really?"

Anna spoke carefully. "I want to. I'm trying."

"That sounds like wiggle room. Does Jules know that? That there's wiggle room?"

"Jules is cutting me a lot of slack. For now. My mother died."

"Mine did too. What a coincidence." Laney leaned around to put her face in front of Anna's, so that eye contact was unavoidable. "What's going on with you guys? Who were you texting with while Dad was rambling?"

"No one. A friend from work."

"The same no one you were with that night?"

"What night?"

"Please. Don't insult me. You said you were going home, you weren't at home and Jules didn't know where you were and your phone was off for a long time. The longest time ever. Literally."

"I'm sorry. How many times can I say it? I can't make that night un-happen. It's the worst thing that's ever happened to me."

"The worst thing that's ever happened to you! It was a whole lot worse for me than for you! I was in the apartment with a dead person! For a really long time."

"Well, no, I think it's always worse for the person who's not there because the imagination—"

"Oh, for God's sakes, Anna. Of course you can't make it unhappen. But you can tell the truth. At least to me."

Anna said again, "I want to. I'm trying."

Keith approached and Laney waved him away.

Anna said, "Yes, I love Jules. Yes, I met someone else for a drink that night. I don't know what I'm doing. I don't have a plan. Nothing ever works out anyway."

Laney dropped her head to her sister's shoulder. She said, "Okay. That makes sense. I don't know what I'm doing, either." She picked up the edge of her crazy skirt and gave it a shake.

Anna tipped her head to Laney's and rubbed her scalp against her sister's, making a papery, whispery sound deep down that each of them, only, could hear. The sound of a mother's fingertips stroking a child's head.

"By the way, Elena, the name 'Sad/Happy Hour'? A flash of brilliance. Because I am. Sad. Yet Happy."

"What's your 'Happy' part?"

"It's almost over. They're still talking in there. Dad thinks we should speak. It would be the signal that the evening has concluded."

"So go speak."

"You do it, Lane. You should."

"Why me?"

Anna looked into her sister's eyes, a pale version of their mother's. "You're not as mad at her as I am."

"I'm not mad at her, but I fucking hate everyone else." Laney stumbled off the bar stool and pointed a toe. "Okay, I'll do it. I've got my skirt. My boots are ready. And I did happen to make a few notes."

Anna said, "I see that," and she wet a cocktail napkin with vodka and soda and scrubbed at the ink stain along the side of Laney's left hand. They wrapped their arms around each other and rocked together for a full minute. They pressed foreheads and merged memories, sharing a sister-brain slide show: a blue bed, a cell phone clattering across the floor, wrong last words, a white knit cap with a skull. Joanna was memory for everyone else, but she pulsed between her daughters, not gone, not by a long shot.

Not gone for Tom either, who dragged Jules over and pushed his big brown body into the small space between the sisters. Jules handed the leash to Laney. "He seems really nervous. He's whining. I'm kind of done with the dog thing."

Anna said, "Okay, let's wrap up and get him out of here."

In the dining room, the three young women took a table next

to the poster of Joanna. Tom stared at it, or into the recesses past it. Laney looped his leash around the leg of her chair. She pushed at his haunches, urging him down, until he acquiesced and fake-rested his head on his paws under the table. His eyes darted around the dining room.

Anna tapped her glass for attention.

Laney stood and swayed with the effects of alcohol and then set herself. She felt drunk again, so she slowed all her gestures and words, overcompensating. She said, "Hi, everyone," with a wave like she was swatting them away. She dug around in her bag and pulled out pages torn from a spiral notebook. Tom stood too, ready for anything. Anna pushed down on him again and he relented and dropped, but just barely. He was panting with anxiety and Anna thought, *Please calm down, it's almost over.*

Laney looked at her notes and started to read, her husky voice disappearing into her chest. Marie called, "Louder, honey, we can't hear you."

Martin said, "Elena, go stand over there, next to the easel."

Laney faced the guests. Tom's panting was audible. His cocked head followed something only he could see, beyond Laney, beyond the poster of Joanna. Laney looked down at the notes. She looked back up. "First time ever, I think, I'm going with a piece of writing that hasn't been edited by my mother." She looked at the pages again for long seconds. She pressed her fingers against one eye, the one that was missing the contact lens, and looked at the pages for a few seconds longer. She folded them up and stuffed them in her jacket pocket and said, "Fuck it. Then again, maybe I won't."

Family, friends, and acquaintances shifted in their chairs, each willing Laney, little Elena, to be okay. Waiters circulated, pouring steaming coffee from hot pots.

"I just want to say, I guess I have a lot of memories of my mother. Like you all do. And I get how sharing them, you know, helps. But, it's just a couple of weeks. She's not . . . So it's hard for me to just shift gears here, to this part. The memory part. Really fucking hard. 'Cause it's too soon. We're doing this way too soon. In my opinion." She was speaking slowly, to mitigate the slur and the sway.

Heads nodded around the room, both in encouragement and discomfort.

Laney looked at her father and said, "It's too soon, right, Dad?" Martin, on the spot, being held accountable for the glass he'd slammed, for showing he was done bearing the burden of the broken family, was solemn. He adjusted the bloody napkin around his finger.

Laney's eyes welled with tears. She looked at her sister and said, "It feels like she's here, right? Just look at Tom—he feels it."

At the mention of his name, Tom popped up from the down position and bumped his head on the table, and hot coffee sloshed over the rims of shallow cups. The uneasy guests chuckled at the dog. Tom continued to stare past Laney. He was at full-on high alert. Anna half-nodded to Laney, just to keep her going, but was distracted by Tom's focus. She tried to see what Tom was tracking in the ceiling's recesses.

"I'm not ready for her to be a memory yet. I'm kind of not convinced she's gone. I know that sounds crazy. But. How can someone's mother just stop being their mother? I mean, that's just . . . that's what's crazy!" Laney sniffed hard to pull back the mucus running from her nose, and swiped at her tears. She said to the approximate universe, "I'm not the crazy one. You're the crazy one."

She tried to laugh, to make it seem like she was joking, but her voice tore and rasped. She took a deep shaky breath and then another as she tried to do the hardest thing she'd ever done, which was justify the unique, most painful, most private feelings she'd ever experienced, maybe would ever experience, to a crowd of people who seemed to expect her to do so. Who seemed to believe that what had happened, her mother dying when Laney was twenty-two, much too soon, was something she should be able to make sense of. That it was possible to turn her mother into memory because of a date on the calendar, an evite. It felt completely unnatural to Laney, and yet, here she stood.

"But okay. Fine. Memories. So here's a memory. From when I was little."

Laney raised her voice. "I asked my mother what her favorite color was. She said, 'Water.' And I, I was maybe like four or five, and I was like, 'No, Mama, what's your favorite color,' thinking she didn't understand the question. And again she answered, 'Water.' And I got so mad at her. I was a little kid, I just wanted her to say yellow or green or blue or something normal. I thought she was teasing me. I actually had a pretty intense tantrum over it."

By being pushed to talk, to remember, to make the memory, Laney, without realizing it, was finding strength. She looked to her regretful father, and without even hesitating made a choice: to offer amends for the many years of unquestioningly taking her mother's side. She took some of Martin's burden, just by saying, with a little smile in her voice, "You may remember."

Martin laughed a laugh of relief and said, "I sure do."

She continued, "So anyway, I was really pissed at my mother and she put me in time-out, for like, half an hour that felt like half a day. By the time my dad came home, I calmed down, but I still wanted to know. 'What is Mama's favorite color?' And my dad said, 'Oh, blue, everybody knows that. Just look around.'

"I was completely surprised. I hadn't known that. I was disappointed! Blue. Huh. After all that excitement, after me being so mad, getting the time-out, just regular blue. Like practically everybody else! Her favorite color was pretty obvious, it was everywhere in our house. Pillows and towels. Rugs and dishes and walls. All I had to do was look around. Regular old blue. All I had to do was notice."

"I think about that a lot. All the time. I mean, her answer. It was so. I don't know. True, I guess. To her. And to me. She couldn't just say, 'Blue.' That was too obvious, that was an easy answer. She wanted me to stop and notice the blues. That everybody has their own blue. Her blue was water, just like she said."

The room was quiet in remembrance of summers and seas, winter skies and eyes, and worn jeans and pools and moods and moons. Laney drank, and then raised her glass in the direction of the photograph of her mother, floating. "So, Mama, there you are. I get it now. The color of water." She finished off her wine.

Anna had stopped listening. She was watching Tom, who was compelled—commanded—by something only he could see that had him practically levitating out of the sit position. His whine rolled to a low growl that he kept on simmer. He rose up, and his hackles rose too, but his tail wagged hard, and with perfect timing, Jules moved wineglasses out of the way.

Anna leaned to Tom and tried to coax him back down, but he ignored her, so avid was he to respond to whatever—whoever—demanded his attention. The wagging tail thrashed. The low growl became his clipped *Hi Mom!* bark, short and insistent, *Bark, bark, bark*. He leaned forward hard, his entire body aimed toward the poster—or, to Anna's *X-Files* fangirl, the-truth-is-out-there determined eye, something up in the restaurant's rafters.

Laney took her seat on the chair with the leash looped around its leg, and as she was trying to replay her words in her head to count up how many times she dropped the F-bomb while eulogizing her mother, Tom, with the confidence of a much smaller dog, lunged in the direction of the poster, yanking Laney's chair with him. She whooped and flew backward, grabbing a fistful of tablecloth with one hand and the back of Jules's sweater with the other. The young women crashed to the floor. Empty glasses and full coffee cups, candles sitting in pools of hot wax, plates and forks and creamers and sugar bowls and crumbs all flew too.

Tom smashed the easel-and-poster setup, but stuck the landing beautifully. His front paws took down the buffet table, lined with platters of fruit and cookies and a tall pedestal of cupcakes. He stood amidst the fallen bounty, a dog's dream, so much accessible forbidden food, but his attention never wavered from what lurked above, what had him riveted, what prevented him from taking advantage of the excellent mess he'd made. He was a dog on duty, ready to serve his master in need, even as Anna struggled to haul him away.

11

Damn your love, damn your lies.

I love this song. During *Rumours*, the band couldn't even stand to be in the studio together. Separate tracks were taped and sliced with razor blades and spliced to make "The Chain." All the connections between Fleetwood Mac, professional and romantic, had been hacked, Stevie and Lindsey spit words at each other, but they were forever linked by betrayal.

Never break, never break, never break.

I know what you're thinking. All this mooning over Ned while everyone who loved me better than he did, the people who actually stuck around, sing my praises in Harvey's. The gang's all here, my dog, my friends, my family, my music and food and alcohol.

My daughters. They touch shot glasses and foreheads. I hear Anna say, "You're not as mad at her as I am." I hear Laney say, "I fucking hate everyone."

Whatever. I churn past all that. None of that is useful to me. Grief-addled daughters don't matter.

I hover. Mirrors see me, so I avoid them. Marie, my old friend, looks old. I pass across her and I think, *A little lip gloss, Ree,* and she shivers and reaches for her bag. Glasses clink. Ice clinks. A little bit of Martin's pink scalp shows where he missed a spot in the comb-over. I pass across him and think, *You missed a spot, Marty,* and he touches his hair. I make his scotch on the rocks explode. I scare him and scar him for old times' sake. My mother's sister, Aunt Faye, clutches the hand of my cousin Jean. Hi, Pam from yoga. Hi, Sharon from the nail salon. There's Angel, from the dry cleaner's. College friends. Work people. Jason, the windbag.

Hey, there's the old me, the photograph from the reconciliation vacation, posterized. I'm smiling like a happy idiot. *We're getting married!*

Tom feels me. Tom is making me nervous. I hide from Tom. He trembles. He pants. His nose twitches. He is a poodle, not a pointer, but he aims like an arrow in my direction. I pull in tight and narrow, I go very small but I feel pinned back by Tom trying to see past the phantom I am now to the dog-mom I used to be. His hackles stay up. He keeps nosing Anna while his eyes search the ceiling.

I'm fast. The need to move moves me. I go between blinks and breaths and beats of music. I head up and up and find the room's corners. Tom's eyes follow. Here comes the searchlight sweep of Anna's gaze, right behind the dog's.

Elena speaks. She says, randomly, "You're the crazy one," to a roomful of my mourners.

Guests shift, ready for dessert, a hit of sugar and the trip home to where they can go back to pretending they're never going to die. The atmosphere, the rhythm of the night, the food, the moods, the exploded glass, Laney's tears, me in the shadows, all of it is too much for Tom. Tom is done with the good-dog act. Tom is done obeying. He is a man on duty. He is at the ready.

I'm desperate to keep out of range. I still don't know what

I'm doing. I don't have the control to manage his undivided attention, his relentless devotion, his love. I think a thing and a thing happens. I am like a joystick but the opposite of joy. Bitterstick? Sadstick?

I see it coming. It's in his eyes. I panic. From lifelong dog-owning habit I think, in ultrasonic, dog-whistle range, *Stay, Tom, stay!* My voice vibrates in his central nervous system, I guess. He does what he must. He leaps.

I cower, I corner, I shy. Anna shouts and wrangles him. *Bad dog!* Jules and Laney are in a heap on the floor. Laney is laughing or crying hard. It's chaos. The playlist shuffles to Cat Power, "Manhattan." Great choice, girls. *Howling at me howling at you.*

That's my cue. I surge away and out out out, and up over Broadway, to the Titania. I'm coked up and buzzy, anxious from the press of love. I accelerate to burn off the sticky cling of friends and colleagues, the fumes of Martin's regret, Anna's pungent anger, and slurry, sad Laney.

Chaos, that's what I do.

I turn in on myself and cycle away, above the buildings, the vents and the ductwork, the water towers and tarpaper, the roofscapes of Morningside Heights, on my way home.

Big D the UPS guy steps back from the open rear door of his truck in front of the Titania. He balances a mix of boxes, Amazon and Apple and Zappos, for drop-off at the concierge desk. I pass through him and think, *Hey, Big D,* the usual hello. He convulses in a shudder of big-man proportions and snaps his head around to see what has borne down on him. It's just me, the ghost of DeAngelis, 11B, Amazon Prime all the way. The boxes fall. The doorman leaves his post and steps out into the night to help Big D.

My building. My Art Deco doors, my lobby. One mahogany-paneled wall holds a gallery of framed newspaper clippings commemorating a visit from Eleanor Roosevelt in 1932. It was the year her husband was elected president, and Eleanor, already in love with reporter Lorena Hickok, reacted to winning the White House by telling Hick, on the record, “Now I shall have to work out my own salvation.”

I hear ya, FLOTUS.

The dull gleam of brushed nickel is everywhere, and I throw shadow. I mark my territory with my noxious scent. I hurtle through carpeted corridors, hushed, past red doors, listening, past where I lived my beautiful life.

I’m home. My home.

The lights are off but I don’t need them. I see everything to its bones. Whites, luminous. Dark things like mercury. I spin slow through the foyer, past the console table. There are my keys. There’s my wallet, the long blue zip-around. Both sit useless in the big capiz shell bowl I bought in Montauk. My favorite umbrella is hooked on the back of a chair, waiting for bad weather. My sneakers, still tied, kicked off last summer, hold the crumpled heel made by my impatient foot. Hooks hang jackets by their necks, limp without the shape of my shoulders.

I move through the foyer down the long hallway hung with photographs of family and friends. How many times I’ve passed these familiar faces of strangers, relatives I recognize but never knew, the long-dead hung there too, and the newly dead, me, and I don’t know any of us anymore. We are all stopped in a moment, the moments framed to show that we are connected by blood, tribe, habits, bone structure, stance, something that was ours, something that means us, our family, something that we carry forward. I put those photographs there to show Anna and Laney—and me too—who we were, who we came from, who we are.

They mean nothing to me now.

The kitchen. I always wanted to redo it, it’s well-used, nothing is new, I wanted sleek and gleaming like Marie’s, white stone and stainless steel, not a sponge or salt shaker on display, but I was nervous to spend the single-mom money, and also I couldn't imagine demolishing the energies—the tasks of meal preparation, the aromas so savored—so I stuck with the old subway tile backsplash, the scarred butcher-block countertops, the open shelves piled with mismatched dishes and bowls. The kitchen table—my mother's—is set against a wall of energy-squandering, draft-allowing casement windows that look down on the skeletal trees of Riverside Drive. The table is cluttered with mail, magazines, peanut shells, an uncorked wine bottle, a juice glass smudged with fingerprints and grainy with red wine dregs.

Fine, whatever, Elena.

I move toward a sound deep in my apartment. Someone breathes. I know the breathing well. I used to lie awake long after he fell asleep, trying to match mine to his. I know the breathing well from deep mornings, as it chugged and accelerated and imploded while we fucked in my bed.

I follow the breathing.

Ned freezes, alert as a dog. He is backlit by the moon above and the streetlights below the tall windows near my desk. He's got the manila envelope I left for him in his hand. He peers hard into the dark. My dark. Mine.

He calls out, "Who's here?"

It's a little bit of a cliché, I admit, but, come on, it's funny, too, isn't it? I mean, I haven't axed through the door, I can't stick my head through the splintered wood and leer like a maniacal motherfucker, Ned is not shaking and quaking like Shelley Duvall, not yet, but I can deliver the line just like Jack, terrorist-husband possessed by the ghosts of the Overlook Hotel.

Heeere's Joanna!

I intensify. I shoot too fast past a tall, leaded crystal vase, my mother's mother's, still filled with dry condolence flowers, mine, sitting in rank water. The vase crashes to the floor. I think, *Fuck*, and at the same time Ned shouts, taut, loud, "Fuck!"

He steps away from the desk to the center of the room. Glass crunches under his thin, Trudi-approved Italian-soled loafers. His shoes are ridiculous.

Ned shouts, "What? Who is that? Is someone here? Tom?"

It's a habit, I can't help myself. I move on him. I hunt for his scent, his essence. I sniff at his neck, his scalp, my favorite spots. I inhale Ned just like old times. The smell of him, *Ooohhh*, I moan—theatrical, I admit. Like a ghost.

Ned jerks away with the same involuntary reflex that afflicted Big D just before he dropped the boxes.

It's good to be invisible. I surround him again. I take my time. I am vaporous and languid. I move up from his ankles, under the cuff of his jeans, I crawl his skin, winding myself around his calves, right, left, to his knees, his thighs, up farther between his legs, I linger at the crotch, I reach behind, I linger behind, I slip up his spine, I turn and spread myself across his chest and his shoulders and wind around and around his throat, in and out of his ears, I idle under his nose, his very nose, so we can breathe each other again. I move up to the scar that paves its way up his cheek through his brow and across his forehead. I am about to enter his mismatched eyes.

Ned waves at the air in front of his face. He flaps and ducks. "Jo?!" He calls my name. "Jo, is that you?!" Ned is pale. He backs away. He steps on fallen flowers and broken glass, stems and shards.

I dismantle him with spectral vision. The fear center of his brain pulses and glows like a heat map. Rigid muscles sheathe his bones. The whites of his eyes bulge, and his optic nerves quiver with the effort to see something they can transmit to the primary visual cortex. The manila envelope is in his shaking hands. His knees shake too. He is terrified and geared up to run. Here he stands, in my living room, in my home, the home I made, the home I shared with him, steps away from the sofa where he left me as I slept off cancer, last August.

Ned, looking to bolt, again. Ready to run, again.

I spin from invisible skeins, I spin from the traces of nothing to silver nothing, sharp like shards, sharp like a broken scotch rocks glass slammed down hard, sharp like a broken crystal vase. I churn and I surge, getting strong, stronger and I narrow and aim like the hurled blade of hurt that I am and I hurtle myself at Ned, needing, needing, needing to cut Ned, to leave Ned in pieces. Pieces of flesh, splatters of blood.

Closure time, Doc.

He tries to twist away from me, from whatever I am that he can't see but knows is coming for him. He keeps flapping at the air in what he thinks is my general direction but I'm everywhere. He calls out, "No!" or "Jo!" from his gut, it's a high-pitched noise I've never heard him make before. He shrinks and cringes. I slice at him. He rears back and swats with the manila envelope. I make a clean, short tear across his name.

I whisper to him, in him, *I'm here, Doc, I'm here, I'm here.*

I shoot straight through Ned, me, Joanna in full, Joanna at full throttle. I slam into that thing he calls a heart. Behind it, his lungs contract hard, jacking for oxygen. I squeeze. He folds in on the pain, I recognize his dilemma, he can't bear the pain, the pain is all he is, he needs to gasp, but at the same time, he can't breathe. Oh, I know his pain. He bends over, clutching and sputtering, and he loses his footing and slips on wet, broken glass and dead flowers and slimy flower water.

When he hits, his bones rattle, they really do. His head bounces hard on my former floor, and that's nice too.

12

Ned opened his eyes to a meaty tongue hanging over him. A drop of dog saliva fell onto his cheek. He blinked to focus.

"Hey, buddy, hiya," he said. He didn't recognize his own voice. His hearing was muffled. He worked his jaw slowly. He ran his tongue along his teeth. He lifted one arm and looked at his hand. He saw blood, but all his fingers were there. He repeated the effort with the other arm—more blood, all the fingers.

Meanwhile, Tom bounded around him and pawed and prodded with a cold nose. The dog was beside himself. He was torn between supine Ned, his long-lost puppy-daddy, available for unrestrained licking, and something that flickered and pricked at his canine sensors at the ceiling near the top of the bookshelves.

Jules turned on lamps around the room. Laney pulled Tom off Ned as he struggled to get to his feet, picking glass from his bloody palms, shaking shards from his hair. He pressed a bloody hand against his chest to quell his frantic heart.

Anna said, "What are you doing here? What the fuck is going on?"

"I'm sorry. I'm really sorry." Ned was as pale as paper. One bleeding hand cradled the other, which still held the manila envelope. "I came to return your mother's keys. And to get something she left for me." He waved the envelope as evidence of innocent intent. "I didn't want to disturb you. At this time. And I don't know . . ." He gestured to the broken vase. "I was about to clean it up," Ned lied. "I must have . . . slipped."

Anna said, "You broke it. You're bleeding all over the place. Are you drunk? Get the fuck out of here before I call the police."

"She sent me a text." Ned tried to punch up the passcode on his phone to show Anna the text, to prove he had legitimately been invited to use keys, but his nerves were too jangled and his hands were shaking and he could not get the code right. Jules got cleaning supplies from the pantry, pulled her winter gloves back on, picked up the biggest shards of crystal, and dropped them into a brown paper bag. She swept the wet mess into a dustpan and dumped that in too. She wrapped the brown paper bag with duct tape and put that into a trash bag. "That was a lot of vase."

"Yeah," Anna said. "My mother loved that vase." She went to her pocket for her phone. "I'm calling the cops. Seriously."

Laney said, "Anna, for God's sakes, that's ridiculous. Mama told him to come. Tom! Off! Off him! Ned, it's fine, just take your envelope. Are you okay?"

Ned explored the back of his head, felt a goose-egg, and made an ouchy face. Laney, soft, said, "Do you need ice?"

He muttered, "No, I'll have it neat," for the benefit of his old collaborator. Laney crossed her arms against Ned, although she looked to Tom to stop herself from smiling. Tom was fixated on the ceiling.

Anna said, "No fucking way! Don't you dare pour him a drink!"

Jules said, "Baby, it was a joke."

"A joke? He's making jokes?!"

"No, no, I'm going." Ned, bloody and dazed, clutching the envelope, his inked name sliced and smeared, moved in the direction of the front door. "Look, I just . . ."

The women looked at Ned. They waited.

"Yes? You just what?" Laney said, prompting him to speak, to explain himself, with actual sentences, one after the other, on purpose, to communicate something meaningful. To admit the truth: He'd been a dick to Joanna. And he'd been a dick to Laney too, treating her as if she hadn't even existed, as if they hadn't once been a kind of family. She prompted with intent eyes, to get Ned to say anything that might be construed, even loosely, as amends. Any remorse would be too little, too late, but would be acknowledgment that he felt bad about how things had turned out.

Ned was distracted from his point by Tom, who was riveted by something beyond his canine ken in the high shadowed corner of the bookshelves. "He sees something."

Tom whined in response. Laney followed Ned's squint into the shadows. She said, "A mouse maybe? Or a squirrel? Aren't we too high up for that? I hope it's not a bat, I heard—"

"Why are you being so nice to him?" Anna grabbed the manila envelope from Ned and stamped to the front door, to encourage him out. "You're lucky your name is on this. I don't even want to know what's inside. Just take it and get out of here."

"Okay, okay. I know. I just want you to know. Your mother's vase, I don't know what happened. I was here, but I was way over there by the window. Nowhere near it. I'm sorry it broke. But I didn't break it."

"How does a heavy crystal vase just fall off a table? Was there an earthquake? Maybe a fifty-mile-an-hour wind blew in? Or maybe it was a ghost. Fucking typical. Try taking responsibility for something for a change."

Ned met and held Anna's glare. "It wasn't an earthquake and it wasn't the wind. I don't know what it was, but it wasn't me."

Jules stepped in and said, "I like the ghost idea." She extended a hand to Ned. "I'm Jules. We haven't met."

Laney shivered. "Is there a window open?"

"That's what I mean. Why is it so cold in here? And do you smell that? What is that? It's like Freon. Maybe we should check the refrigerator."

Anna went to the windows. They were shut tight. She snapped on brighter, overhead lights. She said, "There's no 'we,' and don't tell me what to do in my house."

Laney was spooked. She wanted the night to end. She pulled at Ned's sleeve and walked him to the door. She said, "Keys, please," and looked him in the eye, giving him a last chance to acknowledge their friendship, his disappearance from her life, and their mutual loss. She telepathically urged, *Ned, say something.*

Ned, frightened and injured, too close to the truth, heard Laney, knew what he should do, what he should say, but he stayed mute and moved to hug her instead. She stepped back from the embrace and closed the door against him.

Tom fretted and circled at the bottom of the bookcase.

Anna said, "Good riddance to that asshole. Tom, dude, you've got to chill. Seriously."

Laney said, "I hope he's not having some kind of breakdown. He seems freaked."

Anna said, "Who cares?! How can you be so nice to him? Both of you! The three of you! How dare he use Mom's keys! He didn't even offer to replace the vase! I should have called the cops!"

"I wasn't talking about Ned being freaked. I was talking about Tom. Now who's the asshole." She turned from Anna, went to her room, and slammed the door as hard as she could.

Anna looked to Jules. "I guess you're on her side. Me, right? I'm the asshole?"

"I don't know what you are. I thought I did, and now I don't. "

"Can't I just be pissed off? Am I supposed to be understanding of Ned McGowan? He dumped her when she was sick! He broke in! He destroyed a cherished family object. Is that all just okay with everybody?"

"That's not the asshole part. It's your attitude. On top of being majorly distracted all night by texts from who knows whom. I mean, I get that this is all too much. I do. But. It seems like, I don't know. Like you're policing everyone but yourself."

"Whatever drama you're about to start, Jules, whatever you're about to analyze to pieces, I can't do it now. I just can't."

Jules rolled a hair grip from her wrist and swept her dark hair into a high ponytail. She gathered up the cleaning supplies and stowed them in cabinets, shutting doors hard in retort.

Anna said to Tom, "Another door slammer in the crew."

Tom yawned loudly, dropped to the rug, and pushed his fore-paws until he was stretched out. He was exhausted. Anna looked at him and said, "And you! You cost me money tonight! You wrecked the restaurant! How could you still love Ned McGowan, Tom? Don't you have some special dick detector? I can't believe it."

Jules said, "Love is blind. Tom loves you, and you're kind of a dick."

Anna slumped to the floor next to Tom. She rested her head against the dog's heaving side. "I'm an asshole, I'm a dick. I'm not fit for society. I'm really just not."

Jules said, "The first step is acknowledging it."

Tom let his big head rest, but his haunches stayed tense and his eyes continued to work the edges of the room, tracking the thing he was longing to see.

Stop and go. Stop and go.

Ned's cab stuttered down the West Side Highway.

The back of his head throbbed. His shaking hands—covered by ineptly applied Band-Aids from the Duane Reade on Broadway—throbbed. His chest and ribs were sore. Only a few months past his thirty-sixth birthday, Ned wondered whether he'd had a stroke, or a heart attack. He remembered that a murmur had been detected when he was a kid. He resolved to make a doctor's appointment.

In his gut he knew his heart had indeed been attacked and that it had nothing to do with his health. Ned played the evening's events over and over again. First, the Peck encounter, then a text from the dark side, then next-level flirting in Starbucks with Lauren, his teaching assistant, and then whatever the hell had occurred—attempted murder!—at the Titania.

The stench of it—her, Jo—was still in his nostrils, and the cold was in his bones. Rehearing the auto-tuned version of Joanna's voice impersonating Jack Nicholson in *The Shining—Heeeere's Joanna!*—made him wince. Re-sensing the thing swooping toward him made him flinch. He closed his eyes and leaned his head against the frigid cab window, but the feeling of her—it—was there, too, in the fragmented headlights and streetlights and fog, coming for him. The taxi trundled through traffic and Ned reviewed his scant science knowledge for factoids about electromagnetic fields, and Einstein, and how the heat and light and chemistry of a life force like Jo's—a human being—did not die, but was transformed into something else. A new energy texting, attacking. A ghost. Was that a real thing? Ned shuddered. He'd involuntarily called her name, her name blurted from his throat, and she had come at him.

The manila envelope, scored, lay across his lap. Ned could feel the outline of a packet inside but couldn't bring himself to open it. Whatever it was, he wasn't sure he wanted it. He involuntarily checked his phone for a new text, as if the ghost of Joanna would certainly follow up after kicking his ass, and then he checked two minutes later, and two minutes after that. When his phone did finally ding, he went cold. The convulsive shaking in his hands resumed. He blanked on his passcode, once, twice, and finally he broke through, but it was only Trudi texting: *Im back where r u?*

Ned thought, *Fuck, fuck, what the fuck.* He'd hoped he could sneak in and shower at Trudi's—he could never bring himself to call her place "home"—before she returned from another monumentally important business trip.

He texted: *in cab on my way.* Ned felt queasy. He had to avoid looking at the dried blood on his jeans and the cuff of his shirt. The cabdriver was a start-and-stop jockey, hitting the pedals two-footed, riding both gas and brake, exacerbating the churning in Ned's gut. He cracked his window and icy March air stung his face.

He'd have to concoct a story for Trudi to explain his injuries. He wouldn't—didn't usually—tell her the truth, and at any rate, Trudi probably didn't even remember that Jo had once existed.

In the beginning, when he and Trudi were exchanging romantic histories, Ned had skimmed over the Jo years, and she'd asked no questions. Ned's cleaned-up version neatly fit the couple-narrative Trudi immediately envisioned with him. Trudi's orbit was all-encompassing, and once he was pulled in, not much about Ned pre-Trudi counted, particularly a fling with an older woman that sounded to Trudi like something bucket-list-y and checked off.

That had all been fine by Ned. The more details he was asked to reveal by any woman at any time, on any topic, the less secure the perimeter of the Ned-zone of plausible deniability. He'd dubbed it "the Ned-zone" in college, for laughs with his buddies, as he honed his skill of deploying truthiness to get with women. He was a legend, high-fived and bowed to in the bars, but that was a long time ago. The buddies had moved on, were married, were family men.

For Ned, the truth was still a minefield, rigged with devices—women—that could blow at any time. Every question he got from a woman seemed like a ticking bomb. He spent a lot of time trying to not get blown to pieces. He had become a master at stalling, rhetoric, redirects, reframes, hemming, hawing, and outright ignoring the question until he had cooked up an answer that would fit the story line to integrate into their happily-ever-after scripts, which, Ned believed, was all women really wanted anyway.

He'd learned to lie as a boy in order to survive being parented by a perennially disappointed mother, herself a nonpracticing attorney. Pat Kinney had worked her way through Hofstra and Fordham Law, gone out to celebrate the night she got her congratulations letter from the New York Bar Association, and six weeks later realized she was pregnant by a guy whose last name she didn't know, whom she didn't know how to contact, and whom she didn't want to know. It had warranted no more than a shrug from Pat's own mother: *That's life, deal with it.*

Slender Pat—dark curls, light eyes, extravagantly freckled, and rounding out quickly—had squeezed into a white skirt suit from Macy's and married her best friend and Fordham classmate, Eddie McGowan. Eddie was newly "of counsel" at an academic publishing company hungry for growth, and he had a real future ahead of him negotiating their expanding media acquisitions. He was a gentle man and a good catch. He wanted a family and, so, needed a wife. Eddie and Pat were each other's fail-safe choices.

Just as she was getting her life back after giving birth to Keira, just as the days were sorting themselves out and starting to seem manageable, just as she was thinking about signing up for refresher law courses and interview-skills classes, Pat was pregnant again with Kristen. And then Ned. Three kids, four years.

That's life. Pat's disappointment was like having a terminally ill family member sleeping in the guest bedroom. For years, out of respect for that disappointment, the McGowans lowered their voices, dimmed the lights, navigated the clutter of neglect. Pat's disappointment drove Eddie away to nights in Manhattan with his more sophisticated colleagues, his bachelor friends. McGowan home life became nearly impenetrable with cigarette smoke and secrets and slammed doors. Murky deals had been struck that Ned knew nothing about, but had blindly sworn to uphold and enforce. It was like growing up in a congressional back room. Keira and Kristen kept themselves busy with grooming, with local schools and boys and making small, safe plans. Young Ned, the only son, was the self-appointed protector of the big fat fiction of a normal suburban family, ceaselessly plotting his getaway.

The night before Ned was to leave for freshman year at Amherst, having agreed to aim for prelaw while secretly eyeing art, Eddie McGowan sat the kids down. Pat was bleary-eyed and tight-lipped next to him, leaning away as if he were contagious. Their father told his family that when he came back from driving Ned to school he would be moving out of their Syosset splanch to live in a studio apartment in the city, in Chelsea. He gave no real reason except to say it was for the best.

Pat raised her glass and said, "To Eddie—his new life," and slugged her wine. She'd smirked and said, "I mean 'Edward.' "

Late that night, Ned, packed for school and then, with a bad feeling, wandered downstairs and found his mother slumped across the kitchen table, breathing heavy and slow, in a too-deep sleep. A deck of cards was meticulously laid out, a strong solitaire hand in progress. Broken glass graveled the floor and a cigarette still burned on a dessert plate half an inch away from the sleeve of her nightgown. Ned was transfixed at the sight of his mom, undone by the truth—later he learned that she had known of Eddie's fluid attractions since their college days; it was his public declaration she could not abide—and nearly setting herself on fire to avoid it. He helped her upstairs, where his dad was snoring in the forlorn marriage bed.

Every lousy impulse Ned had to lie, evade, obscure, omit, and deny was completely vindicated. Truth was dangerous. Pat continued drinking and smoking and playing solitaire into the late, late nights. Edward McGowan's attempt to live his truth became Pat's defining moment and, so, the whole family's. Ned did get away to Amherst, but he partied too hard, totaled his roommate's father's car, and had washed out by Thanksgiving. He stayed home and got an associate's degree from Nassau Community College before transferring to Columbia. Eddie McGowan Senior never moved to Chelsea.

The cab stopped for traffic alongside Trump Place in the West Sixties. It depressed Ned. Tall buildings with thousands of dark windows looked down on blank boulevards in what felt to Ned like a gated community misplaced on the far West Side of Manhattan, once the funky fringe of the city, once home to rail yards and car dealerships and car washes and strip clubs and cabbie diners, and the ass-side of Lincoln Center.

As always, it looked deserted. Ned pictured Hong Kong investors, Dubai merchants, Russian oligarchs, multiracial models, Nigerian identity thieves online in their home countries, buying "units" sight unseen, never actually coming to New York, never turning the lights on in their fake-swanky apartments on fake Riverside Boulevard in the fake Manhattan neighborhood, Trump Place.

Traffic crawled. The driver seemed unable to find the rhythm. He sped ahead and jammed on the brakes. He came within inches, every time, of smashing into the vehicle in front of them. He wore an earpiece and spoke high-volume without stopping for breath in a language Ned could not identify, seemingly shouting at the windshield. The radio was loud, too, exhorting in another, different language Ned could also not identify. The video screen mounted at his knees would not turn off, Jimmy, Kelly, Kathie, their forced laughter, the same clips repeated, no matter what degree of pressure Ned applied to the touchscreen to shut them up.

Stop and go. Stop and go. He was a bloody, nervous wreck. He lurched with each acceleration but was unwilling to risk criticizing the driver by asking him to lower the radio, slow down, stop riding the brake, and quit yelling. The meter showed twenty-three, twenty-four, twenty-five dollars. He leaned into examine the official Taxi & Limousine Commission identification card tucked behind milky, scratched, hacked-at plexiglass in the window behind the driver's head, maybe catch a name, make an appeal to get off the West Side Highway. Ned could decipher only that the ID photograph did not appear to match the back of the driver's head, nor the eyes in the rearview mirror. There was not even a cousinly resemblance to the fellow who continued to shout back at whoever was speaking into his earpiece.

Stop. Go. They were crossing Thirty-fourth Street, the beginning of downtown, almost home or, technically, almost home to Trudi's home. Life with Trudi Mink was easy, and Ned let himself look forward to sinking into her plush armchair with a glass of something expensive, applying expensive salve to his wounds.

The relationship with Dr. Trudi bestowed upon Ned the holy grail he hadn't realized he was seeking until he'd met her: an all-access pass. She circled the globe in an exclusive constellation of famous people whom everyone else looked to, Ned included. He worked the access, had compromised every core ideal he had for access, could no longer imagine life without access. His old ambition, to be a respected writer, a novelist, embarrassed him when he was with Trudi, who simply and without any pretense could not comprehend the commitment, the time-suck writing required. It was so much more satisfying to plane surfaces, to smooth lines and bumps, to fill up and filter away the deep gray crevices of solitude creativity demanded.

Ned felt like a fraud, 24/7. He was tagging along on Trudi's ride on Trudi's dime. He was working on the money part, but there was no way he could compete with EternaPlast money. Trudi's money operated on a level of exponential growth and complexity he didn't understand, not really, and he could not hope to come close to it on ShameShame's diminishing advertising dollars. ShameShame was now competing and losing against fully staffed, better-moderated, sharper, corporate-owned blogs. He should have sold ShameShame when he had the chance, years ago. TV spots and an adjunct professorship yielded relatively meager incomes, and so naturally Trudi paid for everything; it was not a question, even though Ned reached for his wallet every time and got an eye-roll, every time.

He pictured a long future of being underestimated, of the bar being set low just for him, a bar he could step over with no trouble. He could practically feel his own expectations of himself contract as his world expanded with the people, places, and things that mattered so much to Trudi. That didn't matter to Ned. Or that hadn't, once.

There was the baby thing too. It was already part of Trudi's constellation, already looked up to. Actually, it was a pre-baby, a baby bump, idolized and photographed for the internet without even needing to be born. Ned felt perversely doomed by the pregnancy, yet, also perversely, relieved because his all-access future was secure.

Ned looked at his bandaged hands. He felt the lump at the back of his head. His future was secure, but Ned missed the past. *Let's pile on that I'm being hunted by my dead ex,* Ned thought. The cab lurched forward as if in response. Ned looked out the window and said softly, "Hello? Jo? You here?" and the driver shouted at Ned in the rearview mirror, "What? What?!"

Ned said, "No, no, man, nothing, it's nothing. Talking to myself." The driver snorted in abject disgust for Ned, another crazy New Yorker occupying his backseat.

In his head, Ned conversed with Jo. *Fine, I suck. What do you want from me?* He let his bandaged hands hover over the manila envelope like it was a Ouija board, and waited for an answer to emerge from whatever ephemera of their love lay within.

The cab stuttered forward. Zoom and slam. Zoom and slam.

He and Jo had been out of touch for a year before the cancer summer. He'd been preoccupied with keeping up with Trudi, but as soon as his head hit her silk pillow at night, he was tormented by cinematic, loud, high-production-value dreams of trenches and mud sucking him under, impeding his desperate mission over uncrossable fields, through deadly waters, against hooded enemies keeping him from Jo, in trouble.

One morning in early summer, he fell out of a dream of himself on horseback racing to a figure in white who called to him from a distance that he could not traverse, no matter how hard he rode. He woke with his fingers grasping the sheets as if they were reins, with his legs trembling as if gripping a galloping horse, with sweat beading his upper lip, and the hardest hard-on he'd had in months. He thought, *I need to go home.*

He watched through Harvey's window as Jo rounded the corner and struggled with the heavy door. He jumped up to guide her in. She was pale, an apparition in white flowing pants, a baggy sweater, white sneakers without laces. Still, her hair streamed behind her and her blue-denim eyes held his. She tried to stop her smile but couldn't, and even though she was sick, her smile lit her up. Skeptical of him, not trusting him, sick of him in a fundamental sense, still she shined for him. He helped her up onto the bar stool. She gave his shoulder a little bump and said, "Hey, Doc." Ned breathed free again.

June; just last June. Ned didn't even have to try to stay off Trudi's radar. She was in her first-class, cashmered, silk-sleeping-masked element, leveraging her brand and locking down new franchisees at EternaPlast meetings around the world: in Buenos Aires, Melbourne, Sao Paulo, on to Hong Kong and Paris and Cannes, Milan and Moscow and Madrid, Stockholm, Dubai, and London, and back to New York at summer's end.

Stop and go. Ned and Jo.

They began again. He cooked for her and washed her hair and sat with her in waiting rooms and took notes when doctors talked. He got repairs done around the apartment, and watched old movies or baseball games. When Jo napped, he walked around the corner with his laptop to his old studio apartment, the escape hatch never sold, all his ratty grad-student furniture still in place. Alone, out from under the sludge of media, away from red carpets and the glitterati, he tried to revive *The Angry Intern.*

He walked through the Metropolitan Museum of Art alone, Mets cap covering his giveaway hair, relaxed and anonymous and open to thinking about art. He fantasized about painting, his secret Amherst aspiration. He planned extended trips to beautiful places where he and Jo could look at art together, where Jo could lose the chill that enshrouded her and maybe heal. He walked Tom. For ten weeks, they were shut away in the strange cocoon that grows around sick people and their caregivers and holds its own unexpected comforts. For ten weeks, they were exempt from participating in the regular world. For ten weeks, even as Jo weakened, life was good, at least for Ned. Ned was happy.

He wanted to stay with Jo, see it through. He wanted to be a man of character, true to himself, like his father had tried to be, before he got trapped by guilt and a life that was a lie. Ned could not let that happen to him. He resolved to go downtown and tell two minutes of truth to Trudi when she returned, and then walk away. She would hate him. The internet and the media would tear him apart, all access would cease, but maybe he did not care. He wanted to be a man of character.

He left Jo dozing, Tom nearby.

When he got to Trudi's, Ned noticed that Trudi's ankles were so puffy they seemed about to snap the straps on her sandals. She flashed an uncharacteristically big smile (she hated her teeth) and rubbed her belly. Ned was incredulous. They barely ever fucked; she was always too full (lemony kale, almonds, two micro-cupcakes, and a glass of wine), too tired, too wired, too freshly manicured, threaded, waxed, lasered, massaged, shopped, or tweeted out. Too preoccupied with looking desirable to feel desire. She was eight weeks pregnant, and biological-clock-stoppingly triumphant. She'd already texted their families with the news. She'd Instagrammed the pee stick internet-wide.

Ned buckled. He could not tell her he did not love her, he could not tell her he did not want a child with her. It was beyond his capacity to disconnect this moment—Trudi nattering on, describing whole new shopping horizons to reach for—from the memory of his sad mother playing out her lifetime of solitaire.

Truth, Ned's kryptonite, to be avoided at any cost. Even losing Jo.

And so the Ned-zone was secure. To rationalize, he mustered and inflated a prick of pride at the idea of having a kid, the thing so definitively off the table with Jo. The thing they had discussed only once, when he vowed it didn't interest him, and Jo chose to believe him. He basked in numbing relief at not having to confront Trudi, and if he were being honest with himself, at not losing the EternaPlast-funded lifestyle.

But right now he was gridlocked. The cab lurched forward and then abruptly stopped. They were surrounded by cars and trucks. To the east was the city, to the west was the *Intrepid*, the Hudson, New Jersey. The driver shut the engine. Other drivers emerged from their vehicles to check out what was going on, to stretch their legs, or to take pictures of the traffic and confer, with the instant intimacy of New Yorkers unsurprised by turns of events. A young couple in matching puffy black coats leaned against each other on the hood of their puffy black Escalade. She turned her face up to his, and he lowered his to hers. Ned was touched by the tenderness between them. He was jealous of strangers, a couple who were indifferent to the traffic, who cared only about being in love.

Fate had pushed him to Trudi when Jo needed him most. The way forward had been ordained for him—a baby!—and he'd let himself be carried along. What else could he have done? He'd hidden behind events as they unfolded, promising himself every single day that this would be the day he would talk to Jo, make Jo understand he'd had no choice. Each day that passed made it harder to do.

He'd been under siege by a barrage of communications from her. It seemed possible she might never stop texting, e-mailing, and calling him, demanding and then begging for him to account for himself. Anyway, that he had fucked up was no surprise. He'd disappointed her before. He'd practically proposed in Belize, and then when he'd sobered up and saw the yes in her eyes, the hope, he'd panicked and shut it down.

Yes, he was a sack of shit, just like she said, just like the men he outed and analyzed on ShameShame, on Fox, just like John Edwards, one woman pregnant, one woman dying of cancer. Ned, like the politician, had a character problem.

Ned sat forward and craned his neck through the open plastic sliding window that separated the taxicab's front seat from the back to make contact with the driver. He said, "Hey, man," to get the driver's attention, find out if dispatch had alerted cabbies about trouble on the highway. The driver, distracted by his intense cell phone conversation, possibly on purpose, grabbed the slider without looking and jammed it along its track, inadvertently closing it with all his strength. Like a guillotine, the thick plastic window hit Ned full force on his left cheek, the site of the old line drive to the face, scoring his skin. At the same time, the traffic unlocked itself, and the driver hit the gas.

"Jesus fucking Christ," Ned said as he was thrown back hard against the seat. The driver, unhesitating, in one fluid motion, punched at the meter and swerved right, hard, crossing three lanes of suddenly fast-moving traffic to a nonexistent shoulder of the highway, beyond the Piers. In flawless English he said to Ned, "Get out of my car. Pay first. Language is not allowed. I am Christian."

Ned, thrown off, said, "What the fuck! I'm Christian too!" He had no idea if lapsed Catholics were technically Christians. The side of his face felt seared and wet. For the second time that night, he ran his tongue along the inside of his mouth to make sure his teeth were intact. The driver found Ned in the rearview mirror. With hard eyes he said, "No language! No language! Get out. Pay first."

The video screen ceased its laughing and became an invoice screen, showing Ned the fare: forty-two dollars. He fumbled for his wallet and found his credit card. The same paralysis that had afflicted the screen earlier froze it again. He tapped, he swiped, the screen stayed static. He tapped, he swiped, the screen did not change.

"Card decline."

"Oh for God's sakes, the card's fine, your thing isn't working!"

"Card decline."

Ned was desperate to leave the taxicab, even though he was being deposited on a dangerous bend of the highway on a cold March night with cars, finally released from traffic's trap, speeding along at a roaring clip. He dug in his wallet for cash and came up with three twenties. He slid them through the slot, across the punishing divide between himself and the driver, whose name he still could not decipher.

"I need change," Ned said. "Ten bucks back."

The driver's phone trilled. He resumed shouting into the earpiece.

Ned shouted, "My change! My fucking change!" He rapped on the plexiglass, which surely now held bits of his own skin and blood. The driver, without interrupting his conversation or even turning around, reached under the seat and waved a hammer.

Ned picked his way through glass and weeds and gravel to the bike path that ran along the Hudson River. He walked the long, cold blocks from Chelsea to Trudi's place in the Meatpacking District in a tweed sports jacket, the wind whipping his injuries and ruffling the hair on his tender head, galled most of all at having been threatened into tipping the cabbie eighteen dollars.

The manila envelope with the tear across his name lay forgotten on the floor of the cab.

13

The bones when they rattle, the head when it bounces.

Violence, ladies. Who knew! I was raised pre–Jerry Springer, I'd never seen women lunge or throw punches, not even in the movies. I never hurt anyone physically in my entire life. I'd yanked the dog's leash, gripped the upper arm of an obstinate daughter, and once when I shouldered past Martin during an argument he bumped hard into a wall, which caused *me* to apologize.

But attacking someone? Seeing fright rise in the eyes? How satisfying. Who knew.

Ned's circuitry of fear hummed. I heard it. Data collected, interpreted, organized, and disseminated to equip him to fight—as if—or flee. And to file the threat for next time. Good idea, Doc.

Ned reeked of fear in my living room. Ned's fear smelled familiar. I'd sniffed it one time before at the neck, and let me say, it was intoxicating. Primal, sexy, yummy.

We were on the A train at two in the morning, coming back from some art thing at the edges of Brooklyn, and three shirtless, dropped-pants, tightly wound and wired boys hustled on, and started in. There were only a couple other people in the subway car and the atmosphere, previously quiet and tired, got tense fast. The boys surrounded a very old Chinese guy, hollering, taunting, and doing pull-ups on the poles and standing on the seats and stomping. The old guy was smiling and shrugging, but his eyes were frightened. A woman in scrubs near us shut her eyes and pretended to doze. The boys did handstands right next to the old guy, and tipped over on to him and laughed maniacally. The old guy actually had his arms up to protect his head. The boys' eyes were hard.

I felt Ned decide to intervene, he was coiled and his feet were set and he was leaning forward, his thigh tight against mine, and I put my hand on his arm and he whirled on me and burned a stare into me and said through gritted teeth, "Just please do what I say. When the doors open at Nostrand, get off. Get off the train. If I'm not behind you, call 911."

The force of his conviction shut me up. I was scared. I nodded. The boys noticed Ned, saw his chest puff, and I did too, that actually happens, the chest actually expands, and he stood, and they lost interest in the old guy and got very interested in Ned. One of the boys stepped forward and his wingmen dropped back. It was choreography, they knew exactly what they were doing, they'd done it before, they knew how to intimidate, they were very good at it. Ned stepped forward too. I remember that, the one step he took into it. He put his body and his face right up against the lead kid, who was built like a welterweight, who was all muscle and smile, who was enjoying himself. Ned opened his arms, palms up, in a faux-submissive let's-not-do-this gesture.

The boy said, "How is this your business?" and he and Ned shit-talked back and forth, spitting in each other's faces, foreplay to violence. The old guy slid down the subway bench until he was right next to the doors. The woman in scrubs did the same, and so did I. The train swayed and shifted and slowed slightly, something we'd normally not even notice, but Ned had known that was coming, so I was waiting for it. Ned was timing the confrontation. Ned was playing the kid, providing the distraction necessary so that the old guy, the other woman, and I could get off the train.

The wingmen were getting antsy, it was time for the shit talk to end. One of them jabbed at Ned and he put his arm up to fend it off, and I could feel the blunt bulk of violence accumulating in the space around the four men as the brakes finally screamed at Nostrand, and the doors opened and the old guy and the woman in scrubs launched off the train, and I did too. The next thing I know the recorded voice, always hearty as hell, reminded us to "Stand Clear of the Closing Doors." Close they did, and we were safe on the platform. Ned, too.

The train sat for a few seconds. Two of the boys were up against the windows, knocking and waving and laughing, and the other was back to doing pull-ups on the pole. They looked like regular, annoying teenagers. And then the train pulled away. The Chinese guy and the woman in scrubs nodded at Ned, shook their heads the New York way—*What can you do, this is our lot*—and disappeared into the city. I put my arms around Ned. I was shaking. He was shaking. I put my nose to his neck. He smelled like scalp and skin oil and soap and Tic Tacs, his Ned smell, but also, now, sweat and ammonia and something else, too, something from the earth, damp and fleshy, up from under, like mushrooms. Fear.

Bravery was in there too. Ned protecting me, so erotic. We got into a cab, and I unzipped him and held him, he was crazy hard, crazy hot, and when we got home we barely made it through the front door. He pushed me up against it, he pushed up against me. He said, "No more talking."

The memory of desire ignites desire, doesn't it? I'm disembodied but still wired to want it. I'm discarnate, but vibrating with the carnal knowledge I will never un-know. I can't forget, dead or alive. I'm wound up.

Swoony subway memories notwithstanding, putting Ned down physically at the Titania felt good. It was my first time, I let my anger rule, I raged in Ned's direction to hurt him, and I did, I smelled fear, but I want more. I want accountability. He needs to know, and I need to know he knows I know.

Post-attack, I flew to the moon and I mingled with my kind, seeking some ritualistic bonding to acknowledge the first revenge notch on my belt. Some kind of poltergeist high-five. But no. Let me just say, there is no such thing as a friendly ghost. I joined in the aura of the moon where phantoms buzzed and sniped and rehearsed their howls, their moans, their spooky voices. They chewed and savored insults and injuries. They flew solo. Definitely no bonding. They can't stand themselves or each other. They are a bunch of neurotic narcissists.

When I say "they," I guess I mean me, too.

I peep in on the Titania from my lair, a scaffold across the street, twelve stories up.

I've got an excellent view of the windows of my old apartment. Once a New Yorker, always a New Yorker, smug about real estate. I cycle back and forth, back and forth on the swaying platform. I slither between the knocked-together pipe joints and the black netting that surrounds the thing to keep debris from pelting passersby. The metal riggings holding my home together bang and screech in the wind.

I'm trying to wind down.

The moon moves, and the windows of the Titania reflect like mirrors. I see me, a phantom with a dead-mouse-gray sheen. Horrible. I moan. I flail and twist and billow. It hasn't escaped me that I was with my daughters tonight, at home. They bickered, they moved past framed photographs, they reached for cleaning supplies. I saw the old interplay of gestures, heard the weave of voices, understood the shoulder's set and the skin's cast in the lamplight of home. The way Anna pulled at Tom, the way Laney closed the front door. My babies.

Stop it. Stay on track.

I bet Ned is concocting the lie for Dr. Trudi right now about the goose-egg at the back of his head and his bloody hands. I bet he leaves out the part about me. No doubt he dismissed me years ago in his sincere voice with his sincere look and the sincere tilt of his head in her direction, as he snapped the lie into place: *We had a thing. It was nothing. She was older. She can't move on.*

I know Dr. Trudi well, everyone does. She posts, uploads, links, likes, tweets and retweets a comprehensive rundown of her beauty routines, her pricey products, her favorite haunts, her anemic plates of artsy food at breakfast, lunch, dinner, caloric intake righteously noted. Wardrobe dilemmas: Prabal or the McQueen? Her white apartment in the Meatpacking District. Her boyfriend.

My boyfriend.

At my end, after Ned's exit, bedridden, heartbroken, of course I followed Dr. Trudi. How could I not? He was ignoring me. Tracking him through her was my only option for contact. And there it was, right there on my phone. I was one of hundreds of thousands, day after day. She provided filtered, curated access to her glossy world. She gave her followers, aspirationalists all—me and @botoxboi and @goguccigo and @eterna4eternity and so many others—the opportunity to congratulate her on having things we wanted but could not possess except through retweeting and proffering likes or hearts. We gasped at pictures of cliffside cocktail parties in exotic locations. And how about that Clearblue pee stick, delicately held by cobalt fingertips? Everyone, absolutely dying over Dr. Trudi's bundle-of-joy-to-be.

Dying. Especially me.

Tracking their vacations, their meals, their friends. I couldn't get enough of seeing Ned trotted out, all cleaned up for the internet. You tell me. Is that cyberstalking? Didn't she invite it? Didn't he expect it?

Ned should have demurred until I was dead. Ned should have pulled back, lain low for a while. He knew I was watching. I texted him. I begged him. Instead, he was busy with this life, these pictures, this record of betrayal, this betrayal of me with this woman and her fingernails and her urine-soaked pregnancy test. This woman of success, excess, access.

At least, at the very least, he should have dropped his gaze, averted his eyes, narrowed his smile, backed up out of the frame until I was out of the picture. Instead he looked straight into the lens and onto the screens of thousands of devices, including mine. He knew I would see.

It's not easy to wind down.

I'm a ghost living on a scaffold, peering into windows, waiting for my next shot at revenge, my next shot at redemption, while Ned—whom I let live—and Dr. Trudi are in their Meatpacking District aerie, surrounded by swag, their well-furnished heaven on earth, waiting for their little angel to arrive.

Me and Ned, we were never nothing. Dr. Trudi needs to know that. He was right about one thing, though. I definitely can't move on.

14

"Emotional cheating? Don't accuse me of some internet syndrome that doesn't actually exist." Anna's indignation was fake, and cunning. She was dismissing the accusation from Jules on a technicality. It wasn't all that emotional, it was just plain cheating.

They sped south to Brooklyn, away from the night's wreckage at Harvey's and her mother's apartment. In the passenger seat, Jules, head bent over phone, texted support to Laney, uptown, agitated and restless, too, after the jagged evening. The orange Wrangler, a summer car, did not hold the weak heat that puffed from its vents. The steering wheel, the gear stick, and the frame supporting the convertible's soft top were brittle with cold. The stiff vinyl seats crackled like ice breaking as they bounced and bumped over ruts and potholes.

Jules said, "You say something's from the internet just to make it sound cheesy." Anna's cell phone chirped. "There's the syndrome that doesn't exist, texting you. Again."

Despite the speed and the freeze and the jolts, the atmosphere in the Wrangler was ready to flare. Anna took the phone from the console between them, glanced, pressed hard at the Off button, and slipped it into her coat pocket. She stared straight ahead and made her voice neutral. "That's my sister. I'm done with her for tonight."

"Your sister." Jules looked out her window. "She must be a hell of a multitasker all of a sudden, since she's texting me, too. She wants you to come over tomorrow, go through some boxes."

The new lie hung in the air between them. Finally, Jules said, "Say something."

Anna said, "I have nothing to say. I'm just tired," when really, she was wired with lies and secrets, and knew that it showed.

"Obviously, there's something up. It would be better if you just said what it was."

Anna kept silent. They were about to enter the tubes of the Brooklyn-Battery Tunnel and she had to concentrate. She hated tunnels, and this one was the worst. At the southern end of the West Side Highway, two very narrow lanes narrowed to one, due to a years-long construction project. Orange rubber batons were set in the median, flimsy barriers against oncoming traffic. The lighting was nonexistent at the tube's mouth, and cars fed themselves into an unfathomable recess with zero visibility, the longest underwater underpass in North America. Once lighting was restored, the eighty-year-old, cinderblock-y walls were visibly wet, and Anna gripped the wheel and tried to think through escape scenarios for when the walls buckled and the water rushed in. She cursed her perverse fascination with disaster movies and heard her sister's wry commentary each time they settled in to watch one: "Try to remember, it's not a documentary."

Jules didn't register the terror of the tunnel at all. She slumped in her seat and said, "Well, then let me put words in your mouth. Thank you, Jules, for your help tonight. Thank you for dealing with my drunk sister, my morose father, nine old ladies, the self-help hippies, and the deranged poodle. And thank you, Jules, for cleaning up the mess at my mother's. And for not interrogating me about texting and sneaking looks at my phone every five minutes."

After a deliberative silence, Anna chose a version of the truth, her best lie. "It's nothing. Okay, yes. There's someone, from the hospital. Asking me how tonight went. But it's nothing."

Jules's face glowed greenish in the tunnel's light. "Someone from the hospital."

"I can't do this. I'm concentrating."

It was way too soon for a crush, Anna knew. She and Jules were together for less than a year, managing nascent careers, discovering each other, navigating Joanna's illness and death. If it were not for Jules, Anna would have been unable to surf the ocean of loss of the past few months, waves that rose and threatened, waves that had not yet ebbed. Jules held them afloat and loved Anna, and Anna was not pulled under, and Anna wanted to love Jules.

They were both first-year residents in the three-year pediatric program at Kravis, the kids' hospital at Mount Sinai. Anna was thrilled to have gotten into a residency back home in Manhattan, after the hurry-up-and-wait pace of four years of med school in Birmingham, at the University of Alabama. At Kravis, she trailed her green-scrubs-and-clog-clad fellow residents as they toured the hospital, one of an annual herd shuffling through. She watched real doctors and nurses moving with the purpose she wanted and envied.

Within the first hour of the first day of her first week, when the residents circled to listen, avid, to the chief resident, Anna had sized up her competition and kept returning to one open face. She could not take her eyes off Jules, who'd looked right back at her and winked. Everyone else blurred, like in the movies, but Jules was clear.

They worked eighty hours a week, toasted day's end, rehashed colleagues, kids, cases, and fell into each other, exhausted, each night. They were lusty, fearless explorers across the continents of their bodies, finding landmarks on the skin. No meal, no song, no moon, no breast or fingertip existed until they made it so, made it new, for each other.

As a couple, life was a laughing matter, the darker, the funnier. What better way to cope with the adult-onset realization that there was no threshold to step across marked "Grown-Up" where, on the other side, you called the shots? What better way than to couple up, laugh it off, and carry on? To collude in the myth that together you would be safe. That it was possible. Anna was happily spellbound.

The spell broke the day she'd found out that Joanna was sick again. The prognosis was bad. Keswani said, "Your mother has known for some time. She chose a less aggressive path."

On Anna's watch.

Anna envied and resented Laney, unfazed by the urgency of the details of caregiving. She herself attacked a to-do list almost before her eyes opened in the morning. It was quite a list: judgment calls and phone calls, caregiver interviews and supervision, equipment rental and maintenance, arranging and rearranging the apartment, medication schedules, monitoring side effects, doctor visits, mad dashes to satisfy food cravings—smoothies one day, fast food the next—when Joanna expressed the slightest interest in eating.

None of it made any difference. Joanna had succumbed as Anna sat at a bar with a Tito's and soda and a sexy nurse in hand. Irrational as it was, she believed her mother had chosen a moment when Anna's back was turned, after months of vigilance.

She'd shut off her phone. She'd been unreachable. She was whirling with vodka and the proximity to Kai in Tap-a-Keg. They stumbled to the street, laughing like maniacs. The sidewalk sparkled with mica and Anna remembered thinking, *We're walking on diamonds*. In a pocket park at the intersection of Broadway and West End at 106th, they happened upon a memorial to the Strauses, who died together on the *Titanic*. Kai googled and read to Anna the romantic story of Ida, who chose to stay behind with Isidor rather than join the other women and children climbing into lifeboats. An inscription was carved: *Lovely and pleasant were they in their lives and in their death they were not parted*. Anna flashed on cemetery visits with her mother to view her grandparents' headstone. She tried to remember the inscription, but lost the thought when Kai pushed her up against Ida and Isidor's memorial and kissed her hard. Zippers and buttons came undone. The night of her mother's death. When they raised their heads, they noticed music thumping from the Underground on the corner, they went inside, they ordered more drinks, they did karaoke. Drunken idiots.

Outside the Underground, finally, a couple of hours after they met up, Anna powered her phone back on. Laney, Jules, Martin. Laney, Jules, Martin. Texts, voice mail, even e-mail. She ran home to find Nick, the Titania's superintendent, grim-faced. He ushered her into the elevator and accompanied her without looking at her, presumably because she reeked of booze and cigarettes, maybe even sex. The apartment was bustling with EMS workers. Tom, panting, underfoot. Laney, stricken, hiding inside her hoodie. Jules, dark-eyed, eyes averted.

Two hours. The freest hours she'd had in so long became, in an instant, the worst night of her life. She thought of holding the karaoke microphone, screaming out, *Touch me baby, tainted love*. She pictured herself where she should have been, at home with her sister, at her mother's bedside, her head bowed, waiting for her mother's fingers to stroke her hair with a last caress, the caress that had soothed her since the day she was born.

Anna thought, *That wasn't gonna happen anyway, she was already checked out. It didn't matter if I was there or not*. She felt rejected and unloved, the wrong kind of grief. She flushed with shame. She conjured images for the hundredth time: Laney hearing the monitor's alarm in her sleep and stumbling down the hallway to the bedroom with Tom barking, Laney punching at her phone, and then Laney waiting for Anna to check in. Waiting for her big, mature sister who was pounding shots of whatever was put down on the bar, having sex in a park, screaming to that stupid song, laughing and laughing and laughing.

One night off, too many drinks, bad behavior. Her diligence, her preparedness had made no difference at all, it was all a crapshoot, and bad things happened, prepared or not, and would just keep on happening, and love did not save the day. It was all random. Including the advent of Kai.

Anna drove on, conscious of the tension in the right side of her body, her shoulder, her neck, rigid and on guard against Jules in the passenger seat, reading her.

Jules did not do random. Jules had firm convictions about a big karmic checklist in the sky. She believed what went around came back around because actual, literal cosmic forces were at work.

It was a perspective Anna had trouble with. From age six, when her grandparents died, shockingly, suddenly, and then for the next twenty years, buffeted by her father's money troubles and her mother's health troubles and the divorce, and now, her mother dead, it seemed more like what went around kept going around and around, circling you, tightening, until you were tied up and twisted and breaking into a sweat every time the telephone rang, always braced for bad news. For a while when Anna was a kid, her mother, as a joke—a joke!—answered the phone with "No bad news!" instead of hello, as if that faux-funny plea could ward off whatever was incoming. Laney used to run from the room with her fingers in her ears.

Anna did not run from the room. Anna the good scout equipped herself with compass and cap, sturdy shoes, pockets full of rations, and a getaway plan. She spent childhood days stomping through the woods behind the house, building forts and securing rope ladders and forging secret pathways. After 9/11, thirteen-year-old Anna lay awake at night mapping escape routes in her head. She asked for a Go Bag one Christmas, batteries for her birthday, a Leatherman for graduation. She did not enter a club or a concert venue without noting where the exits were. She listened closely to preflight safety demonstrations on airplanes and followed along with the card. Always braced, always prepared.

Because bad things happened to good people all the time, and kept on happening. It was no consolation when Jules offered up woo-y reasons, like "Karma's a bitch," or the heart-stoppingly glib, "You've had your share." Meaning, so much has happened, your bad-things quota has been reached. It made Anna scream inside: *Shut up, they'll hear you!* Forget karma—it was the gods of irony that held the cards. Sending platitudes out into the ether felt like dangerous provocation.

Anna instinctively looked out the windshield and up into the sky, full of moon. *Are you there, Ma? It's me, Crazy-pants,* she thought. She could still feel Tom's haunches quivering under her palm as she tried to push him to the down position at the restaurant. Anna played the scene over in her mind, trying to retrieve a visual, trying to see what Tom saw when he leapt past her mother's poster to the ceiling. She could almost capture the disturbance wavering in the atmosphere, something hovering at the edges of the evening, hiding from her.

That's guilt, Anna thought. She flashed on Laney obsessively rubbing a vodka-soaked napkin over her boots. "Ma said." *We're both crazy-pants.*

Unlike Jules, she had never believed in heaven or hell, or in anything at all after death. There was no higher power pulling strings. She had faith in schedules and process and to-do lists, in chemistry, in medicine. Even the concept of "soul" was hard for Anna to wrap her mind around.

When they first met, Jules had argued heatedly in favor of the reality of soul mates, which Anna dismissed as nonsense, considering there were seven billion people on the planet; even filtered by demographics of age, gender, orientation, cultures, language, proximate geographies, ad infinitum, it was statistically impossible that there was one "the one." They'd launched into their first serious disagreement. Jules had said, "Not everything makes sense. Because fate. And wind and tides. And art! Because there must be more meaning than what data means. Because I am me. Not a photo, not a chat, not a post or a click, not a target or a market. Not a list of characteristics. I am Me. With You."

Anna had to admit, having one's mother die certainly made concepts she once dismissed—fate, God, soul—appealing. Maybe religion was just one supereffective magnetic force field, pulling away paralyzing grief over who we lose, and the knowledge that we are next. Maybe concepts she'd previously dismissed were ways to navigate the short, stark arc of little human lives. Because even though she saw the body lifted and carried out, even though she had dealt with the grim details and made the arrangements, Anna couldn't bring herself to accept that Joanna, her mother, no longer existed. Apparently, Tom couldn't accept it either. Or Laney, still hearing motherly admonitions at the memorial service. *Or Ned McGowan*, she thought, and shook the thought away.

They were through the tunnel and she un-tensed, and as always, she noticed the wide sky over Brooklyn, and navigated the borough's meandering streets, so different from Manhattan's tight grid just a few miles away. Their building sat at the edge of Red Hook, close to the city waters of upper New York Bay flowing to the Atlantic, not far from the bars and coffee shops, stores and boutiques that came and went, while the abandoned buildings, hardscrabble lots, and decaying piers hung on forever. Wrangler parked, bags hoisted, they climbed the five flights to their overpriced three-room apartment. When they got to the top, Anna took the knapsack from Jules's shoulders, and unhooked her own, and dropped them in front of their apartment door. She reached for Jules's hand and said, "Let's keep going."

Their Red Hook roof offered a wide vista of downtown Manhattan. They were protected from the wind even on a deep March winter night. Anna lay flat out on the surface with a Frisbee under her head, and Jules was beside her, resting her head on a mostly deflated beach ball. The young women stared up into the glow of a moon mixed with city lights, holding hands. The moon was bigger and closer than Anna had ever seen it.

"Cold?" Anna leaned over and fussed with Jules's puffy coat.

"It scares me when you shut down. When we disconnect. I don't like it."

Anna pulled her wool cap over her eyes to keep Jules out. "We're okay. I'm sorry."

"Don't apologize. I'm trying to have a conversation."

"I'm sorry."

"If we've moved too fast, tell me. If we're too tight, tell me. I can take that. I can handle that. That would be fair."

"I don't think any of those things. I—"

"What I can't handle is, I don't know. Thinking we feel the same way, saying we feel the same way, that we're going in the same direction, and then one of us going off. And doing something else. With someone else. That's not what I thought we were doing."

"I don't want to do anything else. I don't. I just wanted to . . . I don't know. Mess around. Not be a good girl." Anna made a sound like laughing. She sounded false to her own ears, again, as she used a targeted truth to defuse the Kai sex bomb that went off on the night of her mother's death. "Now that my mother's not paying attention anymore."

Every single hour of every single day of Anna's whole life,

Joanna had been a listening or whispering presence just at the edge of her consciousness and her conscience. Awake, dreaming, far away, up close. Continents and oceans apart, it didn't matter. Always there, even when not. It simply wasn't possible that she was gone. Anna thought, *She must be able to see this moon.*

Jules said, "Well, now I'm paying attention. I'm not going to ask you about that night. That's your truth. But I'm paying attention."

Anna brought Jules's gloved hand to her mouth. She pulled the leather away from Jules's wrist with her teeth and blew hot breath into the glove. "I love you."

Jules turned to Anna. "I don't want to just be in love. That's easy. I want it to work. I want to make it work."

"Me too. But I don't know if I know how. Or if it's even possible. For anyone."

"I can guarantee that texting with someone else and hiding it from me is not the way to go."

Anna said, "You make me feel like it's possible—you do," because at that moment she believed it could be true.

They got closer for warmth. "Your mother must be able to see this moon."

Anna smiled up at the sky. "Okay, now you're not playing fair. You plucked that thought right out of my head."

"I'm definitely not playing fair. I want to win."

"Win what? Life? Me?"

"Yes! And points. Credits. Whatever! For trying to be . . . I don't know. It's stupid. It's corny. I want to try hard and be, like, true. Real. True and real to you. To our families and our friends. To myself. You know?" Jules traced Anna's eyebrows with her gloved finger. "I want to be where I am. Not always wondering what else there is. I want you to feel that way too."

Anna's throat constricted. She wanted to say the right thing, but was afraid to say anything at all. She flashed on Laney at the door of the apartment, imploring Ned to communicate, to honor what they'd shared, friendship and loss. Ned had stayed mute. Anna hated that, the way he pulled focus to himself by saying nothing. She recognized the maneuver. She did it too. She took a deep breath.

"When we were little, she used to get us out of bed and make us lie on the front lawn with flashlights and constellation maps, counting stars in the middle of the night. Pretty crazy. I took it seriously. I had a Go Bag next to my bed with my gear. Laney fell asleep on the lawn every time." Anna gave Jules the memory, precious to her, like a locket or a ring.

Jules accepted. "Well, we're on tar beach in Brooklyn. It's just after midnight in March, and it's about twenty degrees and we're together under this sky. So, the apple hasn't fallen far from the tree, baby. Apple-tree."

"We can almost touch the moon." Anna reached her arms. "Maybe she pushed it close, so we could try."

They kissed, and the kiss tapped at Anna's heart, and she said, "Jules, thank you for everything, thank you so much," and let herself cry and cry and cry.

In bed, Anna dreamt of climbing a fire escape dropped from a void. Rusted, slatted steps creaked and swayed under her weight as she climbed, and there was nothing below and there was nothing above, and she pulled herself up in the dream, and she was on the platform of a scaffold shrouded in black netting, high over the city, and the planked platform was vast and floated like a raft on the night sky, and there was her mother, far away, backlit by the moon, approaching Anna, and the closer her mother got the blurrier she became, her hair, her eyes, her skin, everything was pale and diffused. She trailed extended limbs and tendrils of hair, and reached toward Anna, who backed away, who tripped backward and got tangled in netting, who said, *No, Mama, no, no,* and her mother moved in, her mother was a gaseous, rank thing whose eyes were rushing storm clouds, and Anna felt cornered high over the street on the swaying scaffold, and her mother hovered and her mother reached for Anna and wrapped around her in an embrace with arms that felt like icy, cold bands tightening around Anna until her breath stopped.

She startled awake, gasping and shivering. She despaired. She paced her breath to Jules's. She could hear her own big heart thump. She tried to exorcise the nightmare with an image of her regular mother doing regular mother things: at the stove, behind the wheel of the car, scrolling for a song, running her fingers through Anna's hair. The whispers of her fingertips on Anna's scalp. All she could conjure was Tom, staring, imploring, his body pointed toward the shadows, showing her something in the restaurant, in the apartment.

Maybe the body's vitals stopped, but the essence that Jules was talking about, that indefinable and uncharted thing, that singular Me, the soul, cleaved unto by multitudes wiser than Anna, maybe that thing endured, like another deeper heart, an endless heart, always somehow somewhere. Maybe there really were magnetic fields where unseen forces—restless souls—looked down on the living.

Jules was snoring next to her, curled close. She looked unfamiliar to Anna. Like someone she didn't know, might never know. Could anyone be known? Was anything real? "Real" had become subjective.

"Jules," Anna said out loud, wanting to wake her up, wanting her back. "Jules, I don't think she's gone, not yet," Anna said. "She's not."

Without missing a beat, Jules, completely herself, said from sleep, "Baby, obviously. The dog could've told us that. And I'm not a dog person."

Anna let her curves fit the curves of Jules, and matched her breath to Jules's, and tried to join Jules on the path to sleep so she could begin again tomorrow, a faithful partner, a rational woman, a good girl, but nightmares and lies and secrets bounced in her brain. She buried her nose in Jules's hair, but recalled Kai's scent. She squeezed shut her eyes, but continued to search the recesses of her own spirit for her mother.

More than two weeks had passed since the death, the memorial was a few days behind them, and Laney wanted to look forward to what might be next. She was not sure how to start. Tom wasn't helping.

"Please stop staring at me. I don't speak your language. If you're so smart, just say it already, whatever it is you're trying to tell me!"

Tom was making Laney crazy. He followed her through the apartment like it was his job, bumping her leg or underfoot. He panted and padded along, nosing her hand or thigh every few minutes as if to say, "Focus!" His intense attention was adding to her jumpiness. She'd expected Tom to be mopey and depressed without Joanna, but he was on high alert. His eyes were sharp, his ears quivered, he barked at the front door, waiting for Joanna's key in the lock. His dogly inability to process—accept—Joanna's absence was both irritating and heartbreaking.

Tom tilted his head at her tone. Laney said, "I know, I'm sorry. You're figuring it out. I'm not doing such a great job either."

There was so much to figure out—where to live, where to work, how to grow up. Before her mother died, she came home regularly to get a break from the seven-hundred-square-foot box she lived in with two roommates in Crown Heights. Tension would dissolve from her shoulders and neck as soon as she entered. Home. The scent alone was enough to evoke a yawn and a yearning for a nap. She'd drop her bag and her keys and stretch out and aim the remote control at the cable-channel extravaganza she couldn't afford at her own place, with Tom across her legs. She'd doze, loot her mother's clothes closet, and stare into the refrigerator until Joanna showed up to cook something, listen to her troubles, dispense wisdom.

The sisters discussed listing the apartment for sale in the spring. She'd promised Anna, who had dealt with all the tough logistics for so long, and worked twelve-hour days too, that she would begin the process of cleaning out. Her sister said, "Just get it organized."

Laney wandered from room to room, pretending to assess and plan, but her thinking was fragmented. She didn't know what she was doing. She was motherless, and would soon be homeless. Of course, she could stay with Martin, or Anna and Jules, or find an apartment; there'd be money. She remembered being so desperate to get her own place when she graduated, to be grown-up, finally, and how her mother had shrugged and said, "Okay, give it a try. You can always come home." Laney had been insulted, like she was being doubted or condescended to by Joanna, like she couldn't live somewhere on her own. But living somewhere was not the same as being home.

Chalk it up to grief, call it denial, but she still sensed her mother going in and out of rooms, looking for her glasses, chatting to Tom, starting or ending the day. Laney heard her mother's voice in echo, saw her imprint on a cushion, felt the grip on the worn arm of a chair. She was startled to see her mother's hair on a brush, left by an occupant still so present it felt like vandalism to clean up, let alone pack up. Home. It was supposed to stay intact.

And so, weeks later there was Joanna's cup, still in the sink. And so there were Joanna's keys, still in the bowl. Joanna's bedroom door remained closed, since Laney, bringing up the rear behind the EMS crew wheeling the bier, had pulled it shut.

After Ned left the night of the broken vase, when she and Anna were still sniping at each other, Anna had said, again, "And for Christ's sake, deal with the bed! How hard is that?"

Laney thought, *Okay, how hard is it?*

Joanna had loved that damn bed, which had stayed with her through a long marriage and after. She had brought the babies home from the hospital to that bed. When she was diagnosed with the recurrence, she'd gone to the fourth floor of ABC Home on lower Broadway and splurged on new blue sheets, mixing turquoise, indigo and sky and sea, ultramarine and aquamarine, robin's egg and slate and lake.

Laney thought, *She probably croaked when she heard we were bringing in the hospital bed. The prospect of cheap sheets on a urine-proof mattress probably killed her.* She took a deep breath and opened the door to her mother's room. The trace scent of the last two weeks—bergamot, cotton and cream, too many flowers and stale flower water, everything cut thin by antiseptic—stopped her like a second, invisible portal. She was light-headed.

Really fucking hard, Sis, that's how hard, Laney thought. She leaned against the doorjamb and surveyed. She could not cross the threshold. Tom bumped her in acknowledgment of her anxiety, and she flicked at his curly head and said, "Sucks to be us."

She'd planned to strip the sheets, obviously, as Jules had recommended. She had been embarrassed to ask for more direction. Strip it and do what exactly with the "dirty" sheets? It seemed blasphemous or sacrilegious to dump them in the hamper, where they would sit until laundry day, when all traces of Joanna would be washed away, as if those very sheets had not shrouded their mother. Laney couldn't throw them out—that was worse. And once she decided on a plan for the sheets, what next? Remake the bed as if Joanna would be there again at bedtime, setting her reading glasses and book and cup of water on the nightstand with relish, getting into bed and reading, Mama's big fun at day's end—when she was never coming back? But wasn't it even creepier to leave a bare mattress and uncovered pillows?

She stepped into the drift of scent, and approached the unmade bed. She gave the indigo coverlet a tug. She smoothed the white ruffle of the aqua sheet with one finger. She clamped her eyes shut. She could not un-see her mother's empty being, the vacated body, from weeks ago. Home alone, no caregivers, Martin gone, Anna gone.

Her mother had been breathless, drugged, agitated, but lucid. Her coughing tore Laney's heart. She had prayed, "Make it stop," and then when the coughing stopped, she prayed for it to start again, terrified that she had willed her mother to die. There was a long, trippy minute watching Joanna's chest, waiting for it to rise, and then another minute, watching the breath accumulate so slowly in the sick chest, and then a soft release, and then the rise again. She'd thought it would be okay to retreat for an hour to her room.

After, she could not un-hear the terrible muffled lifting of her mother's body, and her little hat falling off, and then the sound of a zipper, *zzzripp*, closing, and then a settling of the black bag with her mother inside, across the gurney. Anna had gone missing and then turned up, glazed by alcohol, fuzzy with secrets. None of the EMS crew spoke, but there were grunts and mutters and nods of direction and coordination.

Laney saw it again as they wheeled and bumped her poor mother along, navigating the dead weight on the gurney around corners, bumping, bumping, bumping into the elevator. All of them, crowding into the elevator, which, when she thought back, was so stupid! Why hadn't she and Anna hung back, gone down separately?

Laney had gripped the gurney's rail and stared at the floor, at her dirty boots. Anna had her work clogs on. The EMS people wore black Nikes. Her stomach had dropped as the elevator dropped to the lobby, where the doorman and Nick and the neighbors watched as EMS bumped Joanna out of the Titania onto 103rd Street and up onto rollers, and took her away.

It sure as hell wasn't Beaches, she thought.

The weak winter sun was gone. The rooms grew dim. She wasn't hungry. She couldn't handle television, the saturated, blaring, parallel universe. She didn't have the attention span to read. Her nose was stuffy. Her throat was sore. She touched her forehead. Hot. Internal snippets of audio and video of her mother, dying, played in her brain.

Grief was exhausting. Having your mother die was, surprisingly, a lot of work. You are on deadline. Your job is to create another you, you without a mother, but to preserve the old you, and to preserve your mother, and to do that you have to undertake a time-sensitive mission, a search for sounds and images, scents and gestures, the veins on the hand, the arch of an eyebrow, the voice, before it fades, before it fades, so of course you seem to be in a dream, you are, of course you are wandering from room to room, you are, because inside you are busy busy busy digging and uncovering and cataloguing and archiving her whole life—a life that gave you yours and then was lived wrapped around yours—into memory.

It was a lot of work. It took a lot of time. That's why she was so mad at everyone at the Sad/Happy Hour. They were moving too fast to the next part.

She thought, *Maybe I should be writing this down.*

There was an obstacle to doing the work of grief. Laney could not grasp that her mother was actually dead. It seemed utterly impossible. She was spooked, there was no other way to put it, when she turned a corner or passed a dark window or stood outside the bedroom door. And she was embarrassed at how infantile it was.

Her head hurt. Laney meant to nap on the sofa for an hour, to use up an hour. She found herself back in her mother's room. She flicked the bedside lamp on. Tom ticked in too.

"What am I supposed to do?" she said out loud, to the dog, to the room, to the deathbed bedding, to her mother. She let the tears come. She sat on the edge of Joanna's bed, and Tom nosed her and put his muzzle into her lap. Laney dropped her head to touch his head with hers. She hugged his neck and breathed in his dog-smell, park earth and yeast and thick dog-skin, with a hint of puppy.

"I'm a big baby," she said into his fur. He stood braced for her embrace, absorbing her pain until she eased herself back, pulled the quilt over, and soon the blues, the scents, the echo, the left-over particles of her mother's being all mingled to sedate her.

Tom couldn't rest. He set his muzzle along the bed, blinking at Laney in Joanna's bed. He lifted the edge of the quilt with his long nose. He paced around the bed, attempting to settle himself on the floor alongside her. He tried to take up a new post at the foot of the bed, but that was no good either. He stood in the doorway, front paws in the bedroom, back paws in the hallway, watching Laney sleep. Worried. She was in the wrong bed at the wrong time of day. He loped out, uneasy, not wanting to leave Laney, but needing to check his other rooms.

The lights were off in the rest of the apartment. Tom clicked along the hardwood floors through the hallway. He paused in front of each empty room. His brown eyes scanned. He padded to the living room and surveyed. He looked back over his shoulder, down the long hallway, to check Laney again before leaving the sight line.

He moved across the living room to the windows and looked out at the night. Trees shuddered in the wind. His ears twitched with the distant rustle and moan. Something caught his eye. He cocked his head. On a building across the street from the Titania a scaffold, hidden from the moon, creaked and swayed. Black mesh netting, hung to stop construction debris from falling to the street, billowed.

Tom's low-light vision kept him fixed and staring. He trained his eyes. Something there. Something he'd seen before, but maybe not. The netting, moving, but not that. Something brighter. But less there. But more there. Something to do with him. His job. He whined and paced and stared back across the street. He saw, he felt, his ruff rose, he let his eyes search the dark corners of the scaffolding until he could fix on it.

There. A swirl in the shadows, something known to him. Something he did not have to be trained to understand. Something he did not need to remember the words for, that didn't need repeating again and again. He didn't need a treat or a toy or a privilege to know how to be in its presence.

Tom stepped one forepaw and then the next onto the windowsill in order to get a better look. He was unblinking. He pawed the sill. He pushed his wet nose against the glass for a trace of scent. Her scent. He let a cautious growl brew at the back of his throat. His tail, barometer of love, wagged as if his most cherished person of all was close to home.

The two low beams of his vision reached past the black netting, into the recesses of the scaffolding. Narrow, tremulous, but glowing paths of light found her, briefly.

15

It's pregame. I've got the tunes turned up. If I could, I'd sing into a hairbrush. If I could, I'd mix a cocktail.

The truth can't hurt you, it's just like the dark: It scares you witless, but in time you see things clear and stark.

Perfect, right? "I Want You," Elvis Costello, it's a good song, but when Fiona Apple does it live, chills. She takes his stalker-guy croon and turns it into a lament over love's grave, she murmurs and wails and growls as if she's having an orgasm while strangling his neck or straddling his mouth, this man who's done her wrong. She'll snuff him out with her sex. *It's the way your shoulders shake and what they're shaking for.*

She moans like I moan. If I can't have you, no one else will.

Hahaha, shocker, Ned hated the song. He'd put his hands over his ears whenever I played it. Sometimes as a joke, I'd let my hair hang in front of my face and make my eyes really big and sing like Fiona, do a zombie-walk in his direction and he'd back up and laugh and say, *Fucking hell, woman, leave me alone!*

Funny how things that mean nothing turn out to mean something.

The black netting flaps and snaps. I cycle across the scaffold, I swoop, charging and surging. I toss and spin hard. I accumulate rage. I reset my agenda. I am fully charged. I shed the gray sheen and shine silver. I try on a spherical form, a glittering ball of wrong, easy to see. For later. For when I show myself to Ned.

I move out. I streak over the sidewalks of the city. I go downtown. To Trudi Mink's.

I zoom past Symphony Space in the West Nineties, where my former neighbors line up for their culture fix. Past Zabar's and Fairway, same crowd, different fix. I stop at the Apple Store near Lincoln Center. I can't resist the glass facade, I swirl into the gloss, into the white, the matte stainless steel, and up up I slither up the stone temple walls to the floating apple bearing the bite, illuminated in its sky against a glass roof, and I hover there, me and the apple ascendant over the devices and heads bent over devices, and the consumers feel something, of course they do, but they don't look up, of course they don't, they are themselves in a magnetic trance, they are part ghost already, phantasmic traces left to their own devices, residing in devices, in histories, caches, searches both predictive and random, in archives, in old data, in foolish choices and weak moments, in secret moments still long alive long after impulses, choices, consequences, and regrets have stopped throbbing. After memory has been consumed.

Everything remains, filtered forever young over impossible spans of space, of time. In person, face-to-face, in the aging flesh, in real life, don't worry about it, those are now the subsets of self. Cached. Archivable. Retrievable.

Hey, maybe what I am is a subset, too. Maybe I'm the next representation of the self.

Oh what fun to blanket the Apple Store in fog. From Broadway, the interior looks like it's filled with clouds. Now and again, a human emerges from the cloud, a confused consumer, and reenters the labyrinth.

I'm fleet. I fly. I've got this.

Over Lincoln Center the fountain springs to life and dances in black light out of season, for me. Columbus Circle, Central Park, the gray, the steel, the stone, the reaching green, all of my city is mine, it's ours, it belongs to ghosts, if I can't make it here yadda yadda yadda, Manhattan shelters us, we throng here, right through the very heart of it we haunt, we hide, we track and hover, and I haunt, southbound downtown now to make sure Trudi Mink knows that I existed and I still exist. Kinda sorta.

In Times Square I fall into a maze. Reflective facades bounce light. Information zippers about money and conflict circle buildings like lit fuses. Giant screens blaze, Showtime, Discover, Olympus, Virgin. Spires show urgent messages from NASDAQ, Visa, Yahoo, Viva Glam, Forever 21. I lose my bearings. It is hard to know where to go. The way is obstructed by neon, nude adolescent bodies, emaciated but pumped up, spread on billboards across the skyline. A wallscape of an interactive girl with tossed hair and a do-me smile made from countless diodes stops tourists in their tracks. The interactive girl licks her lips. She blows kisses. She emerges from her screen and plucks a pedestrian from the street and tosses him away, while he watches from the sidewalk, his camera held high, filming his own plucking happening, but not really, to him.

I'm blinded and buffeted and dizzied by the wrong lights.

I find Gothic refuge on Forty-sixth Street at St. Mary the Virgin, Smoky Mary's, where I spin in the frankincense and flickering votives, the creak of pews and kneelers, and prayer, echoed in the stone room.

Remember spinning out on the lawn when you were a kid? Defying gravity and balance? Shaking yourself to the core? I'm centrifugal. When I stop, I have resurrected my own ghosts.

I am moored, safe, a child in church, undoubting, standing between my parents at Mass. I hold a white leather-bound Sunday missal with gold-edged pages and a ribbon bookmark. My eyes feel heavy, I'm hot in my winter coat, the cornflower-blue wool with the navy velvet piping. The droning priest and the candlelight, the incense, it's soporific. I lean against my pop, Ben. He leans to me. He touches my face with his worker's hand, grazes my cheek with scored fingertips, and he makes me feel how soft my own skin is through his rough skin. He reaches over my head and gives a light tap to Loretta's gold hoop earring, makes it swing, and Loretta flashes her eyes and shakes her head, *Not in church*, but she smiles, and then she smiles at drowsy me, and then my parents hold hands across me, and I doze against my father at Mass.

Sweet. But not so fast with the "safe."

A telephone rings and Ben is dead, bad weather on a hometown lane he's driven countless times before. My children are little, and when somehow I find the words to tell them Pop is gone, Anna's earth-brown eyes fill instantly, and although Elena's just a baby, her eyes fill, too, not because she understands the sudden shred in the world we've woven, but because she cannot abide seeing her sister sad.

Six weeks later, the telephone rings. Even though she's been rigorously healthy, effortlessly ageless and alive, Loretta's heart stops. It breaks. She too leaves us. Leaves me.

Martin speaks to the children. I have no idea what words he finds.

Once safe, then left behind. Hmmn. Dots connect. I should grasp and examine the truth that emerges, but it's inaccessible and hazy, like angels, like God. Like ghosts.

I ascend eighty feet up to Smoky Mary's rafters, where I vibrate and fret and twist beneath the vaulted cobalt ceiling, a painted sky studded with dirty golden stars. I keen, what else? My keen echoes. My keen calls forth others like me hiding in St. Mary the Virgin in Times Square, abandoned too, entities in the rafters, a forsaken congregation huddling under faux heavens. I take my part in the wretched chorus of homeless souls crying to go home, forever, sick of ourselves and our pain, forever.

Not so fast with the "wretched chorus," either. I've still got Fiona Apple growling in my churn.

I pick up my route at the edge of Hell's Kitchen and follow it down through the Hudson Yards, through west Chelsea, past the art galleries and performance spaces and design studios and restaurants and artisan whiskey bars. I race with rage along the miles of tracks that not so long ago carried animal carcasses to city slaughterhouses and factories and warehouses, to be compressed into meat and refreighted to the rest of the country, the world.

Welcome to the High Line. Even in winter it swarms with beautiful young people from all over the world. They link arms and make their way above all, along its length, to be with each other and look at each other on a curated landscape, posing in front of vistas where they can photograph themselves before descending to the intersection of Gansevoort and Washington Streets to eat and drink and shop and photograph themselves again. The Meatpacking District.

A few slaughterhouses remain. Butchers arrive as club kids head home. In the cutting rooms, men shoulder hindquarters off hooks and press buzz saws into flesh and through bone. I'm inspired. They lean to smoke in bloody aprons against the boutiques and pop-up stores and eateries. Youth and beauty stumble past. Boys, smooth and narrow as curved knives, with steely jaws and sharp, tight pants, walk in pairs, matching strides. Girls like woodland creatures, long-necked, long-legged, step alone across cobblestones, hobbled in high, hoofed shoes. Everyone pauses, poses, snaps, filters, and posts.

Trudi lives at the epicenter in the Porterhouse, named with a retro flair after a cut of steak. Clever, huh? Her exclusive, starchitect-designed building, matte-black exterior with mirrored windows you cannot see into, sits like snapped-together Legos on top of an actual steak house, the Old Homestead, on Ninth Avenue.

I'm here, I'm here, I'm here.

I can barely contain myself. I surge hard through the lobby and the doorman/bodyguard/bouncer/concierge's earpiece screams with static. He yelps in pain and rips it from his ear, and his screens go static, too. I go deeper into the Porterhouse, and haunt to the top, I'm sure they live at the top, it must be the top, so high, so secure—so not—and I ascend and sniff for Ned, and I listen for Ned in hallways humming with young money.

I lust and I am now visible. I'm a crystalline sphere trailing pale gray viscosity, shimmering with silver desire, brimming with the need for release. I push and push my streaming self to the top floor of the Porterhouse. I quiver with a most excellent tension, I arch in anticipation.

I slip in.

Nobody home. The smart apartment blinks to life, programmed to welcome or warn. Beams drop to light art. Lamps light themselves. Cameras nod and try to track me. An iPad, my little friend, flickers awake on the quartz countertop in the kitchen.

I'm inside the much-photographed, much-grammed, much-retweeted space I became intimate with, home away from my deathbed, as I swiped, tapped, scrolled to see Ned in his new life. I've virtually visited this apartment a hundred times. Along with everybody else.

I hunt through a long hallway hung with blown-up photos of oddly cropped aspects of Trudi Mink's face and body, big cut-and-paste jobs from her Instagram feed, appropriated, filtered and defaced by a famous crime scene photographer. Art. Her filtered skin is poreless, luminous, perfect. What might be a lip is slashed cobalt. Vulgar graffiti tags a disembodied breast. Ironic black bars are placed over slices of eyes, as if to protect the identity of the instantly recognizable dermatologist to the stars. I rush past with power and every framed fucking piece of Trudi falls from the walls, toppling in on themselves in my wake. Mirrors, and there are plenty, see me, a silver sphere, a pulsing pearl.

The master suite bears no trace of occupation by real human beings. There is not a tossed towel or shoe or a stray book. Everything made of fabric is silk or cashmere, including the creamy walls, the white rug. All surfaces are clutter-free, arranged. The nightstands! Perfect little tablescapes, a lamp, a precious bowl, an angled book. Christ, I'm trying to picture Ned in this room doing anything at all, let alone fucking Trudi, he who shed bottle caps, chalk, plastic bags, TicTacs, pens, and the *New York Post* as he walked. And yet there is their bed, a confection high and fluffy with a white duvet and white pillows in complementary shapes and sizes.

I'd gone to Ned's grad-student studio apartment only that one time, our first time together. It was air shaft-facing and dark and filthy. Every surface was piled high with books and newspapers and magazines, and it smelled like there'd been a fire. He confided he'd recently passed out drunk, smoking, and his pillow had gone up in flames. Luckily, he had woken up and thrown the burning pillow out the window to the alley below. He opened the window to show me, and yes, there it was, all flattened feathers and charred like a burnt bird. It wasn't funny but it made me laugh. He showed me the curve of his ear, which had been singed, which I stroked, and my clothes came off for the second time, he couldn't get enough of me, he said, *I can't get enough of you*, and we fucked on his bed this time, just a nasty mattress on the floor, minus one incinerated pillow.

It's the way your shoulders shake and what they're shaking for.

I've got this. I don't even have to try. I separate myself into dense, noxious strands of jealousy and mark everything in Trudi's bedroom with my stink. I emit all over the white bed, and then I go faster and then I make sparks, and I spark and I shower the bed, I mark the bed with sparks and they penetrate a white silk pillow, and smolder deep inside the fancy feathers. *Pillow's on fire—got the message, Doc?*

Next, so familiar from the feeds, Dr. Trudi's internet-famous room-sized closet, what she calls her "Wardrobe Archive," a marvel of organization by designer, season, item, and color. An entire wall is mirrored and another wall is fitted around her accessories and another is covered with cutesy Polaroids of Trudi in red-carpet outfits, annotated with the dates worn to prevent repeats at coming events.

At the far end, a section of the WA is hung with Ned's things, his shirts and jackets and suits. His T-shirts and sweaters are folded with retail-store precision, and stacked on shelves. His jeans. Who is this Ned? Images cascade through me, his chest, the V of his torso, his thighs working my thighs open, I picture his jeans, what lies beneath, I feel through my gone fingers the way I used to reach in past his belt, how I had to angle my hand because the belt hung low and the buckle was heavy, and then how I pressed my palm flat against his belly and slid my hand down between the denim and his skin where he was naked, is naked, no tighty-whities, no boxers, he hates them, he goes commando, better for me to avail myself of the velvet skin of his uncurling cock.

In the center of the room sits a tall, antique shoe vitrine, legendary among the fashion-y fanboys and girls who follow Dr. Trudi. The gleaming brass and glass display case showcases and protects shoes it is hard to imagine anyone actually wearing. They are obscenely arched and perched high on needle-thin heels, encrusted with rhinestones, embellished with feathers and lace and studs and silk flowers and satin straps and golden buckles, Jimmy Choos and Prada, YSLs and Brian Atwoods and Jason Viviers and Louboutins and Manolos and Chanels.

Shoes. Shoes! I roar and charge.

Brass bends and glass shatters. Shards scatter among the flung shoes like flung gems. I command the iPad on the kitchen counter and merge the wrecked reality with the machine, and Instagram the destruction, filter Perpetua, from Trudi's account. It spreads across feeds and into four hundred thousand eyeballs, and then a million, and then millions, including Dr. Trudi's, including Ned's, so that now, right now, they can see what just happened in real time in her big closet in her white apartment in the black Lego building in the motherfucking Meatpacking District, and they can haul ass home from whatever exclusive experience they are experiencing.

I hate waiting.

16

For date night they had agreed to power off and reconnect over dinner.

They'd gone to the Gaslight, where Trudi Mink ate beet salad and Ned ate boar and squab sausage and drank four Grey Goose and sodas and two glasses of Beaujolais. He'd been quiet through the meal, lonely without his phone, with a primal need to get drunk. Trudi, swaddled in black cashmere, black jeggings, and black, over-the-knee, open-toed Chanel stiletto boots, frowned, line-free, at Ned's drinking. "We're supposed to be in training. We've got to be able to get up in the middle of the night. Not drop the baby."

"Hey, I got drunk-dropped all the time, and I'm fine." Ned had touched the lump at the back of his head and waved his bandaged hands, then lifted his wineglass in pathetic defiance. "Anyway, I'm still injured. This is my painkiller. All natural." His alibi after the attack at the Titania was that he'd been mugged. Tonight, a week later, a week of living with the reality of his ex-girlfriend, the ghost, he'd been drinking to stave off mind-blowing considerations of vengeful souls—women!—coming for him. Ned was confused and terrified.

After dinner, Trudi called for the check and said, "I'm not sure you're taking the baby seriously, Ned. It's a big responsibility. Things have to change. You realize that, yes?"

Ned had patted his pockets for his wallet, which he located immediately but did not actually retrieve until after Trudi dropped her black American Express card on the silver tray. He'd protested, "Wait, no, I've got this. . . ." The waiter, who knew them as regulars, had witnessed this routine before and didn't bother to see who would prevail over the check debate.

It was a clear New York night, they were in a neighborhood known for strolling and window-shopping and people-watching, just a few minutes from home, but the car and driver idled in front of the Gaslight to transport them because Trudi couldn't trust her boots on cobblestone. She leaned heavily on Ned and dipped into the car, as cautious about the Chanel sheathing her legs as the baby bump at her belly.

Ned reached for his phone. Trudi shook her head. "We're supposed to wait until we get home." She sniffed. "It's not easy for me either." Eye-scanned through security in the lobby, just outside the apartment door they powered back on. Trudi's device chirped and glowed in her hand as Ned slid the key card into the slot.

The apartment's altered atmosphere overtook them in the entryway. He said, "Do you smell smoke?" and then, "Why is it so cold in here?"

Trudi was riveted by the profusion of images on the screen in her hand. "Oh. My God. Ned. Omigod, Ned! Look!" Ned was gaping into the apartment. Together they saw the fallen images of Trudi's body parts art littering the hallway that led to the bedrooms. Ned recognized the chill and the terrifying smell of Freon in the air behind the smoke.

He said, "Jesus," and stepped in front of Trudi. "Don't move."

She gripped his arm and waved her screen at him and hissed, "There's someone in the apartment, look, they Instagrammed!" Ned glanced at Trudi's phone and saw the images of the Wardrobe Archive and the blasted shoe shelves. "Everyone's texting!"

"Stay here!" Ned saw a thread of smoke curling out from Trudi's bedroom. He ran to the pantry off the kitchen and grabbed a miniature fire extinguisher and held it in front of him, a tiny, ineffective weapon. The only path to the bedroom was through the hallway. Ned walked across the toppled Trudi pictures and lost his footing and went down on the heap, breaking frames and glass and ripping canvas and slashing his skin as he struggled to stand.

Trudi tried to get out. The security panel did not respond to her passcode. She punched and tapped and punched. She called to Ned, "I can't get out," and her very pale skin was rash-red from chest to hairline. Just when it occurred to her to call 911, her network vanished. She hopped on one over-the-knee lambskin boot as she peeled off the other, backed herself into a corner, and brandished the stiletto like a shiv.

Ned called, "I'm coming!"

The smoldering pillow had caught, and the surrounding pillows were starting to catch too. He aimed the hose and suffocated the flames. White silk and feathers and fire extinguisher foam made sludge. The bed was ruined.

He understood the reference to their first night: his burnt pillow, their romance ignited. He muttered, "Very funny, Jo."

Ned moved toward the nursery. It was an ovoid, under construction, and had been fitted with curved walls painted blush. A wall of glass looked across Gansevoort, past the slaughterhouses, over the boutiques and restaurants and bars, to the Hudson River. In the near distance were the twin skyward shafts of light, the tribute in place during the years it had taken interested parties to achieve consensus on how to memorialize the September 11 attack on the World Trade Center. The columns of light reached from the crater and seemed to teem with the lost.

A white oak crib sat undressed and empty off to the side in the nursery. A version of Trudi's closet was adjacent, fully stocked and hung with tiny garments on tiny hangers. The baby clothes looked to Joanna like costumes, clothes a baby should not, could not wear. Velvet, silk, and leather. Scratchy wools. Neoprene. Black and gray. T-shirts with ironic or provocative sayings. Tiny motorcycle boots and a jacket with studs and zippers. Little baby socks marked with skulls, the symbol of death and decay. Swarovski crystals embedded into slippers, to bite baby feet.

Inside the egg-shaped nursery of his unborn child, Ned could feel something spin and burn cold. He saw a gathering of energies and then a sphere spun out of the mist, out of the silver, out of the waiting, into a thing he could hardly look at, could hardly believe, could hardly stand. He was inside an odor that made him gag. A moan rose. She moaned for him in the same way she had moaned when she was alive, when he'd grunted into her ear as he pumped between her legs.

She whispered, and the whisper thundered inside him. *I'm coming, too, Doc.*

Ned stood immobilized, gripping the little fire extinguisher.

The ghost of Joanna presented herself to him in classic form: an empty human shape, enormous and all-encompassing and long and lithe and bright white. She was electric, magnetic, all impulse, a pulsing harridan. She streamed and flowed hair and arms and legs that went on and on as she surged and curled around the crib and the clothes and Ned. Her breasts and vagina and mouth and eyes and ears were black holes that flowed, too, sending currents to electrocute him with volts and a million tiny jolts.

Ned staggered backward. The nursery door slammed shut against his escape.

She called up her old voice. She impersonated herself and said, as if he'd just joined her at Harvey's, ready for his cocktail on a regular evening during their regular lives, when she loved him, when he loved her, "How was your day, Doc?"

Ned shouted, "You're dead! You're not here!"

Joanna screeched, *I'm here I'm here I'm here.*

The wild declaration of her existence blew open the drawers and the door of the nursery. Ned rolled and crawled and hauled himself up and out and ran back down the long, obstacle-cluttered hallway, hitting the walls, bouncing off the walls, stomping on the pictures back toward the entryway, where Trudi waited, armed with a boot in one fist and her dead smartphone in the other.

Joanna let Ned run. There was no rush.

In the entryway, Trudi said, frantic, "I can't get a signal. And the door won't open." She shook her shoe in his direction. "Is someone here? Who were you talking to? Did you call 911? I can't text!"

Ned shouted, "Move, move, move," and grabbed for Trudi. Joanna swooped. Trudi swatted at whatever this thing was that was flying at them.

She screamed to Ned, "What is that?! Is that a bat?!"

Ned screamed, "Leave her alone!" He encircled Trudi with his arms and turned her belly away from his dead ex, ready to rain down on them.

The Mink home invasion commanded global attention.

By the time everyone had gone—NYPD, FDNY, the Porterhouse security team, lawyers representing the building's owners and the management company, as well as Trudi's own lawyer, and her assistant, along with her doula, and her obstetrician on Face-Time, once the connection was restored—a compelling story line had emerged that could hold up, even though it was mostly fabricated.

Despite the impossibility of penetrating the fortress-like Porterhouse and its only penthouse apartment, despite the absence of anything unusual in the images from the security cameras, despite the destruction, somehow Instagrammed from Trudi's account, and then the ensuing electronic blackout of all devices, and what seemed like the spontaneous combustion of a pillow, and the weird bat thing that Trudi swore she saw, despite evidence of something otherworldly taking place, the cops decided the intruder was a celebustalker.

Probably the stalker had hacked codes or some such and gotten in, and maybe brought some kind of bird or bat or maybe a drone, who knew, crazy people were crazy, that's what the swooping thing was, and what with the sophisticated capability of hacktivists, the impenetrable had been penetrated, the inescapable had been escaped, and somehow nothing was seen or recorded or filmed. The doorman/bodyguard/bouncer/concierge was fired on the spot.

Ned kept his mouth shut while the cops and security guys pieced together the explanation of events. Trudi bought it because having a stalker, as awful as it was, ratcheted her status. Her followers had embraced, embellished, and promoted the stalker version; they liked it, they retweeted it, and they'd even begun hunting among their own online ranks for the perpetrator.

On no account did Ned feel compelled to interrupt the proceedings and say, "Hey, no, everybody, it's my ex-girlfriend, she's dead, she's a ghost, she's pissed, she wants to destroy me. . . ." Even though that is what he believed to be true.

The apartment was a yellow-taped crime scene, uninhabitable. Ned and Trudi headed down the street to the Gansevoort Hotel to stay until security and order and decor were restored. Ned could think of nothing but his next drink.

As Trudi slept, shaky Ned went to the Incident, the hotel bar. The Incident did not soothe his nerves.

The bar's interior design presented a menacing storybook theme, scary murals and upholstered banquettes showing little kids cavorting across threateningly benign landscapes, like something Henry Darger would draw. The light fixtures were shaped like tangled branches, tables and stools were carved from tree trunks. The deep-woods atmosphere was both sexy and creepy. Sylph-esque staff of indeterminate gender circulated. Body parts pulled Ned's gaze, against his will.

As he waited for attention, trying to keep his eyes averted, he did a panicky click-through in his mind of the neighborhood, trying to place a non-ironic, theme-free dive bar tucked away on a side street where he could hide. No such place existed anymore. A brigade of hosts descended upon him. Chests and rib cages, crotches and buttocks were accentuated by tight, black fabric. Tentative queries in whispery, childlike voices floated in Ned's direction: "Just one?" "Right this way?" Ned followed someone's ass through to the bar to be seated. The bartender was a variant on the host. "Welcome?" "Cocktail?" "Signature, Curated, or Artisan?" "House-made ice or neat?"

It seemed like every question required him to buzz in with the right answer in the right format in order for him to make it to the next round, closer to a drink. "Please, just pour."

Salivating for alcohol as minutes ticked by, Ned watched the bartender, with cut black arms in a tight black T-shirt, wearing goggles, hack at a huge block of ice. Her arm rose and plunged like a piston. Her dreads bounced.

Served, finally, Ned drank deeply and tried to normalize his body and his mind. He'd seen a ghost.

He stared into his small-batch vodka and vintage seltzer water and house-made ice, and let his thoughts settle around the reality of Joanna's existence, and her capabilities.

She nearly burst his heart!

She controlled technology, she texted and Instagrammed!

She set a pillow on fire!

She made sex sounds only they knew, and had mocked him with them!

He'd heard her say, "I'm coming, too," and it had made his flesh crawl and his cock hard, and his cock stirred now, recalling that phrase, because Joanna the ghost was using Jo's voice, it was Jo talking dirty in his ear, real as anything, her breath hot, her old sex song sung for Ned, that only he could coax from her throat, with his thrust or his tongue or his fingers on her, in her. She had used their sex talk against him. The voice was dead but alive, a promise and a threat from inside his own brain.

She was sexually harassing him, on top of everything else.

Ned tried to remember ghost movies he'd seen. He remembered *A Christmas Carol*, a VHS tape relic that had scared him when he was a little kid, three ghosts representing the past, present, and future, sent to terrify Scrooge into being nicer to poor people and those with disabilities. Then *Ghost*, a dead guy, Patrick Swayze, humping Demi Moore at a potter's wheel, while she manipulated squishy, wet clay, the movie memorable only for provoking a hard-on for teenage Ned. *Ghostbusters*, where the ghosts invade Manhattan, and it too was noteworthy for Ned because it was hard-on-inducing, Sigourney Weaver in a flimsy red dress all over Bill Murray. *The Sixth Sense*, dead people mingling with the living, or living people who don't know they are dead, and the one with Native American spirits yanking a kid into the television set.

Ned considered himself something of an intellectual, on television anyway, who scoffed at his Catholic mother's bedrock conviction that troubled souls and restless spirits lingered and made nuisances of themselves until they were set to rights. No amount of reasoning across holiday tables could shake Pat McGowan's faith in the rules of order governing the ascent of the soul. She was as familiar with the byways of Heaven and Hell as if they were the two towns adjacent to Syosset, and understood Purgatory as the waiting room for the unresolved dead. Ned had teased her mercilessly, unrepentantly. He could picture her being unsurprised by the turn of events, nodding and squinting at him through cigarette smoke.

Like in a film, the Incident's guests moved in motion blur around Ned, leaving streaks of light in their wake. Seats around him were occupied and vacated, occupied and vacated. Eventually, a handsome woman or a beautiful man, hard to tell and didn't matter, sat next to Ned and gestured at the bartender toward Ned's drink, asking for the same, asking for two. Ned noticed nothing.

The woman gave him a little jab with her elbow. "Hey," she said.

Ned registered her. She was turned to him and he saw that her forehead was so preternaturally smooth and expertly highlighted it was iridescent, that her eyes were wide and sharp on either side of her sculpted nose, and that her cheeks were high and globular. It was impossible to guess her age. She had mermaid hair flowing around bare shoulders, layered and waved to highlight a well-defined Adam's apple. Her breasts, globular too, situated on either side of her sternum, spilled over her bodice.

The woman said, "I bought you a drink—say thank you," and pushed her glossed duck pout out.

Ned looked at his glass. "Oh, right. Well, hell, I apologize. I didn't notice. I've got a few things on my mind tonight. But yeah, thanks."

"Good things or bad things?"

"Crazy things."

"I'm Dana." She stuck her hand out and shook his with intent. "You're Doc McGowan, aren't you? On Fox?"

Ned switched on his full attention. He turned to her, he cocked his head, he assembled his famous bicolored squint-and-smile. "I turn up there now and then, yeah. You a fan?"

Dana, in New York as mergers and acquisitions lead for a search engine behemoth in San Francisco, said, "No. I hate television."

She was, however, a client and a follower of Trudi's. She considered herself practically a FOT—Friend of Trudi—and was sure they had close friends in common. She scrolled through her smartphone, rattling off contacts to uncover the connection. She used her body unsubtly to communicate that she was available to Ned if that would reduce the degrees of separation between herself and Trudi. Ned was drunk, but from long habit he easily worked out the logistics of cheating, rationalizing that he could use—no, he deserved—a couple hours away from the tales from the crypt unfolding around him. He thought, *Why not? A couple of hours with Dana, not famous, not dead, just a regular woman. Or close enough!*

As he entertained the distracting thought, the piston arms of the bartender pumped and ice shards flew like shrapnel. Ned took a series of startling, stinging slices to his face and neck. He raised his arms in defensive posture, fearing for his eyes, and toppled his bar stool. On the grimy floor, Ned felt blood trickling in rivulets from several spots.

No one paused, no one glanced at Ned, no one noticed except Dana, of course, who, instead of helping him to his feet, squatted next to him like a linebacker. "Oh my God, this is so cool!" With her stubbled cheek next to Ned's bloody one, she stretched her arm and aimed her phone and the selfie was posted before Ned got to his feet.

Ned staggered from the Incident. He bumped tables and chairs and trees in the lounge, crowded now with beautiful, tall people, people towering over him, smiling down on him. He stumbled past the illustrations of retro children in ankle socks and sturdy, old-fashioned brown shoes, running, looking back over their shoulders, through an ominous wallpapered land of make-believe, frozen in the moment of everything adult and dark bearing down on them.

Ned looked over his shoulder. Everything bore down on him, too. He felt like the little storybook boy and wondered if he'd be looking over his shoulder for the rest of his life, if Jo would let him live, if there was a rule of law or statute of limitations on ghost revenge.

Or maybe she would consume him, just like he had always secretly worried that she would—that any woman would, that all women would, because they all saw he could never be counted on, could never be faithful, and he had fucked her and fucked her over and left her, with cancer, because he could never reveal himself, the real Ned, because once revealed he would be obliterated like his dear old dad had been obliterated.

Fear gathered behind his balls and zoomed up his spine and prickled at the back of his neck. Trudi knew Ned sucked and did not care. In fact, she was absolutely fine with living a life of half-truth, semi-truth, truthiness, all the time. Truth screwed up perfection. That's why they were so right for each other. He lied, but she wasn't really listening.

Outside the bar in the lobby of the Gansevoort, he remembered again. The lost envelope. He had replayed the moment of losing it over and over since last week's cab ride from hell, away from the Titania. He pictured himself leaning forward to talk to the angry driver, and he had a sense memory of the envelope slipping from his lap to the floor. Maybe its contents held instructions or an incantation or penance or whatever he needed to do to get Joanna off her wrath path. Joanna wasn't finished with him, he knew that. He was out of the Incident and into the hotel elevator, and he said out loud, in case she was close, "I'm sorry, all right?! I don't know what else to tell you."

As he rose to Trudi's room in the low-lit elevator, he drunk-googled terms: "ghost revenge"; "ghost catcher"; "ghostbuster"; "ghost hunter." The sheer volume of search results was astonishing to Ned. What would his friends say? Unfortunately, he couldn't think of one. He had freedom, he had access, he had contacts, lots and lots of contacts, a decent number of followers, but no friends, not for years, not since Jo and Tom and Laney.

The thought of Laney was an epiphany. What *would* Laney say? Laney, who was real and intuitive, and so smart, Laney who listened and considered and, once upon a time, looked up to Ned. Ned felt a longing like homesickness.

He stumbled through the hotel maze, forbidding door after forbidding door, until he found Trudi's room. He patted his pockets for the key card, exhausted, weepy, drunk. He tried his jeans, front and back pockets, his jacket pockets, his inside pocket, his shirt pocket. He flipped through the many cards and receipts and bits of paper stuffed in his wallet. He fumbled the wallet, and then his phone. Everything scattered. Ned crawled along a blood-red carpet, collecting his droppings in the hallway, looking for his key card.

He tried to muster the nerve to knock hard and wake Trudi to let him in. Trudi loathed being summoned from behind her wall of sleep. Access, but no place to rest his head. He slumped against the wall and let his fingers touch the wounds he'd sustained from the flying ice, from the crystal shards and the bounce on Joanna's floor, the fall in Trudi's hallway. He tipped his head back to doze away nausea, dizziness, pain, and shame.

The phone in his hand dinged and glowed. Ned roused himself and checked the screen.

One word appeared in the message field, a directive he recognized immediately, a meeting place, not the Titania, not Harvey's, but their other place, their late-night, let's-dance-dirty dive for all the years they were together, Ned and Jo, Jo and Ned, a dark and

divey bar with a great jukebox, no irony, Tap-a-Keg, whose motto was "A Hell of a Joint," where they closed out the day or the week or a project or a disappointment or a success, eager to drink with each other, touch each other, show themselves to each other, always sexed up and loose for each other, going back to the beginning, drinking, dancing, desirous.

One word glowed on Ned's small screen: *Tap.*

Ned swiped to delete the text, which would not disappear. *Tap.* He said out loud, "I've got the message. But not tonight, dear. You've worn me out." He leaned against the door of Trudi's hotel room and scrolled through hundreds of contacts in the palm of his hand to find Laney, the only person he might call a friend, who might listen.

17

I'm home. Scaffold-home. My ego's bruised. I mean, seriously. "What is that?! Is that a bat?"

Can you believe she said that? I thought that was just plain mean, but sticks and stones, and hey, I was already poised to break her birdy bones. I thought, *Yeah, an old bat, bitch*, and I was activated, I was ready, I was supercharged, I towered, I loomed, I aimed, the long-game goal in sight.

And *pfftt*. Fizzle. One good look at Dr. Trudi, the real Dr. Trudi, and I lost my hard-on, so to speak.

Because oops, there it was: round and taut and straining against cashmere. The much-celebrated baby bump, the baby bump Ned helped plant inside the rich, famous, fertile vessel he chose instead of postmenopausal me.

I saw tangled limbs in motion. I saw the tucked head, the curved spine, the cushioned bottom. The perfect number of fingers and toes. I felt the beat, and out of somewhere from within my churn I pulsed with the memory of the beat before breathing. I felt the origins of Anna my first, imprinted like a cameo relief inside me made from cells and memory, a tiny pre-fish girl, a deep diver at my core, Anna my first, finding the apparatus of me and breathing through me and then breathing for herself, and becoming herself and swimming to the surface to sustain us anew, me and Martin, and then later, Elena. Martin put Anna in my arms. Fingers and toes. Anna in my arms. My first. We blinked semaphores at each other, and I saw a horizon in Anna's eyes.

So sure, when I saw there was an actual kid in Trudi's belly, I choked. I lost my form. I reverted to sphere and went invisible. I had to quit her place. What else could I do? Trudi's big belly spoiled my fun. Motherhood, it's complicated. It derailed me in the Porterhouse.

Now I'm out under the moon. It's like a lit scrim behind the horizon. I play across the face. I can't get enough. I'm cracked out. I flash on Cher slapping Nic Cage across the face in *Moonstruck*. "Snap out of it!"

She meant snap out of the spell of love. Cher's name was Loretta in the movie, my mother's name. I always thought of my mother as a "Snap out of it!" kind of woman. Once upon a time for some people, a lot of people, marriage, and staying married, was the central fact of their existence. Loretta and Ben spent fifty years being married. It was a daily commitment, a daily recommitment. Work, every day. There was nothing moonstruck about staying married for fifty years.

The marriage was so central to their existence that when Ben died, Loretta followed six weeks later. That's a lot of happily-married to not be able to live up to. Martin got the call this time. He came home, his face ashen and drawn in on itself. My mother had had a massive heart attack.

I said, "What?! What?! What?!"

We dropped the girls with Marie and rushed to the community hospital in my old hometown. We waited in a room filled with rows of empty beige plastic chairs, each joined to the next. Martin stood at the desk. Tilted stacks of files were piled behind it. An admin gave Martin her practiced smile.

I sat and waited. I tried to project an air of calm, of confidence, of reasonability. I tried to project myself to the next morning, drinking coffee, relieved, a person whose mother had experienced a close call. I tried to believe I'd had my share, that the universe could not possibly deliver this blow so soon after the death of my Pop.

My chair felt askew. I scooted forward to line up, and all the connected chairs scraped the floor in a way that sounded like the world, torn. Like screaming. The admin pointedly did not look at me. She maintained the fake half-smile, trained on Martin. Fluorescent lighting buzzed. A television, precarious, vibrated at the end of an extension arm hung from the ceiling in a far corner. The blare was incessant. I squinched my eyes shut and put my hands over my ears. Inside, my head roared. Inside, I swear, I could feel my cells plot to go bad and divide and fan out. Or maybe not. That's probably not possible. But that's what I remember.

I tried my distraction techniques, my huffpuff breathing, just like I was taught, and concentrated myself dizzy to stay positive, to breathe through it, to get to the other side where Pop was gone, fine, but Ma was not following him, where maybe I could find myself on the other side of chaos, that was my hope, what I held on to in the waiting room, the waiting room, and I squinched my eyes tighter, dizzy to visualize Loretta recovering, but no, instead I saw the girls, my babies, that's what rose up as I waited to see my massively heart-broke mother, up rose Anna in a white captain's cap marching across a sloping lawn, Elena dawdling behind, talking to the trees. The little girls revolved inside me like the lights of a magical lamp.

Martin came and sat next to me. I said, "Oh my God, is this happening?"

A big, loud family arrived. They increased the television's volume. I hid my face against Martin. "Don't let them look at me." Martin took off his jacket and put it over my head, one of the kindest things anyone has ever done for me. I breathed my husband. I breathed my husband and I waited until I heard my name called and then my throat closed.

A kid from high school, Mickey Allardo, someone I'd been dismissive of way back in time—a man now, the head nurse—had seen my mother's name on a list. He escorted us in.

She was intubated, but perfectly coiffed and manicured and made up, head to toe, I swear to God. I laughed! I was relieved! She looked good! When she saw me, Loretta got fired up. She grasped at her tubes, tore at the mask, made grunting noises, with those eyes flashing the whole time, those eyebrows, arched as high as they could go. She looked like she could lift the bed if they'd only unhook her. Nurse Mickey Allardo requested more of whatever was not keeping Loretta calm.

So I thought there was time. So I didn't take off the mask. I went close and said, *Relax, Ma, it's okay, I'm here, they're going to fix you up.* The eyes said no. The eyes were wild. She was trying to talk to me with her wild eyes, trying to say something important. Trying to talk. I didn't realize. How stupid.

I dozed on a chair against Martin. An hour later, Mickey Allardo handed me an envelope with Loretta's glasses, her gold hoop earrings, her wedding ring. He handed me a plastic bag with her clothes and shoes. He pointed at the bottom of a form and I signed my name. He gave me a cup of water, and put a soft hand on the small of my back. I said, "I'm sorry about high school," and lost my legs. I went down. He lifted me, that nice, nice man, Mickey, and I remember dark spots on the shirt of his scrubs from the water I spilled, from my tears, my running nose.

Loretta left me wondering for the rest of my numbered days what she wanted to say to me, and why oh why didn't I think to take off the mask so she could say it? I got left wondering how she could have checked out on us. How she could have been so feisty, so ready to lift the bed, so insistent, and then just so dead? So so dead, with Pop not yet cold, with his headstone not yet carved.

In the black asterisk of time that I did not remember until now, right now, high as I am on the dope of moonlight and the violence at the Porterhouse, in the black asterisk of time of the days that followed the deaths of Ben and Loretta, which I'd blocked out until now, I did many things. I spoke to people. I cared for my children. I cooked, I dressed, I drove, I probably laughed. I stepped through the days. I canceled Ben DeAngelis's headstone and bought one for the two of them. I made a joke to the stone salesman. "Can it say, 'Joined at the hip'?"

I chose "Together Forever." That's a lot of happily-married to not be able to live up to.

Everything happened and then more happened. We divorced. I got cancer.

I mean, it wasn't just woe-is-*me*. There were the girls. Anna and Laney, they were little, they needed grandparents, they needed Loretta after we lost Pop. They got left behind too. They needed her! And me too. I needed her, my mother.

My mother. She checked out. It felt personal. Okay, Ma? It felt very personal.

The dark did not lift, not really, until I met Ned. Maybe the asterisk dropped away, I don't know. Maybe falling in love with a younger man rolled back the years to before I saw how sad I was in the mirror. I don't know.

I met Ned and for a little while, time slowed, cells behaved. My hair flowed. I showed myself.

Doc. The stakes were high, like I said. The stakes were high.

So yes, I faltered when confronted with Ned McGowan's unborn child nestling in Trudi Mink's uterus. I faltered, I paused, I reflected, I wallowed in the apparatus of breath, the forever of mothering, my own parents, my own husband, my own loss, my own grief, my own little girls and the scent of their baby heads.

I'm only human. Or was.

But better late than never, right? Maybe that's the lesson. Feel it all, feel it all, leave it all behind. Love it and let it go. Maybe that's the lesson, my lesson, and maybe within that awareness, ta-da, the path I need to the light of peace will be revealed. Right? Hey, that's what the self-help books tell you. That's what the Buddhists say, or something along those lines. Eat, pray, love, release, and die right. Maybe it's not too late for a *Beaches* ending to the movie.

Because that would be the way to go, wouldn't it? That would be the Oprah way to go, on a cloud of aphorisms, consolations, tweeted wisdom, socially mediated condolences. So much easier. Right?

Yeah, no.

By the way. I'm not blind. Ned loves her. In his stunted way. He does. I saw. He surrounded her. He protected her. Them. Ned loves them. I saw. Love, marriage, baby carriage, so old-school, so forever, fuck that, I'll show you forever.

Off goes the text, brief, to the point. He'll know.

Tap.

Fuck love. I'm going to snap out of it, and I'm going to double-down.

18

At the old Bondi Blue iMac, left behind when she'd gone to Boston, Laney killed time. Tom snored at her feet.

There was a comforting, house-pet quality to the iMac that sat, still eager, on the dinged-up desk in the corner of her bedroom. She cupped the hockey-puck mouse in her right hand and held a goblet of Chianti in her left, with an American Spirit dangling between her fingers. She was new to smoking and working on being adroit with the gestures, smooth on the inhalations, effortless with the ritual. Smoking at home, in her own girly high school bedroom, was both a satisfying and frustrating desecration. Smoking was a little bit punk. If only there were someone around to be repelled by it. She practiced smoke rings. She drank and surfed and searched.

what is a normal amount of sleep

what is normal > am I normal

normal BMI

which has fewer calories red or white wine > fewer calories white wine or vodka

am I an alcoholic

Petfinder NYC: puppies

how to get rid of cigarette smell

cool people smoking

how to quit smoking

smoking cancer > american spirit breast cancer > breast cancer family history > breast cancer mother

my mother died

She got 113,000,000 results in twenty-six seconds. Laney thought, *I guess that means I'm some version of normal.*

stages of grief > what grief stage am I > how to get over grief

On the floor nearby, Tom paddled through a dream. He made tiny yipping sounds. His eyes fluttered. Laney searched.

what do dogs dream about

do dogs know when someone dies

Petfinder NYC: puppies

what should I be when I grow up > how to make decisions > decision-making matrix > career decision-making

Petfinder NYC: puppies

huffington post > politico > ShameShame >

Doc McGowan

She hit Enter and her search was derailed by a cascade of hot new results for Ned, loading and reloading. Ned and Dr. Trudi were trending over the internet, the news, the blogs, Twitter, Instagram. There was some bizarre break-in at Trudi Mink's swanky apartment and the whole world was theorizing about celebu-stalkers and drones and cyberbullies. It was all Laney could do to remove herself from the soul-sucking morass.

She shook her head. Ned. She couldn't believe it. It was still hard for her not to think of this internet personality as "our Ned." Laney got up to refill her wineglass in the kitchen. She was surprised to see that hours had passed. She lit up again. She inhaled and exhaled the most relaxing breath she'd taken in weeks on a plume of cigarette smoke. She leaned her forehead against a cold, loose pane of the casement windows and looked down over Riverside Park. The treetops were bare, the branches were gray. The sidewalk was patchy with ice. She watched a runner stamp through the dark, undaunted by the slick streets. She thought deeply about her hopes, her beliefs. How to know them. How to protect them in a world that seemed uncaring at best, cruel at worst. How to stay idealistic, not get cynical and ironic and smirky, the hipster default, or overly earnest and annoying, the nerd default. How to be authentic but pragmatic. Collect a paycheck without turning into an asshole. Go places to know the world, not show the world on Instagram. How to be original when it was so tempting, so easy to copy, to sample, to mash up, to crowdsource everything, even feelings.

Do all that and then find someone great and fall in love equally, eventually. When she was ready. Which she was not. She was startled when she heard the twangy chug of the opening bars of "I Walk the Line" and ran to her phone although, somehow, she knew who it was before she saw her screen.

"Yeah?" She didn't know if they were friends or enemies. Involuntarily she thought, *We're frenemies*, and secretly vowed to cut back on time spent on the internet.

"Hey, Lane, hi."

"Yeah. Hi. Why are you calling me?" Laney was working to keep the least bit of happy out of her voice.

Ned was working to sound sober. "Well, look. I know things are tough. I wanted to call. And, you know. Say hello."

"You wanted to say hello? You must be kind of tired, no? You're all over the internet. With your girlfriend. Your pregnant girlfriend. And her wrecked apartment." Laney tried to muster anger as Anna would, on behalf of their mother. "Kind of a weird time to, you know, reach out."

Ned, downtown at the hotel, leaned against a window and looked down on young people crossing and weaving in tight groups through traffic on Washington Street, laughing, calling, drunk. He closed his eyes and said, "Yeah, I know. It's weird. It's actually very weird. Everything is. That's kind of why I'm calling. Kind of."

"What does this have to do with me? And I'm not sure I want to be having a conversation with you. You broke our vase." Laney knew she sounded petty and petulant like a kid, the kid Ned first met.

"I get that. I do. I don't want to mess with you, Lane. I just wanted to, you know, talk."

"Talk about what? Something specific?"

"No. Yes. Yeah, something specific."

"Like what?"

"Well, look, can we get together? Can I buy you a beer some night? Or maybe we can meet up at the park? Give Tom a run? You still on dog-duty?"

Laney relented. "Yeah, I am. Tom's driving me crazy. He's been so agitated. I think he's waiting for my mother to get home." Her voice caught, and Ned choked up too.

"Okay, so let's tire him out. We can meet? The steps at 103rd Street? A few days? Maybe at like nine o'clock? We can let him off the leash. I'll text you. Does that work? The middle of the week?"

"Fine." She'd given away more than she meant to. She heard her sister's admonition, *Why are you being so nice to him?*

Back at her desk Laney thought, *I don't have to meet up with Ned, I'll cancel, I just said "fine" to get off the phone*, but in truth, she felt a lift in her heart to think she might have a conversation with someone she once trusted. Who was close, but not too close.

She tried to think like Anna. What was Ned's angle? What was he after? Something to do with her mother, obviously, maybe the envelope he picked up. She replayed his "everything is weird" comments and flashed on Tom's leap at Harvey's, Tom's obsession with something at the top of the bookcases. She wasn't sure why, but the empty security camera footage of Trudi Mink's corridors and apartment, the images from the internet of the destroyed shoe shelves all flashed too. As if reading Laney's thoughts, Tom lifted his head and looked at her. Laney couldn't resist. She whispered, "Where's Mama . . . ?"

Tom jumped to attention and cocked his head. He stood at the ready, his tail tall, his eyes sharp. Laney sighed. "That was mean, I'm sorry. I shouldn't have done that. Relax, buddy, okay? Relax."

She picked up her Search. She typed "women historians" into the search bar and scrolled and read. She typed "feminist history," scrolled and read some more. She typed "feminist American politics," and "Monica Lewinsky" caught her eye. She clicked. Laney waited thirty-nine seconds for 1.130 million Monica results to appear.

She was intrigued to see where the internet had led her. Monica and Bill, the intern and the president of the United States. At the time, the president was forty-nine and the intern was twenty-two. Laney, twenty-two too, clicked back and forth between the Web, Images, News, Videos, and Books. She returned to Images and sat back. Monica's tossed brown mane, her bright white teeth, her merry eyes. Her sweater-girl, pinup, body-proud confidence. A grinning girl, slightly goofy-looking, overdone, trying too hard, crushing on the most powerful man in the world. Laney could almost picture Monica doodling Bill's name with a heart over the letter *i*, and practicing *Monica Lewinsky-Clinton, Monica Lewinsky-Clinton* over and over.

Laney remembered the ShameShame dinners with her mother and Ned. The anonymous young women at the center of scandals. Everything Laney didn't know about Monicagate waited for the click of her mouse. She scrolled and clicked and read. She clicked and watched videos. President Clinton, so busted, dissembling on nightly news clips, working to distract everyone from cigars and semen stains on a blue dress, from "that woman." His quavering voice, his damp eyes, his performance calibrated to incite the press to do the dirty work of sending up the nutty-and-slutty dog whistle, his banking on the public's willingness to drop Monica—*same age as me*, Laney thought—into the stalkery, psycho-nympho bucket. Monica, as rabid as a teenager on a mission to fall in love, to have the coolest guy on the planet love her back. Laney pictured Bill Clinton—*Slick Willie!*—and his creepy old pals, convened in the Oval Office to manage Monica.

Laney thought, *Poor kid.* Monica was no innocent, but she did seem to be in it for some warped version of romance. Bill's motivation was banal: another woman on her knees, a new mouth, new eyes shining up at him.

In the vortex of the internet, Laney eventually succumbed to the grinding power of accumulated time online, and shopped. On Amazon, she clicked and bought books about the president and the intern for later.

She typed into Search again, with amped-up intent.

Master's degree American studies

graduate schools womens studies

columbia womens studies graduate programs

columbia institute for research on women gender sexuality

admissions > application

She had two other schools on her list, but was only interested in Columbia. She stared at the fields of the online form. She clicked back and forth between deadlines, financial aid, requirements, the fifteen-page Statement of Academic Purpose, a "focused essay that examines an article, book, exhibit or event relevant to your field of interest."

A Statement of Purpose was a good place to start. She looked to Tom for his reliable, unqualified support, but he was gone from the room. He'd taken up his new post at the living room windows, staring at the scaffold that shrouded the building across from the Titania.

19

The moon was gone and the sky was low with gathering snow. March snapped through city streets.

At ten-thirty, Willa, known to her regulars as Wills, looked up from her Sudoku and through Tap-a-Keg's windows onto nighttime Broadway. She watched Columbia undergrads, enthusiastic, novice drinkers, hustle past Tap for a big Saturday night elsewhere. She thought, *Keep heading downtown, kids, it's hipper, and I'd like a nice easy shift.*

She drew a beer, punched at the cash register, counted out dollars, and wiped down the bar. She tried to settle back to her puzzle, across from Albert, who had managed touring and so much more for the Ramones long ago, and now nursed scotches on rocks and followed Wills upstairs a few nights a week. She said, "I'm in some mood tonight."

"What mood would that be?"

"In the good old days, it would have been a Jack-and-Coke

mood. And then some coke, too. There's something in the air, no? Am I imagining it?"

"It's the weather. Snow."

"And what's going on with the heat? It's so freakin' cold in here."

Wills had been behind the bar for more than a decade. She understood each wheeze of pipe and wink of bulb in Tap, ignored what transpired in dark corners, respected the burdens of the hard drinkers, and put up with no shit from the lightweights. She was once a kid from somewhere else with talent, struggling to stand out as a young dancer in the corps of the New York City Ballet, but no matter how little she ate, how many hours at the barre, how many years shaved from her age, she was rarely chosen to perform in the company's productions. A procession of adolescents with formidable build, bearing, and bone structure from tip of bun to mangled toes glissaded through annual auditions, each one aiming for Wills's spot. She understood in her late twenties it was time to quit.

She did have some luck with real estate, no small feat in Manhattan. Tap-a-Keg's landlord offered her rooms at the top, a sunny floor-through over Broadway. From her apartment, it was a short climb to the roof, where she tended a container garden, and a short commute down a flight of stairs, where she tended the bar. Tap's motto, right there on the awning, "A Hell of a Joint," amused Wills every time she unlocked the door and wondered if she should sniff for flames as she stepped across the threshold to hell.

The regulars were assembled on this evening, scruffy and bedheaded, folded into corners in tatty sweaters or curved over beer mugs in tired fleece jackets, some with dogs at their feet, all part of the décor, nearly indistinguishable from a palette of rust stains and gray shadow and brown leather and wood and yellow light. The fixtures in Tap, human and not, were redolent with whiskey and smoke. Like Wills and Albert, everyone in here had been someone else once, before alcohol: poet, bass player, printer, athlete, opera singer, lawyer. Somewhere along the way each had fallen in love with beer and wine and whiskey to the exclusion of all else, and so, lost all else, except evenings at the bar.

Eduardo, in fingerless gloves and a tricked-out wheelchair, rolled up to the digital jukebox and swiped his card and hit at his favorites. Wills called, "No fucking U2, Eduardo."

Eduardo's Rock-Ola selection rose to the rafters.

Stop making sense, stop making sense . . .

The room filled with the stutter and yelp and clipped rhythms of the Talking Heads. The regulars were restless. They pulled jackets and sweaters tighter and tapped the rims of their beer mugs and shot glasses, *Another one*. The dogs were restless. They whined and strained at their leashes. There was a scuffle between two, unusual, and their owners hauled them apart. Wills looked around, poured, unsettled by whatever had disrupted the predictable atmosphere of the bar. She felt a damp edge to the cold, and detected a faint chemical odor. She said to Albert, "Can you go down and have a look at the boiler?"

David Byrne's strained voice shrugged and hiccuped again and again as if caught on a scratch on a vinyl record. Repetition was part of the song, and Wills had been slow to catch that it was a skip until the skip had become a groove in her brain. It was a nervous song, making her nervous. "Jesus, what's with the machine?"

Stop making sense, stop making sense . . .

The song was stuck. The Bubbler, Tap's hulking old juke, had been moved to a corner a couple of years ago, a shrine to the olden days. The Rock-Ola, with a touchscreen list of digital downloads and a swipe to pay, was incapable of sticking. The new box was more likely to go silent, trapped in its mysterious task of buffering, or as Albert called it, "clearing its head." He said, "Hand me the remote," but finding the black object in the tangle of bar drawers was impossible. He passed the Rock-Ola on the way to the basement and threw a useless elbow to try to unstick it. The dogs trembled at the ready, watching everything with on-guard eyes. The few Columbia kids who'd stopped in to tank up before heading downtown cashed out.

The skipped song, the anxious dogs, a chill, an odor, and the feeling that something was happening out of her view, just under her bar-radar, was making Wills thirsty for a beverage stronger than beer, but she measured doses of Stella into a shot glass to help stop her craving for whiskey. Close to midnight, she took inventory and confirmed that everyone in the bar was a familiar face doing familiar things: reading, shooting pool, tapping at screens, staring at the television, staring into a drink. She locked the front door and flipped the "Private Party" sign that hung there for "emergencies," meaning when she wasn't in the mood for tourists or slumming rich locals or college kids. No one else was getting in. The smokers—practically everybody—could just light up in here.

Later, she remembered the instinct to lock up, and wished she hadn't given in when there was a *rap-rap* on the glass door, a guy ignoring the sign, wanting in, a guy with mismatched eyes and a skunk-white stripe of hair, and a grin. She recognized him. He used to come in all the time with a blonde woman. They'd sit at the bend of the bar and go over pages and drink, and sometimes dance. She could almost remember his name. Dan? Ted?

Ned tipped his head, and worked his smile at Wills. She unlocked the door and held it wide and Ned stumbled into his old haunt, a young woman at his side. "Hey, thanks, great, shelter from the storm. It's starting to come down. Come on, Lauren, come on in. . . ."

Earlier, against his better judgment, chased and battered and spooked, not to mention staring into the looming long tunnel of fatherhood, Ned had succumbed when he ran into Lauren at an earlier event on campus and she suggested they continue on into the night. He knew he was an item to be checked off her to-do list: double major, semester abroad, sleep with girls, seduce professors. He was fine with that. Totally fine with it.

They had barhopped their way down Broadway to Tap and were already drunk; Wills wished she'd seen that before she opened up for them. The young woman was wrapped in a cropped down jacket and scarves, with long legs in skinny jeans accentuated by Uggs, sexy in spite of themselves.

Ned took his former favorite bar stool and Lauren wedged in next to him. There was no doubt in her mind that he wanted her, it was now just a matter of time and alcohol, and deciding if she wanted him. Youth was on her side. She was assisting Ned on a new novel idea, while *The Angry Intern* languished in a desktop file that hadn't been opened since last summer at Joanna's. He didn't have much more than the title, *The Porn Papers*, and the pitch, a little thin: rock-star professor embarks on a global sex odyssey to research his book, a contemporary—less science, more kink—Kinsey Report.

This girl, all girls, actually, had gotten very bold since Ned had begun teaching five years ago. Lauren neither blinked nor blushed at the "research" for *The Porn Papers*, and sent him screenshots and video and links he might find useful for the book. They'd meet in his small office, and she would pull a chair close and review sexual imagery and practices, keeping Ned tense with titillation, making him squirm, with her tank tops in the dead of winter, and her neon bra straps peeking out, the two of them "reviewing" imagery, analyzing what the human body was capable of in its endless quest for pleasure and/or pain. How very many variations on that theme existed. None of it seemed discomfiting or remarkable to twenty-one-year-old Lauren.

At the bar, Ned patted at his pockets, twice, and turned each one out, taking his time, looking for his wallet to pay for the drinks. Bits and ends fell to the floor. Excruciatingly carefully, with two fingers as though it were alive, he extracted his cell phone and set it facedown in front of him. He was neither drunk enough nor distracted enough by Lauren to block the fact of the lurking text from Jo, that she had attacked him, twice now, had come after him, and was still coming. He was making a heroic effort to let the booze and the blonde grad student do the work of blocking out the newest text invitation, to which he had succumbed: *Tap*.

Ned peeked at his key ring and was comforted to see the set to his old apartment, the escape hatch, just a couple blocks away. He tried to picture whether or not the mattress on the floor had sheets on it. He was momentarily confounded trying to sort out exactly whom he was about to cheat on, Trudi or Jo, with Lauren.

He fanned cash and winked and squinted at Wills. "Remember me? I used to come here a lot. Ned. I'm Ned." He stuck out his hand. Wills expertly turned away the instant she saw he meant to shake hers.

Nuh-uh, thought Wills. He was with a girl too young, too obviously a student. "Sure, I remember you. Quite the dancer." It was Wills's turn to throw a wink, at Lauren.

Lauren widened her eyes as Ned dropped his. "Really, Ned? You told me you don't dance, ever, under any circumstances." She turned to Wills. "Really? He dances?"

Wills side-eyed Ned and asked him, as she tipped her head toward the girl, "New friend?"

Ned was embarrassed and shook his head definitively, *No*. He shook it to mean, *No, not a new friend, not a real friend, not like my other friend*. For some reason it was important to Ned that Wills not think he was with Lauren. Wills, who'd set eyes on him and Jo together when things were right, who was in a way, part of their story.

Ned pointed to his phone, as if Jo resided there. "My, uh, other friend. I used to come in with her." He couldn't think of how to put it. "She. She's not around anymore."

Wills said, "I can see that." She wanted to punish Ned a little, though she wasn't sure why. He seemed to inspire it.

Ned felt called out. He thought, *What the fuck. Women.* He was just out to have some fun, some drinks, find a little sanctuary from the creepy events that had transpired over the last weeks. That thing after him, that thing on him. Jo. Ned looked up to the ceiling. He wondered if she was watching him right now. He leaned back and looked down the bar to the far corner of the room where the pool table sat empty but waiting, balls racked, sticks leaning, grass-green felt illuminated by a hooded light fixture that swayed.

He picked up his phone, looking to defend himself against Wills's intense dislike of him. "Yeah. No. She died." On cue, Ned's phone dinged and lit with the text that wouldn't quit. He laughed unhappily and said to the screen, "I'm here! I'm here!" He shrugged to Wills. "She still texts me. I think . . . she's having a hard time. Moving on."

"She died. Wow. I'm sorry to hear that." Wills assessed Ned's mental state. She hated the bartender-as-therapist demands of her job. She was terrible at mustering sympathy for drunks trapped in a headlock by their demons. Curious as to whether he was normal-crazy or crazy-crazy, she probed, just a bit. "She died. But she's texting you."

Lauren said, "Wait, who's texting you? Are you double-booking on me? Do you have a backup plan for later?"

"No, fuck no, that's crazy, no." Ned pulled Lauren into the V of his open thighs. "I'm with you."

She did things to his ear with whispers and wetness. Ned was aroused. Wills, disgusted, turned her back on them.

He drank more. Everything—the media mouthpiece he'd

become, orbiting Planet Trudi like a lesser satellite, his failed tenure attempts, ShameShame on the wane, two furrows deepening between his eyes, so obvious in high-def, drinking too much and getting frisky with a young girl. He barely recognized himself. Or he recognized himself too clearly. He was a dick, there was no doubt about it. Jo was dead, Trudi was pregnant, and he was doomed to a life sentence of cheating and lying and denying with her, a woman he did not love. Obviously, he would cheat on Trudi. Here he was, on the verge.

Nah, he rationalized. He just had a good case of the hopping guilts, that was all, like he'd had a million times before. They would quiet down once he pushed them away, once he got free of all this . . .

All this what? Ned shut his eyes to pull the word, but the only one that came was not what he expected, and tears sprang to his eyes. All this "grief." He wasn't grappling with anything otherworldly, it was just a mass pileup of grief and guilt. He was traumatized. He'd had an anxiety attack at the Titania. Leftover texts, lost texts, his phone was fucked up, he needed an upgrade. It *was* a celebustalker at Porterhouse. The shock of Jo's death, the guilt, Trudi's crazy life, the copious drinking he'd been doing—in the olden days it was called a "bender"—all the internet and television eyes watching him, judging him, evaluating him. It was all getting to him. Toss in pure terror at the prospect of a child with Trudi. His eternally disappointed mother. Those were the ghosts that chased him here tonight and that might chase him forever if he didn't pull himself together.

The Rock-Ola righted itself and the playlist resumed. Ned signaled for shots. The alcohol did its work. Lauren nosed his neck. Ned turned his attention to the girl rubbing up against him, crowding him with cleavage. She wheedled and pestered, "Dance with me, Professor, come on, come on, come on." Ned yielded. Were he to misplay it, he would miss out on fucking Lauren tonight in the studio. That was all that was real, and for now, that was all he wanted to be real.

For a couple of minutes, Ned played his old game. He let Lauren pull him off his bar stool. He had a cocktail in his hand, a cigarette dangling from his lip, and Lauren, a living, breathing girl with barely contained tits, bumping up against him. A real girl in the mood to dance.

For a couple of minutes, Ned convinced himself to ignore Joanna one more time.

20

Fuck love. I seep through Tap-a-Keg, the black site of our romance, the arena for our showdown.

I stream between the regulars, disturbing dogs, fluttering newspapers and napkins. I roam behind the bar. I make it cold, I make it rank, I make the lights flicker, I make the jukebox skip, I make it start up again. I head up to the dark eaves above the pool table, where I bank back and forth, weaving strands of need and want, need and want. I watch.

Doc's on his same old bar stool and his legs are spread wide, and she's right in there between them, this not–Dr. Trudi, the blonde grad student. Lauren. Lauren is young. She's ripe. Her skin has what beauty experts call "volume." It catches light. She pushes out lips and breasts. She uses her hair to veil and to tickle. She grinds on his thigh. Her crotch presses. He must feel her heat through his jeans.

Doc and the girl telegraph and choreograph through scents, eyes, bodies, gestures, through the booze and the dark and the music. The tableau of drunken romance is so familiar, the heart I no longer have aches, my phantom nipples pop with desire, I pink with how it felt to be next to Ned on a night like this in this place: his skin, his breath, his fingers. His drinking ritual, the old half-smirk smile, the long pull of his scar slightly skews his gaze, the almost feminine, coy way he slows down and talks low and uses his hands. The intimate way he leans in, and then pulls back.

I join in. Now we're a threesome.

The song is "Sideways," Santana and Citizen Cope. The song is late-night sticky-sexy. She whispers, "Come on." He leans back, I've seen it a million times, I see it now, and his lids go soft and heavy, he's calculating his odds if he turns her down. He fits a cigarette between his lips and pats himself again: matches. It's a stall. She wants to dance. He doesn't want to dance. I want them to dance.

Lauren takes his hands and puts them on her hips. She twitches, left, right, and brings his hands along for the ride. Ned moves his feet, a polite shuffle left, shuffle right, not really dancing. He hopes this will appease her, I know him, just one song, he smokes through it, his chin is tipped up, the cigarette's lit end is bouncing a little bit in rhythm. I can see he's not into it, he's not snaking around her yet. Yet. The girl backs up to him. She bends from the waist, her hair, her long hair, brushes the barroom floor. Ned can't ignore her ass. This is his thing. He takes her hips, drawing her to him.

Drawing me to him, once upon a time, and most definitely, knocking me sideways. Forty-six. Thirty-one.

We roll in from the street. There's the ballerina bartender with the long braid, there's the big guy at the end of the bar. The regulars are there, and the dogs too. We order up, we lean into each other at the Bubbler, we tap for songs, my Doc in his gray shirt, his jeans, his brush of hair. His wonky eyes slow-lidded and glinting beneath the booze, fixed on me. We laugh at each other.

I do teasing c'mere-go-away dance moves, I twirl in and offer it up, like Lauren is doing, I turn away from him and he dance-follows me, he pushes himself against my ass, and then I throw an arm around his neck and bury my nose there, at his collar, and I breathe him and he smells like a carnivore, like tallow and skin, and he snakes his arm around my waist and pulls me in close and breathes me back, and we trip over each other and kiss with whiskey and cigarettes and we grind into each other from our hot middles. I follow the path of his neck to just beneath his collar, and then down his shirt farther and farther, chest, belly, this side, that side, to the bulge. I use my thumb, back and forth, back and forth, over the denim.

Like Lauren is doing.

Everyone is watching. The bartender calls out, "Can somebody punch up the next song!"

Look at desire. Look how it rises. I surge. I want to blanket Tap in a fog of despair, blind everyone in the room, including the dogs, everyone with eyes watching Ned's cock against this girl's ass, her reaching around to touch him, the irresistible, pornographic display.

I need to come, out of shadow, out of churn, out of memory. I want him to see me: a long, lithe, terrifying gray glittering death trace of a woman. Scorned, haunting, hunting. I burn to make my limbs ribbons, to reach for him and wrap around him and wind tight and tighter and squeeze him dry. I burn to feel him shudder inside me like he used to, and go soft and pale and useless. I want to make him die, but only a little. See how he likes it.

The song ends. The jukebox whirs and waits. The dogs are up again, staring into the ceiling. The regulars tense with the silence I've imposed. The bartender, Wills, she knows something this way comes.

And it is coming, my bitch-surge. That's right, that's right, right there, there. *My* rage, my fury, my pain, my release. Right there. Ned. Ned. Ned.

He calls that dancing? He wants to dance? Fine.

I know the playlist. Let's dance.

21

Let's dance. Lauren squealed because she recognized a radio hit. "See! We have to keep going!"

Ned was at capacity. He was finished with the charm offensive. He was a talker and a drinker, not much of a dancer, despite Wills's taunt. He tried to herd Lauren away from the center of the room, maneuver them back to the bar, his smile tight. Lauren danced away from him, holding her arms above her head to help him stay focused on her rolling body.

Wills's irritation meter hit "high." The little sex show had gone on too long. She wiped down bottles and the bar top with a snap. The dogs searched for something they could not see in the eaves, their eyes wide, bloodhound-alert. Wills stepped out from behind the bar and shouted over the music, "Why don't you two take a break—it's on me," and pantomimed knocking back a shot.

Lauren ignored her. She had felt Ned's hard-on, she'd expended this much energy getting Doc McGowan where she wanted him, and she was not stopping now. The vibe darkened and a few people hustled into coats, headed out into the night. The barroom got cold and then hot and then cold again. An iron radiator hissed and dropped a beat like a drumstick on a cowbell. Condensation beaded and ran down windows and mirrors. Something tainted the air. Wills sniffed and threw a look to Albert, *What's that smell?* It was an odor she might have chalked up to the old freezer, but she'd gotten rid of it months ago.

Ned was now on Wills's last nerve. Albert gave her a questioning look back, *Should I bounce them?*

Wills shrugged, *Let's see.*

Ned was morose. Tangled realities were bringing him down. He had given up on the idea of fucking Lauren. She had gone from tantalizing possibility to demanding female, while he'd gone from drunk and horny to headachy and cranky. He was at the point in an all-day drinker's trajectory where he was not sober, but not drunk. A new life for which he was responsible was on the way, a baby, and an old one, an ex, would not exit, for which he was also somehow responsible. The story of his life. The bartender, Ned groused to himself, might as well be his mother standing back there, stink-eyeing him.

The music was strange. The music was not helping. It was the sound track of the best nights of his life, fuck access, fuck red carpets, fuck the world of Trudi and EternaPlast. The best nights had been right here, in a dive bar with Jo, talking about his work and his hopes and laughing and drinking and dancing, Talking Heads, Citizen Cope, Bowie. Ned sucked deep on his cigarette, and exhaled slow. Jo's face assembled itself in front of him in the smoke, or in his memory.

It was the face that felt like forever the first time he'd seen it. She had raised it to him in Harvey's, she had buried it in his neck, he had become an avid reader of that face as it moved, and moved him, with curiosity or anger or delight, and sorrow too, and everything etched her smile, etched her frown. She thought, she connected, she understood, she was skeptical, her brow furrowed, her brow rose. Lines formed and lingered. She had been in the sun, had kids, hated gyms. She'd been in pain; that was there too. She was sick and getting sicker. But they had been happy.

Maybe she would have gotten better.

Ned shivered. He shook his head to clear it. It was a thought that ticked constantly within him. Sickness was like that, right? You could turn things around with your mind. Could you turn things around with your mind? Even cancer? It drove him crazy. Might she have lived if he had kept her safe, like he promised? If he'd come back that August day, like he promised?

Right here at this bar, last summer, Jo, weakening, trying to have a night out, sipping club soda, had asked him point blank, "Ned, are you telling me you will give up everything you've got going on downtown, your big fancy life, for this?" She'd gestured at the barroom. "This?" She'd clasped her hands over her diseased chest. "If you are asking me to wait for you, I will. But hurry." Her eyes filled. His eyes filled too, and Ned said, "Yes, wait, please," and when he said it, he'd meant it. The very next day he had gone downtown to do the breakup and there was Dr. Trudi with her swollen ankles and her pee stick.

He was struck dumb that end-of-summer day by a run-of-the-mill, mind-boggling reality: fatherhood. It was a simple twist of fate, and he could not bear to tell Jo that this little gestating reality was bigger than their love, bigger than her cancer. Was utterly intimidating and unspinnable. In an instant, everything previously denied, delayed, and whitewashed, all of Ned's tactics and strategems, all of it, was rendered ridiculous. A baby. He was a dick, but he'd had his reasons. Ned had never seen Joanna alive again.

Ned pinched the bridge of his nose hard. He couldn't bring

himself to look at Lauren bouncing to the music. The jukebox seemed programmed to taunt him. Was it his imagination, or had the music gotten louder? He was officially done with this night. He was miserable in his miserable skin. He hated himself.

You taught me how to treat you, Doc, better late than never.

Later, in the ER, Ned recalled her voice sparring with his thoughts as memory and grief and fear and great guilt coalesced inside him.

Joanna chose the moment. She showed herself. She unfolded in the shadows into a stretched-out, long thing, a silent scream of milky silver limbs and hair that insinuated and streamed, a toxic bloodletting of bad juju. She swirled against the ceiling in ancient form, a woman scorned, left behind, disintegrated and reconstituted into bitter bits and pieces. She was a beautiful nothing, luminous dust and mist, humid and deadly, unable to let go.

Hello, Doc. I'm here I'm here I'm here.

Ned, about to go to the bar and settle up and head out, stopped cold and shuddered with a whole-body quake.

Wills thought she saw something, it was just out of range, but it crossed her atmosphere. She said to Albert, over the music, "What the fuck was that? Did you see that? Something flew by." Albert reached behind the bar for the baseball bat and walked the length of Tap, searching for the bird or whatever had infiltrated the bar. The regulars didn't know who to watch, Wills on high alert, Albert wielding his baseball bat, or sexy Lauren on the dance floor.

Joanna cued a song that started out shy, with a wobbly guitar, restrained, but raw, with a stop-motion, tentative catch in the melody. *You can get addicted to a certain kind of sadness.* The words got taut, drawing the music taut too, like a bow, Gotye before Kimbra, feeling sorry for himself, justifying himself, trying to dismiss her: *You're just somebody that I used to know.*

Ned changed course, and headed back toward the center of the room. His face was slack and dark, his eyes seemed to set in deeper, and he appeared to be drunker. He arched and bent and thrust with the beat, in place at first, and then moving his feet. He spilled his drink and dropped his glass. He ignored Lauren. The dogs crouched and growled, ruffs up, trying to get a fix on what hovered.

The volume increased. Kimbra's voice sliced back in accusation: *You're just somebody that I used to know.*

Lauren, intoxicated by her own special potion of alcohol and estrogen and youth, hadn't yet noticed that something had shifted in Ned. She stepped up her moves, made herself slinky and drew *Pulp Fiction* V-fingers across her eyes.

Joanna made Ned step it up too, and he drew V-fingers across his eyes back at Lauren, uncharacteristically vamping, and he looked surprised by himself and out of control of himself, although he had not had any more to drink since he took the dance floor.

A new song banged in with psychedelic, hip-hop guitars and Questlove's crashing cymbals. Black Thought rapped, *Knocked up nine months ago*, teasing out Cody's vocals. Ned bent and moved around Lauren. He let the music punctuate his slide, his sidestep, his angles. He let the music twist him.

Joanna outgrew the shadows. She was engorged with the music as she DJ'ed her way to revenge. She got big with it, she arched with it, it stretched her, it widened all the openings she had given up to him when she was alive, openings that once needed coaxing by a needy tongue or fingers or cock to yield; openings now widening and closing and widening and closing, her once-female places, like something hungry from the sea, great gaps, great maws.

Ned became a dervish, Ned went out-of-body, with a deep-brain comprehension: Joanna had taken hold of him, was pressing in on him from inside of him.

Lauren was thrilled with the victory of getting Ned back to the dance floor, to see him dance like this. She thought, *He's so wild!*

mistaking it as testament to his desire for her. She looked around Tap-a-Keg for her audience, but no one was watching Lauren anymore. All eyes were on Ned. A few patrons stood and conferred with Albert about what was wrong with the guy, what was wrong with the Rock-Ola, how to shut it down, while Wills dug in drawers for the remote. It was time to stop the music.

Ned was no longer conscious of Lauren. Ned was dancing for Jo.

Joanna pushed the music into him.

She shuffled a flip-book of grotesque moments within his brain: Pat McGowan pulled hard on her cigarette, side-eyeing him; Peck smirked; manuscript pages flew away; dick pics and bathroom-mirror chest-selfies of headless politicians cascaded; Tom, freakishly huge, towered over him; angry Anna punched at her phone for the cops; Laney slammed a door in his face, over and over. A dead woman, a ghost, growled at him in an unfinished nursery with a black crib; weird Darger children in wide-striped T-shirts and brown leather shoes ran through; dark forest creatures on twig stilts with hooves instead of feet looked down on Ned while piston muscles stabbed and shards flew and a pansexual lawyer scratched cobalt-blue fingernails along his thigh.

Ned jerked and staggered with the visions.

He was losing himself, from the toes up. His feet were numb. His legs were liquid. His thighs quivered. From a distance, he felt sweat trickling from the middle of his back to the crack of his ass. His arms lifted and swayed over his head. He ran his fingertips along his neck, almost coy, down his forearm, stroking himself seductively. His muscles tightened, too tight. Ned felt panicky inside, aware of what was happening, too aware, and utterly unable to stop moving. Inside he was screaming for Jo to make it stop.

For Joanna, there was only one thing left to do. Make it worse.

The Rock-Ola whirred and searched and shuffled and found songs that did not appear on its playlist. The box glowed brighter.

The box went louder than it was ever programmed to go, very, very loud. Ned could no longer distinguish his heartbeat from the downbeat or the bass from his breath or the bass from the blood thumping in his ears. He was forced by Joanna to shake, rattle, and hum. Diving at him from above, Joanna tripped along the wires of his nerves and penetrated his bones, his very bones, what held him up, what held him together, the structure of him, and she spread through his bones like cancer, of course she did, she ate into his bones to deteriorate him, to wreck his foundation. Just as he had done to her.

Lauren leaned against the bar, bored with the night, bored with Ned, fixated on the blister that had sprouted on her heel, and confused at being irrelevant. She thought, *What a freak! He must have taken, what, molly, to be raving around like this, in this dump. He's actually pretty threatening! I'm not comfortable with this! It's actually inappropriate! I'm a student!* She tugged up the scoop of her shirt and went to her back pocket for her phone, wondering what else was happening tonight. She looked over at Doc McGowan, still ignoring her, and thought, *Pics or it didn't happen, bitches.*

Lauren loved Instagram. Her idea was contagious. The remaining customers in Tap brandished their smartphones too.

Ned tranced, a manic marionette going low and doing a sinewy, spine-twisting crouch near the floor. Joanna popped him back up and bounced him on the balls of his feet, tossing his head from side to side. He looked gray and desperate to catch his breath; spittle flew from the corners of his mouth. Still, Ned, limp, grabbed his crotch and turned around and around until he was dizzy. He threw his arms out for balance. He pumped his fist at all the phones held high, recording him. He caved his shoulders in, held his wrists as if cuffed, shuffle-walked as if chained, forward and back, lost to himself, moving because Joanna wouldn't let him stop moving.

Deep inside, Ned felt like he might die. Deep inside he screamed, *Go away go away go away.*

Behind the bar, Wills felt uncharacteristically panicked. This guy was not right in the head, he was bad news, she had known it, he was too drunk, the girl he was with was too young, he'd babbled about texts from a dead person, and still she had served him. He was hopping around on the dance floor like he had taken something on top of the drinking, Ecstasy or speed or meth or whatever the hell people take these days, or he was having a seizure. Her regulars were riveted, the phones were out and held high, and the dogs were pacing. Albert was crouched under the Rock-Ola looking for a plug, a wire, anything, knowing nothing was as simple as pulling a plug anymore.

Wills had to make the music stop.

She pawed through the junk drawer for the remote control, pulling at tangled chargers and long-forgotten bar bills and receipts, greasy menus, torn corners of paper scrawled with telephone numbers without names, a stapler that hadn't been refilled since the nineties, notes on napkins, half-filled inventory sheets, dried-out Sharpies, pencils without points. She found three remotes, but not the remote she needed. Wills moved booze nobody ever ordered, sticky, dusty bottles of peppermint schnapps and Blue Curaçao and bitters, crème de menthe and monk-shaped Frangelico. She cursed for the millionth time that she hadn't cleaned this crap out, once and for all.

The song changed.

Despite the dramatic scene being played out, the regulars raised a collective groan when "One" rang out, because everybody loved that song and everybody hated that song, especially Wills, who had so emphatically banned it from this box because she could not bear it, because she had loved it once, so much, that now, when Bono's questions came, she nearly leapt out of her skin, her teeth rattled and every fiber of her being said *For fuck's sake, no!* because "One," by U2, was not on the Rock-Ola, so it could not be playing.

But it was.

Wills thought, *Okay, this is now officially bizarre.* It was an epic heart-hammer of a song, a painful and raw reminder of her own long-gone love, her true love, and a U2 fanatic if ever there was one, who had gotten cold feet and run out on Wills, who she would never stop loving even after how bad he'd hurt her, even with good Albert in her bed.

Glasses and mugs rattled. Framed photographs and mirrors trembled. The whole place rumbled with "One." She found the remote control and with great and focused intent, Wills aimed it at Bono blaring from the box. Off, Mute, Volume, Shuffle. Nothing. She could not shut Bono up.

Ned twitched in time. It occurred to Wills that the box had a mind of its own. It occurred to Wills that the box was providing this asshole with a very specific sound track, at ear-splitting volume. It occurred to Wills that Ned might seize up right here, have a heart attack, and it would be up to Wills to save him (granted, it wouldn't be the first time somebody had expired at the bar). Passersby on Broadway peered into Tap's front windows, wondering why the door was locked, why the music was so insanely loud.

Albert went to Ned and put a heavy bouncer's hand on his shoulder, *Settle down, man*, but Ned whipped away and flailed and fell backward into tables. Albert tried to bear-hug him from behind, but Ned broke away and continued to thrash, lunging and hurling himself as if he were in a mosh pit. He fell backward into the cue stick rack and sticks fell and Ned fell, too. He was unmoving. Albert yelled to Wills: "911." Ned was still.

Wills was already talking into her phone, giving the address.

Tap's patrons looked up. Something raced and banked above them, frenzied too, keeping time with Ned, making a sound they could hear under the music, a rhythmic moan, low-pitched and precise. *That's wailing*, Wills thought, *like a banshee*. Everyone crowded up against the walls, but, New Yorkers, they had no intention of fleeing this scene, a real I-was-there event. A ghost or an alien, in Tap-a-Keg! On video! Eduardo was already thinking about slogans for T-shirts. A hell of a joint, living up to its name.

Wills and Albert, Lauren, Eduardo, the growling dogs, the rest of the crew all looked to the ceiling to watch whatever it was circle her prey. They held phones high.

There was no ignoring her. She was pain, externalized and expansive. She got bigger, became a gritty cloud of hurt, and she swallowed the oxygen in the bar. She consumed the atmosphere and clipped the breath in the lungs of everyone in the room as the room was enveloped by her pungent gas.

She was what she was, eternal and terrifying: a woman sprung from the traps of youth and beauty and good health, fueled by disappointment, come too late to wisdom, refusing to exit, powered by rage. A crone. A hag. A ghost.

Ned felt her. He felt her in his shaking legs, his exhausted arms, his sweat, his heaving chest, his throat clutched with fear. He could move nothing. He could not turn away. His eyes were pinned open. He was like an insomniac suspended in the moment before consciousness is lost, exactly where she wanted him. She had split his soul and splayed it, she penetrated and injected him with her poison, she fucked him there, so he would know, and he would die from it like she did, and she would be free.

But there was one more song, and there was all the time in the world before the ambulance arrived.

Joanna cleared the atmosphere to wipe the phones clean, all except Lauren's. She shut down everything else in Tap. The Rock-Ola went dark and silent, suddenly irrelevant, the bar phone was dead, useless, and the house lights blacked. Every living thing in the bar was mute, waiting for what was next. There was no hum, there was no power, only the shuffling, tired sound of Doc McGowan being hauled back up onto his feet.

She gave him the spotlight he'd so desperately wanted when they were together, that he had so ambitiously acquired on the arm of Dr. Trudi. Under a beam, Jo outlined Ned with the fluorescent aura of a man posed like some Kurt Weill version of a Bob Fosse dancer, his head dipped, one shoulder up, a toe pointed, poised to embody and perform some dark fetish in dance.

And perform he did.

The ghost blasted a misogynist's anthem, a delicious, politically incorrect snarl of a song, all old-school fuzz bass and marimba. Joanna knew that Ned had a special affection for the song. It used to be his karaoke go-to. He'd actually performed it for her in a little Korean joint in the East Thirties back when she was stupid and alive and in love with him. *Sweetest pet in the world.*

"Under My Thumb" came from everywhere, deafening and sinister.

Lauren filmed. Ned Mick-mimicked his way through the song, his pitch-perfect Irish tenor urgent and nasty, his lip curled. He sang directly to Lauren's smartphone. He was a lurching zombie-Ned, the dancing dead. There was no there there. His eyes were blank, glazed with booze and Joanna's domination.

Lauren held her phone out in front of her like a shield, thinking, *He's not even cute anymore! His face is weird! He's mad old!* She Instagrammed and tweeted Ned's rendition of "Under My Thumb" with a few taps of her own thumb, easy as you please, far and wide.

Lauren thought, *Mission accomplished!*

Joanna thought, *Mission accomplished.*

Ned bent in on himself and slid to the floor, a spotlight from nowhere still shining down on him. Joanna beamed everything bad into Ned, she hurt Ned and scarred Ned on the inside, so he would feel and never un-feel this: that the truth, the whole truth—*I can't love you, like I promised*—the whole truth spoken by

Ned into Joanna's eyes at the end, out of respect for what they had, who they had been with each other, would have made it all okay. Not fine, but okay.

Wills pushed through the group and dropped down on her creaky knees and pulled off her sweater and tucked it under Ned's head. Ned pushed weakly at her. His legs twitched and his eyes were wild, searching and frantic for a glimpse of Joanna. She had been in him, she had torn at his soul, and he was now nearly expired with exhaustion and fear.

He could do nothing but let Wills cradle him and pat his heaving back as he cried in her lap, *Jo, Jo, Jo*, and as sirens cried too in the night, and as all the house lights leapt up bright, and as Joanna dematerialized back to churn, back to black.

22

It was over.

He lay on the barroom floor, afraid to move, and inventoried body parts. Zones of pain revealed themselves: legs, lower back, upper arms, neck. His chest, his chest, his chest. His clothes felt stuck to him with sweat. He was freezing. His eardrums reverberated with all the songs of the night, and Bill Wyman's last bass line. Agitated faces appeared and disappeared above him, their mouths working. The bartender slid something under his head, and that human kindness made him cry. Past the commotion and blur of tears, Ned saw an apparition's contrail leading out of Tap-a-Keg, over Broadway and up into the dark. He called after her, *Jo Jo Jo.*

EMS clapped a mask on Ned, hoisted him from the barroom floor, strapped him to a gurney, bumped him out Tap's door and down the curb and up the ramp into the ambulance. The siren blared as they rushed south to the emergency room at St. Luke's. In between perfunctory ministrations, the crew bent to their phones, snickering and sharing their screens across him. Ned understood, distantly, that they were laughing at him—literally over him—as, in the course of thirty blocks, he achieved the next level of internet-famous. He was a viral sensation, and a joke.

Joanna made sure that Lauren's pictures and video clips were the only ones that survived of the smartphones recording inside Tap-a-Keg. Ned's rendition of "Under My Thumb" yielded snagged images cascading one after the next, past real, past surreal, into pop art born on the internet—the gif. The gifs—self-referencing, compressed, low-resolution, creepy—were fortified and enhanced by the many images of Ned that already existed from television and appearances with Trudi.

As he was sped to St. Luke's, citizen journalists from around the globe worked on generating more gifs of Ned, making him an internet star: sexpert Ned, yakking on television; red-carpet Ned, with a fake, cool smile, half a step behind Dr. Trudi; professorial Ned behind a lectern—familiar images edited and spliced ingeniously with Tap-a-Keg's leering Ned; crotch-grabbing, sweaty Ned; foaming-at-the-mouth Ned; and Mick-Ned. The video versions, via YouTube, Vine, and a dozen other channels, were all scored to "Under My Thumb," and that too was precisely auto-tuned and processed with Ned's snarling karaoke rendition. The countless re-creations and reanimations were short, hilarious, and nasty. They looped forever. Headlines and captions proliferated: *Porny Horny Prof, The Pervy Professor, Karaoke Kreep, Dr. Trudi's Bad Boy*, and so forth and so on.

The EMS crew parallel-parked Ned's gurney and oxygen trolley in a packed corridor of the ER. The waiting room was crowded with stretchers supporting other occupants who seemed unusually calm in the wake of whatever chaos had landed them there. The walk-ins leaned wearily against walls that vibrated with machinery lurking behind them, cupping or cradling vulnerable, broken body parts: a wrist, an elbow, an ear, an eye. Partners, spouses, and friends, small children and the elderly knew how to behave, knew how to wait. Everyone seemed stolid, resigned, experienced.

Ned pulled himself up, and looked around for whoever was in charge. He raised his mask and called to the staff for attention, or at least information on how long he'd be parked in the hallway, and was ignored. He noticed people noticing him, and then he realized they were all holding phones, checking screens, looking at him, tapping and texting the sighting of Dr. Trudi's boyfriend.

Ned gave into the unspoken emergency room protocol of accepting insult on top of actual injury while waiting for care and sank back down and checked his own phone. In addition to the supernatural, forced occupation of his body in Tap and his almost dying from dancing, in addition to the bizarre post-disaster/pre-disaster atmosphere of the ER on a Friday night, Ned had to contend with one big *WTF DUDE* coming at him from every direction through his phone. Ed Senior and Pat, Kristen and Keira, colleagues from the J-School and Fox, faux friends and frenemies and old acquaintances he hadn't heard from in years were all clamoring to know what had happened to push Doc McGowan from the coattails of fame to internet notoriety. With realization spreading like thin ice in his veins, he knew that come Monday morning, he was absolutely sure, Dean Peck's own version of *WTF DUDE* would no doubt land in his in-box. Hello, Pervy Professor; goodbye, Columbia.

Ned was finally wheeled behind a curtain. Nurses circulated. A monitor was clipped to his finger. The oxygen deepened his breathing, the opiates relaxed his muscles. The clanking and beeping of the emergency room, the continuous in and out of attendants, their voices, the ticking of the fluorescent light fixture above him, all helped distract him from what swarmed on the internet.

He mumbled to himself, "Let me think." He still had Trudi. And a baby on the way! She'd hear his side of it, she'd help him ride this out. They were about to be a family. He'd made a mistake.

He was an ambitious man and ambitious men fucked up. It was practically part of the job description!

Trudi would be fine. Trudi wasn't as idealistic as Jo, with her too-high expectations, her impossible-to-meet twentieth-century standards. Like somebody's mom. Like his mom! He'd never realized their relationship—his and Jo's—followed the old Pat McGowan blueprint. Of course he would fuck up, because it was assumed he would fuck up, because he was a born fuckup.

Ned bobbed and drifted toward the Ned-zone of plausible deniability. "Let me think."

Trudi would look past this, he was sure. She'd rather have a fuckup than a nobody. He just had to get his story together. This is what he did best. He was great at it. He had to go slow, think it through. Certainly there was no trying to explain that he was being hounded from the grave by his ex-girlfriend. Surely Trudi would not connect this Tap situation with the vandalism at the Porterhouse, or with the cuts and bruises he sustained the night of the attack at the Titania.

Doc McGowan worked on his version.

Okay, yes, he was out drinking with Lauren and shouldn't have been, fine, he sucked for that. But what could he do, Trudi was always away, always so fucking busy, and he was lonely for her and their unborn baby, so he was flirting a little bit, yes, he was busted on that, he would cop to that. Fine! Who knew Lauren would turn out to be crazy. Stalker-level crazy! Probably slipped something in his drink! And then filmed his meltdown to ruin him and blackmail him! For a grade!

Even doped up, Ned was a master at turning himself into the aggrieved party.

Trudi wouldn't push him, she didn't want to know. She just needed the right story to post, to tweet, to embed, to encrypt, to show and tell, for the masses, her followers, her friends, her brand. Ned could deliver that, no problem. It's what he'd been doing all along. Not too much detail, not too much remorse. Some confusion, light doses of double-talk, peppered with righteous indignation. And the classic passive-evasive nonapology: *Mistakes were made. If I've done anything to hurt you or upset you, I'm sorry.*

Before he fell away into a druggy sleep, Ned let his mind wander to the possibilities of life, post-scandal. Rehab and redemption, multimedia deals, an internet persona he could leverage once he understood which way the wind blew. He could position himself as Dr. Edward McGowan, representative of the Men's Rights Movement, MRM, a guy with a strong masculine energy who had been politically corrected, testosterone-suppressed, bitch-slapped to the point of finally letting it blow when he was targeted by Lauren, a calculating, privileged young woman.

Or, he could be Doc McGowan, neofeminist, undone by the tawdry world he inhabited for work, corrupted like the men he talked about on television, himself a StickyFigure spiraled down into booze and babes before bottoming out, and then converted and redeemed. His penance: to challenge the high-pressure culture of masculinity itself.

Ned drowsily reviewed the two post-scandal options as if they were displayed on websites and magazine covers, in interviews, on television, with the paparazzi on his trail as he took the kid—baby whomever-whatever—to the park. In his mind, his rebranding strategy featured pictures of himself in a baseball cap, behind sunglasses, hiding, but not really. Very DiCaprio. The tantalizing phrase "scandal groupie" popped into his head.

Under the drugs and the clamor of the ER, the way forward came into view, and it made all the madness of the past few weeks worth it: If his situation wasn't a surefire reality television show, he did not know media. Trudi would love it—another payday, another stream flowing to the mighty river of the EternaPlast brand! In fact, now *they* would be the brand, Dr. Trudi and her rehabbed Ned. It was so Kardashian. It was almost as if he had orchestrated the whole thing, really, wasn't it? To think that just a few hours ago he was worrying about getting tenure and getting laid.

Maybe he was too drugged. Maybe he was too traumatized. Maybe he was in denial. Ned refused to replay the beat-down in the bar. He willed himself to believe that she was done with him, that she had gotten what she wanted. Ned refused to write the ghost, Joanna, into the plotline of his redemption tale.

Hours later, morning, Ned, holding a white plastic Duane Reade bag, a dripping seltzer bottle, a soggy *New York Post*, and his book bag, let himself into Trudi's place in the Porterhouse. The apartment hummed with refreshed security and data and technology, green numbers glowing time, flicks of light indicating steady systems, fuzzy cones of light illuminating circles of handpicked, matte-finished, white-oak plank flooring.

The seamed wall panels that lined the entryway were actually closets fronted by doors without handles. They completely confused Ned. He could never decide which panel held coats, and no amount of touch or pushing caused the walls that were really doors to yield to Ned. Consequently, he never knew where to put anything in the empty foyer, although for a change, he did remember to take off his shoes because once the door clicked shut, a Siri-like voice, a premium mindful-home feature upgrade since the invasion, said, "Shoes, please." He padded in his socks to the kitchen, fearful of setting things down on precious surfaces, still wearing his coat and scarf.

Within just a few days, all traces of the home invasion were gone from the apartment. It was as if it never happened. The Instagram artsy images of Trudi had been reprinted and rehung. The vitrine's vintage beveled-glass shelves had been sourced, shipped, and replaced, undoubtedly at great expense, and the unwearable designer shoes were refurbished and set back on their perches. The burnt bedding was gone and identical clouds of white silk and down were in its place. The silk walls had been cleaned and fumigated to eliminate any traces of smoke. Sensors and cameras of an even higher magnitude of amplification and detection than before were implanted and every wall virtually and literally hummed, restored and fortified.

Ned arranged his meds ostentatiously mid-counter—painkillers, antibiotics, tranquilizers, sleeping pills—so that Trudi would not be able to ignore evidence of his trauma, validated by ER doctors and endorsed by the sly, hot Latina pharmacist at the Duane Reade who'd reached for her phone to tweet Doc McGowan's scrip particulars before Ned had even left the counter.

Bag-, coat-, seltzer-, and newspaper-laden, he made his way to Trudi's bedroom, hoping to put his feet up and rehearse his story before she returned from who-knows-where, obviously having seen the shit storm on the internet, in her texts, in her feeds.

Trudi was on the bed, napping. Her long black hair was knotted at the back of her neck. She was tiny, curved around her huge belly like a fetus curled around a fetus. She was wearing a black bra and panties. Ivory skin, flawless from face to feet, showed nothing mottled or scarred or bumpy or uneven, showed not a mole or the pocky shadow of an old acne outbreak. Not a blue vein or stretch mark could be seen, even on the belly, or the slope of breast, or the thighs thin enough to be arms. Her back looked as though small perfect stones had been implanted along her spine.

Ned stopped in the doorway to psych himself up. He tried to picture Forever. He tried to connect to Family. He tried to feel Love.

"Trudi? Hey, Trude?" He sat next to her on the bed, letting his bag, his seltzer, and his newspaper drop to the floor. He touched her hair to wake her.

"Oh, hey, hi." Trudi shivered. "Cold."

"Yeah, hi. When did you get home? I was going to order some food. Want something?" Ned took off his outdoor jacket and draped it, tenderly he thought, over Trudi, who immediately made an "ick" face and shrugged it off.

"Hang that up." Trudi rubbed her belly.

Ned put his hand on her shoulder, squeamish about making contact with the stretched, alien surface of her belly skin, barely able to contain a human girl baby who would soon slither out, and soon see through him too.

Trudi pulled the quilt over herself. "I told you I'd be home this morning. The red-eye? Remember? Although. You've been pretty busy."

Ned braced. "I was in the ER. Overnight. They kept me."

"Uh-huh. I saw."

Ned nodded. "Yeah, I know. It looks pretty fucked up. But I got hurt. I wanted to talk to you. Tell you what happened."

Trudi tightened her mouth and did something subtle with her permanently un-furrowed EternaPlast-blasted brow to indicate skepticism. Ned was thrown off. Was she doubting him already? Was she being confrontational? He could not read her controlled face. He said, "Well, come on. Let's go into the, uh, living room. I was going to call for some food. What do you want? Egg whites?"

Trudi rolled off the bed and stood and stretched. Ned looked away from her distorted body. She went to the bathroom and emerged in a long black cashmere robe. It was then that Ned noticed her feet, swollen to twice their normal size.

He pointed. "Ouch."

"They don't really hurt. Mostly numb. Tight. No Louboutins. And no standing. Or walking."

Ned couldn't tell if she was kidding about standing and walking. "Have you talked to Goren about it? Can he give you something?"

Trudi sighed and said, "Ned, my feet have been like this for two months. I've mentioned it to you half a dozen times. I think you've promised me three massages."

"Of course, I know. I'm just saying. Maybe Goren—"

"Forget Dr. Goren, will you? Dr. Goren is my business. And pick up your things. You're leaking all over my rug."

Ned, in his socks, carrying his pile of stuff, followed Trudi down the long, low-lit hallway. She arranged herself on the ivory leather sofa and looked funereal, sunk inside her black hair, her black cashmere, in her matching ivory skin. Her fat feet were tucked underneath. She took her smartphone out of the folds of her robe and tapped it with her head bent.

"You're a sensation today, Ned."

Ned sunk into the depths of an iconic chair that had a name he could never remember. His jeans felt dirty. His socked feet looked misshapen. He squinted at Trudi from under his lids, attempted the old cocked eyebrow, attempted to muster authority in his voice. "Now listen, I know how it looks. But it's bullshit. It's the internet. Everything seems worse than it actually is. You can't believe things happening in real time. You need the context before you judge."

Trudi did not look up from her tapping.

"The girl I was with . . . she was just some kid who wanted to talk about class. About a grade. You know how they are. Demanding special treatment."

Silence.

"I was walking to the train and she tagged along. She wouldn't give up. So we went to some dive in my old neighborhood to talk about it. That's all." Ned couldn't stop explaining. "I didn't even drink that much. A couple beers, I swear to you. Maybe she dropped something in my drink. She was freaked about the grade. She was coming on to me. To get me to change it. Her old man's some big CEO. Some big tyrant."

Ned checked Trudi's impassive, perfect face, still bent to her phone. "Trudi? I'm talking to you here. Are you listening?"

"The girl. You mean Lauren." Trudi said, "Her father is a client."

Ned worked to stay on message. "Well, obviously I didn't know that, and I'm sorry about that, but really, it's not how it looks. We were at Tap, it was no big deal. Okay, fine. There was some flirting, absolutely, I take responsibility for that. I do. But, believe me, it was nothing. Nothing. She's this rich kid thinking she can get anything taken care of, right? Lousy grade, whatever, snap your fingers. I mean her fingers. But I wasn't playing along, I really wasn't."

"He's a client with a wife and a lot of friends who are clients. And Lauren—Lauren, your student—has been working with you. On your sex book, I think?"

"We'll get through this. I love you. I love . . ." Ned gestured in the general direction of Trudi, her belly, her sofa. "Everything. I'm, you know, excited. Happy and whatnot."

"Happy and whatnot."

"You know what I'm trying to say. The baby. The baby. I wouldn't fuck that up."

Trudi stood and wrapped her robe tighter. She crossed the living room to the kitchen, ignoring Ned's meds on the counter. A cabinet sprang open at her touch and she selected a paper-thin wineglass. She bent and took out an already-opened bottle of white burgundy from the wine refrigerator, pulled the cork from the neck with her teeth, and poured herself a respectable amount. She took one test sip and then another, less delicate.

"Trudi," Ned said, alarmed at the sight of her slugging wine, mid-morning, with a protective hand on her belly.

"Yes, Ned."

He got up to come to her, but she held up her hand. "Stay, please." She took another sip. "I'm having 'the baby'—who, by the way, is not some generic, un-sonogrammed, nameless creature—in less than six weeks."

"I know that. Of course."

"You do? You know that? Okay, Ned, what's the due date?"

"I know the due date, for Christ's sakes. It's like, end of April, right? Thereabouts."

Trudi smiled and topped off her glass. "Ah. Thereabouts. Right. Well, it doesn't matter. Don't block off your calendar."

"What do you mean, don't block off my calendar? I didn't cheat on you! She was just some stupid kid! She was practically stalking me! She put something in my drink, that's what they think at St. Luke's! And then she took the video on purpose, to fuck things up for me! I know it's fucked up but this will be history in a week! Come on! We can get past this! I love you!"

Trudi shook her head. "Ned, I'm having my daughter—Sevigny—by myself. I've discussed with Mother, and the board and management. I'm staffed up. There's the doula, of course, a Pregnancy Event Coordinator and a Labor Coach, and nanny interviews start next week. You're out."

"Out? What the fuck are you talking about, out? I can't be out! You can't fire me, I'm the father. This is crazy. You don't want this. We're in this together! I want to marr—be with you! You and . . . Sidney!"

"Sevigny, Ned, not Sidney."

"Whatever! Whatever name you want! But we're about to be a family! This is my kid! You can't just cut me out!"

Trudi nodded. "You'll get a check, and it will be a lot more than the average sperm donor winds up with, that's for sure. And you'll get papers, too, from Amanda, spelling the whole thing out. Proscribing things. Proscribing you, basically. Permanently, basically."

Ned was stunned.

Trudi continued. "I don't need a husband, Ned, and I don't think Sevigny needs a dad. Raising a child takes a village, and I've built one. We have our little EternaPlast community. We'll be fine. It's all worked out. You do what you want, obviously, once you get the papers. I mean, if you want to take it further. If you want to, like, fight me."

She attempted a frowning pouty face like a little girl threatened with no dessert. She held up her smartphone and tapped her passcode, turned the screen to Ned and waggled it. "Under My Thumb" started up. A tiny Ned glowed from across the room, pushing his face out, curling his lip, grabbing his junk. "That's entirely up to you," she said.

Trudi took her wineglass, and with her left arm curved around her cashmere-wrapped belly, walked regally from the kitchen through the living room, toward her white silk bedroom. As she passed Ned, she tapped at his old tweed jacket sleeve. "You look terrible, Ned. Keep the Botox appointment if you want. It's on me." She gestured vaguely behind her. "Oh, and meet Joel."

A large, bald man in a big suit stepped from a recess in the room. He extended his hand to Ned. "Nice to meet you, Ned. I enjoy you on TV." Joel gestured to the front door with a tilt of his shaved head. "This way, sir."

Ned said, "Now, wait a second. Wait. This is my . . . What about . . ."

Trudi was already gone, back to her bedroom, but Joel said, "It's all taken care of, Ned. All sent uptown. Nothing to worry about. Time to go."

Shoes forgotten, out on the street in his socks, still holding the white plastic bag and the *Post* and his seltzer, Ned was shocked by the blue day. So much had happened to him in the past twelve hours, but still, dark had yielded to light, snow to warm sun. Beautiful girls and boys rushed past him. He was about to raise his hand to hail a cab to take him up to 102nd Street, to the studio—obviously Trudi had known it existed, and thank God it did—when a taxi screeched to the curb in front of him. A dusky, compact man got out of the driver's seat and rushed at Ned, who thought he looked familiar but could not place him.

The cabdriver said, "I found you! McGowan! Google!" He thrust out the manila envelope with Ned's name slashed across the front in Jo's handwriting, the envelope that he'd left in the cab on the terror trip downtown, when he was dumped along the West Side Highway in the dark on the night he was first attacked by her ghost.

Ned was shocked to have it back. "Wow . . . Hey, thank you so—"

The intense cabbie moved in right next to Ned, shoulder to shoulder, and held up his phone. He pointed a gun-finger at Ned and snapped a selfie with the trending, pervy professor and then hustled back to his taxicab. Ned said, "Wait, can you take me up—"

The cabdriver slammed the door against Ned's entreaty and tore away from the curb.

23

I'm here, I'm here, I'm here, blah blah blah.

Ned danced like the little bitch puppet I commanded him to be. My directorial debut—Lauren's video—continues to deliver across the internet, it's beyond viral, it's metastatic, it's killer. Ned was undone in Tap, utterly undone. I did that, and then I swooped away from the heap of broken man on the barroom floor, a man I had so desperately wanted to fuck, to marry, to kill.

Even Bono worked with me. On repeat.

I made Ned know me anew, this terrible me. I injected my pain into his soul. I made him take me in, all at once, there, on the barroom floor. I wasn't looking for remorse. I was past that. I wasn't looking for him to drop dead. That would have let him off too easy. Instead, I left him with my pain, living outside his own beautiful life like a ghost looking in, but worse, if you ask me. I, at least, am actually dead, for the most part.

Jo Jo Jo.

I want to exult in triumph. I want to gloat. How's the tenure track, Doc? How's the high life along the High Line with Dr. Trudi? How's the fatherhood fantasy? But. But.

I'm suffering from PRDD—post-revenge depression disorder. I'm still here. No signs, no exit, no light.

The only new thing I find inside my spectral self is what was coiled inside Ned when I plugged him into my pain.

I can't un-see little-boy Ned, trying to understand the secrets swirling through his Syosset home.

I can't un-see college-bound Ned, helping his mother climb the stairs, cleaning up broken glass, realizing in the dark of that dark night that the truth was too heavy for her to bear.

I can't un-see Ned, now, bleached out by the glare of Trudi's constellation, Ned, superfluous, Ned, scrounging for meaning in his land of truthiness. Ned, trying to save himself.

But. Who isn't?

We'd had a lush spring, a scorching summer, a melancholy fall, and a nuclear fucking winter, but Ned is no villain. Ned is just a boy trying to be a man, a boy who learned early to bend truth, to see women as inquisitors and marriage as a lifelong exercise in plausible deniability. Those are the components that equal love for Ned. He simply had no idea it could be different. At least not with me.

Are you here for forgiveness? Or to raise the dead?

The song remains the same, and the song asks the same questions, but those questions no longer sound like they are meant for Ned. They sound like they are meant for me. Fucking Bono.

I ask myself, Well, Joanna, have you? Have you come to raise dead memories of disappointment and regret, eternally, like a song stuck on repeat? The questions are for me. Let me think. Let me think.

Me, taking cover from cancer in the make-believe of my rom-com script, where I am young and desirable and healthy.

Me, under siege, terrified, shutting out my girls, leaving them motherless before I died.

Me, left behind by my father, and by my own mother, especially. Motherless too.

I feel it all. I feel it all. But.

Let's face it, we all have tombs in our eyes. We move through as best we can, with a Sudoku puzzle, a song lyric, a glass of red wine, with screens in the palms of our hand, in the arms of someone unexpected, leaning on the braced back of a big dog. We move through as best we can, in the ritual of shutting down each day, same as before, wiping surfaces clean, drawing blinds against the past, to tidy up today so tomorrow can unfold.

We are all only entities looking for a well-lit path. We move through hoping guides wait for us, hoping we will recognize them. Our lights. If only I recognized them. My lights.

Anna and Laney, and Tom.

Tom's eyes pierce the dark and find me like ancient wolf eyes. He puts his front paws up on the sill, *I see you.*

I leave the scaffold. I go close. I am at the window. Tom's tail whirs. His back end shimmies.

Elena sleeps in my bed. Her breath quavers on the intake. It works itself past her stuffy nose, and dissolves into the same sighs she's always sighed in sleep. It is breath I know better than the breath that was once my own. I was a young mother. I listened, torn by every ragged inhale, every asthmatic cough across the hall. I eased her breath as best I could, covering her bluish mouth with a plastic mask so she could inhale steroids to quell the inflammation in her lungs, while little Elena, a talker, chattered away. We sat, she on my lap, on an old wooden chair in our big bathroom in our house on the hill in the woods, next to the scalding, pounding shower, towels smothering doorjambs and windowsills, my girl limp against me, talking, rasping, the two of us stuck together in our damp nightgowns, wet arms entwined, in the hot thick steam.

I can see inside Elena, the slow blood, the slow beat, how grief has muffled the hum of her, how even in sleep she is sad.

No, Mama, no, no.

Now I trance, now her breath is my mantra, now I breathe like her mother, vigilant and calm.

Now I look again.

In her beautiful brain power gathers, the power to swim the endless rise and pull of riptides, disappointment and expectation, despair and hope, to go under and then surface. Elena sleeps and grieves, but in sleep, in grief, she heals, too, and underneath it she's excited, her expectations are perilously high, she's twenty-two, she's swimming parallel to the shore, she's under but she'll surface, I see that, I love that, and Tom sees me, Tom sees what I see, Tom showed me, just by waiting at the windows of home.

So, okay, I'll wait too. It's always only been a waiting room, after all. I will wait. For what happens next. Because this part will end.

This will end. I will it so.

Yes, Ned is undone, but revenge is beside the point. Ned is beside the point.

I will it so. Better late than never.

24

At the end of her shift, Anna slipped out the Mount Sinai doors and threaded through the phalanx of Access-a-Rides, yellow and green cabs, and private cars depositing and receiving patients and their families and caregivers. She crossed through Fifth Avenue traffic, and leaned to breathe for a few minutes at the Central Park stone wall, watching the procession—the comings and goings of people afflicted or blessed, their people helping them, the intensity of expressions on faces, the concentrated tender touches, and all the ways of facilitating locomotion into or away from the hospital: crutches, wheelchairs, fracture boots, canes, walkers, a steady shoulder, a hand gripping an arm. Infant car seats and strollers.

She tried to stretch her facial muscles, un-set her jaw, un-furrow her brow, un-clench her teeth. She clasped her hands together and stretched up. She rolled her head and winced at the creaks in her neck. She scratched all along the rim of her wool cap. She was in scrubs, or she'd sneak a cigarette. She watched the action in front of Mount Sinai for a while, and then trotted back across Fifth, half a block north to the Guggenheim Pavilion and up the stairs to Hatch.

Anna's habit was to retreat to the often-empty hospital chapel, away from the temptations of Kai, the instincts of Jules, and the needs of the sick Kravis kids. The chapel was interdenominational, a spiritual free zone, and the long, narrow room's muted acoustics and palette, its noncommittal stained glass and low ceiling offered sanctuary.

The last time her mother had recurred, before February, she'd spent considerable time in a different hospital's sanctuary, the All Faith Chapel at Memorial Sloan Kettering, where she waited and worried so often she might as well have been praying. MSK had been the center for Joanna's treatment after her first diagnosis, when Anna was an undergraduate at NYU, before med school. It was Anna, before she was a doctor, before she was a grown-up, really, who'd helped Joanna navigate the formidable maze of buildings and outposts, the specialists and lab results and records, the many appointments, the administrative and financial challenges—eventually, collectively *as* stressful—associated with breast cancer. Anna was her mother's chemo buddy. Anna was her mother's "person," accompanying her to surgeries. She'd say, again and again, "Relax, Ma, it's okay, I'm here, they're going to fix you up."

She hadn't chosen the job, it had chosen her. Who else was there to do it? Laney was too young, Martin was too complicated, and later, last, Ned was completely unreliable, as she had known he would be from the day they met. Breast cancer was a fact of their lives, had changed them, had changed Anna. She wondered where she'd be, whether or not she'd have even gone to med school if it weren't for her mother's disease. Yet, if it weren't for her mother's disease, there might be no Jules or Kai, or the epic bond with Laney.

Now, at the chapel, she sat fiddling with her smartphone in her favorite spot midway along a bench, second-to-last row. Her scalp tingled, and had done so to varying degrees of intensity since the night of her mother's death, the night of her encounter with Kai. Today the tingle was in high gear. Full itch. She'd heard of people clawing at imaginary mites on the skin. Anna tapped at her phone and queried Dr. Google about the myriad bizarre afflictions she might have, including delusional dermatitis, which, Anna was sure, was guilt-induced.

Or Mama-induced, she thought.

She tapped to the clip of Ned performing "Under My Thumb." Since they'd emerged, the images from Tap-a-Keg had played on an endless loop behind Anna's eyes, and the Rolling Stones song had infected her brain. She was now a one-woman internet search party, and it was making her crazy. Crazier. She'd sat for hours in front of her laptop, or hunched over her phone's small screen, reviewing Lauren's clip. She'd run it many times, peering with her finger poised to hit Pause so she could examine grainy recesses and shadows of the online micro-movie. Seconds of video consumed hours of her time as Anna searched the footage. She was literally scratching her head over the questions that nagged at her.

Why were there no lights on in the bar? Why did it look like there was a spotlight on Ned? What form did the dull reflection in the bar mirror show? What was that? Why did the clip show the small group of Tap's patrons in the background, holding up phones, recording, and yet only Lauren's video had turned up on the internet? She clicked her way over to the Facebook page for Tap-a-Keg: A Hell of a Joint, and read posts about the moon and magnetic fields: a jukebox with a mind of its own, malfunctioning cell phones. Lots of chatter about Ned's antics, and observations divided along gender lines, either slut-shaming or defending Lauren, but only one lone, fuzzy-memory, hangover-tainted comment about something else having taken place. About something that was there but not there.

Anna the doctor relentlessly analyzed Ned's convulsive movements and blown pupils, considering the possibility of a central nervous system disorder. His skin was pallid. He was foaming at the mouth. Was he having a seizure? Was he evidencing symptoms of acute psychosis? A psychotic or schizophrenic break? Or an overdose of MDMA? No theory or diagnosis aligned with the footage of Ned, dancing like a marionette. He didn't look drunk or drugged. He looked vacant, but frenetic and frightened. The whole thing had a forced feel, and despite the internet's condemnation of Ned as a sexual predator, it was obvious to Anna that Ned's performance had nothing to do with Lauren.

Ned was a dick, but he was not a creep.

She was startled when her phone dinged with a text from Jules.

Still here?

Anna texted back, *Yes, Im done. R u?*

Nope.

Jules was on guard. Anna knew she was being checked up on, and knew it was justified. She'd admitted to being out with Kai the night her mother died, admitted to drinking and carousing, but nothing more. She used shock and grief to maintain distance from Jules's probing looks and pointed comments, and kept her fingers crossed that Jules would not, out of respect, push further, not now anyway. Anna kept the sex stuff private, until she herself could make sense of it. But she knew she would keep it to herself forever, when—if—she let the Kai thing go. She would live the lie, afraid the truth would be a deal-beaker for Jules-who-believed-in-soulmates.

Now, this new distraction: ghost-hunting. Anna widened her eyes at the improbability of everything, and let her neck rest on the back of the bench and rolled it against the cool wood for one more moment, and then left the chapel for the third floor, with a stop at the gift shop first.

Jules sat on the floor of the family lounge closest to the neonatal intensive care unit, hugging her knees. She wore green scrubs and black Crocs, and her dark hair was held in a high ponytail. She was looking up from under her long bangs, listening to the kid sitting in the chair next to her, who seemed to have a lot to say. The little boy was deep in explanation about the blue stuffed bear he clutched, pointing and gesturing and shrugging. Jules spoke softly to him, reasoning. Anna felt everything she'd always hoped she would feel for a partner, and wondered why she was jeopardizing it.

Jules saw Anna and almost smiled, almost forgot the tension between them. Anna held up the peace offering she'd picked up in the gift shop—a pink poodle with a white bow in its topknot and a rhinestone collar.

Jules said, "Perfect. Bring it over."

Anna crouched to kiss Jules on the cheek. "It's a pink poodle. Who's your friend?"

"This is Lester. He has a brand-new baby sister." Jules tightened her mouth and tipped her head toward the ICU.

Lester said, "She doesn't have a name yet."

Jules held out the pink poodle and said, "Anyway, look! Can you believe it? Let's name the poodle for now."

The boy's eyes widened. To make Jules smile, Anna said, "Okay, but Lester's already got a bear. The poodle's for you."

Jules said, "No, this is much better. He hates blue."

To see if it was really okay, Lester looked from Jules, who rolled her eyes for his benefit at Anna's comment, to Anna, who winked, and then he smiled, let the blue bear drop to the floor, and reached for the pink poodle.

Jules and Anna hung out with Lester. When the boy's parents came out of the ICU, they peeled off yellow isolation gowns, latex gloves, shower caps, and face masks, wiped at sweat and tears, shifted their sorrow and surrounded Lester, hugging and fussing over him as they admired newly christened Rosie, the better stuffed animal.

Jules said, “I’m going to hang out for a while, in case,” and so Anna went home alone, full of need: the need to stop thinking, the need to stop making sense, the need for no thoughts, just touch, just touch. Back in Brooklyn, she closed her eyes and could still see Jules sitting on the floor next to the little boy who wasn’t getting the baby sister he’d been waiting for, whom he already loved even though she hadn’t yet had a name. Anna missed Jules fiercely, and she missed her mother, and so it was no wonder that after three glasses of wine, when her phone lit with a new text, she let herself ignore the consequences, again.

She saw Kai as soon as she entered the park on the pier. From a distance, through the dark, Kai looked motionless, sculpted and aglow, and past her, rising up from the dark water, the Statue of Liberty’s green gown and torch glowed, too.

“Hey.”

“Hey, hi.”

“Cold, huh?”

Anna sat and said, “This is really bad.”

“Meaning?”

“Meaning, I don’t know what I’m doing here. It’s late. It’s cold. I’m sorry.”

Kai shrugged. “You told me to text you. I texted you.”

“No, I know. It’s my bad, definitely. I know that.”

“That’s a lot of negativity sixty seconds into meeting up in the park. Nothing’s happened.”

Anna pushed the conversation to where she wanted it to go. “Yet.”

“Yes,” Kai agreed. “Yet. Not to mention, again.” She smiled a dark smile and glanced at Anna.

Anna thrummed with cold and desire. Her wool beanie exacerbated her itchy head. She jiggled her legs. She took off her gloves in anticipation of Kai's skin and rested the hand closest to Kai on the bench between them. She pushed her other hand into her pocket and fiddled with her keys, lacing her fingers through and twisting the chain, threading the keys around and around on the ring. She looked over and saw paw prints in the frozen earth, fossilized from a long-lost day of mud and sun and dogs on the run, and said, "My mother has a dog. Had one. I mean, we still have him. He's still around."

Kai nodded. "I have two. Rescues. Sugar and Doc."

"You're kidding. You have a dog named Doc?"

"Uh, yeah. Why is that weird?"

"Eh, it's a long story. To do with my mother. And that freak on the internet. Have you seen that guy? Doc McGowan, perving out on his grad student? The video that's all over the place? The front page of the *Post*?" Anna let her chin sink into her scarf. "I know him. That's Ned. Our Ned. I don't mean *our* Ned, but . . . he's . . ."

Anna slumped lower on the bench and shut her eyes against the cold. She was here, next to Kai, in an attempt to escape everything, cheat, and she could not stop talking about her mother, about Tom, about Ned McGowan.

She said, "Do you believe in ghosts?"

Kai pulled in her brows and side-eyed Anna. "You mean, like dead people who aren't dead?"

"Well, yeah, but no. I mean, there's a little more to it than that."

"Do tell."

"Yeah, actually, there are different orders, like levels. Higher-order ghosts with spiritual levels above thirty percent are more evolved, so they have other . . ." She heard herself, heard how she sounded, cursed the internet, and tried to laugh it off. "No, I mean, it's bullshit, but. Well. I don't know. Kind of interesting."

Kai shook her head and raised her eyebrows. "If you say so."

"I don't know." Anna tried to find her voice of reason. "Sometimes I like to think about what happens, after. Don't you ever think about that? Like, with the kids at the hospital? The ones that you just know aren't going to make it? There was a baby girl today. She didn't even have a name yet. But her parents, her little brother, they already loved her. I can't get with the idea she's just . . . erased . . . after all that . . . possibility, I guess? All that love waiting for her? Doesn't that have to go somewhere? Maybe she's zooming around, soaking it up." Anna pointed to the sky.

Kai was silent.

"Anyway." Anna shook her head to clear it. "Never mind," she said. "Don't listen to me. I'm shutting up."

"Okay, never mind." Kai elbowed Anna. "Look, so far, no offense, I'm not having that much fun." Kai gave Anna a teasing, testing smile. "If you are too weirded out by this . . . by us . . . let's just bail. I'm cool with that. Really. But if you want to check it out, let's go get a drink. Either way, it's cool."

Anna twisted her keys. Jules was probably home from work, maybe upset about Lester, his unfathomable loss. "I don't know. Can we sit here for a minute? Would that be cool?"

Kai stood and said, "It's freezing, right? We can sit somewhere warm, and still be cool."

She leaned down and put her hands on the bench, on either side of Anna, corralling her. Their tongues met inside each other. She pulled away and gave Anna a long look and said, "Come on," and headed toward Coffey Street and the bars on Van Dyke just a few blocks away. Anna watched Kai's stride, Kai, a moving, hot human, beckoning Anna by turning away from her, and Anna bargained with her conscience, *If she looks back at me, I'll go to the bar; if she doesn't look back, I'm going home. Where I'm supposed to be.*

Anna put her gloves back on. Her house keys were cupped in her palm, and they felt pliable and warm. She stayed on the bench for a long time, tracking the frozen paw prints with her eyes. She could still feel Kai's lips burning against her own. Her eyes teared with the thrill of a new mouth and what it could do, and the great disappointment she felt in herself for wanting someone other than Jules.

Kai looked back. Anna got up but did not follow. She kicked at the rutted tracks the dogs had made, and then walked them as if they were a trail she was looping and backtracking. Walking the maze of paw prints made her dizzy. Anna thought about dogs running and splashing in mud, mad with joy. She picked up a crusty tennis ball, pocketed it for Tom. She watched Kai's form diminish in the distance.

Anna felt sick—homesick, grief-sick, sick with desire and guilt. The sickness was acute at night and nearly unbearable in the mornings. An empty trough, like a moat, had settled around her heart. She closed her eyes and could swear she felt it. A loss of something, something corporeal, inside. Loss had penetrated her, her heart and mind and gut, the filaments of hair on her head, loss residing, settling in, not yet acclimated, loss not yet absorbed, nor processed, nor managed. Making her itchy. It was work. In a breath, in a blink, with a nod, she saw the work of it, the big, big work of it. Grief. She had to do the work.

Luckily she had help. She texted and sent, *Took a walk, on my way back*. She texted and sent, *Love you, Lane, miss you*. She shut her phone to stop the world.

It was time to go home. The keys were in the palm of her hand.

Jules opened the building's lobby door before Anna had her gloves off. In the time it had taken her to walk the cold blocks home from the park, texts had accumulated. Jules said, "I've been trying to reach you. It's Laney."

25

Earlier in the evening, at the appointed hour, Laney clipped Tom's leash to his collar and just as she'd done a hundred times, put on the down parka that hung near the door, took a hat and gloves from the pockets, and stepped into her mother's winter boots.

The sidewalks were slippery with the mid-March remains of snow and ice. Tom was excited to be outside in the brittle cold, away from the complicated vibe in the apartment. He was long-legged, waist-high on Laney, and strong; he bounced and pulled and skittered from right to left in front of her as they walked. Tom exploited walks with Laney. He knew she wasn't the disciplinarian that Joanna had been, or that Anna was, where a walk was a businesslike undertaking. He bounded unexpectedly when he saw another dog, nearly yanking her off her feet. He darted toward squirrels, and hardy birds who stayed in New York for the winter or had come back north too soon. With Laney, Tom got twisted in his leash and she had to stop and untangle him again and again.

She worked to slow him down so she could stay on her feet on ice. She tried to nudge him into walking at her heel, and said, "Tom, you're gonna kill me."

Riverside Drive stretched north and south, with only an occasional car at this time of night, at this time of year. Laney crossed the Drive at 103th Street, toward the steps that lead down from the promenade into Riverside Park, to meet Ned.

As she and Tom approached Ned, his heart accelerated. It looked like Joanna coming toward him. The hair, long and blonde and streaming from under a knit hat, just like the night they first met, when he walked her home. The big puffy coat. She passed under a streetlight and he could see the inward pull of her lips against a smile, her smile restrained, as if she didn't want to be happy to see him.

He watched Laney struggle across the wide Drive with Tom, and then in an instant Tom caught the scent and sight of Ned and his tail wagged madly, and his whole body wiggled forward, straining to get to Ned, dragging Laney behind him. Laney, despite her resolve to be serious and adult and reserved with Ned, even angry, smiled and shrugged as the dog pulled away from her and ran toward him.

"Okay, okay, man, calm down, it's okay, I'm here." Ned crouched to Tom's height and they were entangled in a licking and snuffling embrace. Ned buried his face in Tom's neck and held on for a long time. He pressed into the dog's fur, and his eyes filled with tears. It felt like his best friends, the only friends he'd ever had, had turned up to support him in the wake of his public humiliation.

The three of them walked north in the park for a while, with Tom looking over his shoulder every few seconds to check on them with a dog-grin of happiness, as if relieved that the universe had reunited Laney and Ned, two of his most beloved people, together in his beloved place, Riverside Park, and that he could again take up the important job of herding them along. Ned released the leash and Tom took off, but circled back to them, and encircled them, before running off and returning, again and again.

"I like your coat." Ned looked sidelong at Laney. "I thought you were your mom for a minute."

"I have all her stuff on. I forgot. I keep forgetting."

"I don't think she'd mind."

"No, I know. It seems weird, though. But I don't know what's weird or not weird anymore. Everything's weird."

"I know what you mean." Ned let that hang. They walked along. "How's it going? At the apartment?"

"I don't know. Fine, I guess. Anna's in Brooklyn, she's got Jules and work. She took a little bit of time off, but she really can't. With the residency. Mama will kill her if she gets sidetracked now. I mean, would have killed her."

Ned nodded. "What about you? You feeling sidetracked?"

Laney puffed out a breath. "I'm just up taking care of Tom for now. Trying to figure out what to do next." Laney took a breath. "And thinking about things. Future things."

"Any specific future things?"

"Maybe school. Columbia, actually. This fall. I hope. I'm applying to a few places, to be safe. But I want to stay around. Near my sister." She kept her tone noncommittal, although she'd been feverishly working on her essay. The application deadline was a few weeks away.

"Your concentration? Can I ask?"

"I don't know. Women's Studies, I think. I'm doing the Statement of Purpose now. I'm out of practice. Writing."

"What's the topic?"

"Actually . . ." Laney hesitated. "It's kind of about Monica Lewinsky. The nutty-and-slutty thing. Slut-shaming, I guess. Something like that."

Ned smiled. "That's really good, Lane. I like your angle. A lot to think about there." He said, carefully, "Well, let me know if I can help with the essay. I'd like to help. Like old times."

She remembered how angry she was supposed to be with him. "Anyway, never mind. You can stop acting concerned about me. I should be the concerned one. Considering you're, like, a predator, according to the internet. I can smell alcohol on you."

Ned nodded. "I have been drinking. No point in denying it. But I think you know the other isn't true."

"Then what's your deal? What were you doing in Tap-a-Keg, with that student?"

"I don't know. I don't know what my deal is. And I don't know what I was doing. To tell you the truth, everything has gotten epically fucked up. Since your mother. Died and all."

Laney struggled to keep her voice steady, struggled not to cry. "So, what? You're blaming my mother dying for you, like, sexually assaulting a teenager in a bar? It's your fault that she died! Everything was your fault! Long before the bar!"

"I know how it looks. I know what you think. And just a technical detail, she's not a teenager."

Laney pushed back. "My mother. She was . . . really upset. That last day, the day she died. She was very, very upset with you. And not just then. For a long time before. For months. She did not do what the doctors told her to. They wanted her to do chemo again. She didn't even tell us! She stopped trying. She stopped caring about anything. After whatever happened. With you."

Ned looked ahead, up the trail. "Things . . . important things . . . got complicated. For me. I didn't want to make it harder on your mom."

"What's that supposed to mean? What things? She was dying. You supposedly loved her. How could anything have been more important than that?"

"I thought it was better if I wasn't around. I'm really sorry. I really am. Believe me, she was better off without me."

"Obviously! And it's way too late to apologize! To her, or to me." Like the teenager she was when they met, when they became friends, Laney said, "I stuck up for you! I always stuck up for you!"

Ned nodded. He said nothing. Laney got quiet too. They walked in the dark. They picked through patches of black ice on the high path; at one point, Laney lost her footing and Ned grabbed her arm, and she let him. Even after everything, they walked companionably, because the worst had happened to them together, they had lost someone they loved together.

They climbed the long slope up around the bird sanctuary, wound their way down the steps, and stopped at the tennis courts. They leaned on the fence and looked across the rubbled surface, the faded green, the fallen branches and dirty snow at the edges of the cracked courts. Tom ran the perimeter, nosing the underbrush for stray balls.

"She was a terrible tennis player," Laney said.

"That's true. She hated running backward. And she took her eye off the ball." Ned bumped his shoulder into Laney's. "We should maybe play sometime. In the spring."

"I will beat you. I'm younger. And faster. And I'm not afraid of running backward."

Tom came back to them with two tennis balls bulging from his mouth. He tried to drop them at Ned's feet, but couldn't dislodge them. He shook his great head and swiped a big paw at his snout to loosen the balls. Ned and Laney laughed at the dog's dilemma, and Ned pried the balls free. He threw a ball across the court and Tom raced for it. For a couple of minutes, the three of them were happy.

Then Ned said, "You watched it, right? The video? Me singing and whatnot?"

"Oh my God, please do not make me talk about this. It's too . . . I don't even know. 'Creepy' isn't even the right word. Beyond creepy."

"That's what I'm saying. It was weird, right?"

"That's an understatement! It's borderline criminal! I'm surprised you're not in jail or something!"

"No, Laney, listen for a sec. I mean, like truly weird. In a . . . a freaky way. Like, spooky."

" 'Spooky'?" Laney enunciated as though Ned's word choice was absurd, although it fit.

"Well, yeah. I mean, didn't I seem kind of out of it?"

"I assumed you were high, Ned. Everyone does!"

"I wasn't high, Laney. I don't do drugs. It was spooky. A few things have been kind of spooky lately. Know what I mean?" Ned glanced at her, gauging her reaction.

Laney said, "No. I don't know what you mean." They turned from the courts and followed the park's trail south toward home. Ned threw a tennis ball. Tom ran for it, brought it back, and stared Ned down until he threw it again.

"Like that night at your place. When I was getting the envelope your mother left. When the vase broke."

"You mean when you broke the vase?"

"I didn't break that vase. It just went flying off the table. I was nowhere near it."

"Okay, so it just went flying off the table. Right." Laney understood that this conversation was why Ned had called her, why they were here, together in the park.

"Well. I don't know. It was like someone knocked it over while I was on the other side of the room."

"Are you saying someone else was in the apartment?"

Ned was quiet for a bit. "Yes. Kind of."

"Kind of?"

"I know this is bizarre. Just hear me out."

Laney stopped and looked into Ned's eyes. "Just say what you're saying. For a change."

That was almost impossible for Ned, to muster the truth and say it, without equivocating, and they both knew it, so the time ticked away, and then he could not hold on to it anymore.

"The vase went flying off the table, and I went over to see what was going on, and then I went flying too and cracked my head and sliced up my hand. But."

"But what?"

"I thought I'd had a heart attack, I swear."

"Well, maybe you did."

"I didn't, Lane. Something . . . someone pushed me. Really hard. But like, pushed through me. I . . . I had this intense feeling. Like . . . like a feeling that your mom was there."

Laney stared Ned down. "You're saying you think my dead mother smashed her grandmother's vase, then dive-bombed through your chest and knocked you down? And then followed you and possessed you and made you act like a perverted fucking maniac in Tap-a-Keg? I suppose she forced your little girlfriend to record it and post it all over the internet. That too?"

"Well," Ned said, trying to sound sober and sane. "Actually, yes, I think . . . I think yes, that's what happened. Is happening."

"What does your fancy fiancée think of your theories, may I ask? Have you tested them out on her, or am I the only lucky one?" She called to the dog. "Tom! Tom, come! Right now!"

Laney grabbed the leash from Ned, and her resolve not to cry crumbled. "Leave us alone. I don't know what happened to you! What's wrong with you?! I used to like you! We trusted you! TOM!"

"Laney, hold on a sec, just listen. There was more, some other stuff happened at . . . at my . . . friend's place. Trudi's. Stuff got destroyed, and the bed was set on fire. Some vandalism nobody could explain. Because you can't get into that building, it's like a fortress. With cameras and motion sensors and everything."

"I know! Everyone knows!" Laney backed away. "Your 'friend'

Trudi? The whole world knows she's pregnant! She was pregnant when you were with my mother at the end of last summer, and it made my mother so sad she didn't want to live anymore. She didn't want to stick around for anything, including me and my sister. You need to leave me alone. You are seriously fucked up."

Ned said, "It made her sad, it did. But also, really, really mad. So mad that maybe she's not done being mad. And needs to, I don't know, get back at me or something. I'm just asking you to think about it. That it could be true. That maybe you've noticed things too."

Tom bounded up to them and reared back in a play bow, nosing the soggy tennis ball, still optimistic that Ned might continue the game of fetch, despite the anxiety of the voices crossing above him.

"Get over here! You come when I call you!" Laney grabbed Tom's collar and angrily clipped the leash. "We're going home, come on!" She pulled furiously on Tom, who resisted and leaned toward Ned. Ned distractedly put the tennis ball in his coat pocket, and Tom became fixated on the hidden ball.

Laney pulled harder on the leash. "Tom! Let's. Go."

"Laney, please. I know how crazy this sounds, but she was so mad at me, she was just so mad, I know she was. And you were too. You are. I get that, I do. You all hate my guts. I beat myself up about it every day. But this is something else. I have this feeling. All the time. She's . . . I think your mother is . . . not gone."

"I said leave me alone! You just feel guilty so you're drinking too much and getting high and acting like an asshole. The asshole you always were. I'm such an idiot. My sister was right about you!" Laney's eyes and nose streamed in the cold night air. "You should have been there to help. At the end. She needed you. I needed you! You just walked away from us! To trade up or something!"

Laney dragged Tom up the steps and out of the park. Tom

dug in, trying to get back to the tennis ball in Ned's pocket and Ned.

Ned said, "Go, buddy, go. Go with Laney. Lane, I'm sorry you're upset. I'm sorry. I'll e-mail you. Send you some ideas. For the essay."

"Don't e-mail me! I'm going to delete you! Just like my mother should have!"

Laney struggled up the steps to Riverside Drive with Tom. She pulled him to the crosswalk at 103rd Street so they could cross to home. They were thirty yards from the lobby of the Titania. Tom kept twisting around, kept looking back, trying to keep Ned in his sights, agitated that one of his humans was out of his herding zone, and that the ball was still in Ned's pocket. Ned hung back to let Laney get her distance and control of Tom and to wait for the tremors in his hands and legs to subside.

Laney had to get away from Ned and get home, to think about everything he said, and how it all fit around her own restless, jumbled feelings—how her mother refused to become memory, how home seemed haunted, for sure, where Tom waited for something. Someone.

She gave Tom one more hard yank and trotted across the empty highway, against the light. Without warning, in the middle of the northbound lanes, Tom wrenched around one more time to see where Ned was, to see if Ned was coming along. Steps from the sidewalk, Laney pulled hard against Tom's powerful will. He knew he wasn't supposed to dawdle as they crossed the highway. Tom reared back and twisted around and his collar slipped up over his ears and over his head and off and he ran to Ned, who had just ascended the top step to the promenade.

Ned saw the running dog. He put up his hands and screamed, "NO! STAY! STAY!" and "STOP! STOP!"

Laney held the slack leash with the empty collar for another second or two, and then she understood this moment and the next and said, "Tom," and sunk to her knees and covered her eyes. Tom bounded to Ned, possessed by love, as a beater Camry with tinted windows and busted headlights pounded north at a roar out of nowhere, into Laney's mother's dog.

26

A deep kinesthetic shock rocks me from inside. The reverberation says: *Elena.*

My combustion is propulsive. I surge. The scaffolding rumbles with the force of it. The platform breaks free of its moorings and wrenches away and drops and tilts above the sidewalk across from the Titania. Black net tangles with broken pipe and cracked wood. I fly.

Elena is on her knees, but Elena is safe. She is bowed in sorrow, but she is alive.

Tom has taken the hit. Tom's body soars, describing an arc over the trees, and he crashes through bare branches, breaking them. He smashes into earth. Ned runs to the dog shouting, *No no no.* Across the highway, my daughter, on her knees, drops her head to the iced pavement in a child's pose of despair.

Tom's soul, sleek as a just-born pup blinking to life, emerges, rises up, and leaves a broken carcass of bones and bloody fur behind. Tom, my good boy, my protector, my provider of unconditional love. My dog, who, when his siblings hustled for attention in a sweet puppy tumble, sat apart with his eyes locked on me, to show me which pup to pick. My dog, the best dog, who moved me up and out and forward with purpose into each blue morning or indigo evening for years.

Loyal, trustworthy. Faithful Tom. Old-fashioned words. My goes-without-saying components of love. It had never occurred to me to ask Ned—or Martin, for that matter—if those were the goes-without-saying components of love for them too. Between people, words turned and meaning shifted and in the turning and shifting the words became broken vows.

But Tom rises up.

Tom, who loved me when I hated myself.

Tom, my last dog on earth, rises up, overjoyed to be with me again.

Tom chases across the night sky above the Hudson and circles back, forever unleashed. He orbits and encircles me. We move across the moon, a woman and her dog, far above the skeleton branches of linden trees. Tom herds me forward, what he was born to do. What he died to do. He leads because he knows where I need to go.

I hadn't lifted the mask, because I wanted Loretta to keep breathing.

I hadn't looked into my daughters' eyes, because I didn't want them to see the sickness in me.

Words unsaid, eyes unseen, raging cells, broken hopes or hearts, speeding cars, blood, fur—none of it matters anymore.

There's no more confusion. I have help. How lucky am I? I have Tom. It's the same as it ever was.

No more waiting. Tom rises up and I follow.

27

Although it was midnight, everything was on and loud. The radio played in the kitchen, the television in Laney's bedroom was on, and the television in the living room was on. Texts and calls hit Laney's phone, alternating a bell ding with the "I Walk the Line" ringtone. Anna's phone trilled the default.

Jules, well-meaning, had posted of Tom's demise on Facebook. Condolences were flying. Anna suppressed a half-sob, half-giggle. First their mother, now Tom—double tragedy. Throw in the Karaoke Kreep connection, and it was social media crack. Stretched out on one end of the sofa, she took the phone from her sister, who dozed at the other end. She turned it off, and turned hers off, and aimed the remote and whispered a little "Yay" when the *Law & Order* logo came up. The voice intoned, "In the criminal justice system, sexually based offenses are considered especially heinous. . . ." Da-dum.

Perfect timing: weirdly soothing heinosities solved in less than an hour. She loved this episode, had seen it half a dozen times:

In the interview room, Stabler shreds ballsy ADA Sonya Paxton, gets his face slapped, and laughs it off. Anna thought Ned's Tap-a-Keg video could be an especially heinous sexually based offense, too, and fantasized that she and Laney could write a "ripped-from-the-headlines" episode and sell it to *L&O.*

Laney's eyes were closed but she wasn't asleep. She tried to tune in to the episode and tune out the visuals and sounds of Riverside Drive that played behind her lids. She flashed on arguing with Ned, remembered the metallic rage that rose in her throat, and her eyes going hot, and then trying to get away from Ned and struggling to control Tom, who had his own ideas. Tom galloping across the dark Drive to Ned, or so it seemed, and being, for an instant, illuminated. By headlights?

So it seemed, in memory. Laney had a distinct visual of Tom illuminated, she could see it again in her replay, but the Camry's headlights were out. She recalled no lights approaching on Riverside in the moments before the dog was hit. She'd crossed that stretch dozens of times, she knew how the road rose from the south, and fair enough, there was a bit of a blind curve, a car could be coming and be seen just a little bit late, making you run across to safety if its approach was fast, but there is no way she would not have seen headlights on that dark stretch.

Laney wondered why Tom was illuminated in her brain's replay.

After, she and Ned stood waiting for the vet to send a van, more removal specialists. The city was positively teeming with noble occupations she had never considered—workers who scraped dead squirrels off the street, or cleaned up when a body went off a building, or expired in a blue bed, or was hit by a car on Riverside Drive.

Ned had said, "It was a Camry. No headlights. They never saw him, and then they took off," and Laney had nodded.

A cop car pulled up and waited with them. Ned covered Tom with his coat, and was shaking with the cold. Anna arrived, and

Ned went over it again: Tom on a mission, unstoppable. Camry from nowhere, no headlights.

Anna commented darkly about the number of fatalities associated with one's attachment to Ned, then took a blanket from the backseat of the Wrangler and handed it to him for warmth, without looking at him. The three of them, united by another death, watched as the dog's body was tended to with fearsome efficiency. Eventually, the van pulled away, and the cops pulled away, too, and Ned wandered back to his studio with Anna's blanket around his shoulders.

Anna put her arms around her little sister and turned her away from Riverside, and talked with her voice pitched low as she guided Laney half a block home, through the Art Deco doors of the Titania, past the concierge and neighbors who'd already heard about the accident via the doormen in the surrounding buildings, and Anna kept talking, low and soft into her baby sister's ear, *Come on, Elena, let's go, I'm right here, I've got you, come on, you're okay, we're okay, let's go, let's go home.* For Laney, it was like listening to a bedtime story or a lullaby, so that by the time they'd ridden the elevator up and arrived on the twelfth floor, she was nearly limp with the need to sleep.

She could not sleep. She stretched out on the sofa and slid her feet under Anna's legs.

Anna said, "Cold? Hungry?" Laney shook her head no; Anna covered their legs with a throw and handed Laney half an English muffin with peanut butter and peach jam anyway. They watched Stabler destabilize. Laney tried to be distracted by *Law & Order.* Da-dum.

She couldn't stop the torrent of hit-and-run images, instances and sounds that passed across her mind's eye, her mind's ear. She let them come and then started them from the beginning again, to see what was missing, what was off, like in those side-by-side photographs at the back of gossip magazines, where you have to compare every detail to find out what tiny thing they've photoshopped out of the picture. What was off?

Tom broke away, Tom ran, Tom got hit by a car. Tom lit up as he soared, but she swore there were no headlights.

What else? Something else.

In her brain's replay, Tom was not headed toward Ned. Ned had not actually come up from the park yet. He had hung back to give Laney a chance to get the resistant dog up the steps and across the street. Tom ran, and in the aftermath, in the conferring with Ned, they naturally assumed the dog ran back looking for Ned. To get at the ball in Ned's pocket. To herd his person.

Laney's hand was sore. She still felt the force of Tom's resistance and her own retaliatory yank back. She still felt Tom's big-dog power, combined with his instinct to round up Ned. He'd flagrantly disregarded the rules of walking calmly on the leash, of no fooling around when crossing streets, of obeying, no matter what. . . .

What else? Something else. Laney started the movie in her brain again.

Tom moves in a different direction, not toward Ned at all. Tom swerves, pulls toward a spot twenty-five feet south of the steps, toward the stand of linden trees whose branches look etched on the moon. Tom runs, looks up into the trees, and is hit hard, and then he arcs with the impact, and then it gets surreal for Laney, she keeps seeing the oddest thing, but it is only memory, so fickle, it's all in her mind, and she's so exhausted from everything, and there's so much to do, and why bother with all this analysis of what happened with Tom, it's making her even crazier than she's been.

Even so.

Tom, hit by a car and hurled, does not seem rag-doll limp, as would be expected. He actually seems unhurt, in control of his trajectory, his flight, and he yearns on and up, toward something, going farther than the impact should have propelled him, going up with intention, and he sort of seems to soar. And he is illuminated! As if he were a winged, celestial creature of some kind, rising above the trees. A glowing, winged poodle traveling with intention.

And then the rest of it comes: the descent, the weight of the carcass dropping, the dry noise as the branches give way, and the bad thud as Tom hits earth. Ned runs to him. Laney runs to him. It gets very real.

Laney was startled out of this deep reconsideration of events when Anna said, "Can you handle another episode? I can. I'm thinking we binge for the next four or five hours or so. I'll replenish supplies. I'll be right back."

Laney needed to test it out. She needed to rehearse what it would sound like when she said all this to Anna, because she had to. Anna was her sister and Anna's DNA and her own DNA were nearly identical and Anna would know if she were completely fucking cray-cray. Anna was a doctor.

She shut her eyes and practiced, saying her crazy theory out loud, while Anna was busy in the kitchen. "I lost control of Tom and he twisted away from me, he was on a mission, it had nothing to do with Ned, and he ran, it was like he just ran into the dark, all happy, and then he got hit and he flew, but luckily he turned into a winged poodle and was illuminated, a light shone on him, maybe showing him the way, or maybe he was the light, I can't tell, but he soared to the sky, unbroken, to meet . . . Well, obviously, to meet up. With Mama."

Anna stood at the end of the sofa, holding a bottle of champagne and two of their mother's best flutes. She said, "Who are you talking to?"

Laney opened her eyes. She muted the television. She nodded. "I'm talking to you. It's true. Tom was not running to Ned. And there were no headlights, but some kind of glow was shining down on him or through him, I swear. He looked like he was flying. On purpose. His body language, or whatever. He was psyched. Like when he sees—saw—Ma."

Anna lifted the bottle and said, "Well, then I guess champagne is the right choice. We don't have to wait for a special occasion. It seems like they just keep on coming." She popped the cork and poured. "So?"

"I don't know. So nothing. Do you believe in ghosts?"

Anna drank the champagne in her flute, all at once. "It's funny you should say that. I found myself in this very same insane conversation, not three hours ago. It did not go well."

"I knew it! You agree!? It's Mama!"

"Yes. No. Keep going."

"We met in the park because Ned wanted to tell me something. Along these same lines."

"Okay, but Mr. Never Accountable, though, right? Blaming unseen forces. Seems pathologically dissociative to me." Anna was not ready to reveal how many hours she'd spent watching YouTube, trying to diagnose Ned, and looking past Ned in the video, to see evidence of something she knew did not exist, and yet needed to find. The rational, big-sister part of her brain restrained any impulse she had to acknowledge Laney's implication.

They drank the champagne. Anna refilled the flutes. They drank more. And more. Another heinous crime unfolded mutely on the television screen. The sisters emptied the first bottle.

Anna said, "I don't know. Maybe things didn't wind up the right way. For us. Me and you. Mama checked out on us. Maybe you're coming up with crazy theories just to try and make it better."

"Maybe." Laney rose and paced. "But Ned's coming up with crazy theories, too. And you had an insane conversation about it just tonight. It didn't wind up right for Mama. Maybe she's out there, trying to make it right. That's what Ned thinks."

Anna snorted and poured. "Well, she's still getting it wrong.

It's still all about Ned McGowan, isn't it? If she wanted to make it right, what about us?"

"I know! We're the injured party! We're the abandoned children!"

"When you say 'we,' you secretly mean you, don't you? Right? Admit it."

"Fine. But I'm needier."

Anna said, "I'm not so sure about that." She scratched at her scalp. "My head is so itchy."

Laney sat back down and pulled her sister over so that Anna's head rested in her lap. She raked her fingers through Anna's hair perfectly and Anna closed her eyes and let herself luxuriate in the touch, and said, "It's kind of cool, actually. If she were, like, taking care of business. Finally holding him accountable. It's badass."

The girls were tipsy and giddy. Laney laughed. Her cheeks were flushed and her eyes were bright. "Totally. The big editor in the sky, rewriting the ending. Gotta have the right ending, even if it's a tragedy. Like *Beaches*." She yelled, "Mama! Gotta do it like *Beaches*, right? Hey, Ma! *Beaches*, bitches!"

Anna said, "Ma, you didn't have to murder the damn dog on top of destroying the pervy professor!"

Laney went for a second bottle, popped it, and poured. She moved close to Anna and rested her head on her sister's shoulder. "You were with Kai?"

"Yes. I had to . . . I don't know. Test myself, I guess. One more time."

"How'd you do?"

"We'll see. It's up to Jules." Anna drained her glass and aimed the remote at the television to un-mute Benson, mid-interrogation. "Anyway, considering the two times I've sneaked around with Kai a death has occurred, I think monogamy is my best bet."

Laney laughed, and then her laugh faltered and dissolved into rasps and sobs. Her voice stopped and started and she gulped. She said, "I was so mad at him."

Anna said, "Ned?"

"No, not Ned, Tom! I mean, yes, Ned, but I took it out on Tom. I kept dragging him and he kept resisting me. The next thing I knew, he took off across the highway." She covered her face and pressed her fingertips into her eyes but the tears did not, could not stop. "I can't believe it. He just took off. I couldn't hold on to him. I lost him."

Anna said, "But okay, just listen, okay? Just think about it. Think about what you were telling me. About the flying poodle."

Laney curled her fingers into her palms, made fists, and pressed her knuckles hard against her burning, brimming eyes, but listened.

Anna said, "Maybe it wasn't such an accident. Maybe he needed to get to her. Be with her, or something."

"What do you mean, be with her?"

"I don't know. I don't think spirits . . . I don't think they want to be here. From what I've read."

"Spirits? Meaning ghosts. You've been reading about ghosts. Remind me to question everything you ever tell me from now on."

"From what I've read, they're miserable in their in-between zone. They're trying to leave. Get to the right level. Light. Whatever. You know what I mean."

Laney squinted and shook her head. "I most certainly do not." She used a corner of her shirt to wipe her eyes.

"Maybe Tom knew Mama . . . needed help. Like he always did. Like how he waited for her when she was getting out of bed? How she held on to him? Well, maybe he knew she was stuck, and he went. To help her get where she needs to go."

Laney wound back to Tom's flight. She let it replay against the backdrop of Anna's theory.

Tom's body language. Tom, not battered from the impact, Tom, not limp and lifeless. Tom in control of his trajectory. He soared, illuminated. He was on the wing to the sky. He was traveling with intention.

Laney wrapped her arms around Anna. She breathed the scent of her sister, their childhood, her own complicated self. She sighed deeply. She said, “Okay, but let’s keep drinking.”

Anna stood, wobbled, straightened herself, extended a hand to Laney, and grabbed the champagne with the other. She said, “Okay, but let’s be productive, too,” and hauled her sister from the sofa so they could, almost a month after their mother died there, deal with her bed together.

28

My babies, my babies. They're drunk.

Who can blame them? It does feel, as Anna says, like some kind of occasion.

In my old room they pretend to hold their noses and squinch their eyes shut. They stuff sheets and pillows and the skater beanie with the black skull into a garbage bag. There is a white fringed linen throw on a chair, and Laney puts it over her head and reaches her arms and lurches toward Anna, saying, "Woooo, woooooo," like a cartoon version of a ghost. They laugh their asses off and get the job done.

I could swoop in and confirm their theory, but maybe it's better for all of us if I leave them in the zone of . . . plausible deniability. Just in case someday, they prefer to disavow the existence of ghosts. Just in case someday, they want to chalk me up as a phantasmagoria of grief.

I can understand that. I want them to be okay. I think they'll be okay. But.

I can't help but think. Had I been in my right mind.

If I had taken Keswani's advice. If I had reached for my girls, instead of reaching for Ned. If I had never, ever, ever let my beautiful life tick to his time.

If I had taken the mask from Loretta's face and let my mother speak, at her end.

If I had let myself speak, at my own.

I like to think Loretta and I, giving voice to our last words, words for daughters, would have each let the clichés roll, post-irony, post-cynicism, clichés of mothering soaked in the sweet syrup of sentiment, thick with feelings bigger, stickier, more meaningful than the words created to convey them, the clichés of deep and deepest truths.

I am your mother. That's a natural fact.

I'm not your friend, but I'm the best friend you'll ever have.

You'll always be my baby, so don't be afraid to grow up.

You're not perfect because that's impossible, and you are full of possibility, and you are perfect.

Rise and shine. Always make the bed. Look both ways. Don't smoke after twenty-five. Three drinks maximum. Have fun but stay safe. Make your own money. Don't have a boss—be the boss. Dance, in the car, in the supermarket, on graves. Barefoot whenever possible.

Count the stars. Count your blessings. Do it, right now. Let me hear you.

I hear you.

I made you. More important, you made me.

I am always watching you and someday, my eyes will look out from the face in your mirror.

I am the voice in your head, and someday, my words will come out of your mouth.

Someday you'll recognize me in you. It will be the ghost of your mother stopping by, and you'll be overjoyed to see me.

Forgive. Especially yourself.

My mother and I would have said, Get a dog. Your time together will be short, but it will be time enough for you to become the human being he already knows you to be.

We would have said, Love saves the day.

29

Before she opened her eyes, before she was fully awake, she heard the anxious ticking of a pacing dog's paws on wood floors, on the other side of the apartment. She resisted. She wasn't ready. She wanted to turn over, pull the quilt up, keep hiding from the spring sun.

But she was needed.

Laney called, "Hey! What are you up to out there?" and the dog, Laney's dog, skittered through the apartment and into her room. After several failed attempts to jump onto the bed—it was high and the dog was built low to the ground—the dog was scooped up by Laney. "Good girl, good morning, good morning." The dog burrowed into the quilt. She nosed it with her narrow, pointy muzzle, urging Laney up and out. "Ooh, you're a smarty. You want me to get up too, yes? Okay, okay, I'm coming."

They walked into the almost warm Manhattan morning. The little dog was about a year old, a rescue, a hard mix to decipher, maybe pit bull and dachshund. Her belly nearly touched the ground because her legs were so short. She was broad and chesty, with serious eyes set wide across her brow, a big, square head with silky ears like flags, and a wiry whip of a tail. Her coat was as black and shiny as a seal's. She had the confidence and gait of a dog who'd had some love, who'd come from a good home, had maybe gotten lost, but was not abused or abandoned. She listened attentively, she was a little bit fat, and she was happy. She walked at Laney's heel, she waited at the curb, she was all business until Laney unleashed her, and then she trundled across the park with dog-joy.

Finally, last night, they named her. She and Anna and Jules had been drinking, getting to know the dog—which Anna thought an insane acquisition, coming at the worst time, considering they were sitting amongst cardboard boxes, packing tape, and bubble wrap; but Laney took the dog home anyway—and drunk-googling names for superheroes, celebrity babies, foodstuffs, movie dogs, baseball players.

Anna threw out "Dumpling" and "Fatso" and "Butterball." She tried "Pokey" and "Dash" and "Shorty." Laney considered "Hillary" and "Hudson" and "Girl"—just plain "Girl." Jules said "Blue" and Anna said "Indigo" and Laney nodded and said, "Indie," and thought. *"Indie," like "independent,"* and Indie it was.

She'd gotten her acceptance letters, including Columbia's, in early April. She had not re-signed her Brooklyn lease and had a few months to find a place to call home. With Indie. The apartment at the Titania was sold and the closing was in a few weeks. They would sign it over, get checks, say goodbye to Riverside Drive and head out to Montauk for a couple of days of festivities to honor Martin and Margaret on the occasion of their wedding.

Back upstairs, yellow squares of morning sun tiled the wood floors. With Indie following, Laney wound through the apartment, assessing what was left to do. Her mother's room was completely empty.

It was time to tackle the rest of it. Closet doors were ajar, drawers extended, cabinets opened. Contents spilled out. Everywhere there were disorderly piles of possessions, not sorted, not organized, everything revealed, everything on display. When the offer had come, the one they accepted (mostly because she and Anna were done with the process, but also because they liked the buyers—an older couple from out on Long Island who wanted to "retire" to Manhattan and be in the middle of everything), Laney had started cleaning out.

She wasn't like Anna. She didn't plan all the steps. She wandered from task to task, depending on her mood and her attention span. She started here, and then thought about something compelling over there, and then remembered the other thing she'd wondered about, elsewhere.

Maybe after the sale, she'd be able to buy an apartment of her own in Brooklyn, near Anna and Jules. Maybe a little yard for Indie. There was a lot to do, including figuring out how to afford living alone. But she had a little money and a little time.

Time she would never have again. Time to wander through the place where so much had happened. To look into closets and cabinets and drawers. To let her eyes slide along shelves, considering everything. Contemplating possessions. What her mother would want her to have, would want Anna to have. What she had always secretly coveted or hated. So what if things were being done haphazardly? So what if her method was to drag it all into the open, everything, and give it a long, hard look? The possessions were themselves possessed, as was the apartment, as was Laney, by the spirit of Joanna, and Tom, too. Maybe hauling things out to call forth past lives, justify existence, reveal fate would help Laney know what to do with what. What to do with herself.

She had time.

Laney was twelve and Anna was sixteen when everything bad happened between their parents, and there was no more money, and the telephone was ringing constantly and their world had been invaded by grim men, her own father among them, wearing nearly identical suits and ties that looked to Laney like the uniform of impending doom: lawyers, doctors, accountants, businessmen. Realtors, brokers. The press of papers and voices, meetings, conference calls, debt and deadlines and deals, all communicated by strangers—it must have frightened her mother to the core.

And so Anna, and so Laney.

Joanna would be shocked to hear that both girls had been so tuned in to the terror of massive loss within such a short time frame. And then there was cancer and their mother went into protective overdrive. When she'd started daily radiation treatment, Joanna told her daughters not to worry, it was like going to a tanning salon, no big deal. When she faced months of chemotherapy, she said the infusion center was like a spa dispensing healing cures. When Martin moved out, she told the lie she wanted to be true: "We love you. Nothing will change."

They sold the house with the porch on the hill at the edge of the woods, an even greater blow for Joanna than being diagnosed with cancer and losing her breasts, hair, and faith in any future at all, let alone a financially secure one. Home, gone. She shrugged it off, *That's life*, scoffed at the suburbs, the city was better anyway—all to protect the girls, the girls, the girls. With blind determination, Laney's mother steeled herself again, again, to get them through yet another run of great loss and profound disappointment. She had believed with animal intensity that she was shielding her girls from the worst of it.

It was delusion. They were the finely calibrated daughter-barometers she had raised them to be. They missed nothing, especially when it was not said out loud.

Laney remembered walking the streets of their little town feeling useful, holding a sheaf of flyers. Anna wielded a staple gun. Signs went up: "Moving Back to the City! Everything Must Go!"

They'd spent a couple of days tagging their stuff for a yard sale. Red tag stays, green tag goes.

Joanna put on the Clash and made it a game while they sorted through their things. *Should It Stay or Should It Go?* She turned the song up loud. Laney was still young enough to be distracted into thinking they were having fun. Just the three of them, building piles of the things they could no longer keep, on dusty floors they no longer owned.

On the day of the yard sale, cars and neighbors ascended the steep driveway and descended on their belongings. Joanna, popping the well-timed tranquilizer and sipping vodka and lemonade from a travel mug, wore a half-apron stuffed with price lists and cash and fixed her face with a wrought smile. She quipped about the things she sold as if they meant nothing to her. She laughed, hollowly. She pretended not to notice Laney and Anna sneaking their baby books back inside the nearly empty house while she made change for strangers.

Now, Laney thought, *it's my turn to clean out.*

She scanned along the bookshelves, bringing her mother's books into focus, touching spines, tracking Joanna, unwilling yet to dismantle the stacks, make the piles, decide. Stay, or go. Guides to skies and tides and birds and gardens and foods and places. And coasts. Poets, all women. Fiction, all men. Laney thought, *Hmn, I never noticed that.*

She moved along the shelves: brain coral, a glass fish full of seashells, rocks with personality, art cards from museums around the world. Framed photographs stood in between books and objects, from when Anna and Laney hugged and smiled against the sky (and Laney felt Anna's strong arms now, crushing her with sister-love); from when Joanna bent low to Laney, her head tilted, offering her ear, to show Laney that she was listening; from when Anna, so proud, had cut her own hair and stared, solemn, defiant, into the lens; from when Laney, at the shore, seemingly mid-sentence, shouted to the waves, apart from everyone, with Loretta and Ben in the near distance, watching, smiling.

The photographs were Joanna's favorites. They showed her daughters stopped in the moment of who their mother believed them to be. *That's why these photographs are here*, Laney thought. *These photographs. She's showing us who she thinks we are.* Laney surveyed the images and understood what her mother had seen in them: Anna, fierce and protective, self-sufficient. Laney, always caught about to say, needing to say, mid-sentence, or hollering at the ocean.

Laney saw what her mother did not see: Anna, overly worried about the next disaster, battle-ready, even as a child. Laney, shouting to hear her own voice amidst the cacophony of myth, party line, bad news, lyrics to every song her mother turned up the volume on, signs pointing to the things they could not keep. Both girls, afraid to hold on, afraid to let go, listening, listening, listening, finally, for the right last words, the ones that never came.

Something solid occupied space up in the top corner of the shelves, something she hadn't noticed in a long time. Joanna's old typewriter, a Selectric, jutted from a high spot near the window, the spot that had so captivated Tom the night of the incident with Ned and the vase. A relic of the long-ago yard sale, something no one wanted then and everyone wanted now, like vinyl records. The typewriter was from IBM's heyday, a revolutionary machine for revolutionary times, with a groovy sixties feel.

Laney unfolded a stepladder in which she had no confidence. Indie scooted away from the shape-shifting noisy metal thing and took up her safe position on the other side of the room.

Laney thought, with an internal, eternal Clash sound track, *Stepladder goes.* She climbed and reached. The typewriter was bulky and heavy and hard to get ahold of. Her arms trembled with the angle and the weight as she inched it from the back to the edge of the shelf. Her fingers didn't know where to grip the machine's curves, and she was tentative as she tipped and lowered it carefully, carefully. She remembered just in time to keep her head turned away, hearing Joanna, *Those beautiful teeth, God forbid!*

Her ankles wobbled as she backed down the wobbly stepladder. Indie whined. Laney thought, *What am I doing? I am going backward on a rickety stepladder, my fingers are cramping, I have a twenty-pound machine bearing down on my chest. This is a mistake.* Still, she backed down the steps, carefully, and her arms were shaking, and then she was on the ground, bearing the weight of the Selectric. Laney bent low, coaxing, coaxing herself to be careful, hearing her mother, hearing her sister—*Laney, go slow!*—and trying hard to obey, and finally she was able to set the Selectric on the floor, and have a look.

The keyboard nestled perfectly in the body of the blue machine. A silver sphere like a golf ball was set in the trough. The typewriter housed elements that, when you looked at them, made perfect sense. A ruler along the back. Sliders in front of the paper roll, to set the margins. A rod to hold the paper fast. It was hard to believe the machine was obsolete.

Two #10 white envelopes were tucked there, one with *Elena* written in blue ink across its face, and the other, *Anna.* Her mother must have climbed the ladder with the remains of her strength, after hospital, before morphine. The sight of Joanna's expressive, confident script, her angles and loops, the ink trails rendering their names, was as startling to Laney as if her mother had just whispered in her ear. It wasn't only Ned who'd been left an envelope.

Laney considered getting up, going for her phone to text Anna, to ask Anna, to share this important discovery—letters—with her sister, her better self, who would know what to do. But Laney realized she didn't need any advice. She knew what to do. She sat cross-legged. The back of her neck vibrated. Her fingertips tingled. There it was, the envelope with her name, meant for her, meant for Laney, at this moment, a moment Joanna had known would come. Had planned for. Of course it would be Laney, the secret writer, reckless, who would climb up to claim the Selectric. Anna would never in a million years climb the stepladder and try to move that machine. The finding was part of it. The finding was part of it.

Indie made her way over and flopped against Laney's leg. Time was Laney's. She had nowhere to be but right here, on a sunny, almost spring morning, with the radio playing somewhere back in her bedroom, familiar New York cadences of traffic, weather, banter, a dog snoring at her side, all reassuring her that a day, just a day, was unfolding all around the city, and unfolding here too. A day for Laney.

She picked up her letter and pressed it to her breast. For the first time in months she did not feel sad. Her heart hammered with hope. She opened her envelope with shaky hands and as she had known, as she had hoped, even though the envelope was in her mother's handwriting, the letter itself had been typed on the Selectric.

Laney closed her eyes to extend time. She saw her mother rolling paper into the carriage, setting margins, inspecting the machine's globe, its letters and symbols, the little fonts carved in steel. She could see Joanna looking down into the blank white page, intent. She saw her mother's fingers hover and then fly and she heard keys clacking as the words that had gathered in her mother's heart were inscribed, for Laney, for Anna.

Their good, good mother.

Laney read slowly, savoring the words, not wanting to gulp down too many at once, knowing it was her time, her day, just a day like all the other days except this day was its own, it wasn't the past and it wasn't the next, it was just a day in which you'd hear your mother call, hear her remind you for the thousandth time to slow down, to take it easy. Her mother, Joanna. Mama.

Dear Laney,

I am picturing you. Just up, moving pretty slow, I bet. Looking for your glasses. Making coffee. Is Tom staring you down? He's used to going out before coffee! He knows how to put the pressure on. Luckily you have incredible powers of ignoring him!

Dear Laney, I am picturing you. They took you out of me and your dad put you in my arms and you were scrunched up and lumpy, with merry eyes that locked on mine immediately and stay glued to mine even as the nurse was taking you away to clean you up. You moved your head around to find me. Your dad said, Obviously, you two have met before!

Dear Laney, I am picturing you at the beach, looking back at me as you ran along the shore, naked as a cherub. You stopped at the edge and yelled at the ocean, Come back, Go away, Come back, Go away! Poppy gave you a conch shell and told you to listen for the sea, and you used it like a microphone instead.

Dear Laney, I am picturing you with your head bent over one journal after another. Or bent over your guitar, or a scrapbook, or a chopping board. Needing to get your hands on everything, to get in deep, to touch and understand from the inside, find the essence and then express it.

When you were little, do you remember? You asked for business cards—six years old! I thought it was funny, so I indulged you. You wanted to start a detective agency. You chose a Sherlock Holmes cartoon guy with a giant magnifying glass for the card! And the tagline was: We'll figure it out.

Laney, you will, I promise. Just don't wait until you figure it out to talk about it. About anything and everything. Figure it out, out loud. Holler at the ocean. Write.

I'm still picturing you. My eyes are closed but I see you. And I always will, always and forever, Mama

PS: Walk the dog!

Finally, the voice she knew, the voice that lived inside her, the voice—the direction—she'd lost, was living inside her again, for now. Finally, the right last words.

Laney uncoiled the Selectric's ancient cord, thick and umbilical, and crawled to the wall to make the connection. She said to the machine, "Don't be broken. Don't be broken," and pushed the power button. The machine hummed and vibrated, ready for touch like no computer ever could. She put her hands on its sides and found a tag taped there long ago, with her mother's Sharpie scrawl. *Stays.* Laney said, "I get it, I get it," and went to find paper.

30

She watched 5:59 roll to 6:00 A.M., set bare feet on worn wood floor, reached for jeans, slid into deck shoes, shrugged into a gray hoodie, and put the hood up. She tucked the quilt around Jules, who said *No!* while smiling from inside a dream.

Anna hustled down three flights and stepped out, aviators in place, into Brooklyn. The building's door closed and locked itself behind her and she had the gratuitous moment of panic that occurred every time she left home. She reassured herself for the third or fourth time since leaving the bedroom, patting pockets for her wallet, her keys, her phone.

The sky was big and white. Anna walked along empty city streets, passing a lone teenage couple in love, genders indeterminate and irrelevant, sitting on a curb wrapped around each other, in matching narrow pants and dark layers and sneakers, not finished with the night before. She bypassed a sleepy Starbucks and a couple of cafes, and headed to the overly lit, high-fructose, crazy-carb, palm-oil-saturated, spotless Dunkin' Donuts, run with gratifying efficiency by an Indian family, all of whom had regal posture and carved facial structure and incredible hair.

Anna was a regular. She didn't have to place her order, and that gave her secret pleasure. She made eye contact with the owner, and two coffees were handed to her sixty seconds later: tall, iced, milk and sugar. This silent, daily exchange had become ritual for Anna, and it triggered a gratitude prayer she used to start each day. "Gratitude prayer" was just a new age-y way to juice up a cliché, her mother's reminder at bedtime, *Count your blessings, let me hear, say them out loud*, words before sleep, the white noise of childhood, repeated and repeated, unheard until needed, and then unexpectedly a cliché became so necessary it could save your life.

Today she sipped her sweet coffee and thought, *Thank you, world. The sunshine. The teenagers in love. This beautiful family, their great posture, the glossy hair, the cleanliness, caffeine and sugar, the remembering of me. Not a bad way to start the day.*

A big day. Lots to accomplish, once the world woke up. Once Jules woke up, and they continued to work their way back to each other, post–dead mother, post-Kai. They had prevailed, for now, after months of strife. Residency pressures, money stuff, the grief, the exhaustion, their quick, sharp mouths, too much drinking, not enough kindness. Anna had been hurt by her mother, and so, hurt Jules. Anna pushed Jules away. She had acted out precisely the behaviors she felt most aggrieved by, as humans do.

And then one day, in such an ordinary way that it was magical, without any special words or conversations, just by accumulating days, regular days, anger got too heavy, too hard to carry, too tedious to track. It lifted and left and love was back. Love saved the day.

Today was spring. Today, the road trip. She wanted it to go well.

To be okay for everyone. Martin was marrying Margaret on Sunday in Montauk. Laney and Anna and Jules had a ceremony of their own to attend to as well.

Anna thought through the order of the morning: Get the car, check the oil, check the tire pressure, gas it up, maybe buy new flares; she couldn't remember how old the old ones were. Monitor the weather and the traffic reports. Pack it up. Car wash. Or no, do that later, once they were on the road. Jules loved the car wash. Anna smiled to herself. Jules was good. Jules would have a stocked cooler, the right music, word games. Jules was a good traveler, and that was important to Anna.

Anna took the steps back up to the apartment two at a time. The sight of Jules in their bed flooded Anna with the same warm-cool mix of protectiveness and lust and calm as when she first saw her, just a little over a year ago. She placed a glazed Munchkin in Jules's curled palm, proximate to her nose, and wondered, science-wise, how long it would take for nose to alert brain to rumble stomach, and prompt eyes to open.

Anna brought the iced coffee and her laptop to a sunny corner of the sofa. She checked weather: smiley faces. She checked routes: all clear, no obstacles. She watched a couple minutes of the Montauk surf cam: wild, good. She texted Laney: *GET UP.* She checked her bank balance. She allowed herself ten minutes of BuzzFeed, letting images of puppies remind her of Tom, and of his serious, intent eyes, always fixed on Joanna as if to say, "Okay, boss, what's next?"

Indie was a very different dog. Anna had laughed, relieved, when Laney told the story of picking the rescue mutt: Indie had been the only one to sleep, unperturbed, in a long row of caged, whining, nervous, unhappy castoffs. Indie slept through the noise and ordeal of her own cage being opened, and an attendant pulling her out and placing her in Laney's arms. She finally woke up once they were outside and Laney set her down on the sidewalks of New York, where she shook off her nap, looked up at Laney, wagged her tail, and dropped back down for a follow-up rest.

Finally Anna could wait no longer. She clicked over to e-mail, fingers crossed, and there it was, the sender's name now familiar, the subject: Confirming + Directions. Inside, the note she'd been waiting for. Anna added a new location, a detour, to the Google Map on her phone that plotted their return route from Montauk.

She clicked a link inside the note and revisited the photos of the gleaming object of her desire. She heard Jules getting out of bed. She called, "There's coffee."

Jules came up behind Anna. "Thank you for the Munchkin, munchkin. Ready to do this weekend?"

Anna left her screen in view for Jules to see.

Jules said, "Wow. What's that?"

"A horse."

"Ah, humor. Why am I looking at this?"

Anna stared at her screen, mentally maneuvering herself to return the incoming volley of questions from Jules.

Jules said, "So? What? You're buying a motorcycle off craigslist?"

"Thinking about it."

"Wow." Jules, careful, said, "A motorcycle. Have you ever ridden one before?"

"Mmn-hmn."

"Okay. Wow again. I did not know that. See? Still learning about each other. That's a good thing. I think."

"At school. Ryan had one." Anna let herself look at Jules. "Come see." She patted her lap. Jules sat. "It's a 2002 Indian Scout. 19,780 miles, one owner, a woman. Look what it says. 'Mild weather only, easy rider.' I love that. Carfax says no accidents. $9,399."

"Okay. Nice. I mean, this is one of the few topics I know absolutely nothing about, so, yeah. Cool."

"It is nice, actually. And cool. And we can look at it on our way back. Take a test drive. After the weekend. It's in Bethpage." Anna waited for Jules to catch up.

Jules tucked the perpetual stray lock of hair behind Anna's ear and said, "Okay. But a motorcycle? We already have a car, right? Unless you're gonna vroom vroom around Red Hook? I have to admit, you'd be the darling of the hipsters. More than you already are."

"The car is for here."

"And the motorcycle is for?"

Anna skimmed her finger along the track pad of her laptop, bringing another screen into view. It was a map, with a bright green line lighting a route that began in Brooklyn, New York, and ended in Memphis, Tennessee.

Jules glanced at the screen and looked at Anna. "You do realize we have less than one month off this summer, right? My residency starts up again the third week of August."

"I do realize that. Mine, too."

"I can't just bail on everything. Colleen and Jacob are getting married in August. And my parents want to come up. After that, we'll never see anyone again. We'll barely have time to see each other."

"That's why." Anna jiggled her knee to dislodge Jules. She went to the dresser and found a book, *Travels with Charley*, by John Steinbeck, about the writer's 1960 road trip across America with his big poodle. She took out an envelope that she had pressed between the yellowed pages. "My sister found this."

Anna's name was written across the envelope's face in cursive, looping like a blue pulse. "Oh, wow. Your mom," Jules said.

Anna put the envelope to her nose, smelling for skin. "Laney got one too. Last words, I guess. Better late than never, I hope." She flattened the envelope across her forehead. It was as cool as her mother's palm on her brow.

"You haven't read it yet?"

Anna shook her head. "I've had it for a while but still. I don't know. I can't open it. Maybe she's giving me instructions I should have seen sooner. Things to do. At the end. That I didn't do. For everyone."

Jules shook her head no. "Okay. But maybe it's something else. I bet it is. I think you should read it. Do you need some privacy?"

Anna shook her head again. "No. I waited. For you. Until we were okay. I want you to read it. With me. To me, actually."

Jules found Anna's eyes with her eyes. "Okay. Of course."

Anna handed the envelope to Jules.

"Are you sure? Maybe it's private."

"Obviously it's private. She was, like, dying."

"Well, yes, I know that, but I mean . . ."

"What you mean is, maybe she's said something about you? Like, get the hell away from Jules, that woman is hell on heels. Like that?"

"If these are her last words to you, I'm gonna assume she didn't waste any of them on me, as difficult as that is for me to accept. I haven't been around long enough."

"Oh, you've been around long enough. It took my mother seven whole minutes to size someone up." Anna took Jules's hand and they moved to the sofa, each tucking into a corner. "Read, please."

"If you're sure." Jules opened the envelope and took out the letter, typewritten on plain white paper. She waved the page a little to shake it alive. She cleared her throat and looked at Anna.

Anna shut her eyes and leaned her head back against the arm of the sofa. She touched her feet to Jules's feet. Jules shut her eyes for a moment and then read in her clear, strong voice.

Darling Anna,

It's a cliché, but I when was a teenager my favorite book was Catcher in the Rye. Not very fashionable these days, I guess Holden seems like kind of a jerk, but back then it was a revelation. Teenagers talking about what an awful place the world was, how phony and empty their parents' lives were, a young person "cracking up"—pretty intense stuff back then.

I loved the title. Holden hears a little kid singing an old folk song: If a body meet a body coming through the rye. It sets him wondering what job he can do to feel proud of, to feel good about himself, and not turn into a phony too. He thinks how great it would be to protect little kids coming through the rye who might not see danger up ahead. He'd be the catcher, their savior.

When Elena was just born, and you were 4? I was in the porch swing with her, milk drunk, sprawled across me. You came out of the house wearing your white cap, your pockets bulging with supplies for whatever yard expedition you had planned, it was always something, and you stood on the top porch step and squinted and then shaded your eyes like a little sea captain looking for land, and I heard the words, clear as a bell inside me, If a body meet a body coming through the rye, and I felt like I could see inside you, and that even as small as you were, you possessed the purest heart I would ever encounter.

And now here you are, devoting your life to protecting little ones from sickness and pain. A catcher in the rye. It's you.

You caught me when I fell. You got me up and walked me forward. You made me laugh when I didn't want to. You showed me love in all its glorious forms. Pure of heart, my champion, my daughter. What a gift you are. Love, Mama.

After reading "Love, Mama," Jules said, "Shit."

Anna said, "She said, 'Love, Mama,' and then 'Shit'? Like that? That is a very strange way to close."

"No. Sorry. I meant, shit, there's a PS."

"Okay. Don't tell me. It says 'Just Kidding.'"

"No, it says, 'Hi, Jules!' With an exclamation point."

After a few minutes, Anna nodded, satisfied. Of course her mother would know she'd share this letter with Jules. "I guess she liked me. I sound kind of awesome."

Jules said, "'Love in all its glorious forms.' That means me, right?"

"Only if you take a road trip with me. On a motorcycle! Your champion. Your savior. Your gift." Anna put her feet under Jules's tank top and kneaded her belly with her toes.

Jules set the letter aside, moved Anna's feet, reached for the laptop, and brought it back to life. Her eyes followed along the green route. "Honestly, if I have to go to another fucking artisan Brooklyn wedding, I may do violence."

Anna shrugged and said, "Exactly."

Jules said, "So, what, like, Graceland?" and Anna moved in close to show her the way.

31

Ned couldn't help but congratulate himself on keeping the studio.

Just off the escape hatch's entry was the kitchen, or more accurately, a short wall of sized-down appliances, with a sink and a cabinet. A few steps farther, one hardback chair attended a battered wood table cluttered with tabloids, gossip magazines, and gaping take-out containers whose congealed innards seeped through the cardboard. Deeper in, there was a mattress on the floor, partly exposed, with deflated pillows and gray sheets puddled in its vicinity. A stand of black garbage bags filled with Ned's clothes and shoes and grooming things sent from Trudi's sat in the middle of the bed, unpacked. Across from the bed, a fiesta-striped love seat, which Ned had scrounged from the street on trash pickup day, was living out the last chapter of its life piled with clothing and the blanket Anna had handed him on Riverside Drive back in March.

After "Under My Thumb," Lauren's father threatened action against Ned and every department possible at Columbia, and it had taken a university disciplinary committee all of a day to hand over a decision to Dean Peck, which Peck, vindicated, delivered to him. Ned was forced to take an indefinite unpaid leave of absence immediately, while the university decided whether it and Ned McGowan had a future together. Ned understood the formalities of the process, and that the conclusion had already been reached.

Ned had watched the baby bump's last weeks of expansion on screen. He'd tapped and swiped, searching Page Six, *People*, and *Us*, Trudi's Instagram and Twitter, tracking tweets of twinges and the baby's descent. And it—she, Sevigny Mink—had emerged. Ned saw the first posted pictures of his daughter, her pitch-black hair pointing in all directions, her new pink skin, the baby already outfitted in a fashiony way that made Ned sad. She had that infant look, as if she'd just arrived from somewhere in the cosmos, somewhere pure blue and vast. She was snapped at by smartphones and her innocent image was sent all over the world, while Ned, her unnecessary father, sat on the other side of his screen, as close as he would get, and studied her from far away.

He tried to work up feelings of loss and outrage. He tried to muster up the fury required to fight Trudi's army—her "village," she called it—of lawyers and advisors retained for the sole purpose of keeping him away from his daughter. It would take years to meet Sevigny Mink, assuming he was ever successful in his quest. He didn't have it in him, yet, to start that quest.

He couldn't face his parents and sisters, either.

He was preoccupied.

It was a high corner apartment facing north and west. Two wide windows met, affording Ned a view of the Hudson and the cliffs of New Jersey, a wider view of the trees of Riverside Park. At night, car lights intermittently swept across the pavement where Tom had been hit. Ned sometimes got lost watching headlights, counting the seconds before they brightened as they got close and then illuminated Tom's spot.

Ned also had a perfect view of the Titania and Jo's south-facing apartment. Both places were on the twelfth floor. In the very early days of their romance, when every new fact murmured was like a lyric auto-tuned by limerence, enhanced to confirm that they were destined to be together, the lovers sent signals shining from their phones, *Come to your window*, and stood nude, framing themselves for each other.

At the windowed corner with the complicated view, Ned had erected an easel. He had the desire to paint, and now, the time. A canvas was propped on its ledge. A photograph was taped to the upper left corner. A standing, swing-arm work lamp aimed at the photograph and the canvas. More canvases of all sizes, some painted and complete, a few half-painted, some blank, leaned in shadow against every wall. A small dresser, originally meant for clothes, was arranged kitty-corner to the easel. It was cluttered with jars of water and thinner and brushes and rags and tubes of paint. A hardback chair faced the easel. Surrounding the setup was a half-circle of bottles: beer, Jack, Black, and a couple of empty white wines. Amidst the bottles was the tennis ball Ned had tucked into his pocket the night of the walk in the park with Laney and Tom.

Ned took up his post and closed his eyes to wait. He breathed and prepared. He took a deep, long drink of Black, straight up, and waited for the alcohol to burn and spark inspiration inside him. He went still at this moment every evening, to immerse himself in the losses he'd suffered over the last few months. Jo, Trudi, Tom, baby Sevigny, hope for friendship with Laney. His lifestyle, teaching and television, his reputation, his writer dreams, his very idea of himself. His access. All gone. Gone, gone, gone.

His gut roiled with booze and no food. His heart thrummed

with old sorrows. All he had left was the cash from the baby buyout, the rent-controlled studio that he thought of as his garret, and the contents of the manila envelope Jo had left him, scattered now on the floor around him, fifty or so photographs, taken on their travels around the world and from their life together in Manhattan.

The physicality of the pictures was mesmerizing, really, on the studio floor. They practically pulsed with love. There were stiff Polaroids from a vintage camera (Jo trawled for film on eBay) and snapshots from her Olympus. There were matte and glossy finishes, vivid color and black-and-whites, three-by-fives, four-by-sixes, a couple of overblown eight-by-tens; nothing was cropped or filtered, nothing came from a phone or a screen, they were real photographs on real paper, images framed through Joanna's viewfinder . . . Jo, who'd found the view, who'd framed it for Ned.

They'd argued about photographs more than once. She'd complained that he never wanted to take any pictures, and that he never wanted to look at them with her, that he was aggressively uninterested in seeing the two of them as a couple stopped for a real moment in their relationship, stopped in a moment of truth, in a moment of happiness. Jo was worried, she became fixated with worry, that he didn't like the photographs because in them it was obvious that she was older, the fifteen-year difference was stark, and she worried his desire for her would round off, and he would bounce away.

That was her worry, but that's not what had stopped Ned from taking or looking at pictures of the life they'd made.

He hadn't wanted any proof of their commitment to exist; it was that simple. He hadn't wanted images that would jeopardize the plausible deniability he might need, later, the escape hatch he might want to squirm through. It was as if the photographs from his relationship with Jo were evidence he might someday need to refute. Evidence that he'd had a great love that he'd fucked up and lost.

There it was in the pictures. He was surrounded by it. Love on the wing. Love, smiling all around the world. Love drinking. Love napping on stone walls, love in the ruins, in churches and temples, in the dust, on higher ground, in the sun, under the stars. Love squinting, shading eyes, pointing to the sea. Love shaking sand from a blanket on a wild, rocky shore.

Her last wish was that he take possession of the pictures, of the two people they had been, two people who had met in a bar, miraculously, and had crossed borders into each other to love each other. And an even greater miracle: they had expanded themselves, each to reach each, with that love. They had accomplished that hard thing. They had existed. She had existed. Love did not simply die, because how could it? Here was the proof, in a manila envelope with his name written with her hand, in her hand, "Doc McGowan," underlined, and then later, scored by her anger, punctuated with a slice right through his name.

Now she was talking to him through the photographs.

Jo had been here. He knew that to be true, and that she would be back if he waited patiently. She had come for him at the Titania. She had revealed herself to him at the Porterhouse. She had met him in Tap, and she had showed him—and the world—his cruelty by turning him into a strutting, sexist, opportunistic attention whore. She'd opened him up and put her pain inside him. He understood completely her need for revenge, and he was ready to allow her to do with him whatever she needed to do. He owed her that. In fact, he looked forward to it.

He wanted her to come for him. He invited her, through the paintings. He waited.

With eyes closed, Ned counted breath, in through his nose. He filled his chest, one, two, three, four. He held breath deep inside, one, two, three, four, five, six, seven, until his lungs burned. He pushed it out, counting it away until he was light-headed. To open himself, to make himself available.

Ned finished his mindful breathing and his scotch. He was poised. He called up the image, now burned onto his retinas, of a woman made of sparkling mist swirling in the nursery, swirling in the eaves of Tap-a-Keg, streaming toward him, wrapping him tight, tight, in the shredded ribbons of her soul. He was ready. He had desire. He had his muse and his subject and his colors, his brushes.

Ned smiled. For weeks he had been confused about what to paint. For weeks he sat in front of his first blank canvas, staring down at scattered pictures, entranced with the memories, blinded by the love, paralyzed with the abundance of the life they had shared, that he had discarded, the life she had lost.

He waited for her to tell him what to do with all the left-behind love, and one evening, she had. After a quick trip to the liquor store, he came home to find one particular photo of Jo tucked under the front leg of the easel, having been deliberately segregated from the others. He knew immediately that it was Jo's doing. But her choice of photograph surprised him. He'd expected she'd want him to paint another kind of image, more serious, deeper and more melancholy, showing her sadness, rebuking him. To have him memorialize her that way, so he would never forget what he did to her. To punish him for the pain he put in her eyes. But in the photograph she chose, there was no rebuke, only joy.

Ned focused on the photograph, now taped to the easel. It was one of the very few photographs of Jo he'd taken. In Belize, the morning after he'd sort of asked her to marry him. She was in a white bathing suit on a round pink float in a turquoise swimming pool holding an orange drink, with clouds and sky behind her. Her head was thrown back. She was laughing at something Ned had said. She was in the float on the water, she was buoyant, she was laughing. Her hair was blonde and silver, her head was tossed back, her face was turned to the sun. Happiness creased her eyes and the corners of her mouth. A crescent scar made a sharp turn around her right breast and followed down into the deep V of her white bathing suit. Her arms and thighs were soft.

He wanted to capture it. Ned angled the lamp and moved in closer. To remember her skin. Her skin looked like it was strewn with confetti. Her skin showed the terrain of fifty years, a life lived under the sun, standing too close to a flame, hitting the brakes too late, showed notches and puckers and lines and furrows, trails into and out of her past, showed tattoo-blue veins that traced the flowing blood that carried the cells that would kill her. She knew. But at that moment, she didn't care. She was ecstatic.

He painted it again and again and again. Over and over—the blue pool, the blue water, the pink float, the blue sky, the white clouds. From up close. From far away. The pool, the water, the float, the sky, the clouds, in the exact palette of the photograph.

He wanted to capture it all, but still, the one thing missing from the paintings: Joanna. In his unfinished paintings there was a pool and it held the water and the water held the float but the float was empty.

Ned was waiting for her, now. Right now, tonight. And every night. Painting the empty water, the empty float. The canvases piled up against his walls. Bottles were added to the circle, take-out containers to the tabletop. Now and then he bounced or kneaded the tennis ball he'd pocketed the night Tom was hit by the Camry. He waited for Jo to come back, to crash into him again so he could come into her again, in a boy's dream of love, so he could dance for her again, with her, so she could leave him weak again and haunt him over and over, so he could try to paint her back into the float under the sun, to paint her laughing again into the sky, to bring her, and bring himself, alive.

32

It was the wrong direction, but Anna and Jules headed north from Brooklyn to pick up Laney and Indie on the Upper West Side of Manhattan for the trip out to Long Island. Laney was intractable. She refused to even discuss taking a cab from the Titania to Red Hook, schlepping the ashes of their mother in one container and the ashes of the damn dog in another, trapped in a taxicab with a potentially erratic driver and Indie.

So she was leaning against the building, yawning, a pack strapped to her back and a battered L.L. Bean white tote bag with dark green handles and trim and the monogram JMD, for Joanna Mary DeAngelis, in the other, with Indie sprawled on the sidewalk next to her, when Anna and Jules pulled up.

"Lane!" Anna shouted, and waved above the six noisy cylinders of the hot-orange Wrangler. "Elena! Come on! Come on, little sister! Come on, Fatso!" The chugging Jeep's bikini top was in place, and provided a canopy for the front-seat passengers while leaving the rear seat open to the elements. Anna said, "Just throw your shit in the back. Jump in. Come on!"

"Don't body-shame her, please," Laney said. "She's on a diet." She unhooked the backpack from her shoulders and tossed it on top of the gear already in the car. Laney encouraged Indie to jump into the backseat. The short dog looked dubious. Anna and Jules joined to cheer Indie on. "Jump, jump, Indie, come on!"

Indie made several starts at a leap, but the distance from sidewalk to seat proved insurmountable. She turned and waddled back to the Titania, intending to sit this trip out. Laney scooped her up and deposited her. "Anyway, good try."

She held the tote bag up and shook it. "Please. Somebody take this. I've been babysitting it for days. It's freaking me out." She held it toward Anna and Jules.

Jules took the tote and looked inside. "Ooh, weird. And heavy! That's how they come? Plastic bags inside cardboard boxes? I pictured urns."

Laney said, "Mama's were mailed. Nick buzzed me to come down. I had to sign because it's Return Receipt Requested, from a crematorium. You have to keep the slip with important papers. Proof of delivery. Nick patted the box. Which was so sweet. I picked up Tom's from the vet. Same exact box. It's like, cremains transport regulation, I guess."

"Cremains? Is that really what they're called? That's kind of hip." Anna got out too, and inspected the contents of the tote bag with Jules as Laney hauled herself up into the back next to the dog. "Huh. I was picturing urns, too." Anna checked her sister with a glance. "Did you open them?"

Laney said, "God, no. I used rubber gloves when I put them in the tote bag. In case of, you know, seeping dust or whatever."

"'Seeping Dust and the Cremains,'" Anna said. "Our new band name."

"I'll take it up front with me. I love this kind of thing." Jules climbed back into the car and arranged the tote between her feet. "Okay. Sitting pretty."

Laney tightened the seat belt across her chest and lap and said, "Why do I always have to sit in the back? I can never hear anything. It's too open. It's too bumpy. I'm going to fly out. The dog too. You won't even know we're gone until we get there. Why am I up this early again?"

"That dog is too fat to fly, thank God. I think we've had enough flying dogs for one lifetime."

Jules said, "Can there ever be too many flying dogs?"

Anna adjusted the mirrors and the tilt of her captain's cap, once again admiring the anchor emblem and gold braid, that she'd rescued from a box marked "Goes," destined for the trash in the wake of the sale of her mother's apartment. She rolled her sleeves high on her inked biceps to get some color as they drove. Jules and Laney compared and shared hair elastics and lip gloss and sunscreen. The three girls donned cheap sunglasses. Jules plugged an iPhone into the radio, hit Shuffle, and turned the volume up on the Talking Heads' "Naive Melody." Anna drove them south on Riverside Drive.

Anna traveled the spine of the city with the rest of the Friday morning getaway traffic, and then she pushed through the Brooklyn-Battery Tunnel without a care, without a thought to collapsing walls or rushing waters, or any disasters at all, and they emerged, blinded, into a big sun. She dropped the Wrangler's visor. She threaded her car, steady and quick, across cracked, narrow highway lanes, making good time, in between and alongside thousands of other drivers, her fellow New Yorkers, through the boroughs. It was a joy to be driving, even in traffic, even in an old car, even over potholes, even with her dead mother and a dead dog reduced to ash in boxes bouncing on the floor of the car.

Anna picked up the Gowanus, found Interstate 278, and zipped across Brooklyn, through Queens. Not too many miles later, trees outnumbered buildings, and then buildings disappeared altogether. Traffic got lighter and faster. They traversed the Belt Parkway and hit the Southern State, Route 27. They crossed a border into Nassau County and the Southern State Parkway became Sunrise Highway became Montauk Highway, which would take them all the way. They drove on.

Laney said, "Let's play."

Anna said, "No, it's not fair to Jules. She doesn't know this game."

"She'll catch on. It's not rocket science, Anna."

Jules looked at Anna in mock shock. "You truly think there is a game invented I cannot beat you at? You do remember that it took you over a year to post a winning Scrabble score? And then by only thirty points, I might add."

"Mmm, no, it's not that kind of game. It's more like a mindfuck. From when we were little."

Laney said, "'Mindfuck'! What a disrespectful thing to say, with Mama in the car. I'm telling." She leaned forward and talked at the tote bag on the front floor of the car. "Ma! Anna cursed!"

Jules persisted. "What's the game? Tell me! And explain it all the way through. Don't spring new rules on me once you're losing."

Anna said, "It's not really a game, it's more like . . . like a quiz, I guess. We used to play it in the car when we were little. It was our family's version of I Spy With My Little Eye, which my parents couldn't bear. 'Too juvenile.'"

Laney said, "They wouldn't let us watch cartoons, either. 'Too juvenile.' I had to sneak Barney. Pee-wee Herman, no problem, but Barney didn't pass the smell test."

Anna smiled at her sister in the rearview mirror. "She was suspicious of Mister Jasons for a while. 'Too nice.'"

"He finally won Ma over," Laney said. "She decided he was the kindly gay neighbor."

"Anyway," Jules said. "What's the quiz?"

"It's a music quiz. Dad called it Heroes." Anna closed Pandora on her phone. "Lane, you go first."

"Okay. Give me a minute. I have to remember." Laney shut her eyes and listened to the white rhythm of black tires rolling on gray road and the memory of that same rhythm from when she was a kid on a car trip with her family. "I was little. Anna was older than me. But they made me play, like, for real. None of this 'Let the youngest win' shit in our family." She smiled. "Once on our way out east, my car seat wasn't secure. And I guess neither was my door. We were doing the quiz, and Mama took that hard left just before you pick up 27 again, past Stargazer, that giant deer sculpture thing. Right before Southampton. My door flew open on the turn. The car seat started tipping out."

"Yikes," Jules said. "That's so scary."

Anna said, "She was fine. I grabbed it."

"You're kidding! How lucky is that? Was everyone freaking out? Poor Laney! You were almost roadkill!"

Laney said, "Well, no, that's the point. Anna grabbed the car seat and pulled me back in, but they all just kept going with the quiz. She was shouting out answers the whole time. Mama pulled over and hopped out, and came around and locked me in. Anna was still playing the quiz."

Jules was silent, both impressed and dismayed.

Anna said, "It was cutthroat, I tell ya. I couldn't let up."

"All right. Heroes. We'll start easy. Give Jules a chance." Laney paused for dramatic effect and said in a game show host voice, "Okay, here we go. Jules, who is the King of Pop?"

Jules said, "Easy, Michael Jackson."

Laney said, "Right. And who is the Queen of Soul?"

Jules said, "Aretha? Franklin?" Anna nodded encouragement.

Laney said, "Now we're gonna step it up. Who is the Chairman of the Board?"

Jules wrinkled her brow. "The Chairman of the Board? I've heard that before. I know I have."

Anna said, rolling her eyes, "That would be Frank Sinatra. Okay, my turn."

Laney said, "Bring it."

"Who's the Boss?"

Jules shouted, "Bruce Springsteen!" Indie snored.

"The Godfather of Soul?"

Jules shouted, "B. B. King!" The sisters groaned.

"No, baby. It's James Brown."

Jules, addicted, said, "Keep going!"

Laney said, "Who is known as the Killer?"

Anna gave Jules a polite nanosecond, then cut in with "Jerry Lee Lewis. Who married his cousin. Who was fourteen!"

"And the Godfather of Funk?"

"Funk." Anna thought for a minute. "George Clinton?"

"George Clinton is correct. You go."

"Okay. Jules, you can get this, I've seen your playlist. Who is . . . the Queen of Country!?"

"I know this, my father loves her. It's Kitty Wells. Kitty Wells!"

Anna tooted the horn and Laney clapped. Jules said, "More, more!" Indie twitched awake, looked around, and yipped half-heartedly.

"Okay. The Man in Black?"

"Johnny Cash!"

Laney said, "Okay, we're gonna go deep now. Ready?"

Anna smirked and said, "You cannot stump me."

Laney said, "Who. Is. The Lizard King."

"Oh, please. Jim Morrison."

"Who. Is. The King of Pain."

Anna said, "The King of Pain? That's not a thing."

"Yes, it most certainly is. A thing. The clock ticks, Sis. Who is the King of Pain?" Laney doo-dooed the countdown music from Final Jeopardy.

Anna shook her head. "You can't mean Sting. 'King of Pain' is a song, not his, um, Hero name. That doesn't count. Dad made that up. That's bullshit."

Laney turned to Jules. "Have you seen the sore-loser side of my sister? Okay. I'll give you a chance to redeem yourself. Who is the Pope of Mope?"

Jules screeched "Morrissey!" so fast and so loud that the sisters were startled into silence and Indie yipped and yapped and hopped in excitement.

Laney poked Anna and said, "Uh-oh, she's gaining on you."

"Fine." Anna sulked for a minute. "My turn. Who is Lady Day?"

No answers. Anna answered herself. "Billie Holiday."

"And who is the First Lady of Song?" No answers. "That would be Ella Fitzgerald."

"One last one," Laney said. "On the count of three, okay? Who. Is. The Godmother of . . . PUNK! The Godmother of Punk! One two three!"

Anna and Jules shouted, "Patti Smith! Patti Smith!"

Laney shouted back, "Fuckin' A right it's Patti Smith." She leaned across Jules and talked to the tote bag again. "Fuckin' Patti Smith, right, Ma? Fuckin' Patti!"

Jules was ready with the playlist. They sang at the top of their lungs, and Indie, a soprano, howled, "Frederick," Patti's song for Fred "Sonic" Smith, her husband who died too soon.

Kiss to kiss, breath to breath, my soul surrenders, astonished to death
Hihi, Heyhey, maybe we will come back someday

The women, both species singing loud and howling, continued south and east.

33

We watch them meet, we watch them go.

We know their route, south and east. We hear them singing each to each on Sunrise Highway.

Let's go, let's go. Let's go to the beach.

I forgot how good it feels to leave the city. No more surging, no more churning.

Tom and I, we skip along the Hudson, from the Upper West Side of Manhattan to the Rockaways, where we find the Atlantic. We shimmer and bob along one hundred miles of coast, undeveloped, protected, public: Long Beach and Point Lookout, the oceanfront state parks, Jones Beach and Robert Moses.

We lift and dip under a white sun. Tom loves the sky.

We'll go to the beach. Tom loves the ocean.

I charge out of the car before Pop gets the key out of the ignition, I hop across the hot asphalt of the parking lot, my feet slap the gritty slats of the boardwalk, I run and the sand shifts, I thread between blankets and chairs, I head straight for the wild water, wild to get in. Loretta calls, *Joanna, Joanna, slow down! Watch the current!* I go into the blue, into the current, into the pounding, thrilling depths of blue, so many blues, I am thrown and tossed, almost lost, and then I find myself, right myself, reach feet to the bottom and emerge. Loretta calls, *Can you stand? Are you sure you can stand?*

Farther and farther, east and east, over the pine barrens, over the olive trees and the stunted oak, over low cliffs, over dunes lined up to look at the sea, Tom and I skim and surf waves and clouds, waves and clouds, and there is no difference between them.

I am moving. I move. I am all spirit, silvery and sleek like a fish swimming in my element, air, soaring in my element, air, with Tom, the two of us, and we slow down, we find the currents that carry us, the currents we ride to Montauk.

We go to Hither Hills, set between Napeague and the Point. I camped there as a high school girl. I got kissed and stroked by a different beautiful boy each summer. Our hearts were strong. My soul was young, unmated, all mine. I took my babies there. Anna built moats. Laney called to the sea. I loved the passage of time. Who knew what was next?

Tom and I are in the Walking Dunes. The dunes migrate. They are marched south by northwest winds, moving, changing position, building and remaking themselves on the headlands, adapting, marching alongside the ocean. Parabolas of sand rise and Tom and I curve with them, watching the ocean too while the sun watches us. The sun is so high.

Everything is blue and sand and white and gold. And we are.

My girls are here. My babies, my babies. Now love plus two, with Jules and a blue-black dog in the magical mix. They descend to the shore, single file. Anna leads and Elena holds the tote bag while Jules follows with Indie, who lags, who keeps looking to the clouds, nose twitching for a known scent, a scent known from her new home, the scent of Tom.

The young women step carefully and purposefully through a fragile environment, along a shifting path above a seductive sea. They find their way down. They chatter and laugh. They are in high spirits. It's the thrilling atmosphere: unfamiliar terrain, undeterred winds, bright sun, crashing, crazy ocean. It's relief. They are together, they are strong, they are prepared, they will figure it out, they will do this day and move on to the next. They are a new kind of girl. They are themselves accepting themselves unfolding themselves, letting themselves be, letting themselves become.

Did I find you or did you find me? You are my flesh, my blood, yet I will never completely know you. You are my mystery achievement, my daughters, and you step high surer than I ever was, into the wonder that is every hour of every day, every year of your own lives, into something or someone you can't yet know, but know will transform you.

The wind picks up. They are at the water's edge. They work with the choreography of sisters. They lift the boxes that hold the ashes of Joanna and Tom from the monogrammed bag. They set the boxes in the sand at the water's edge and open cardboard flaps and plastic bags and look in and stand back and confer. They talk to each other in the secret sister language of love and loss and music and laughter.

They have their backs to the sea. The tide. The tide comes closer to the strong feet of the young women. I see them, my babies, and I see their fat, succulent baby feet that have grown into these feet and these legs astride, planted firm, a new kind of girl, standing ground, and I see them, their reaching arms, lifting, and their changing shapes and sister heads bent now in humor and wonder and confidence, again and again across the years, and I see I see the slope of their shoulders and the paths of their necks and the slide down to their beautiful beautiful breasts.

At the water's edge in the wind. Their hair whips, Anna's hat flies, what happens next is they run for the captain's hat, and the funny little dog runs too, and barks, and they are all running for the hat as it wheels and skims on the rising wind, and the sun is high and the tide moves in and three young women and a black dog chase a white hat on a beach, and next the tide moves in and the wind lifts and dips, and next the gray ribbons of dead dust rise, the wind lifts the ribbons of dust, the wind takes what's left and empties the forgotten boxes and tosses the boxes and they tumble, empty, down the beach after the women, and what's left, every last particle, every speck, every trace becomes sand, not dust, no longer ash, but sand, and next the tide surges and churns, surges and churns, just like always, and rushes the sand forward and back and away. Into the sea. Forward and back and away.

The last time I see my daughters they are shrieking and pointing as the boxes tumble along the shoreline. Their eyes are wide, their mouths are open. Their mouths make the shapes of each other's names: Anna! Laney! Jules! Their calls are lost in the wind or I am far away. Like muses, they lace fingers and turn, they laugh and hug and turn and stagger in the shifting sand, laughing, turning, laughing, turning. Astonished. Ecstatic. With dog.

I turn. Tom follows. I go to the edge. Tom follows. I know the sea, I know the sun. My skin is gold, my hair is silver. The waves curl high and then flatten and reach to the shore, whitecaps aflutter, like the white ruffled edge of a sheet shaken high and fanning out above a blue bed that will be fixed and tucked, readied for the next good night's sleep.

I go in first. I swim. With my hands together like praying, I reach my arms long toward the horizon with my hands pointed at the horizon, and then my hands part and I make a heart-shaped arc around myself, frog-kick, push the sea behind me, push the sea to shore, create my wake. Again. Again. I pray, I reach, I point, I arc, I kick again. I propel my self, this perfect, sleek, phosphorescent self, straight to the horizon, straight to the sun, where there is no horizon, where there is no sun, where there is nothing above or below the surface, the surface is gone, it is only light, there's the light, I swim for it, all the body is gone, and I am gone, and I am gone gold and I am gone light and gone clear and I am gone.

Tom follows.

ACKNOWLEDGMENTS

I have been carried by:

Sophia Marie Hoffman and Grace Dover Hoffman, good good daughters.

The memory of my parents, Thomas and Marie Gangi.

The memory of Jonathan Kaplan, who double-dared me.

The memory of writing teachers Robert Creeley, Leslie Fiedler, June Jordan, Michael Kalter, and Eugene Murphy.

Bess Weatherman, constant, honest, supportive, and true blue.

Melissa Glassman, Anna Hammond, Philip Hoffman, Janet Dulin Jones, Adele LaTourette, Beth Ann Maliner, Diane Martin, Ann Patty, Jessica Retan, Mary Root, Lynn Rozzi, Melanie Sonderman, and Joanne Vitale, each of whom knows why.

And Enzo, who nosed his way in to where he belonged.

I thank:

Nancy Eichenbaum and Roger O'Sullivan, Judy Lee Hartnett, Karen and Dan Stewart, friends who gave me the gift of places to write.

Valiant readers and advisers: M. Blair Breard, Sharon Dolin, Celia Fogel, Sam Gentle, Catherine Heraty, Joel Hinman and my Writers Studio classmates; and Shaziya Keswani, Sarah Key, Joseph Krongold, John Morris, Tracy Rhine, and Theresa Rich.

Neil Lester, the closest reader of all.

The crew at Jane Rotrosen Agency: Jane Berkey, Andrea Cirillo, Chris Prestia, Annelise Robey, Meg Ruley, Amy Tannenbaum, and Julianne Tinari.

The crew at St. Martin's Press: Tom Cherwin, Caitlin Dareff, Jennifer Enderlin, Olga Grlic, Brant Janeway, Kim Ludlam, Sally Richardson, Lisa Senz, Nancy Trypuc, Dori Weintraub; and Elizabeth McNamara.